THE DUST FLOWER

THEN SLOWLY, SLOWLY LETTY SANK ON HER KNEES, BOWING HER HEAD ON THE HANDS WHICH DREW HER CLOSER   [See p. 350]

THE
DUST FLOWER

BY
BASIL KING

AUTHOR OF
THE STREET CALLED STRAIGHT,
THE EMPTY SACK, Etc.

ILLUSTRATED BY
HIBBARD V. B. KLINE

NEW YORK
GROSSET & DUNLAP
PUBLISHERS

Made in the United States of America

THE DUST FLOWER

Copyright, 1922
Harper & Brothers
Printed in the U. S. A.

M—W

The Dust Flower

Chapter I

IT is not often that you see a man tear his hair, but this is exactly what Rashleigh Allerton did. He tore it, first, because of being under the stress of great agitation, and second, because he had it to tear—a thick, black shock with a tendency to part in the middle, but brushed carefully to one side. Seated on the extreme edge of one of Miss Walbrook's strong, slender armchairs, his elbows on his knees, he dug his fingers into the dark mass with every fresh taunt from his fiancée.

She was standing over him, high-tempered, imperious. "So it's come to this," she said, with decision; "you've got to choose between a stupid, vulgar lot of men, and me."

He gritted his teeth. "Do you expect me to give up all my friends?"

"All your friends! That's another matter. I'm speaking of half a dozen profligates, of whom you seem determined—I *must* say it, Rash; you force me to it—of whom you seem determined to be one."

He jumped to his feet, a slim, good-looking, well-dressed figure in spite of the tumbled effect imparted by excitement. "But, good heavens, Barbara, what have I been doing?"

"I don't pretend to follow you there. I only know the condition in which you came here from the club last night."

He was honestly bewildered. "Came here from the club last night? Why—why, I wasn't so bad."

Standing away from him, she twirled the engagement solitaire as if resisting the impulse to snatch it off. "That would be a question of point of view, wouldn't it? If Aunt Marion hadn't been here ——"

"I'd only had ——"

"Please, Rash! I don't want to know the details."

"But I want you to know them. I've told you a dozen times that if I take so much as a cocktail or a glass of sherry I'm all in, when another fellow can take ten times as much and not ——"

"Rash, dear, I haven't known you all my life without being quite aware that you're excitable. 'Crazy Rash' we used to call you when we were children, and Crazy Rash you are still. But that's not my point."

"Your point is that that infernal old Aunt Marion of yours doesn't like me."

"She's not infernal, and she's not old, but it's true that she doesn't like you. All the more reason, then, that when she gave her consent to our engagement on condition that you'd give up your disgusting habits ——"

He raced away from her to the other side of the room, turning to face her like an exasperated animal at bay.

The room was noteworthy, and of curiously feminine refinement. Expressing Miss Marion Walbrook as it did, it made no provision for the coarse and lounging habits of men, Miss Walbrook's world being a woman's world. All was straight, slender, erect, and hard in the way that women like for occasions of formality. It was evident, too, that Miss Walbrook's women friends were serious, if civilized. There was no place here for the slapdash, smoking girl of the present day.

The tone which caught your eye was that of dusky gold, thrown out first from the Chinese rug in imperial yellow, but reflected from a score of surfaces in rich old satinwood, discreetly mounted in ormolu. On the French-paneled walls there was but one picture, Sargent's portrait of Miss Walbrook herself, an exquisite creature, with the straight, thin lines of her own table legs and the grace which makes no appeal to men. Not that she was of the type colloquially known as a "back number," or a person to be ignored. On the contrary, she was a pioneer of the day after to-morrow, the herald of an epoch when the blundering of men would be replaced by superior intelligence.

You must know these facts with regard to Miss Walbrook, the aunt, in order to understand Miss Walbrook, the niece. The latter was not the pupil of the former, since she was too intense and high-handed to be the pupil of anyone. Nevertheless she had caught from her wealthy and public-spirited relative certain prepossessions which guided her points of view.

Without having beauty, Miss Barbara Walbrook impressed you as Someone, and as Someone dressed by the most expensive houses in New York. For beauty her lips were too full, her eyes too slanting,

THE DUST FLOWER

and her delicate profile too much like that of an ancient Egyptian princess. The princess was perhaps what was most underscored in her character, the being who by some indefinable divine right is entitled to her own way. She didn't specially claim her way; she only couldn't bear not getting it.

Rashleigh Allerton, being of the easy-going type, had no objection to her getting her own way, but he sometimes rebelled against her manner of taking it. So rebelling now, he tried to give her to understand that he was master.

"If you marry me, Barbe, you'll have to take me as I am—disgusting habits and all."

It was the wrong tone, the whip to the filly that should have been steered gently.

"But I suppose there's no law to compel me to marry you."

"Only the law of honor."

Her whole personality was aflame. "You talk of honor!"

"Yes I talk of it. Why shouldn't I?"

"Do you know anything about it?"

"Would you marry a man who didn't?"

"I haven't married any one—as yet."

"But you're going to marry me, I presume."

"Considering the facts, that's a good deal in the way of presumption, isn't it?"

They reached the place to which they came once in every few weeks, where each had the impulse to hurt the other cruelly.

"If it's so much presumption as all that," he demanded, "what's the meaning of that ring?"

THE DUST FLOWER

"Oh, I don't have to go on wearing it." Crossing the room she pulled it off and held it out toward him. "Do you want it back?"

He shrank away from her. "Don't be a fool, Barbe. You may go too far."

"That's what I'm afraid of—that I've gone too far already."

"In what way?"

"In the way that's brought us face to face like this. If I'd never promised to marry you I shouldn't now have to—to reconsider."

"Oh, so that's it. You're reconsidering."

"Don't you see that I have to? If you make me as unhappy as you can before marriage, what'll it be afterward?"

"And how happy are you making me?"

Holding the ring between the thumb and forefinger of the right hand, she played at putting it back, without doing it. "So there you are! Isn't that another reason for reconsidering—for both of us?"

"Don't you care anything about me?"

"You make it difficult—after such an exhibition as that of last night, right before Aunt Marion. Can't you imagine that there are situations in which I feel ashamed?"

It was then that he spoke the words which changed the current of his life. "And can't you imagine that there are situations in which I resent being badgered by a bitter-tongued old maid, to say nothing of a girl—" He knew how "crazy" he was, but the habit of getting beyond his own control was one of long standing—"to say nothing of a girl who's more like an old maid than a woman going to be married."

With a renewed attempt at being master he pointed at the ring which she was still holding within an inch of its finger. "Put that back."

"I think not."

"Then if you don't ——"

"Well—what?"

Plunging his hands into the pockets of his coat, he began tearing up and down the room. "Look here, Barbe. This kind of thing can't possibly go on."

"Which is what I'm trying to tell you, isn't it?"

"Very well, then; we can stop it."

"Certainly—in one way."

"The way of getting married, with no more shilly-shallying about it."

"On the principle that if you're hanging over a precipice the best thing you can do is to fall."

He continued to race up and down the room, all nerves and frenzy. "Don't we care about each other?"

She answered carefully. "I think you care about me to the extent that you believe I'd make a good mistress of the house your mother left you, and which, you say, is like an empty sepulcher. If you didn't have it on your hands, I don't imagine it would have occurred to you to ask me."

"Well, that's all right. Now what about you?"

"You've already answered that question for yourself." She stiffened haughtily. "I'm an old maid. I haven't been brought up by Aunt Marion for nothing. I've an old maid's ways and outlooks and habits. I resented your saying it a minute ago, and yet it's true. I've known for years that it was true. It wouldn't be fair for me to marry any man. So here it is, Rash." Crossing the floor-space she held out the ring again. "You might as well take it first as last."

He drew back from her, his features screwed up like those of a tragic mask. "Do you mean it?"

"Do I seem to be making a joke?"

Averting his face, he swept the mere sight of the ring away from him. "I won't touch the thing."

"And I can't keep it. So there!"

It fell with a little shivery sound to a bare spot on the floor, rolling to the edge of a rug, where it stopped. Each looked down at it.

"So you mean to send me to the devil! All right! Just watch and you'll see me go."

She was walking away from him, but turned again. "If you mean by that that you put the responsibility for your abominable life on me ——"

"Abominable life! Me! Just because I'm not one of the white-blooded Nancies which your aunt thinks the only ones fit to be called men——"

But he couldn't go on. He was choking. The sole relief to his indignation was in once more tearing round the room, while Miss Walbrook moved to the fluted white mantelpiece, where, with her foot resting on the attenuated Hunt Diedrich andirons she bowed her head against an attenuated Hunt Diedrich antelope in bronze.

She was not softened or repentant. She knew she would become so later; but she knew too that her tempers had to work themselves off by degrees. Their quarrels having hitherto been rendered worth while by their reconciliations, she took it for granted that the same thing would happen once more though, as she expressed it to herself, she would have died before taking the first step. The obvious thing was for him to pick up the ring from off the floor, bring it to her humbly while her back was turned on him, and beseech her to allow him to slip it on where it belonged; whereupon she would consider as to whether she would do so or not. In her present frame of mind, so she told herself, she would not. Nothing would induce her to do anything of the kind. He had betrayed the fact that he knew something as to which she was desperately sensitive, which other people knew, but which she had always supposed to have escaped his observation—that she was like an old maid.

She was. She was only twenty-five, but she had been like an old maid at fifteen. It had been a joke till she was twenty, after which it had continued as a joke to her friends, but a grief to herself. She was distinguished, aristocratic, intellectual, accomplished, and Aunt Marion would probably see to it that she was left tolerably well off; nevertheless she had picked up from her aunt, or perhaps had inherited from the same source, the peculiar quality of the woman who would probably not marry. Because she knew it and bewailed it, it had come like a staggering blow to learn that Rash knew it, and perhaps bewailed it too. The least he could do to atone for that offense would be to beg her, to implore her on his bended knees, to wear his ring again; and she might not do it even then.

The dramatic experience was worth waiting for,

THE DUST FLOWER

however, and so with spirit churning she leaned her hot brow against the thin, cool flank of Hunt Diedrich's antelope. She knew by the fierce grinding of his steps on the far side of the room that he hadn't yet picked up the ring; but there was no hurry as to that. Since she would never, never forgive him for knowing what she thought he didn't know—forgive him in her heart, that was to say—not if she married him ten times over, or to the longest day he lived, there was plenty of time for reaching friendly terms again. Her anger had not yet blown off, nor had she stabbed him hard enough. As with most people subject to storms of hot temper, stabs, given and received, were all in her day's work. They relieved for the moment the pressure of emotion, leaving no permanent ill-will behind them.

She heard him come to a halt, but did not turn to look at him.

"So it's all over!"

As a peg on which to hang a retort the words would serve as well as any others. "It seems so, doesn't it?"

"And you don't care whether I go to the devil or not?"

"What's the good of my caring when you seem determined to do it anyhow?"

He allowed a good minute to pass before saying, "Well, if you don't marry me some other woman will."

"Very likely; and if you make her a promise to reform I hope you'll keep your word."

"She won't be likely to exact any such condition."

"Then you'll probably be happier with her than you could have been with me."

THE DUST FLOWER

Having opened up the way for him to make some protest to which she could have remained obdurate, she waited for it to come. But nothing did come. Had she turned, she would have seen that he had grown white, that his hands were clenched and his lips compressed after a way he had and that his wild, harum-scarum soul was worked up to an extraordinary intensity; but she didn't turn. She was waiting for him to pick up the ring, creep along behind her, and seize the hand resting on the mantelpiece, according to the ritual she had mentally foreordained. But without stooping or taking a step he spoke again.

"I picked up a book at the club the other day."

Not being interested, she made no response.

"It was the life of an English writing-guy."

Though wondering what he was working up to, she still held her peace.

"Gissing, the fellow's name was. Ever hear of him?"

The question being direct, she murmured: "Yes; of course. What of it?"

"Ever hear how he got married?"

"Not that I remember."

"When something went wrong—I've forgotten what—he went out into the street with a vow. It was a vow to marry the first woman he met who'd marry him."

A shiver went through her. It was just such a foolhardy thing as Rashleigh himself was likely to attempt. She was afraid. She was afraid, and yet reangered just when her wrath was beginning to die down.

THE DUST FLOWER

"And he did it!" he cried, with a force in which it was impossible for her not to catch a note of personal implication.

It was unlikely that he could be trying to trap her by any such cheap melodramatic threat as this; and yet ——

When several minutes had gone by in a silence which struck her soon as awesome, she turned slowly round, only to find herself alone.

She ran into the hall, but there was no one there. He must have gone downstairs. Leaning over the baluster, she called to him.

"Rash! Rash!"

But only Wildgoose, the manservant, answered from below. "Mr. Allerton had just left the 'ouse, miss."

Chapter II

WHILE Allerton and Miss Walbrook had been conducting this debate a dissimilar yet parallel scene was enacted in a mean house in a mean street on the other side of the Park. Viewed from the outside, the house was one of those survivals of more primitive times which you will still run across in the richest as well as in the poorest districts of New York. A tiny wooden structure of two low stories, it connected with the sidewalk by a flight of steps of a third of the height of the whole façade. Flat-roofed and clap-boarded, it had once been painted gray with white facings, but time, weather, and soot had defaced these neat colors to a hideous pepper-and-salt.

Within, a toy entry led directly to a toy stairway, and by a door on the left into a toy living-room. In the toy living-room a man of forty-odd was saying to a girl of perhaps twenty-three,

"So you'll not give it up, won't you?"

The girl cringed as the man stood over her, but pressing her hand over something she had slipped within the opening at the neck of her cheap shirtwaist, she maintained her ground. The face she raised to him was at once terrified and determined, tremulous with tears and yet defiant with some new exercise of will power.

"No, I'll not give it up."

"We'll see."

THE DUST FLOWER

He said it quietly enough, the menace being less in his tone than in himself. He was so plainly the cheap sport bully that there could have been nothing but a menace in his personality. Flashy male good looks got a kind of brilliancy from a set of big, strong teeth the whiter for their contrast with a black, brigand-like mustache. He was so well dressed in his cheap sport way as to be out of keeping with the dilapidation of the room, in which there was hardly a table or a chair which stood firmly on its legs, or a curtain or a covering which didn't reek with dust and germs. A worn, thin carpet gaped in holes; what had once been a sofa stood against a wall, shockingly disemboweled. Through a door ajar one glimpsed a toy kitchen where the stove had lost a leg and was now supported by a brick. It was plain that the master of the house was one of those for whom any lair is sufficient as a home as long as he can cut a dash outside.

Quiveringly, as if in terror of a blow, the girl explained herself breathlessly: "The castin' director sent for me just as I was makin' tracks for home. He ast me if this was the on'y suit I had. When I 'lowed it was, he just said he couldn't use me any more till I got a new one."

The man took the tone of superior masculine knowledge. "That wasn't nothin' but bull. What if he does chuck you? I know every movin' picture studio round N'York. I'll get you in somewheres else. Come now, Letty. Fork out. I need the berries. I owe some one. I was only waitin' for you to come home."

She clutched her breast more tightly. "I gotta have a new suit anyhow."

"Well, I'll buy you a new suit when I get the bones. Didn't I give you this one?"

She continued, still breathlessly: "Two years ago— a marked-down misses' it was even then—all right if I was on'y sixteen—but now when I'm near twenty-three—and it's in rags anyhow—and all out of style— and in pitchers you've gotta be ——"

"They'se plenty pitchers where they want that character—to pass in a crowd, and all that."

"To pass in a crowd once or twice, yes; but when all you can do is to pass in a crowd, and wear the same old rig every time you pass in it ——"

He cut her protests short by saying, with an air of finality: "Well, anyhow I've got to have the bucks. Can't go out till I get 'em. So hand!"

With lips compressed and eyes swimming, she shook her head.

"Better do it. You'll be sorry if you don't. I can pass you that tip straight now."

"If you was laughed at every time you stepped onto the lot ——"

"There's worse things than bein' laughed at. I can tell you that straight now."

"Nothin's worse than bein' laughed at, not for a girl of my age there ain't."

Watching his opportunity he caught her off her guard. Her eyes having wandered to the coat she had just taken off, a worn gray thing with edgings of worn gray squirrel fur, he wrenched back with an unexpected movement the hand that clutched something to her breast, thrust two fingers of his other hand within her corsage, and extracted her pay-envelope.

THE DUST FLOWER

It took her by such surprise that she was like a mad thing, throwing herself upon him and battling for her treasure, though any possibility of her getting it back from him was hopeless. It was so easy for him to catch her by the wrists and twist them that he laughed while he was doing it.

"You little cat! You see what you bring on yourself. And you're goin' to get worse. I can tell you that straight now."

Still twisting her arms till she writhed, though without a moan or a cry, he backed her toward the disemboweled sofa, on whose harsh, exposed springs she fell. Then he sprang on her a new surprise.

"How dare you wear them rings? They was your mother's rings. I bought and paid for 'em. They're mine."

"Oh, don't take them off," she begged. "You can keep the money ———"

"Sure I can keep the money," he grinned, wrenching from her fingers the plain gold band he had given her mother as a wedding ring, as well as another, bigger, broader, showier, and set with two infinitesimal white points claiming to be diamonds.

Though he had released her hands, she now stretched them out toward him pleadingly. "Aw, give 'em back to me. They'se all I've got in the world to care about—just because she wore 'em. You can take anything else I've got ———"

"All right, then. I'll take this."

With a deftness which would have done credit to a professor of legerdemain he unbuckled the strap of her little wrist-watch, putting the thing into his pocket.

THE DUST FLOWER

"I give that to your mother too. You don't need it, and it may be useful to me. What else have you got?"

She struggled to her feet. He was growing more dangerous than she had ever known him to be even when he had beaten her.

"I ain't got nothin' else."

"Oh, yes, you have. You gotta purse. I seen you with it. Where is it?"

The fear in her eyes sent his toward her jacket, thrown on the chair when she had come in. With an "Ah!" of satisfaction he pounced on it. As he held it upside down and shook it, a little leather wallet clattered to the floor. She sprang for it, but again he was too quick for her.

"So!" he snarled, with his glittering grin. "You thought you'd get it, did you?" He rattled the few coins, copper and silver, into the palm of his hand, and unfolded a one-dollar bill. "You must owe me this money. Who's give you bed and board for the last ten year, I'd like to know? How much have you ever paid me?"

"Only all I ever earned—which you stole from me."

"Stole from you, did I? Well, you won't fling that in my face any more." He handed her her coat. "Put that on," he commanded.

"What for?" She held it without obeying the order. "What's the good o' goin' out and me without a cent?"

"Put it on."

Her lip quivered; she began to suspect his intention. "I do' wanta."

"Oh, very well! Please yourself. You got your

hat on already." Seizing her by the shoulders he steered her toward the door. "Now march."

Though she refused to march, it was not difficult for him to force her.

"This'll teach you to valyer a good home when you got one. You'll deserve to find the next one different."

She almost shrieked: "You're not going to turn me out?"

"Well, what does it look as if I was doin'?"

"I won't go! I won't go! Where *can* I go?"

"What I'm doin' 'll help you to find out."

He had her now in the entry, where in spite of her struggles he had no difficulty in unlocking the door, pushing her out, and relocking the door behind her.

"Lemme in! Lemme in! Oh, *please*, lemme in!"

He stood in the middle of the living-room, listening with pleasure and smiling his brigand's smile. He was not as bad as you might think. He did mean to let her in eventually. His smile and his pleasure sprang purely from the fact that his lesson was so successful. With this in her mind, she wouldn't withstand him a second time.

She rattled the door by the handle. She beat upon the panels. She implored.

Still smiling, he filled his pipe. Let her keep it up. It would do her good. He remembered that once when he had turned her mother out at night, she had sat on the steps till he let her in at dawn before the police looked round that way. History would repeat itself. The daughter would do the same. He was only giving her the lesson she deserved.

Meanwhile she was experiencing a new sensation,

that of outrage. For the first time in her life she was swept by pride in revolt. She hadn't known that any such emotion could get hold of her. As a matter of fact she hadn't known that so strong a support to the inner man lay within the depths of human nature. Accustomed to being cowed, she had hardly understood that there was any other way to feel. Only within a day or two had something which you or I would have called spirit, but for which she had no name, disturbed her with unexpected flashes, like those of summer lightning.

While waiting for the camera, for instance, in the street scene in "The Man with the Emerald Eye," a "fresh thing" had said, with a wink at her companions, "Say, did you copy that suit from a pattern in *Chic?*"

Letty had so carefully minded her own business and tried to be nice to every one that the titter which went round at her expense hurt her with a wound impelling her to reply, "No; I ordered it at Margot's. You look as if you got your things there too, don't you?" Nevertheless, she was so stung by the sarcasm that the commendation she overheard later, that the Gravely kid had a tongue, didn't bring any consolation.

Without knowing that what she felt now was an intensified form of the same rebellion against scorn, she knew it was not consistent with some inborn sense of human dignity to stand there pleading to be let into a house from which she was locked out, even though it was the only spot on earth she could call home. Still less was it possible when, round the foot of the steps, a crowd began to gather, jeering at her passionate beseechings. For the most part they were children,

THE DUST FLOWER

Slavic, Semitic, Italian. Amid their cries of, "Go it, Sis!" now in English and now in strange equivalents of Latin, or Polish, or even Hebraic origin, she was suddenly arrested by the consciousness of personal humiliation.

She turned from the door to face the street. It was one of those streets not rare in New York which the civic authorities abandon in despair. A gash of children and refuse cut straight from river to Park, it got its chief movement from push-carts of fruit and other foods, while the "wash" of five hundred families blew its banners overhead. Vendors of all kinds uttered their nasal or raucous cries, in counterpoint to the treble screams of little boys and girls.

Letty had always hated it, but it was something more than hatred which she felt for it now. Beyond the children adults were taking a rest from the hawking profession to comment with grins on the sight of a girl locked out of her own home. She was probably a very bad girl to call for that kind of treatment, and therefore one on whom they should spend some derision.

They were spending it as she turned. It was an experience on a large scale of what the girl in the studio had inflicted. She was a thing to be scorned, and of all the hardships in the world scorn, now that she was aware of it, was the one she could least submit to.

So pride came to her rescue. Throwing her coat across her arm she went down the steps, passed through the hooting children, one or two of whom pulled her by the skirt, passed through the bearded

THE DUST FLOWER

Jews, and the bronzed Italians, and the flat-nosed Slavs, passed through the women who had come out on the sidewalk at this accentuation of the daily din, passed through the barrows and handcarts and piles of cabbages and fruit, and went her way.

Chapter III

EXACTLY at this minute Rashleigh Allerton was standing outside Miss Walbrook's door, glancing up and down Fifth Avenue and over at the Park. It was the hour after luncheon when pedestrians become numerous. For his purpose they could not be very numerous; they must be reasonably spaced apart.

And already a veritable stream of women had begun to flow down the long, gentle slope, while a few, like fish, were stemming the current by making progress against it. None of them was his "affair." Young, old, short, tall, blond, brunette, they were without exception of the class indiscriminately lumped as ladies. Since you couldn't go to the devil because you had married a lady, even on the wild hypothesis that one of these sophisticated beings would without introduction or formality marry him, it would be better not to let himself in for the absurdity of the proposal. When there was a break in the procession, he darted across the street and made his way into the Park.

Here there was no one in sight as far as the path continued without a bend. He was going altogether at a venture. Round the curve of the woodland way there might swing at any second the sibyl who would point his life downward.

He was aware, however, that in sibyls he had a preference. If she was to send him to the devil, she must be of the type which he qualified as a "drab."

THE DUST FLOWER

Without knowing the dictionary meaning of the word, he felt that it implied whatever would contrast most revoltingly with Barbara Walbrook. Seeing with her own eyes to what she had driven him, her heart would be wrung. That was all he asked for, the wringing of her heart. It might be a mad thing for him to punish himself so terribly just to punish her, but he was mad anyhow. Madness gave him the satisfaction which some men got from thrift, and others from cleverness. He would keep the vow with which he had slipped out of Miss Walbrook's drawing room. It was all that life had left for him.

That was, he wouldn't pick and choose. He would take them as they came. He had not stipulated with himself that she must be a "drab." It was only what he hoped. She must be the first woman he met who would marry him. Age, appearance, refinement, vulgarity were not to be considered. Picking and choosing on his part would only take his destiny out of the hands of Fate, where he preferred that it should lie.

Had any one passed him, he would have seemed the more perturbed because of his being so well-dressed. He was one of the few New Yorkers as careful of appearances as many Londoners. With the finish that comes of studied selection in hat, stick, and gloves, as well as all small accessories of the costliest, he might have been going to or coming from a wedding.

He was imposing, therefore, to a short, stout, elderly woman with whom he suddenly found himself face to face as the path took a sharp sweep to the south. The shrubs which had kept them hidden from each other gave place here to open stretches of lawn. When

THE DUST FLOWER

Allerton paused and lifted his hat, the woman naturally paused, too.

She was a red-faced woman crowned with a bonnet of the style introduced by Mrs. Langtry in 1878, but worn on this occasion some degrees off center. On her arm she carried a flat basket of which the contents, decently covered with a towel, might have been freshly laundered shirts. Being stopped by a gentleman of Allerton's impressiveness and plainly suffering expression, her face grew motherly and sympathetic.

"Madam, I wish to ask if you'll marry me?"

Even a dull brain couldn't fail to catch words hammered out with this force of precision. The woman didn't wait to have them repeated. Dropping her basket as it was, she took to flight. Flight was the word. A modern Atalanta of Wellesley or Bryn Mawr might have envied the chamois leaps which took the good creature across the grass to the protection of a man with a lawn-mower.

Allerton couldn't pause to watch her, for a new sibyl was advancing. To his disgust rather than not, she was young and pretty, a nursemaid pushing a baby-cart into which a young man of two was strapped. While far more likely to take him than the stout old party still skipping the greensward like a mountain roe, she would be much less plausible as a reason for going to the evil one. But a vow was a vow, and he was in for it.

His approach was the same as on the previous occasion. Lifting his hat ceremoniously, he said with the same distinctness of utterance, "Madam, I wish to ask if you'll marry me?"

THE DUST FLOWER

The girl, who had paused when he did, leaned on the pusher of her go-cart, studying him calmly. Chewing something with a slow, rotary movement of the lips and chin, she broke the action with a snap before quite completing the circle, to begin all over again. "Oh, you do, do you?" was her quiet response.

"If you please."

She studied him again, with the same semi-circular motion of the jaw. She might have been weighing his proposal.

"Say, is this one of them club initiation stunts, or have you just got a noive?"

"Am I to take that as a yes or a no?"

"And am I to take you as one of them smart-Alecks, or a coily-headed nut?"

He saw a way out. "I'm generally considered a curly-headed nut."

"Then it's me for the exit-in-case-of-fire, so ta-ta." She laughed back at him over her shoulder. "Wish you luck with your next."

But fate was already on him in another form. A lady of fifty or thereabouts was coming up the path, refined, sedate, mistress of herself, the one type of all others most difficult to accost. All the same he must do it. He must keep on doing it till some one yielded to his suit. The rebuffs to which he had been subjected did no more than inflame his will.

Approaching the new sibyl with the same ceremoniousness, he repeated the same words in the same precise tone. The lady stood off, eyed him majestically through a lorgnette, and spoke with a force which came from quietude.

THE DUST FLOWER

"I know who you are. You're Rashleigh Allerton. You ought to be ashamed with a shame that would strike you to the ground. I'm a friend of Miss Marion Walbrook's. I'm on my way to see her and shall *not* mention this encounter. We work on the same committee of the League for the Suppression of Men's Clubs. The lamentable state in which I see you convinces me once more of the need of our work, if our men are to become as we hope to see them. I bid you a good afternoon."

With the dignity of a queen she passed on and out of sight, leaving him with the sting of a whiplash on his face.

But the name of Miss Walbrook, connected with that of the League which was her pet enthusiasm for the public weal, only served as an incitement. He would go through with it now at any cost. By nightfall he would be at police-headquarters for insulting women, or he would have found a bride.

Walking on again, the path was clear before him as far as he could see. Having thus a few minutes to reflect, he came to the conclusion that his attacks had been too precipitate. He should feel the ground before him, leading the sibyl a little at a time, so as to have her mentally prepared. There were methods of "getting acquainted" to which he should apply himself first of all.

But getting acquainted with the old Italian peasant woman, bowed beneath a bundle, who was the next he would have to confront, being out of the question, he resolved to side-step destiny by slipping out of the main path and following a branch one. Doing so, he came into less frequented regions, while his steps took him up a low hill burnished with the tints of mid-October. Trees and shrubs were flame-colored, copper-colored, wine-colored, differing only in their diffuseness of hue from the concentrated gorgeousness of amaranth, canna, and gladiolus. The sounds of the city were deadened here to a dull rumble, while the vibrancy of the autumn afternoon excited his taut nerves.

At the top of the hill he paused. There was no one in sight who could possibly respond to his quest. He wondered for a second if this were not a hint to him to abandon it. But doing that he would abandon his revenge, and by abandoning his revenge he would concede everything to this girl who had so bitterly wronged him. Ever since he could remember they had been pals, and for at least ten years he had vaguely thought of asking her to marry him when it came to his seeking a wife. It was true, the hint she had thrown out, that he had felt himself in no great need of a wife till his mother had died some eighteen months previously, and he had found himself with a cumbrous old establishment on his hands. That had given the decisive turn to his suit. He had asked her. She had taken him. And since then, in the course of less than ten weeks, if they had had three quarrels they had had thirty. He had taken them all more or less good-naturedly—till to-day. To-day was too much. He could hardly say why it was too much, unless it was as the last straw, but he felt it essential to his honor to show her by actual demonstration the ruin she had made of him.

THE DUST FLOWER

Looking about him for another possibility, he noticed that at the spot where the path, having serpentined down the little hillside, rejoined the main footway there was a bench so placed that its occupant would have a view along several avenues at once. Since it was obviously a vantage point for such strategy as his, he had taken the first steps down toward it when a little gray figure emerged from behind a group of blue Norway spruces. She went dejectedly to the bench, sitting down at an extreme end of it.

Wrought up to a fit of tension far from rare with him, Allerton stood with his nails digging into his clenched palms and his thin lips pressed together. He was sure he was looking at a "drab." All the shoddy, outcast meanings he had read into the word were under the bedraggled feathers of this battered black hat or compressed within the forlorn squirrel-trimmed gray suit. The dragging movement, the hint of dropping on the seat not from fatigue but from desperation, completed the picture his imagination had already painted of some world-worn, knocked-about creature who had come to the point at which, in his own phrase, she was "all in."

As far as this described Letty Gravely, he was wrong. She was not "all in." She was never more mentally alert than at that very minute. If she moved slowly, if she sank on the seat as if too beaten down by events to do more, it was because her mind was so intensely centered on her immediate problems.

She had, in fact, just formed a great resolution. Whatever became of her, she would never go back to Judson Flack, her stepfather. This had not been clearly in her mind when she had gone down his steps and walked away, but the occasion presented itself now as one to be seized. In seizing it, however, the alternatives were difficult. She was without a cent, a shelter, a job, a friend, or the prospect of a meal. It was probable that there was not at that minute in New York a human being so destitute. Before nightfall she would have to find some nominal motive for living or be arrested as a vagrant.

She was not appalled. For the first time in her life she was relatively free from fear. Even with nothing but her person as she stood, she was her own mistress. No big dread hung over her—that is, no big dread of the kind represented by Judson Flack. She might jump into the river or go to the bad, but in either case she would do it of her own free will. Merely to have the exercise of her own free will gave her the kind of physical relief which a human being gets from stretching limbs cramped and crippled by chains.

Besides, there was in her situation an underlying possibility of adventure. This she didn't phrase, since she didn't understand it. She only had the intuition in her heart that where "the world is all before you, where to choose your place of rest, and Providence your guide," Providence *becomes* your guide. Verbally she put it merely in the words, "Things happen," though as to what could happen between half-past three in the afternoon and midnight, when she would possibly be in jail, she could not begin to imagine.

So absorbed was she in this momentous uncertainty that she scarcely noticed that some one had seated himself at the other end of the bench. It was a public place; it was likely that some one would. She felt neither curiosity nor resentment. A lack of certain of the feminine instincts, or their retarded development, left her without interest in the fact that the newcomer was a man. From the slight glance she had given him when she heard his step, she judged him to be what she estimated as an elderly man, quite far into the thirties.

She went back to her own thoughts which were practical. There were certain measures which she could take at once, after which there would be no return. Once more she was not appalled. She had lived too near the taking of these steps to be shocked by them. Everything in life is a question of relativity, and in the world which her mother had entered on marrying Judson Flack the men were all so near the edge of the line which separates the criminal from the non-criminal that it seemed a natural thing when they crossed it, while the women. . . .

But as her thoughts were dealing with this social problem in its bearing on herself, her neighbor spoke.

"Funny to watch those kids playing with the pup, isn't it?"

She admitted that it was, that watching children and young animals was a favorite sport with her. She answered simply, because being addressed by strange men with whom she found herself in proximity was sanctioned by the etiquette of her society. To resent it would be putting on airs, besides which it would cut off social intercourse between the sexes. It had happened to her many a time to have engaging conversations with chance young men beside her in the subway, never seeing them before or afterward.

So Allerton found getting acquainted easier than he had expected. The etiquette of *his* society not sanctioning this directness of response on her part, he drew the conclusion that she was accustomed to "meeting fellows halfway." As this was the sort of person he was looking for, he found in the freedom nothing to complain of.

With the openness of her social type she gave details of her biography without needing to be pressed.

"You're a New York girl?"

"I am now. I didn't use to be."

"What were you to begin with?"

"Momma brought me from Canada after my father died. That's why I ain't got no friends here."

At this appeal for sympathy his glance stole suspiciously toward her, finding his first conjectures somewhat but not altogether verified. She was young apparently, and possibly pretty, though as to neither point did he care. He would have preferred more "past," more "mystery," more "drama," but since you couldn't have everything, a young person utterly unfit to be his wife would have to be enough. He continued to draw out her story, not because he cared anything about hearing it, but in order to spring his question finally without making her think him more unbalanced than he was.

"Your father was a Canadian?"

"Yes; a farmer. Momma used to say she was about as good to work a farm as a cat to run a fire-engine.

THE DUST FLOWER

When he died, she sold out for four thousand dollars and come to New York."

"To work?"

"No, to have a good time. She'd never had a good time, momma hadn't, and she was awful pretty. So she said she'd just blow herself to it while she had the berries in her basket. That was how she met Judson Flack. I suppose you know who he is. Everybody does."

"I'm afraid I haven't the pleasure."

"Oh, I don't know as you'd find it any big pleasure. Momma didn't, not after she'd give him a try."

"Who and what is he?"

"He calls hisself a man about town. I call him a bum. Poor momma married him."

"And wasn't happy, I suppose."

"Not after he'd spent her wad, she wasn't. She was crazy about him, and when she found out that all he'd cared about was her four thousand plunks—well, it was her finish."

"How long ago was that?"

"About four years now."

"And what have you been doing in the meanwhile?"

"Keepin' house for Judson Flack most of the time—till I quit."

"Oh, you've quit?"

"Sure I've quit." She was putting her better foot forward. "Now I'm in pitchers."

He glanced at her again, having noticed already that she scarcely glanced at him. Her profile was toward him as at first, an irregular little profile of lifts and tilts, which might be appealing, but was not beautiful. The boast of being in pictures, so incongruous with her woefully dilapidated air, did not amuse him. He knew how large a place a nominal connection with the stage took in the lives of certain ladies. Even this poor little tramp didn't hesitate to make the claim.

"And you're doing well?"

She wouldn't show the white feather. "Oh, so so! I—I get along."

"You live by yourself?"

"I—I do now."

"Don't you find it lonely?"

"Not so lonely as livin' with Judson Flack."

"You're—you're happy?"

A faint implication that she might look to him for help stirred her fierce independence. "Gee, yes! I'm —I'm doin' swell."

"But you wouldn't mind a change, I suppose?"

For the first time her eyes stole toward him, not in suspicion, and still less in alarm, but in one of the intenser shades of curiosity. It was almost as if he was going to suggest to her something "off the level" but which would nevertheless be worth her while. She was used to these procedures, not in actual experience but from hearing them talked about. They made up a large part of what Judson Flack understood as "business." She felt it prudent to be as non-committal as possible.

"I ain't so sure."

She meant him to understand that being tolerably satisfied with her own way of life, she was not enthusiastic over new experiments.

THE DUST FLOWER

His next observation was no surprise to her. "I'm a lawyer."

She was sure of that. There were always lawyers in these subterranean affairs—"shyster" was a word she had heard applied to them—and this man looked the part. His thin face, clear-cut profile, and skin which showed dark where he shaved, were all, in her judgment, signs of the sinister. Even his clothes, from his patent leather shoes with spats to his dark blue necktie with a pearl in it, were those which an actor would wear in pictures to represent a "shark."

She was turning these thoughts over in her mind when he spoke again.

"I've an office, but I don't practise much. It takes all my time to manage my own estate."

She didn't know what this meant. It sounded like farming, but you didn't farm in New York, or do it from an office anyhow. "I guess he's one of them gold-brick nuts," she commented to herself, "but he won't put nothin' over on me."

In return for her biography he continued to give his, bringing out his facts in short, hard statements which seemed to hurt him. It was this hurting him which she found most difficult to reconcile with her gold brick theory and the suspicion that he was a "shark."

"My father was a lawyer, too. Rather well known in his day. One time ambassador to Vienna."

Ambassador to Vienna! She didn't know where Vienna was or the nature of an ambassador, but she did know that it sounded grand, so she looked at him attentively. It was either more gold brick or else. . . .

Then something struck her—"smote her" would be perhaps the more accurately descriptive word, since the effect was on her heart. This man was sick. He was suffering. She had often seen women suffer, but men rarely, and this was one of the rare instances. Something in her was touched. She couldn't imagine why he talked to her or what he wanted of her, but a pity which had never yet been called upon was astir among her emotions.

As for the minute he said no more, her next words came out only because she supposed them to betray the kindly interest of which he was in need.

"Then I suppose he left you a big fat wad."

"Yes; but it doesn't do me any good. I mean, it doesn't make me happy—when I'm not."

"I guess it'd make you a good deal less happy if you didn't have it."

"Perhaps so; I don't think about it either way." He added, after tense compression of the lips; "I'm all alone in the world—like you."

She was sure now that something was coming, though of what nature lay beyond her speculative power. She wondered if he could have fallen in love with her at first sight, realizing a favorite dream she often had in the subway. Hundreds of times she had beguiled the minutes by selecting one or another of the wealthy lawyers and bankers, whom she supposed to be her fellow-travelers there, seeing him smitten by a glance at her, following her when she got out, and laying his heart and coronet at her feet before she had

THE DUST FLOWER

run up the steps. If this man were not a shyster lawyer or a gold brick nut, he might possibly be doing that.

"It's about a girl," he burst out suddenly. "Half an hour ago she kicked me out."

"Did she know you had all that dough?"

"Yes, she knew I had all that dough. But she said that since I was going to the devil, I had better go." He drew a long breath. "Well, I'm going—perhaps quicker than she thinks."

"Will you do yourself any good by that?"

"No, but I'll do her harm."

"How?"

"I'll show her what she's made of me."

"She can't make anything of you in half an hour or in half a year—not so long as you've got your wad back of you. If you was to be kicked out with your pay-envelope stole, and your mother's rings pulled off your fingers, and her wrist-watch from your wrist, and even your carfare——"

"Is that what's happened to you?"

"Sure! Half an hour ago, too. Judson Flack! But why should I worry? Something'll happen before night."

He became emphatic. "Yes, and I'll tell you what it will be. You put your finger on it just now when you said she couldn't make anything out of men in half an hour. Well, it's got to be something that would take just that time—an hour at the most—*and fatal*. Now do you see?"

She shook her head.

He swung fully round on her from his end of the bench. "Think," he commanded.

As if with a premonitory notion of what he meant, she answered coldly: "What's the good o' me thinkin'? I've got nothin' to do with it."

"You might have."

"I can't imagine what, unless it'd be ———" Realizing what she had been about to say, she broke off in confusion, coloring to the eyes.

He nodded. "I see you understand. I want you to come off somewhere and marry me."

She took it more calmly than if she hadn't thought him mad. "But—but you said you'd be—be goin' to the devil."

"Well?"

His look, his tone, conveyed the idea, which penetrated to her mind but slowly. When it did, the surging color became a flush, hot and painful.

So here it was again, the thing she had been running away from. It had outwitted and outrun her, meeting her again just at the instant when she thought she was shaking it off. She was so indignant with the *thing* that she almost overlooked the man. She too swung round from her end of the bench, so that they confronted each other, with the length of the seat between them. It was her habit to put things plainly, though now she did it with a burning heart.

"This is the way you mean it, isn't it?—you'd go to the devil because you'd married *me*."

The half-minute before he answered was occupied not merely in thinking what to say but in noticing, now that he had her in full-face, that her large, brown irises seemed to be sprinkled with gold dust. Otherwise her appearance struck him simply as burred, as if it had been brightly enough drawn as to color and line, only rubbed over and defaced by the hand of misery.

"I don't want you to get me wrong," he explained. "It's not a question of my marrying you in particular. I've said I'd marry the first girl I met who'd marry me."

The gold-brown eyes scintillated with a thousand tiny stars. "Say, and am I the first?"

"No; you're the fourth." He added, so that she should be under no misconception as to what he was about: "You can take me or leave me. That's up to you. But if you take me, I want you to understand that it'll be on a purely business basis."

She repeated, as if to memorize the words, "A purely business basis."

"Exactly. I'm not looking for a wife. I only want a woman to marry—a woman to whom I can point and say, See there! I've married—that."

"And *that'd* be me."

"If you undertook the job."

"The job of—of bein' laughed at—jeered at ——"

"I'd be the one who'd be laughed at and jeered at. Nobody would think anything about you. They wouldn't remember how you looked or know your name. If you got sick of it after a bit, and decided to cut and run, you could do it. I'd see that you were well treated—for the rest of your life."

She studied him long and earnestly. "Say, are *you* crazy?"

"I'm all on edge, if that's what you mean. But there's nothing for you to be afraid of. I shan't do you any harm at any time."

THE DUST FLOWER

"You only want to do harm to yourself. I'd be like the awful kind o' pill which a fellow'll swaller to commit suicide." She rose, not without a dignity of her own. "Well, mister, if I'm your fourth, I guess you'll have to look about you for a fifth."

"Where are you going?"

He asked the question without rising. She answered as if her choice of objectives was large.

"Oh, anywheres."

"Which means nowhere, doesn't it?"

"Oh, not exactly. It means—it means—the first place I fetch up."

"The first place you fetch up may be the police-station, if the things you said just now are true."

"The police-station is safe, anyways."

"And you think the place I'd take you to wouldn't be. Well, you're wrong. It'll be as safe as a church for as long as you like to stay; and when you want to go—lots of money to go with."

Facing away from him toward the city, she said over her shoulder: "There's things money couldn't pay you for. Bein' looked down on is one."

She was about to walk on, but he sprang after her, catching her by the sleeve.

"Look here! Be a sport. You've got the chance of your lifetime. It'll mean no more to you than a part they'd give you in pictures—just a rôle—and pay you a lot better."

She was not blind to the advantages he laid before her. True, it might be what she qualified as "bull" to get her into a trap; only she didn't believe it. This man with the sick mind and anguished face was non-

40

of the soft-spoken fiends whose business it is to ensnare young girls. She knew all about them from living with Judson Flack, and couldn't be mistaken. This fellow might be crazy, but he was what he said. If he said he wouldn't do her any harm, he wouldn't. If he said he would pay her well, he would. The main question was as to whether or not, just for the sake of getting something to eat and a place to sleep, she could deliberately put herself in a position in which the man who had married her would have gone to the devil *because* he had married her.

As he held her by the sleeve looking down at her, and she, half turned, was looking up at him, this was the battle she was fighting. Hitherto her impulse had been to run away from the scorn of her inferiority; now she was asking herself what would happen if she took up its challenge and fought it on its own ground. What if I do? was the way the question framed itself, but aloud she made it.

"If I said I would, what would happen first?"

"We'd go and get a license. Then we'd find a minister. After that I should give you something to eat, and then I'd take you home."

"Where would that be?"

He gave her his address in East Sixty-seventh Street, only a few doors from Fifth Avenue, but her social sophistication was not up to the point of seeing the significance of this. Neither did her imagination try to picture the home or to see it otherwise than as an alternative to the police-station, or worse, as a lodging for the night.

THE DUST FLOWER

"And what would happen to me when I got to your home?"

"You'd have your own room. I shouldn't interfere with you. You'd hardly ever see me. You could stay as long as you liked or as short as you liked, after the first week or two."

There was that about him which carried conviction. She believed him. As an alternative to having nowhere to go, what he offered her was something, and something with that spice of adventure of which she had been dreaming only a few minutes earlier. She couldn't be worse off than she was now, and if it gave her the chance of a hand-to-hand tussle with the world-pride which had never done anything but look down on her, she would be fighting what she held as her worst enemy. She braced herself to say,

"All right; I'll do it."

He, too, braced himself. "Very well! Let's start."

The impetuosity of his motion almost took her breath away as she tried to keep pace with him.

"By the way, what's your name?" he asked, before they reached Fifth Avenue.

She told him, but was too overwhelmed with what she had undertaken to dare to ask him his,

Chapter IV

"NAO!"

The strong cockney negative was also an exclamation. It came from Mrs. Courage, the cook-housekeeper, who stood near the kitchen range making the coffee for breakfast. She was a woman who looked her name, born not merely to do battle, but to enjoy being in the midst of it.

Jane, the waitress, was the next to speak. "Nettie Duckett, you ought to be ashymed to sye them words, you that's been taught to 'ope the best of everyone."

Jane had fluttered in from the pantry with the covered dish for the toast. Jane still fluttered at her work, as she had done for the past thirty years. The late Mrs. Allerton had liked her about the table because she was swift, deft, and moved lightly. A thin little woman, with a profile resembling that of Punch's Judy, and a smile of cheerful piety, she yielded to time only by a process of drying up.

Nettie Duckett was quick in her own defense, but breathless, too, from girlish laughter. "I can't 'elp syin' what I see, now can I? There she was 'arf dressed in the little back spare-room. Oh, the commonest thing! You wouldn't 'a wanted to sweep 'er out with a broom."

"Pretty goin's on I must sye," Jane commented. "'Ope the best of everyone I will, but when you think that we was all on the top floor——"

THE DUST FLOWER

"Pretty goin's off there'll be, I can tell you that," Mrs. Courage declared in her rich, decided bass. "Just let me 'ave a word with Master Rashleigh. I'll tell 'im what 'is ma would 'ave said. She left 'im to me, she did. 'Courage,' she's told me many a time, 'that boy'll be your boy after I'm gone.' As good as mykin' a will, I call it. And now to think that with us right 'ere in the 'ouse. . . . Where's Steptoe? Do 'e know anything about it?"

"Do 'e know anything about what?" The question came from Steptoe himself, who appeared on the threshold.

The three women maintained a dramatic silence, while the old butler-valet looked from one to another.

"Seems as if there was news," he observed dryly.

"Tell 'im, Nettie," Mrs. Courage commanded.

Nettie was the young thing of the establishment, Mrs. Courage's own niece, brought from England when the housemaid's place fell vacant on Bessie's unexpected marriage to Walter Wildgoose, Miss Walbrook's indoor man. Indeed she had been brought from England before Bessie's marriage, of which Mrs. Courage had had advance information, so that as soon as Bessie left, Nettie was on the spot to be smuggled into the Allerton household. Steptoe had not forgiven this underhand movement on Mrs. Courage's part, seeing that in the long-ago both she and Jane had been his own nominees, and that he considered the household posts as gifts at his disposal. "I'll 'ave to make a clean sweep o' the lot o' them," he had more than once declared at those gatherings at which the English butlers and valets of upper Fifth

Avenue discuss their complex of interests. Forty years in the Allerton family had made him not merely its major-domo but in certain respects its head. His tone toward Nettie was that of authority with a note of disapprobation.

"Speak, girl, and do it without giggling. What 'ave you to tell?"

Though she couldn't do it without giggling Nettie repeated the story she had given to her aunt and Jane. She had gone into the small single back bedroom on the floor below Mr. Allerton's, and there was a half-dressed girl 'a-puttin' up of 'er 'air.' According to her own statement Nettie had passed away on the spot, being able, however, to articulate the question, "What are you a'doin' of 'ere?" To this the young woman had replied that Mr. Allerton had brought her in on the previous evening, telling her to sleep there, and there she had slept. Nettie's information could go no further, but it was considered to go far enough.

"So what do you sye to *that?*" Mrs. Courage demanded of Steptoe; "you that's always so ready to defend my young lord?"

Steptoe was prepared to stand back to back with his employer. "I don't defend 'im. I'm not called on to defend 'im. It's Mr. Rashleigh's 'ouse. Any guest of 'is must be your guest and mine."

"And what about Miss Walbrook, 'er that's to be missus 'ere in the course of a few weeks?"

Steptoe colored, frostily. "She's not missus 'ere yet; and if she ever comes, there'll be stormy weather for all of us. New missuses don't generally get on with old servants like us—that's been in the family for so many years—but when they don't, it ain't them as gets notice."

A bell rang sharply. Steptoe sprang to attention.

"There's Mr. Rashleigh now. Don't you women go to mykin' a to-do. There's lots o' troubles that 'ud never 'ave 'appened if women 'ad been able to 'old their tongues."

"But I suppose, Steptoe, you don't deny that there's such a thing as right."

"I don't deny that there's such a thing as right, Mrs. Courage, but I only wonder if you knows more about it than the rest of us."

In Allerton's room Steptoe found the young master of the house half dressed. Standing before a mirror, he was brushing his hair. His face and eyes, the reflection of which Steptoe caught in the glass, were like those of a man on the edge of going insane.

The old valet entered according to his daily habit and without betraying the knowledge of anything unusual. All the same his heart was sinking, as old hearts sink when beloved young ones are in trouble. The boy was his darling. He had been with his father for ten years before the lad was born, and had watched his growth with a more than paternal devotion. " 'E's all I 'ave," he often said to himself, and had been known to let out the fact in the afore-mentioned group of English upper servants, a small but exclusive circle in the multiplex life of New York.

In Steptoe's opinion Master Rash had never had a chance. Born many years after his parents had lived together childlessly, he had come into the world constitutionally neurasthenic. Steptoe had never known a boy who needed more to be nursed along and coaxed along by affection, and now and then by indulgence. Instead, the system of severity had been applied with results little short of calamitous. He had been sent to schools famous for religion and discipline, from which he reacted in the first weeks of freedom in college, getting into dire academic scrapes. Further severity had led to further scrapes, and further scrapes to something like disgrace, when the war broke out and a Red Cross job had kept him from going to the bad. The mother had been a self-willed and selfish woman, claiming more from her son than she ever gave him, and never perceiving that his was a nature requiring a peculiar kind of care. After her death Steptoe had prayed for a kind, sweet wife to come to the boy's rescue, and the answer had been Miss Barbara Walbrook.

When the engagement was announced, Steptoe had given up hope. Of Miss Walbrook as a woman he had nothing to complain. Walter Wildgoose reported her a noble creature, splendid, generous, magnificent, only needing a strong hand. She was of the type not to be served but to be mastered. Rashleigh Allerton would goad her to frenzy, and she would do the same by him. She was already doing it. For weeks past Steptoe could see it plainly enough, and what would happen after they were married God alone knew. For himself he saw no future but to hang on after the wedding as long as the new mistress of the house would allow him, take his dismissal as an inevitable thing, and sneak away and die.

It was part of Steptoe's training not to notice anything till his attention was called to it. So having said his "Good-morning, sir," he went to the closet, took down the hanger with the coat and waistcoat belonging to the suit of which he saw that Allerton had put on the trousers, and waited till the young man was ready for his ministrations.

Allerton was still brushing his hair, as he said over his shoulder: "There's a young woman in the house, Steptoe. Been here all night."

"Yes, sir; I know—in the little back spare-room."

"Who told you?"

"Nettie went in for a pincushion, Mr. Rash, and the young woman was a-doin' of 'er 'air."

"What did Nettie say?"

"It ain't what Nettie says, sir, if I may myke so bold. It's what Mrs. Courage and Jane says."

"Tell Mrs. Courage and Jane they needn't be alarmed. The young woman is—" Steptoe caught the spasm which contracted the boy's face—"the young woman is—my wife."

"Quite so, sir."

If Allerton went no further, Steptoe could go no further; but inwardly he was like a man reprieved at the last minute, and against all hope, from sentence of death. "Then it won't be *'er*," was all he could say to himself, " 'er" being Barbara Walbrook. Whatever calamity had happened, that calamity at least would be escaped, which was so much to the good.

His arms trembled so that he could hardly hold up the waistcoat for Allerton to slip it on. But he didn't slip it on. Instead he wheeled round from the mirror, threw the brushes with a crash to the toilet table, and cried with a rage all the more raging for being impotent:

"Steptoe, I've been every kind of fool."

"Yes, sir, I expect so."

"You've got to get me out of it, Steptoe. You must find a way to save me."

"I'll do my best, sir." The joy of cooperation with the lad almost made up for the anguish at his anguish. "What 'ud it be—you must excuse me, Mr. Rash—but what 'ud it be that you'd like me to save you from?"

Allerton threw out his arms. "From this crazy marriage. This frightful mix-up. I went right off the handle yesterday. I was an infernal idiot. And now I'm in for it. Something's got to be done, Steptoe, and I can't think of any one but you to do it."

"Quite so, sir. Will you 'ave your wystcoat on now, sir? You're ready for it, I see. I'll think it over, Mr. Rash, and let you know."

While first the waistcoat and then the coat were extended and slipped over the shoulders, Allerton did his best to put Steptoe in possession of the mad facts of the previous day. Though the account he gave was incoherent, the old man understood enough.

"It wasn't her fault, you must understand," Allerton explained further, as Steptoe brushed his hat. "She didn't want to. I persuaded her. I wanted to do something that would wring Miss Walbrook's heart—and I've done it! Wrung my own, too! What's to become of me, Steptoe? Is the best thing I can do to shoot myself? Think it over. I'm ready to. I'm not sure that it wouldn't be a relief to get out of this rotten life. I'm all on edge. I could jump out of that window as easily as not. But it wasn't the girl's fault. She's a poor little waif of a thing. You must look after her and keep me from seeing her again, but she's not bad—only—only—Oh, my God! my God!"

He covered his face with his hands and rocked himself about, so that Steptoe was obliged to go on brushing till his master calmed himself.

"Do you think, sir," he said then, "that this is the 'at to go with this 'ere suit? I think as the brown one would be a lot chicker—tone in with the sort of fawn stripe in the blue like, and ketch the note in your tie." He added, while diving into the closet in search of the brown hat and bringing it out, "There's one thing I could say right now, Mr. Rash, and I think it might 'elp."

"What is it?"

"Do you remember the time when you 'urt your leg 'unting down in Long Island?"

"Yes; what about it?"

"You was all for not payin' it no attention and for 'oppin' about as if you 'adn't 'urt it at all. A terr'ble fuss you myde when the doctor said as you was to keep still. Anybody 'ud 'ave thought 'e'd hordered a hamputation. And yet it was keepin' still what got you out o' the trouble, now wasn't it?"

"Well?"

"Well, now you're in a worse trouble still it might do the syme again. I'm a great believer in keepin' still, I am."

Allerton was off again. "How in thunder am I to keep still when ——?"

THE DUST FLOWER

"I'll tell you one wye, sir. Don't talk. Don't *do* nothink. Don't beat your 'ead against the wall. Be quiet. Tyke it natural. You've done this thing. Well, you 'aven't committed a murder. You 'aven't even done a wrong to the young lydy to whom you was engyged. By what I understand she'd jilted you, and you was free to marry any one you took a mind to."

"Nominally, perhaps, but ——"

"If you're nominally free, sir, you're free, by what I can understand; and if you've gone and done a foolish thing it ain't no one's business but your own."

"Yes, but I can't stand it!"

"O' course you can't stand it, sir, but it's because you can't stand it that I'm arskin' of you to keep just as quiet as you can. Mistykes in our life is often like the twists we'll give to our bodies. They'll ache most awful, but let nyture alone and she'll tyke care of 'em. It's jest so with our mistykes. Let life alone and she'll put 'em stryght for us, nine times out o' ten, better than we can do it by workin' up into a wax."

Calmed to some extent Allerton went off to the club for breakfast, being unable to face this meal at home. Steptoe tidied up the room. He was troubled and yet relieved. It was a desperate case, but he had always found that in desperate cases desperate remedies were close at hand,

Chapter V

"SEE that the poor thing gets some breakfast," had been Allerton's parting command, and having finished the room, Steptoe went down the flight of stairs to carry out this injunction.

He was on the third step from the landing when the door of the back room opened, and a little, gray figure, hatted and jacketed, crept out stealthily. She was plainly ready for the street, an intention understood by Beppo, the late Mrs. Allerton's red cocker spaniel, who was capering about her in the hope of sharing the promenade.

As Steptoe came to a halt, the girl ran toward him.

"Oh, mister, I gotta get out of this swell dump. Show me the way, for God's sake!"

To say that Steptoe was thinking rapidly would be to describe his mental processes incorrectly. He never thought; he received illuminations. Some such enlightenment came to him now, inducing him to say, ceremoniously, "Madam can't go without 'er breakfast."

"I don't want any breakfast," she protested, breathlessly. "All I want is to get away. I'm frightened."

"I assure madam that there's nothink to be afryde of in this 'ouse. Mr. Allerton is the most honorable—" he pronounced the initial *h*—"young man that hever was born. I valeted 'is father before 'im and know that 'e wouldn't 'urt a fly. If madam'll trust

THE DUST FLOWER

me— Besides, Mr. Allerton left word with me as you was to be sure to 'ave your breakfast, and I shouldn't know how to fyce 'im if 'e was to know that you'd gone awye without so much as a hegg."

She wrung her hands. "I don't want to see him. I couldn't."

"Madam won't see 'im. 'E's gone for the dye. 'E don't so often heat at 'ome—'ardly never."

Of the courses before her Letty saw that yielding was the easiest. Besides, it would give her her breakfast, which was a consideration. Though she had nominally dined on the previous evening, she had not been able to eat; she had been too terrified. Never would she forget the things that had happened after she had given her consent in the Park.

Not that outwardly they had been otherwise than commonplace. It was going through them at all! The man was as nearly "off his chump"—the expression was hers—as a human being could be without laying himself open to arrest. After calling the taxi in Fifth Avenue he had walked up and down, compelling her to walk by his side, for a good fifteen minutes before making her get in and springing in beside her. At the house opposite he had stared and stared, as if hoping that some one would look out. During the drive to the place where they got the license, and later to the minister's house, he spoke not a word. In the restaurant to which he took her afterward, the most glorious place she had ever been in, he ordered a feast suited to a queen, but she could hardly do more than taste it. She felt that the waiter was looking at them strangely, and she didn't know the uses of the knives and forks.

THE DUST FLOWER

The man she had married offered her no help, neither speaking to her nor giving her a glance. He himself ate but little, lost in some mental maze to which she had no clue.

After dinner he had proposed the theatre, but she had refused. She couldn't go anywhere else with him. Wherever they moved, a thousand eyes were turned in amazement at the extraordinary pair. He saw nothing, but she was alive to it all—more conscious of her hat and suit than even in the street scene in "The Man with the Emerald Eye." Once and for all she became aware that the first standard for human valuation is in clothes.

In the end they had got into another taxi, to be driven round and round the Park and out along the river bank, till he decided that they might go home. During all this time he hardly noticed her. Once he asked her if she was warm enough, and once if she would like to get out and take a walk along the parapet above the river, but otherwise he was withdrawn into a world which he kept shut and locked against her. That left her alone. She had never felt so much alone in her life, not even in the days which followed her mother's death. It was as if she had been snatched away from everything with which she was familiar, to find herself stranded in a country of fantastic dreams.

Then there was the house and the little back room. By the use of his latchkey they had entered a palace huge and dark. Letty didn't know that people lived with so much space around them. Only a hall light burned in a many-colored oriental lamp, and in the

THE DUST FLOWER

half-gloom the rooms on each side of the entry were cavernous. There was not a servant, not a sound. The only living thing was a little dog which pattered out of the obscurity and, raising his paws against her skirt, adopted her instantaneously.

"He was my mother's dog," Allerton explained briefly. "He likes women, but not men, though he's never taken to the women in the house. He'll probably like you. His name is Beppo. I'll show you up at once."

The grandeur of the staircase was overpowering, and the little back spare-room of a magnificence beyond all her experience outside of movie-sets. The flowers on the chintz coverings were prettier than real ones, and there was a private bath. Letty had heard of private baths, but no picture she had ever painted equaled this dainty apartment in which everything was of spotless white except where a flight of blue-gray gulls skimmed over a blue summer sea.

The objects in the bedroom were too lovely to live with. On the toilet table were boxes and trays which Letty supposed must be priceless, and a set of brushes with silver backs. She couldn't brush her hair with a brush with a silver back, because it would be journeying too far beyond real life into that of fairy princesses. On opening the closet to hang up her jacket the very hangers were puffed and covered with the "sweetest flowered silks," so she hung her jacket on a peg.

But she wasn't comfortable, she wasn't happy. Alice had traveled too far into Wonderland, and too suddenly. Unwillingly she lay down in a bed too clean

THE DUST FLOWER

and soft for the human form, but she couldn't sleep in it. She could only tremble and toss and lie awake and wish for the morning. With the dawn she would be up and off, before any one caught sight of her.

For Allerton had used words which had terrified her more than anything that had yet happened or been said—"the other women in the house!" Not till then had she sufficiently visualized the life into which he was taking her to understand that there would be other women there. Now that she knew it, she couldn't face them. She could have faced men. Men, after all, were simple creatures with only a rudimentary power of judgment. But women! God! She pulled the eiderdown about her head so as not to cry out so loudly that she would be heard. What mad thing had she done? What had she let herself in for? She didn't ask what kind of women they would be— members of his family or servants. She didn't care. All women were alike. The woman was not born who wouldn't view a girl in her unconventional situation, "and especially in that rig"—once more the expression was her own—without a condemnation which Letty could not and would not submit herself to. So she would get up and steal away with the first gleam of light.

She got up with the first gleam of light, but she couldn't steal away. Once more she was afraid. Unlocking the door, she dared not venture out. Who knew where, in that palace of cavernous apartments, she might meet a woman, or what the woman would say to her? When Nettie walked in later, humming a street air, Letty almost died from shame. For one

THE DUST FLOWER

thing, she hadn't yet put on her shirtwaist, which in itself was poor enough, and as she stood exposed without it, any other of her sex could see. . . . She had once been on the studio lot when a girl of about her own age, a "supe" like herself, was arrested for thieving in the women's dressing-rooms. Letty had never forgotten the look in that girl's face as she passed out through the crowd of her colleagues. In Nettie's presence she felt like that girl's look.

She had no means of telling the time, but when she could no longer endure the imprisonment she decided to make a bolt for it. She hadn't been thieving, and so they couldn't do anything to her—and there was a chance at least that she might get away. Opening the door cautiously, she stole out on the landing, and there was, not a woman, but a man!

Joy! A man would listen to her appeal. He would see that she was poor, common, unequal to a dump so swell, and would be human and tender. He was a nice looking old man too—she was able to notice that—with a long, kindly face on which there were two spots of bloom as if he had been rouged. So she capitulated to his plea, making only the condition that if she took the hegg—she pronounced the word as he did, not being sure as to what it meant—she should be free to go.

"Certainly, if madam wishes it. I'm sure the last thing Mr. Allerton would desire would be to detain madam against 'er will."

She allowed herself to be ushered down the monumental stairs and into the dining-room, which awed her with the solemnity of a church. She knew at once that she wouldn't be able to eat amid this stateliness any more than in the glitter of last evening's restaurant. She had yielded, however, and there was nothing for it but to sit down at the head of the table in the chair which Steptoe drew out for her. Guessing at her most immediate embarrassment, he showed her what to do by unfolding the napkin and laying it in her lap.

"Now, if madam will excuse me, I'll slip awye and tell Jyne."

But telling Jyne was not so simple a matter as it looked. The council in the kitchen, which at first had been a council and no more, was now a council of war. As Steptoe entered, Mrs. Courage was saying:

"I shall go to Mr. Rashleigh 'imself and tell 'im that hunder the syme roof with a baggage none of us will stye."

"You can syve yourself the trouble, Mrs. Courage," Steptoe informed her. "Mr. Rash 'as just gone out. Besides, I've good news for all of you." He waited for each to take an appropriate expression, Mrs. Courage determined, Jane with face eager and alight, Nettie tittering behind her hand. "Miss Walbrook, which all of us 'as dreaded, is not a-comin' to our midst. The young lydy Nettie see in the back spare-room is Mr. Rashleigh's wife."

"Wife!" Mrs. Courage threw up her hands and staggered backward. "'Im that 'is mother left to me! 'Courage,' says she, 'when I'm gone——'"

Jane crept forward, horrified, stunned. "Them things can't be, Steptoe."

"Mr. Rash told me so 'imself. I don't know what

THE DUST FLOWER

more we want than that." Steptoe was not without his diplomacy. "It's a fine thing for us, girls. This sweet young lydy is not goin' to myke us no trouble like what the other one would, and belongs right in our own class."

" 'Enery Steptoe, speak for yourself," Mrs. Courage said, severely. "There's no baggages in my class, nor never was, nor never will be."

Jane began to cry. "I'm sure I try to think the best of everyone, but when such awful things 'appens and 'omes is broken up———"

"Jynie," Steptoe said with authority, "the young missus is wytin' for 'er breakfast. 'Ave the goodness to tyke 'er in 'er grypefruit."

"Jyne Cakebread," Mrs. Courage declared, with an authority even greater than Steptoe's, "the first as tykes a grypefruit into that dinin'-room, to set before them as I shouldn't demean myself to nyme, comes hunder my displeasure."

"I couldn't, Steptoe," Jane pleaded helplessly. "All my life I've wyted on lydies. 'Ow can you expect me to turn over a new leaf at my time o' life?"

"Nettie?" Steptoe made the appeal magisterially.

"Oh, I'll do it," Nettie giggled. " 'Appy to get another look at 'er. I sye, she's a sight!"

But Mrs. Courage barred the way. "My niece will wyte on people of doubtful conduck over my dead corpse."

"Very well, then, Mrs. Courage," Steptoe reasoned. "If you won't serve the new missus, Mr. Rashleigh, will 'ave to get some one else who will."

"Mr. Rashleigh will 'ave to do that very selfsame

thing. Not another night will none of us sleep hunder this paternal roof with them that their very presence is a houtrage. 'Enery Steptoe was always a time-server, and a time-server 'e will be, but as for us women, we shall see the new missus in goin' in to give 'er notice. Not a month's notice, it won't be. This range as I've cooked at for nearly thirty years I shall cook at no more, not so much as for lunch. Oh, dear! Oh, dear! What's the world comin' to?"

In spite of her strength of character Mrs. Courage threw her apron over her head and burst into tears. Jane was weeping already.

"There, there, aunt," Nettie begged, patting her relative between the shoulders. "What's the good o' goin' on like that just because a silly ass 'as married beneath 'im?"

Mrs. Courage pulled her apron from her face to cry out with passion:

"If 'e was goin' to disgryce 'imself like that, why couldn't 'e 'a taken you?"

So Steptoe waited on Letty himself, bringing in the grapefruit, the coffee, the egg, and the toast, and seeing that she knew how to deal with each in the proper forms. He was so brooding, so yearning, so tactful, as he bent over her, that she was never at a loss as to the fork or spoon she ought to use, or the minute at which to use it. Under his protection Letty ate. She ate, first because she was young and hungry, and then because she felt him standing between her and all vague terrors. By the time she had finished, he moved in front of her, where he could speak as one human being to another.

THE DUST FLOWER

Taking an empty plate from the table to put it on the sideboard, he said: "I 'ope madam is chyngin' 'er mind about leavin' us."

Letty glanced up shyly in spite of being somewhat reassured. "What'ud be the good of my changin' my mind when—when I'm not fit to stay?"

"Madam means not fit in the sense that——"

"I'm not a lady."

Resting one hand on the table, he looked down into her eyes with an expression such as Letty had never before seen in a human face.

"I could myke a lydy of madam."

At the sound of these quiet words, so confidently spoken, something passed through Letty's frame to be described only by the hard-worked word, a thrill. It was a double current of vibration, partly of upleaping hope, partly of the desperate sense of her own limitations. A hundred points of gold dust were aflame in her irises as she said:

"You mean that you'd put me wise? Oh, but I'd never learn!"

"On the contrary, I think madam would pick up very quick."

"And I'd never be able to talk the right——"

"I could learn madam to talk just as good as me."

It seemed too much. She clasped her hands. It was the nearest point she had ever reached to ecstasy. "Oh, do you think you could? You talk somethin' beautiful, you do!"

He smiled modestly. "I've always lived with the best people, and I suppose I ketch their wyes. I know what a gentleman is—and a lydy. I know all a lydy's little 'abits, and before two or three months was over madam 'ud 'ave them as natural as natural, if she wouldn't think me overbold."

"When 'ud you begin?"

The bright spot deepened in each cheek. "I've begun already, if madam won't think me steppin' out o' my plyce to sye so, in showin' madam the spoons and forks for the different——"

Letty colored, too. "Yes, I saw that. I take it as very kind. But—" she looked at him with a puzzled knitting of the brows— "but what makes you take all this trouble for me?"

"I've two reasons, madam, but I'll only tell you one of 'em just now. The other'll keep. I'll myke it known to you if—if all goes as I 'ope." He straightened himself up. "I don't often speak o' this," he continued, "because among us butlers and valets it wouldn't be understood. Most of us is what's known as conservative, all for the big families and the old wyes. Well, so am I—to a point. But——"

He moved a number of objects on the table before he could go on. "I wasn't born to the plyce I 'old now," he explained after getting his material at command. "I wasn't born to nothink. I was what they calls in England a foundlin'—a byby what's found— what 'is parents 'ave thrown awye. I don't know who my father and mother was, or what was my real nyme. 'Enery Steptoe is just a nyme they give me at the Horphanage. But I won't go into that. I'm just tryin' to tell madam that my life was a 'ard one, quite a 'ard one, till I come to New York as footman for

BY THE TIME HE HAD FINISHED, HIS HEART WAS A LITTLE EASED AND
SOME OF HER TENDERNESS BEGAN TO FLOW TOWARD HIM

Mr. Allerton's father, and afterward worked up to be 'is valet and butler."

He cleared his throat. Expressing ideals was not easy. "I 'ope madam will forgive me if I sye that what it learned me was a fellow-feelin' with my own sort—with the poor. I've often wished as I could go out among the poor and ryse them up. I ain't a socialist—a little bit of a anarchist perhaps, but nothink extreme—and yet—Well, if Mr. Rashleigh had married a rich girl, I would 'a tyken it as natural and done my best for 'im, but since 'e 'asn't—Oh, can't madam see? It's—it's a kind o' pride with me to find some one like—like what I was when I was 'er age—out in the cold like—and bring 'er in—and 'elp 'er to tryne 'erself—so—so as—some day—to beat the best—them as 'as 'ad all the chances ——"

He was interrupted by the tinkle of the telephone. It was a relief. He had said all he needed to say, all he knew how to say. Whether madam understood it or not he couldn't tell, since she didn't seize ideas quickly.

"If madam will excuse me now, I'll go and answer that call."

But Letty sprang up in alarm. "Oh, don't leave me. Some of them women will blow in ——"

"None of them women will *come*—" he threw a delicate emphasis on the word—"if madam'll just sit down. They don't mean to come. I'll explyne that to madam when I come back, if she'll only not leave this room."

Chapter VI

"GOOD morning, Steptoe. Will you ask Mr. Allerton if he'll speak to Miss Walbrook?"

"Mr. Allerton 'as gone to the New Netherlands Club for 'is breakfast, miss."

"Oh, thanks. I'll call him up there."

She didn't want to call him up there, at a club, where a man must like to feel safe from feminine intrusion, but the matter was too pressing to permit of hesitation. Since the previous afternoon she had gone through much searching of heart. She was accustomed to strong reactions from tempestuousness to penitence, but not of the violence of this one.

Summoned to the telephone, Allerton felt as if summoned to the bar of judgment. He divined who it was, and he divined the reason for the call.

"Good morning, Rash!"

His voice was absolutely dead. "Good morning, Barbara!"

"I know you're cross with me for calling you at the club."

"Oh, no! Not at all!"

"But I couldn't wait any longer. I wanted you to know—I've got it on again, Rash—never to come off any more."

He was dumb. Thirty seconds at least went by, and he had made no response.

THE DUST FLOWER

"Aren't you glad?"

"I—I could have been glad—if—if I'd known you were going to do it."

"And now you know that it's done."

He repeated in his lifeless voice, "Yes, now I know that it's done."

"Well?"

Again he was silent. Two or three times he tried to find words, producing nothing but a stammering of incoherent syllables. "I—I can't talk about it here, Barbe," he managed to articulate at last. "You must let me come round and see you."

It was her voice now that was dead. "When will you come, Rash?"

"Now—at once—if you can see me."

"Then come."

She put up the receiver without saying more. He knew that she knew. She knew at least that something had happened which was fatal to them both.

She received him not in the drawing-room, but in a little den on the right of the front door which was also alive with Miss Walbrook's modern personality. A gold-colored portière from Albert Herter's looms screened them from the hall, and the chairs were covered with bits of Herter tapestry representing fruits. A cabinet of old white Bennington faience stood against a wall, which was further adorned with three or four etchings of Sears Gallagher's. Barbara wore a lacy thing in hydrangea-colored crêpe de chine, loosely girt with a jade-green ribbon tasselled in gold, the whole bringing out the faintly Egyptian note in her personality.

THE DUST FLOWER

They dispensed with a greeting, because she spoke the minute he crossed the threshold of the room.

"Rash, what is it? Why couldn't you tell me on the telephone?"

He wished now that he had. It would have saved this explanation face to face. "Because I couldn't. Because—because I've been too much of an idiot to—to tell you about it—either on the telephone or in any other way."

"How?" He thought she must understand, but she seemed purposely dense. "Sit down. Tell me about it. It can't be so terrible—all of a sudden like this."

He couldn't sit down. He could only turn away from her and gulp in his dry throat. "You remember what I said—what I said—yesterday—about—about the—the Gissing fellow?"

She nodded fiercely. "Yes. Go on. Get it out."

"Well—well—I've—I've done that."

She threw out her arms. She threw back her head till the little nut-brown throat was taut. The cry rent her. It rent him.

"You—*fool!*"

He stood with head hanging. He longed to run away, and yet he longed also to throw himself at her feet. If he could have done exactly as he felt impelled, he would have laid his head on her breast and wept like a child.

She swung away from him, pacing the small room like a frenzied animal. Her breath came in short, hard pantings that were nearly sobs. Suddenly she stopped in front of him with a sort of calm.

THE DUST FLOWER

"What made you?"

He barely lifted his agonized black eyes. "You."

She was in revolt again. "I? What did I do?"

"You—you threw away my ring. You said it was all—all over."

"Well? Couldn't I say that without driving you to act the madman? No one but a madman would have gone out of this house and—" She clasped her forehead in her hands with a dramatic lifting of the arms. "Oh! It's too much! I don't care about myself. But to have it on your conscience that a man has thrown his life away——"

He asked meekly, "What good was it to me when you wouldn't have it?"

She stamped her foot. "Rash, you'll drive me insane. Your life might be no good to you at all, and yet you might give it a chance for twenty-four hours—that isn't much, is it?—before you—" She caught herself up. "Tell me. You don't mean to say that you're *married?*"

He nodded.

"To whom?"

"Her first name is Letty. I've forgotten the second name."

"Where did you find her?"

"Over there in the Park."

"And she went and married you—like that?"

"She was all alone—chucked out by a stepfather——"

She burst into a hard laugh. "Oh, you baby! You believed that? The kind of story that's told by nine of the ——"

He interrupted quickly. "Don't call her anything, Barbe—I mean any kind of a bad name. She's all right as far as that goes. There's a kind that couldn't take you in."

"There's *no* kind that couldn't take *you* in!"

"Perhaps not, but it's the one thing in—in this whole idiotic business that's on the level—I mean she is. I'd give my right hand to put her back where I found her yesterday—just as she was—but she's straight."

She dropped into a chair. The first wild tumult of rage having more or less spent its force, she began, with a kind of heart-broken curiosity, to ask for the facts. She spoke nervously, beating a palm with a gold tassel of her girdle. "Begin at the beginning. Tell me all about it."

He leaned on the mantelpiece, of which the only ornaments were a child's head in white and blue terra cotta by Paul Manship, balanced by a pair of old American glass candlesticks, and told the tale as consecutively as he could. He recounted everything, even to the bringing her home, the putting her in the little, back spare-room, and her adoption by Beppo, the red cocker spaniel. By the time he had finished, his heart was a little eased, and some of her tenderness toward him was beginning to flow forth. She was like that, all wrath at one minute, all gentleness the next. Springing to her feet, she caught him by the arm, pressing herself against him.

"All right, Rash. You've done it. That's settled. But it can be undone again."

He pressed her head back from him, resting the

THE DUST FLOWER

knot of her hair in the hollow of his palm and looking down into her eyes.

"How can it be undone?"

"Oh, there must be ways. A man can't be allowed to ruin his life—to ruin two lives—for a prank. We'll just have to think. If you made it worth while for her to take you, you can make it worth while for her to let you go. She'll do it."

"She'd do it, of course. She doesn't care. I'm nothing to her, not any more than she to me. I shan't see her any more than I can help. I suppose she must stay at the house till—I told Steptoe to look after her."

She took a position at one end of the mantelpiece, while he faced her from the other. She gave him wise counsel. He was to see his lawyers at once and tell them the whole story. Lawyers always saw the way out of things. There was the Bellington boy who married a show-girl. She had been bought off, and the lawyers had managed it. Now the Bellington boy was happily married to one of the Plantagenet Jones girls and lived at Marillo Park. Then there was the Silliman boy who had married the notorious Kate Cookesley. The lawyers had found the way out of that, too, and now the Silliman boy was a secretary of the American Embassy in Rome. Accidents such as had happened to Rash were regrettable of course, but it would be folly to think that a perfectly good life must be done for just because it had got a crack in it.

"We'll play the game, of course," she wound up. "But it's a game, and the stronger side must win.

What should you say of my going to see her—she needn't know who I am further than that I'm a friend of yours—and finding out for myself?"

"Finding out what?"

"Finding out her price, silly. What do you suppose? A woman can often see things like that where a man would be blind."

He didn't know. He thought it might be worth while. He would leave it to her. "I'm not worth the trouble, Barbe," he said humbly.

With this she agreed. "I know you're not. I can't think for a minute why I take it or why I should like you. But I do. That's straight."

"And I adore you, Barbe."

She shrugged her shoulders with a little, comic grimace. "Oh, well! I suppose every one has his own way of showing adoration, but I must say that yours is original."

"If it's original to be desperate when the woman you worship drives you to despair——"

There was another little comic grimace, though less comic than the first time. "Oh, yes, I know. It's always the woman whom a man worships that's in the wrong. I've noticed that. Men are never impossible—all of their own accord."

"I could be as tame as a cat if——"

"If it wasn't for me. Thank you, Rash. I said just now I was fond of you, and I should have to be to—to stand for all the——"

"I'm not blaming you, Barbe. I'm only——"

"Thanks again. The day you're not blaming me is certainly one to be marked with a white stone, as the

THE DUST FLOWER

Romans used to say. But if it comes to blaming any one, Rash, after what happened yesterday——"

"What happened yesterday wasn't begun by me. It would never have entered my mind to do the crazy thing I did, if you hadn't positively and finally—as I thought—flung me down. I think you must do me that justice, Barbe—that justice, at the least."

"Oh, I do you justice enough. I don't see that you can complain of that. It seems to me too that I temper justice with mercy to a degree that—that most people find ridiculous."

"By most people I suppose you mean your aunt."

"Oh, do leave Aunt Marion out of it. You can't forgive the poor thing for not liking you. Well, she doesn't, and I can't help it. She thinks you're a ——"

"A fool—as you were polite enough to say just now."

She spread her hands apart in an attitude of protestation. "Well, if I did, Rash, surely you must admit that I had provocation."

"Oh, of course. The wonder is that with the provocation you can ——"

"Forgive you, and try to patch it up again after this frightful gash in the agreement. Well, it *is* a wonder. I don't believe that many girls ——"

"I only want you to understand, Barbe, that the gash in the agreement was made, not by what I did, but what you did. If you hadn't sent me to the devil, I shouldn't have been in such a hurry to go there."

She was off. "Yes, there you are again. Always me! I'm the one! You may be the gunpowder, the perfectly harmless gunpowder, but it would never

71

blow up if I didn't come as the match. *I* make all the explosions. *I* set you crazy. *I* send you to the devil. *I* make you go and marry a girl you never laid eyes on in your life before."

So it was the same old scene all over again, till both were exhausted, and she had flung herself into a chair to cover her face with her hands and burst into tears. Instantly he was on his knees beside her.

"Barbe! Barbe! My beloved Barbe! Don't cry. I'm a brute. I'm a fool. I'm not satisfied with breaking my own heart, but I must go to work and break yours. Oh, Barbe, forgive me. I'm all to pieces. Forgive me and let me go away and shoot myself. What's the good of a poor, wrecked creature like me hanging on and making such a mess of things? Let me kill myself before I kill you ——"

"Oh, hush!"

Seizing his head, she pressed it against her bosom convulsively. By the shaking of his shoulders, she felt him sob. He *was* a poor creature. She was saying so to herself. But just because he was, something in her yearned over him. He *could* be different; he could be stronger and of value in the world if there was only some one to handle him rightly. She could do it—if she could only learn to handle herself. She *would* learn to handle herself—for his sake. He was worth saving. He had fine qualities, and a good heart most of all. It was his very fineness which put him out of place in a world like that of New York. He was a delicate, brittle, highly-wrought thing which should be touched only with the greatest care, and all his life he had been pushed and hurtled about as if

THE DUST FLOWER

he were a football player or a business man. With the soul of a poet or a painter or a seer, he had been treated like the typical rough-and-ready American lad, till the sensitive nature had been brutalized, maimed, and frenzied.

She knew that. It was why she cared for him. Even when they were children she had seen that he wasn't getting fair treatment, either at home or in school or among the boys and girls with whom they both grew up. He was the exception, and American life allowed only for the rule. If you couldn't conform to the rule, you were guyed and tormented and ejected. Among all his associates she alone knew what he suffered, and because she knew it a vast pity made her cling to him. He had forced himself into the life of clubs, into the life of society, into the life of other men as other men lived their lives, and the effect on him had been so nearly ruinous that it was no wonder if he was always on the edge of nervous explosion. His very wealth which might have been a protection was, under the uniform pressure of American social habit, an incitement to him to follow the wrong way. She knew it, and she alone. She could save him, and she alone. She could save him, if she could first of all save herself.

With his head pressed against her she made the vow as she had made it fifty times already. She would be gentle with him; she would be patient; she would let him work off on her the agony of his suffering nerves, and smile at him through it all. She would help him out of the idiotic situation in which he found himself. The other girl was only an incident, as the show-girl had been to the Bellington boy, and could be disposed of. She attached to that only a secondary importance in comparison with the whole thing—her saving him. She would save him, even if it meant rooting out every instinct in her soul.

But as he made his way blindly back to the club, his own conclusions were different. He must go to the devil. He must go to the devil now, whatever else he did. Going to the devil would set her free from him. It was the only thing that would. It would set him free from the other woman, set him free from life itself. Life tortured him. He was a misfit in it. He should never have been born. He had always understood that his parents hadn't wanted children and that his coming had been resented. You couldn't be born like that and find it natural to be in the world. He had never found it natural. He couldn't remember the time when he hadn't been out of his element in life, and now he must recognize the fact courageously.

It would be easy enough. He had worked up an artificial appetite for all that went under the head of debauchery. It had meant difficult schooling at first, because his natural tastes were averse to that kind of thing, but he had been schooled. Schooled was the word, since his training had begun under the very roof where his father had sent him to get religion and discipline. There had been no let-up in this educational course, except when he himself had stolen away, generally in solitude, for a little holiday.

But as he put it to himself, he knew all the roads and by-paths and cross-country leaps that would take him to the gutter, and to the gutter he would go.

Chapter VII

AND all this while Letty was in the dining-room, learning certain lessons from her new-found friend.

For some little time she had been alone. Steptoe finished his conversation with Miss Walbrook on the telephone, but did not come back. She sat at the table feeding Beppo with bread and milk, but wondering if, after all, she hadn't better make a bolt for it. She had had her breakfast, which was an asset to the good, and nothing worse could happen to her out in the open world than she feared in this great dim, gloomy house. She had once crept in to look at the cathedral and, overwhelmed by its height, immensity, and mystery, had crept out again. Its emotional suggestions had been more than she could bear. She felt now as if her bed had been made and her food laid out in that cathedral—as if, as long as she remained, she must eat and sleep in this vast, pillared solemnity.

And that was only one thing. There were small practical considerations even more terrible to confront. If Nettie were to appear again. . . .

But it was as to this that Steptoe was making his appeal. "I sye, girls, don't you go to mykin' a fuss and spoilin' your lives, when you've got a chanst as'll never come again."

Mrs. Courage answered for them all. To sacrifice

decency to self-interest wasn't in them, nor never would be. Some there might be, like 'Enery Steptoe, who would sell their birthright for a mess of pottage, but Mary Ann Courage was not of that company, nor any other woman upon whom she could use her influence. If a hussy had been put to reign over them, reigned over by a hussy none of them would be. All they asked was to see her once, to deliver the ultimatum of giving notice.

"It's a strynge thing to me," Steptoe reasoned, "that when one poor person gets a lift, every other poor person comes down on 'em."

"And might we arsk who you means by poor persons?"

"Who should I mean, Mrs. Courage, but people like us? If we don't 'ang by each other, who *will* 'ang by us, I should like to know? 'Ere's one of us plyced in a 'igh position, and instead o' bein' proud of it, and givin' 'er a lift to carry 'er along, you're all for mykin' it as 'ard for 'er as you can. Do you call that sensible?"

"I call it sensible for everyone to stye in their proper spere."

"So that if a man's poor, you must keep 'im poor, no matter 'ow 'e tries to better 'imself. That's what your proper speres would come to."

But argument being of no use, Steptoe could only make up his mind to revolution in the house. "The poor's very good to the poor when one of 'em's in trouble," was his summing up, "but let one of 'em 'ave an extry stroke of luck, and all the rest'll jaw against 'im like so many magpies." As a parting shot

THE DUST FLOWER

he declared on leaving the kitchen, "The trouble with you girls is that you ain't got no class spunk, and that's why, in sperrit, you'll never be nothink but menials."

This lack of *esprit de corps* was something he couldn't understand, but what he understood less was the need of the heart to touch occasionally the high points of experience. Mrs. Courage and Jane, to say nothing of Nettie, after thirty years of domestic routine had reached the place where something in the way of drama had become imperative. The range and the pantry produce inhibitions as surely as the desk or the drawing-room. On both natures inhibitions had been packed like feathers on a seabird, till the soul cried out to be released from some of them. It might mean going out from the home that had sheltered them for years, and breaking with all their traditions, but now that the chance was there, neither could refuse it. To a virtuous woman, starched and stiffened in her virtue, steeped in it, dyed in it, permeated by it through and through, nothing so stirs the dramatic, so quickens the imagination, so calls the spirit to the purple emotional heights, as contact with the sister she knows to be a hussy. For Jane Cakebread and Mary Ann Courage the opportunity was unique.

"Then I'll go. I'll go straight now."

As Steptoe brought the information that the three women of the household were coming to announce the resignation of their posts, Letty sprang to her feet.

"May I arsk madam to sit down again and let me explyne?"

Taking this as an order, she sank back into her chair again. He stood confronting her as before, one hand resting lightly on the table.

"Nothink so good won't 'ave 'appened in this 'ouse since old Mrs. Allerton went to work and died."

Letty's eyes shone with their tiny fires, not in pleasure but in wonder.

"When old servants is good, they're good, but even when they're good, there's times when you can't 'elp wishin' as 'ow the Lord 'ud be pleased to tyke them to 'Imself."

He allowed this to sink in before going further.

"The men's all right, for the most part. Indoor work comes natural to 'em, and they'll swing it without no complynts. But with the women it's kick, kick, kick, and when they're worn theirselves out with kickin', they'll begin to kick again. What's plye for a man, for them ain't nothink but slyvery."

Letty listened as one receiving revelations from another world.

"I ain't what they call a woman-'ater. *I* believe as God made woman for a purpose. Only I can't bring myself to think as the human race 'as rightly found out yet what that purpose is. God's wyes is always dark, and when it comes to women, they're darker nor they are elsewheres. One thing I do know, and we'll be a lot more comfortable when more of us finds it out—that God never made women for the 'ome."

In spite of her awe of him, Letty found this doctrine difficult to accept.

"If God didn't make 'em for the home, mister, where on earth would you put 'em?"

The wintry color came out again on the old man's cheeks. "If madam would call me Steptoe," he said ceremoniously, "I think she'd find it easier. I mean," he went on, reverting to the original theme, "that 'E didn't make 'em to be cooks and 'ousemaids and parlormaids, and all that. That's men's work. Men'll do it as easy as a bird'll sing. I never see the woman yet as didn't fret 'erself over it, like a wild animal'll fret itself in a circus cage. It spiles women to put 'em to 'ousework, like it always spiles people to put 'em to jobs for which the Lord didn't give 'em no haptitude."

Letty was puzzled, but followed partially.

"I've watched 'em and watched 'em, and it's always the syme tyle. They'll go into service young and joyous like, but it won't be two or three years before they'll have growed cat-nasty like this 'ere Jyne Cykebread and Mary Ann Courage. Madam 'ud never believe what sweet young things they was when I first picked 'em out—Mrs. Courage a young widow, and Jynie as nice a girl as madam 'ud wish to see, only with the features what Mrs. Allerton used to call a little hover-haccentuated. And now—!" He allowed the conditions to speak for themselves without criticizing further.

"It's keepin' 'em in a 'ome what's done it. They knows it theirselves—and yet they don't. Inside they've got the sperrits of young colts that wants to kick up their 'eels in the pasture. They don't mean no worse nor that, only when people comes to Jynie's age

THE DUST FLOWER

and Mrs. Courage's they 'ave to kick up their 'eels in their own wye. If madam'll remember that, and be pytient with them like ———"

Letty cried in alarm, "But it's got nothin' to do with me!"

"If madam'll excuse me, it's got everything to do with 'er. She's the missus of this 'ouse."

"Oh, no, I ain't. Mr. Allerton just brung me here ———"

Once more there was the delicate emphasis with which he had corrected other slips. "Mr. Allerton *brought* madam, and told me to see that she was put in 'er proper plyce. If madam'll let me steer the thing, I'll myke it as easy for 'er as easy."

He reflected as to how to make the situation clear to her. "I've been readin' about the time when our lyte Queen Victoria come to the throne as quite a young girl. She didn't know nothin' about politics or presidin' at councils or nothin'. But she had a prime minister—a kind of hupper servant, you might sye—'er servant was what 'e always called 'imself—and whatever 'e told 'er to do, she done. Walked through it all, you might sye, till she got the 'ang of it, but once she did get the 'ang of it—well, there wasn't no big-bug in the world that our most grycious sovereign lydy couldn't put it all hover on."

Once more he allowed her time to assimilate this parable.

"Now if madam would only think of 'erself as called in youth to reign hover this 'ouse ———"

"Oh, but I couldn't!"

THE DUST FLOWER

"And yet it's madam's duty, now that she's married to its 'ead ——"

"Yes, but he didn't marry me like that. He married me—all queer like. This was the way."

She poured out the story, while Steptoe listened quietly. There being no elements in it of the kind he called "shydy," he found it romantic. No one had ever suspected the longings for romance which had filled his heart and imagination when he was a poor little scullion boy; but the memory of them, with some of the reality, was still fresh in his hidden inner self. Now it seemed as if remotely and vicariously romance might be coming to him after all, through the boy he adored.

On her tale his only comment was to say: "I've been readin'—I'm a great reader," he threw in parenthetically, "wonderful exercise for the mind, and learns you things which you wouldn't be likely to 'ear tell of—but I've been readin' about a king—I'll show you 'is nyme in the book—what fell in love with a beggar myde ——"

"Oh, but Mr. Allerton didn't fall in love with me."

"That remynes to be seen."

She lifted her hands in awed amazement. "Mister —I mean, Steptoe—you—you don't think ——?"

The subway dream of love at first sight was as tenacious in her soul as the craving for romance in his.

He nodded. "I've known strynger things to 'appen."

"But—but—he couldn't—" it was beyond her power of expression, though Steptoe knew what she meant— "not *him!*"

He answered judicially. " 'E may come to it. It'll

81

be a tough job to bring 'im—but if madam'll be guided by me ——"

Letty collapsed. Her spirit grew faint as the spirit of Christian when he descried far off the walls of the Celestial City, with the Dark River rolling between him and it. Letty knew the Dark River must be there, but if beyond it there lay the slightest chance of the Celestial City. . . .

She came back to herself, as it were, on hearing Steptoe say that the procession from the kitchen would presently begin to form itself.

"Now if madam'll be guided by me she'll meet this situytion fyce to fyce."

"Oh, but I'd never know what to say."

"Madam won't need to say nothink. She won't 'ave to speak. 'Ere they'll troop in—" a gesture described Mrs. Courage leading the advance through the doorway— "and 'ere they'll stand. Madam'll sit just where she's sittin'—a little further back from the tyble—lookin' over the mornin' pyper like—" he placed the paper in her hand—"and as heach gives notice, madam'll just bow 'er 'ead. See?"

Madam saw, but not exactly.

"Now if she'll just move 'er chair ——"

The chair was moved in such a way as to make it seem that the occupant, having finished her breakfast, was giving herself a little more space.

"And if madam would remove 'er 'at and jacket, she'd—she'd seem more like the lydy of the 'ouse at 'ome."

Letty took off these articles of apparel, which Steptoe whisked out of sight.

THE DUST FLOWER

"Now I'll be Mrs. Courage comin' to sye, 'Madam, I wish to give notice.' Madam'll lower the pyper just enough to show 'er inclinin' of 'er 'ead, assentin' to Mrs. Courage leavin' 'er. Mrs. Courage will be all for 'avin' words—she's a great 'and for words, Mrs. Courage is—but if madam won't sye nothin' at all, the wind'll be out o' Mrs. Courage's syles like. Now, will madam be so good——?"

Having passed out into the hall, he entered with Mrs. Courage's majestic gait, pausing some three feet from the table to say:

"Madam, things bein' as they are, and me not wishin' to stye no longer in the 'ouse where I've served so many years, I beg to give notice that I'm a givin' of notice and mean to quit right off."

Letty lowered the paper from before her eyes, jerking her head briskly.

"Ye-es," Steptoe commended doubtfully, "a lettle too—well, too habrupt, as you might sye. Most lydies—real 'igh lydies, like the lyte Mrs. Allerton—inclines their 'ead slow and gryceful like. First, they throws it back a bit, so as to get a purchase on it, and then they brings it forward calm like, lowerin' it stytely—Perhaps if madam'ud be me for a bit—that 'ud be Mrs. Courage—and let me sit there and be 'er, I could show 'er——"

The places were reversed. It was Letty who came in as Mrs. Courage, while Steptoe, seated in the chair, lowered the paper to the degree which he thought dignified. Letty mumbled something like the words the hypothetical Mrs. Courage was presumed to use, while Steptoe slowly threw back his head for

83

the purchase, bringing it forward in condescending grace. Language could not have given Mrs. Courage so effective a retort courteous.

Letty was enchanted. "Oh, Steptoe, let me have another try. I believe I could swing the cat."

Again the places were reversed. Steptoe having repeated the rôle of Mrs. Courage, Letty imitated him as best she could in getting the purchase for her bow and catching his air of high-bred condescension.

"Better," he approved, "if madam wouldn't lower 'er 'ead *quite* so far back'ard. You see, madam, a lydy don't *know* she's throwin' back 'er 'ead so as to get a grip on it. She does it unconscious like, because bein' of a 'aughty sperrit she 'olds it 'igh natural. If madam'll only stiffen 'er neck like, as if sperrit 'ad made 'er about two inches taller than she is ——"

Having seized this idea, Letty tried again, with such success that Mrs. Courage was disposed of. Jane Cakebread followed next, with Nettie last of all. Unaware of his possession of histrionic ability, Steptoe gave to each character its outstanding traits, fluttering like Jane, and giggling like Nettie, not in zeal for a newly discovered interpretative art, but in order that Letty might be nowhere caught at a disadvantage. He was delighted with her quickness in imitation.

"Couldn't 'ave done that better myself," he declared after Nettie had been dismissed for the third or fourth time. "When it comes to the inclinin' of the 'ead I should sye as madam was about letter-perfect, as they sye on the styge. If Mr. Rash was to see it, 'e'd swear as 'is ma 'ad come back again."

A muffled sound proceeded from the back part of

THE DUST FLOWER

the hallway, with some whispering and once or twice Nettie's stifled cackle of a laugh.

" 'Ere they are," he warned her. "Madam must be firm and control 'erself. There's nothink for 'er to be afryde of. Just let 'er think of the lyte Queen Victoria, called to the throne when younger even than madam is ——"

A shuffling developed into one lone step, heavy, stately, and funereal. Doing her best to emulate the historic example held up to her, Letty lengthened her neck and stiffened it. A haughty spirit seemed to rise in her by the mere process of the elongation. She was so nervous that the paper shook in her hand, but she knew that if the Celestial City was to be won, she could shrink from no tests which might lead her on to victory.

Steptoe had relapsed into the major-domo's office, announcing from the doorway, "Mrs. Courage to see madam, if madam will be pleased to receive 'er."

Madam indicated that she was so pleased, scrambling after the standard of the maiden sovereign of Windsor Castle giving audience to princes and ambassadors,

Chapter VIII

"I'M 'ere."

Letty couldn't know, of course, that this announcement, made in a menacing female bass, was due to the fact that three swaying bodies had been endeavoring so to get round the deployed paper wings as to see what was hidden there, and had found their efforts vain. All she could recognize was the summons to the bar of social judgment. To the bar of social judgment she would have gone obediently, had it not been for that rebelliousness against being "looked down upon" which had lately mastered her. As it was, she lengthened her neck by another half inch, receiving from the exercise a new degree of self-strengthening.

"Mrs. Courage is 'ere, madam," Steptoe seconded, "and begs to sye as she's givin' notice to quit madam's service ——"

The explosion came as if Mrs. Courage was strangling.

"When I wants words took out of my mouth by 'Enery Steptoe or anybody else I'll sye so. If them as I've come into this room to speak to don't feel theirselves aible to fyce me ——"

"Madam'll excuse an old servant who's outlived 'er time," Steptoe intervened, "and not tyke no notice. They always abuses the kindness that's been showed 'em, and tykes liberties which ——"

THE DUST FLOWER

But not for nothing had Mrs. Courage been born to the grand manner.

"When 'Enery Steptoe talks of old servants outlivin' their time and tykin' liberties 'e speaks of what 'e knows all about from personal experience. 'E was an old man when I was a little thing not *so* high."

The appeal was to the curiosity of the girl behind the screen. To judge of how high Mrs. Courage had not been at a time when Steptoe was already an old man she might be enticed from her fortifications. But the pause only offered Steptoe a new opportunity.

"And so, if madam can dispense with 'er services, which I understand madam can, Mrs. Courage will be a-leavin' of us this morning, with all our good wishes, I'm sure. Good-dye to you, Mary Ann, and God bless you after all the years you've been with us. Madam's givin' you your dismissal."

Obedient to her cue Letty lowered her guard just enough to incline her head with the grace Steptoe had already pronounced "letter perfect." The shock to Mrs. Courage can best be narrated in her own terms to Mrs. Walter Wildgoose later in the day.

"Airs! No one couldn't imagine it, Bessie, what 'adn't seen it for theirselves—what them baggages'll do—smokin'—and wearin' pearl necklaces—and 'avin' their own limousines—all that I've seen and 'ad got used to—but not the President's wife—not Mary Queen of England—could 'a myde you feel as if you was dirt hunder their feet like what this one—and 'er with one of them marked down sixty-nine cent blouses that 'adn't seen the wash since—and as for

87

looks—why, she didn't 'ave a look to bless 'erself—
and a-'oldin' of 'erself like what a empress might—
and bowin' 'er 'ead, and goin' back to 'er pyper, as if
I'd disturbed 'er at 'er readin'—and the dead and
spitten image of 'Enery Steptoe 'imself she is—and
you know 'ow many times we've all wondered as to
why 'e didn't marry—and 'im with syvings put by—
Jynie thinks as 'e's worth as much as—and you know
what a 'and Jynie is for ferritin' out what's none of
'er business—why, if Jynie Cykebread could 'a myde
'erself Jynie Steptoe—but that's somethink wild
'orses wouldn't myke poor Jynie see—that no man
wouldn't look at 'er the second time if it wasn't for
to laugh—pitiful, I call it, at 'er aige—and me
always givin' the old rip to know as it was no use 'is
'angin' round where I was—as if I'd marry agyne,
and me a widda, as you might sye, from my crydle—
and if I did, it wouldn't 'a been a wicked old varlet
what I always suspected 'e was leadin' a double life—
and now to see them two fyces together—why, I
says, 'ere's the explanytion as plyne as plyne can make
it. . . ."

All of which might have been true in rhetoric, but
not in fact. For what had really given Mrs. Courage
the *coup de grace* we must go back to the scene of
the morning.

Ignoring both Letty's inclination of the head and
Steptoe's benediction she had shown herself hurt
where she was tenderest.

"Now that there's no one to ryse their voice agynst
the disgryce brought on this family but me———"

"Speak right up, Jynie. Don't be afryde. Madam

THE DUST FLOWER

won't eat you. She knows that you've come to give notice ——"

Mrs. Courage struggled on. "No one ain't goin' to bow me out of the 'ouse I've been cook-'ousekeeper in these twenty-seven year ——"

"Sorry as madam'll be to lose you, Jynie, she won't stand in the wye of your gettin' a better plyce ——"

Mrs. Courage's roar being that of the wounded lioness she was, the paper shook till it rattled in Letty's hand.

"I *will* be listened to. I've a right to be 'eard. My 'eart's been as much in this 'ouse and family as 'Enery Steptoe's 'eart; and to see shyme and ruin come upon it ——"

Steptoe's interruption was in a tone of pleased surprise.

"Why, you still 'ere, Mary Ann? We thought you'd tyken leave of us. Madam didn't know you was speakin'. She won't detyne you, madam won't. You and Jynie and Nettie'll all find cheques for your wyges pyde up to a month a 'ead, as I know Mr. Rashleigh'd want me to do. . . ."

Shame and ruin! Letty couldn't follow the further unfoldings of Steptoe's diplomacy because of these two words. They summed up what she brought—what she had been married to bring—to a house of which even she could see the traditions were of honor. Vaguely aware of voices which she attributed to Jane and Nettie, her spirit was in revolt against the rôle for which her rashness of yesterday had let her in, and which Steptoe was forcing upon her.

Jane was still whimpering and sniffling:

89

"I'm sure I never dreamed that things would 'appen like what 'as 'appened—and us all one family, as you might sye—'opin' the best of everyone——"

"Jynie, stop," Mrs. Courage's voice had become low and firm, with emotion in its tone, making Letty catch her breath. "My 'eart's breakin', and I ain't a-goin' to let it break without mykin' them that's broken it know what they've done to me."

"Now, Mary Ann," Steptoe tried to say, peaceably, "madam's grytely pressed for time——"

"'Enery Steptoe, do you suppose that you're the only one in the world as 'as loved that boy? Ain't 'e my boy just as much as ever 'e was yours?"

"'E's boy to them as stands by 'im, Mrs. Courage—and stands by them that belongs to 'im. The first thing you do is to quit——"

"I'm not quittin'; I'm druv out. I'm druv out at a hour's notice from the 'ome I've slyved for all my best years, leavin' dishonor and wickedness in my plyce——"

Letty could endure no more. Dashing to the floor the paper behind which she crouched she sprang to her feet.

"Is that me?" she demanded.

The surprise of the attack caught Mrs. Courage off her guard. She could only open her mouth, and close it again, soundlessly and helplessly. Jane stared, her curiosity gratified at last. Nettie turned to whisper to Jane, "There; what did I tell you? The commonest thing!" Steptoe nodded his head quietly. In this little creature with her sudden flame, eyes all fire and cheeks of the wine-colored damask rose, he seemed to find a corroboration of his power of divining character.

It seemed long before Mrs. Courage had found the strength to live up to her convictions, by faintly murmuring: "Who else?"

"Then tell me what you accuse me of?"

Mrs. Courage saw her advantage. "We ain't 'ere to accuse nobody of nothink. If it's 'intin' that I'd tyke awye anyone's character it's a thing I've 'ardly ever done, and no one can sye it *of* me. All we want is to give our notice——"

"Then why don't you do it—and go?"

Once more Steptoe intervened, diplomatically. "That's what Mrs. Courage is a-doin' of, madam. She's finished, ain't you Mary Ann? Jynie and Nettie is finished too——"

But it was Letty now who refused this mediation. "No, they ain't finished. Let 'em go on."

But no one did go on. Mrs. Courage was now dumb. She was dumb and frightened, falling back on her two supporters. All three together they huddled between the portières. If Steptoe could have calmed his protégée he would have done it; but she was beyond his control.

"Am I the ruin and shame to this house that you was talkin' about just now? If I am, why don't you speak out and put it to me plain?"

There was no response. The spectators looked on as if they were at the theater.

"What have you all got against me anyhow?" Letty insisted, passionately. "What did I ever do to you?

What's women's hearts made of, that they can't let a poor girl be?"

Mrs. Courage had so far recovered as to be able to turn from one to another, to say in pantomime that she had been misunderstood. Jane began to cry; Nettie to laugh.

"Even if I was the bad girl you're tryin' to make me out I should think other women might show me a little pity. But I'm not a bad girl—not yet. I may be. I dunno but what I will. When I see the hateful thing bein' good makes of women it drives me to do the other thing."

This was the speech they needed to justify themselves. To be good made women hateful! Their dumb-crambo to each other showed that anyone who said so wild a thing stood already self-condemned.

But Letty flung up her head with a mettle which Steptoe hadn't seen since the days of the late Mrs. Allerton.

"I'm not in this house to drive no one else out of it. Them that have lived here for years has a right to it which I ain't got. You can go, and let me stay; or you can stay, and let me go. I'm the wife of the owner of this house, who married me straight and legal; but I don't care anything about that. You don't have to tell me I ain't fit to be his wife, because I know it as well as you do. All I'm sayin' is that you've got the choice to stay or go; and whichever you do, I'll do different."

Never in her life had she spoken so many words at one time. The effort drained her. With a torrent of dry sobs that racked her body she dropped back into her chair.

The hush was that of people who find the tables turned on themselves in a way they consider unwarranted. Of the general surprise Steptoe was quick to take advantage.

"There you are, girls. Madam couldn't speak no fairer, now could she?"

To this there was neither assent or dissent; but it was plain that no one was ready to pick up the glove so daringly thrown down.

"Now what I would suggest," Steptoe went on, craftily, "is that we all go back to the kitchen and talk it over quiet like. What we decide to do we can tell madam lyter."

For consent or refusal Jane and Nettie looked to Mary Ann, whose attitude was that of rejecting parley. She might, indeed, have rejected it, had not Letty, bowing her head on the arms she rested on the table, begun to cry bitterly.

It was then that you saw Mrs. Courage at her best. The gesture with which she swept her subordinates back into the hall was that of the supremacy of will.

"It shan't be said as I crush," she declared, nobly, directing Steptoe's attention to the weeping girl. "Where there's penitence I pity. God grant as them tears may gush out of an aichin' 'eart."

Chapter IX

BY the time Letty was drying her eyes, her heart somewhat eased, Steptoe had come back. He came back with a smile. Something had evidently pleased him.

"So that's all over. Madam won't be bothered with other people's cat-nasty old servants after to-dye."

She felt a new access of alarm. "But they're not goin' away on account o' me? Don't let 'em do it. Lemme go instead. Oh, mister, I can't stay here, where everything's so different from what I'm used to."

He still smiled, his gentle old man's smile which somehow gave her confidence.

"Madam won't sye that after a dye or two. It's new to 'er yet, of course; but if she'll always remember that I'm 'ere, to myke everythink as easy as easy——"

"But what are you goin' to do, with no cook, and no chambermaid——?"

Standing with the corner of the table between him and her, he was saying to himself, "If Mr. Rash could only see 'er lookin' up like this—with 'er eyes all starry—and her cheeks with them dark-red roses—red roses like you'd rubbed with a little black. . . ." But he suspended the romantic longing to say, aloud:

"If madam will permit me I'll tyke my measures as I've wanted to tyke 'em this long spell back."

THE DUST FLOWER

Madam was not to worry as to the three women who were leaving the house, inasmuch as they had long been intending to leave it. Both Mrs. Courage and Jane, having graduated to the stage of "accommodating," were planning to earn more money by easier work. Nettie, since coming to America, had learned that housework was menial, and was going to be a milliner.

Madam's remorse being thus allayed he told what he hoped to do for madam's comfort. There would be no more women in the house, not till madam herself brought them back. An English chef who had lost an eye in the war, and an English waiter, ready to do chamberwork, who had left a foot on some battlefield, were prepared under Steptoe's direction to man the house. No woman whose household cares had not been eased by men, in the European fashion, knew what it was to live. A woman waited on by women only was kept in a state of nerves. Nerves were infectious. When one woman in a household got them the rest were sooner or later their prey. Unless strongly preventative measures were adopted they spread at times to the men. America was a dreadful country for nerves and it mostly came of women working with women; whereas, according to Steptoe's psychology, men should work with women and women with men. There were thousands of women who were bitter in heart at cooking and making beds who would be happy as linnets in offices and shops; and thousands of men who were dying of boredom in offices and shops who would be in their element cooking and making beds.

THE DUST FLOWER

"One of the things the American people 'as got back'ards, if madam'll allow me to sye so, is that 'ouse'old work is not fit for a white man. When you come to that the American people ain't got a sense of the dignity of their 'omes. They can't see their 'omes as run by anything but slyves. All that's outside the dinin' room and the drorin' room and the masters' bedrooms the American sees as if it was a low-down thing, even when it's hunder 'is own roof. Colored men, yellow men, may cook 'is meals and myke 'is bed; but a white man'd demean 'imself. A poor old white man like me when 'e's no longer fit for 'ard outdoor work ain't allowed to do nothink; when all the time there's women workin' their fingers to the bone that 'e could be a great 'elp to, and who 'e'd like to go to their 'elp."

This was one reason, he argued, why the question of domestic aid in America was all at sixes and sevens. It was not considered humanly. It was more than a question of supply and demand; it was one of national prejudice. A rich man could have a French chef and an English butler, and as many strapping indoor men—some of them much better fitted for manual labor—as he liked, and find it a social glory; while a family of moderate means were obliged to pay high wages to crude incompetent women from the darkest backwaters of European life, just because they were women.

"And the women's mostly to blyme," he reasoned. "They suffers—nobody knows what they suffers better nor me—just because they ain't got the spunk to do anything *but* suffer. They've got it all in their own 'ands, and they never learn. Men is slow to learn; but women don't 'ardly ever learn at all."

Letty was thinking of herself, as she glanced up at this fount of wisdom with the question:

"Don't none of 'em?"

Having apparently weighed this already he had his answer. "None that's been drilled a little bit before 'and. Once let woman feel as so and so is the custom, and for 'er that custom, whether good or bad, is there to stye. They sye that chyngin' 'er mind is a woman's privilege; but the woman that chynged 'er mind about a custom is one I never met yet."

She took him as seriously as he took himself.

"Don't you like women, mister—I mean, Steptoe?"

He pondered before replying. "I don't know as I could sye. I've never 'ad a chance to see much of women except in 'ousework, where they're out of their element and tyken at a disadvantage. I don't like none I've ever run into there, because none of 'em never was no sport."

The inquiry in her golden eyes led him a little further.

"No one ain't a sport what sighs and groans over their job, and don't do it cheerful like. No one ain't a sport what undertykes a job and ain't proud of it. If a woman *will* go into 'ousework let 'er do it honorable. If she chooses to be a servant let 'er *be* a servant, and not be ashymed to sye she *is* one. So if madam arsks me if I like 'em I 'ave to confess I don't, because as far as I see women I mostly 'ear 'em complyne."

Her admiration was quite sincere as she said: "I

shouldn't think they'd complain if they had you to put 'em wise."

He corrected gently. "If they 'ad me to *tell* 'em."

"If they 'ad you to *tell* 'em," she imitated, meekly.

"Madam mustn't pick up the bad 'abit of droppin' 'er haitches," he warned, parentally. "I'll learn 'er a lot, but that's one thing I mustn't learn 'er. I don't do it often—Oh, once in a wye, mybe—but that's something madam speaks right already—just like all Americans."

Delighted that there was one thing about her that was right already she reminded him of what he had said, that women never learned.

"I said women as 'ad been drilled a bit. But madam's different. Madam comes into this 'ouse newborn, as you might sye; and that'll myke it easier for 'er and me."

"You mean that I'll not be a kicker."

Once more he smiled his gentle reproof. "Oh, madam wouldn't be a kicker any'ow. Jynie or Nettie or Mary Ann Courage or even me—we might be kickers; but if madam was to hobject to anything she'd be—*displeased.*"

She knitted her brows. The distinction was difficult. He saw he had better explain more fully.

"It's only the common crowd what kicks. It's only the common crowd what uses the expression. A man might use it—I mean a real 'igh gentleman like Mr. Rashleigh—and get awye with it—now and then—if 'e didn't myke a 'abit of it; but when a woman does it she rubberstamps 'erself. Now, does madam see? A lydy couldn't be a lydy—and kick. The lyte Mrs.

Allerton would never demean 'erself to kick; she'd only show displeasure."

With a thumb and two fingers Letty marked off on the table the three points as to which she had received information that morning. She must say brought, and not brung; she must say tell, and not put wise; she must not kick, but show displeasure. Neither must she drop her aitches, though to do so would have been an effort. The warning only raised a suspicion that in the matter of speech there might be a higher standard than Steptoe's. If ever she heard Rashleigh Allerton speak again she resolved to listen to him attentively.

She came back from her reverie on hearing Steptoe say:

"With madam it's a cyse of beginning from the ground up, more or less as you would with a byby; so I 'ope madam'll forgive me if I drop a 'int as to what we must do before goin' any farther."

Once more he read her question in the starry little flames in her eyes.

"It's—clothes."

The damask red which had ebbed surged slowly back again. It surged back under the transparent white skin, as red wine fills a glass. Her lips parted to stammer the confession that she had no clothes except those she wore; but she couldn't utter a syllable.

"I understand madam's position, which is why I mention it. You might sye as clothes is the ABC of social life, and if we're to work from the ground up we must begin there."

THE DUST FLOWER

She forced it out at last, but the statement seemed to tear her.

"I can't get clothes. I ain't got no money."

"Oh, money's no hobject," he smiled. "Mr. Rash 'as plenty of that, and I know what 'e'd like me to do. There never was 'is hequal for the 'open 'and. If madam'll leave it to me . . ."

Allerton's office was much what you would have expected it to be, bearing to other offices the same relation as he to other business men. He had it because not to have it wouldn't have been respectable. A young American who didn't go to an office every day would hardly have been a young American. An office, then, was a concession to public sentiment, as well as some faint justification of himself.

It was in the latter sense that he chiefly took it, making it a subject of frequent reference. In his conversation such expressions as "my office," or "due at my office," were introduced more often than there was occasion for. The implication that he had work to do gave him status, enabling him to sit down among his cronies and good-naturedly take their fun.

He took a good deal of fun, never having succeeded in making himself the standardized type who escapes the shafts of ridicule. It was kindly fun, which, while viewing him as a white swan in a flock of black ones, recognized him as a swan, and this was as much as he could expect. To pass in the crowd was all he asked for, even when he only passed on bluff. If he couldn't wholly hide the bluff he could keep it from being

THE DUST FLOWER

flagrantly obtrusive; and toward that end an office was a help.

It was an office situated just where you would have expected to find it—far enough downtown to be downtown, and yet not so far downtown as to make it a trouble to get there. Being on the eastern side of Washington Square, it had a picturesque outlook, and the merit of access from East Sixty-seventh Street through the long straight artery of Fifth Avenue.

It was furnished, too, just as you might have known he would furnish it, in the rich and sober Style Empire, and yet not so exclusively in the Style Empire as to make the plain American business man fear he had dropped into Napoleon's library at Malmaison. That is what Rashleigh would have liked, but other men could do what in him would be thought finicky. To take the "cuss" off his refinement, as he put it to Barbara, he scattered modern American office bits among his luscious brown surfaces, adorned with wreaths and lictors' sheaves in gold, though to himself the wrong note was offensive.

But wrong notes and right notes were the same to him as, on this particular morning, he dragged himself there because it was the hour. His office staff in the person of old Mr. Radbury was already on the spot, and had sorted the letters for the day. These were easily dealt with. Reinvestment, or new opportunities for investment, were their principal themes, and the only positive duty to attend to was in the endorsement of dividend checks for deposit. A few directions being given to Mr. Radbury as to such letters as were to be answered, Allerton had nothing to do but stroll to the window and look out.

It was what he did perhaps fifty times in the course of the two or three hours daily, or approximately daily, which he spent there. He did so now. He did so because it put off for a few minutes longer the fierce, exasperating, acrid pleasure of doing worse. To do worse had been his avowed object in coming to the office that morning, and not the answering of letters or the raking in of checks.

Looking down from his window on the tenth floor he asked himself the fruitless question which millions of other men have asked when folly has got them into trouble. Among these thousands who, viewed from that height, had a curious resemblance to ants, was there such a fool as he was? From the Square they streamed into Fifth Avenue; from Fifth Avenue they streamed into the Square. In the Square and round the Square they squirmed and wriggled and dawdled their seemingly aimless ways. Great green lumbering omnibuses disgorged one pack of them merely to suck up another. Motors whirled them toward uptown, toward downtown, or east, or west, by twos and threes, or as individuals. Like ants their general effect was black, with here and there a moving spot of color, or of intermingling colors, as of flowers in the wind, or tropic birds.

He watched a figure detach itself from the mass swirling round a debouching omnibus. It was a little black figure, just clearly enough defined to show that it was a man. Because it was a man it had been a fool. Because it had been a fool it had dark chambers in its life which it would never willingly open. But it had doubtless got something for its folly. It might have lost more than it had gained, but it could probably reckon up and say, "At least I had my fun."

And he had had none. He had squandered his whole life on a single act of insanity which even in the action had produced nothing but disgust. He hadn't merely swindled himself; he had committed a kind of suicide which made death silly and grotesque. The one thing that could save him a scrap of dignity— and such a sorry scrap!—would be going to the devil by the shortest way.

He had come to the office to begin. He would begin by the means that seemed obvious. Now that going to the devil was a task he saw, as he had not seen hitherto, how curiously few were the approaches that would take him there. Song being only an accompaniment, he was limited to the remaining two of the famous and familiar trio.

Very well! Limited as he was he would make the most of them. Knowing something of their merits he knew there was a bestial entertainment to be had from both. It was a kind of entertainment which his cursed fastidiousness had always loathed; but now his reckoning would be different. If he got *anything* he should not feel so wastefully thrown away. He would be selling himself first and making his bargain afterwards; but some meager balance would stand to his credit, if credit it could be called. When the devil had been reached the world he knew would pardon him because it was the devil, and not—what it was in truth —an idiotic state of nerves.

THE DUST FLOWER

At the minute when Letty was leaping to her feet to take her stand he swung away from the window. First going to Mr. Radbury's door he closed it softly. Luckily the old man, an inheritance from his, Allerton's, father, was deaf and incurious. Like most clerks who had clerked their way up to seventy he was buried in clerking's little round. He wouldn't come in till the letters were finished, certainly not for an hour, and by that time Allerton would be . . . He almost smiled at the old man's probable consternation on finding him so before the middle of the day. Any time would be bad enough; but in the high forenoon. . . .

He went to a cabinet which was said to have found its way via Bordentown from the furnishings of Queen Caroline Murat. Having opened it he took out a bottle and a glass. On the label of the bottle was a kilted Highlander playing on the pipes. A siphon of soda was also in the cabinet, but he left it there. What he had to do would be done more quickly without its mitigation.

While Allerton was making these preparations Judson Flack, in pajamas and slippers, was standing in his toy kitchen, looking helplessly at a small gas stove. It was the hour in the middle of the morning at which he was accustomed to be waked with the information that his coffee and eggs were ready. The forenoon being what he called his slack time he found the earlier part of it most profitably used for sleep.

"Curse the girl!"

The adjuration was called forth by the fact that he didn't know where anything was, or how anything

THE DUST FLOWER

should be done. From the simple expedient of going for his breakfast to one of the cheap restaurants with which he was familiar he was cut off by the fact of an unlucky previous night. He simply didn't have the bones. This was not to say that he was penniless, but that in view of more public expenses later in the day it would be well for him to economize where economy was so obvious. He never had an appetite in the morning anyway. With irregular eating and drinking all through the evening and far toward daylight, he found a cup of coffee and an egg. . . .

It was easy, he knew, to make the one and boil the other, but he was out of practice. He couldn't remember doing anything of the sort since the days before he married Letty's mother. Even then he had never tried this new-fangled thing, the gas stove, so that besides being out of practice he was at a loss.

"Curse the girl!"

The resources of the kitchen being few exploration didn't take him long. He found bread, butter, milk that had turned sour, the usual condiments, some coffee in a canister, and a single egg. If he could only light the confounded gas stove. . . .

A small white handle offering itself for experiment, he turned it timidly, applying a match to a geometrical pattern of holes. He jumped back as from an exploding cannon.

"Curse the girl!"

Having found the way, however, the next attempt was more successful. Soon he had two geometrical patterns of holes burning in steady blue buttons of flame. On the one he placed the coffee-pot into which

THE DUST FLOWER

he had turned a pint of water and a cupful of coffee; on the other a saucepan half full of water containing his egg. This being done he retired to the bathroom for the elements of a toilet.

"Curse the girl!"

Washing, shaving, turning up his mustache with the little curling tongs, he observed with self-pity his increasing haggardness. He observed it also with dismay. Looks were as important to him as to an actress. His rôle being youth, high spirits, and the devil-may-care, the least trace of the wearing out would do for him. He had noticed some time ago that he was beginning to show fatal signs, which had the more emphatically turned his thoughts to the provision Letty might prove for his old age.

"Curse the girl!"

It was cursing the girl which reminded him that he had allowed more than the necessary time for his breakfast to be ready for consumption. Hurrying back to the kitchen he found the egg gracefully dancing as the water boiled. He fished it out with a spoon and took it in his hand, but he didn't keep it there. Dashing it to the table, whence it crashed upon the floor, he positively screamed.

"Curse the girl!"

He cursed her now licking and sucking the tips of his fingers and examining them to see if they were scalded. No such calamity having occurred he took up the coffee pot, leaving the mashed egg where it lay. Ladling a spoonful of sugar into a cup, and adding the usual milk, he poured in the coffee, which became a muddy dark brown mixture, with what appeared to

THE DUST FLOWER

be a porridge of seeds floating on the top. One sip, which induced a diabolical grimace, and he threw the beverage at the opposite wall as if it was a man he meant to insult.

"Curse the girl!"

The appeal to the darker powers being accompanied now by a series of up-to-date terms of objurgation, the mere act of utterance, mental or articulate, churned him to a frenzy. Seizing the coffee pot which he had replaced on the gas stove he hurled it too against the wall. It struck, splathered the hideous liquor over a hideous calsomining which had once been blue, and fell to the floor like a living thing knocked insensible.

The resemblance maddened him still more. It might have been Letty, struck down after having provoked him beyond patience. He rushed at it. He hurled it again. He hurled it again. He hurled it again. The exercise gave relief not only to his lawful resentment against Letty, but to those angers over his luck of last night which as "a good loser" he hadn't been at liberty to show. No one knew the repressions he was obliged to put upon himself; but now his inhibitions could come off in this solitary passion of destruction.

When the coffee pot was a mere shapeless mass he picked up the empty cup. It was a thick stone-china cup, with a bar meant to protect his mustache across the top, a birthday present from Letty's mother. The association of memories acted as a further stimulus. Smash! After the cup went the stone-china sugar bowl. Smash! After the sugar bowl the plate with the yellow chunk of butter. Smash! After the butter plate the milk jar, a clumsy, lumpy thing, which merely gurgled out a splash of milk and fell without breaking.

"Curse the girl! Curse the girl! Curse the girl! I'll learn her to go away and leave me! I'll find her and drag her back if she's in. , , ,"

Chapter X

WHILE Letty was beginning a new experience Judson Flack was doing his best to carry out his threat. That is to say, he was making the round of the studios in which his step-daughter had occasionally found work, discreetly asking if she had been there that day. It was all he could think of doing. To the best of his knowledge she had no friends with whom she could have taken refuge, though the suspicion crossed his mind that she might have drowned herself to spite him.

As a matter of fact Letty was asking the question if she wasn't making a mistake in not doing so, either literally or morally. Never before in her life had she been up against this problem of insufficiency. Among the hard things she had known she had not known this; and now that she was involved in it, it seemed to her harder than everything else put together.

In her humble round, bitter as it was, she had always been considered competent. It was the sense of her competence that gave her the self-respect enabling her to bear up. According to her standards she could keep house cleverly, and could make a dollar go as far as other girls made two. When she got her first chance in a studio, through an acquaintance of Judson Flack's, she didn't shrink from it, and had more than once been chosen by a director to be that member of a crowd who moves in the front and expresses the crowd psychologically. Had she only had the clothes. . . .

And now she was to have them. As far as that went she was not merely glad; she was one sheer quiver of excitement. It was not the end she shrank from; it was the means. If she could only have had fifty dollars to go "poking round" where she knew that bargains could be found, she might have enjoyed the prospect; but Steptoe could only "take measures" on the grand scale to which he was accustomed.

The grand scale frightened her, chiefly because she was dressed as she was dressed. It was her first thought and her last one. When Steptoe told her the hour at which he had asked Eugene to bring round the car the mere vision of herself stepping into it made her want to sink into the ground. Eugene didn't live in the house—she had discovered that—and so would bring the stare of another pair of eyes under whose scrutiny she would have to pass. Those of the three women having already scorched her to the bone, she would have to be scorched again.

She tried to say this to Steptoe, as they stood in the drawing-room window waiting for the car; but she didn't know how to make him understand it. When she tried to put it into words, the right words wouldn't come. Steptoe had taken as general what she was trying to explain to him in particular.

"It'll be very important to madam to fyce what's 'ard, and to do it bryve like. It'll be the mykin' of 'er if she can. 'Umble 'ill is pretty stiff to climb; but them as gets to the top of it is tough."

She thought this over silently. He meant that if she set herself to take humiliations as they came, dragging herself up over them, she would be the stronger for it in the end.

"It'd 'ave been better for Mr. Rashleigh," he mused, "if 'e'd 'ad 'ad somethink of the kind to tackle in 'is life; it'd 'ave my'de 'im more of a man. But because 'e adn't—Did madam ever notice," he broke off to ask, " 'ow them as 'as everythink myde easy for 'em begins right off to myke things 'ard for theirselves. It's a kind of law like. It's just as if nyture didn't mean to let no one escype. When a man's got no troubles you can think of, 'e'll go to work to create 'em."

"Didn't *he*—she had never yet pronounced the name of the man who had married her—"didn't *he* ever have any troubles?"

" 'E was fretted terrible—crossed like—rubbed up the wrong wye, as you might sye,—but a real trouble like what you and me 'ave 'ad plenty of—never! It's my opinion that trouble is to char-*ac*-ter what a peg'll be to a creepin' vine—something to which the vine'll 'ook on and pull itself up by. Where there's nothink to ketch on to the vine'll grow; but it'll grow in a 'eap of flop." There was a tremor in his tone as he summed up. "That's somethink like my poor boy."

Letty found this interesting. That in these exalted circles there could be a need of refining chastisement came to her as a surprise.

"The wife as I've always 'oped for 'im," Steptoe went on, "is one that'd know what trouble was, and 'ow to fyce it. 'E'd myke a grand 'usband to a woman who was—strong. But she'd 'ave to be the wall what the creepin' vine could cover all over and—and beautify."

"That wouldn't be me."

"If I was madam I wouldn't be so sure of that. It don't do to undervalyer your own powers. If I'd 'a done that I wouldn't 'a been where I am to-dye. Many's the time, when I was no more than a poor little foundlin' boy in a 'ome I've said to myself, I'm fit for somethink big. Somethink big I always meant to be. When it didn't seem possible for me to aim so 'igh I'd myde up my mind to be a valet and a butler. It comes—your hambition does. What you've first got to do is to form it; and then you've got to stick to it through thick and thin."

To say what she said next Letty had to break down barrier beyond barrier of inhibition and timidity. "And if I was to—to form the—the ambition—to be —to be the kind of wall you was talkin' about just now ———"

"That wouldn't be hambition; it'd be—consecrytion."

He allowed her time to get the meaning of this before going on.

"But madam mustn't expect not to find it 'ard. Consecrytion is always 'ard, by what I can myke out. When Mr. Rash was a little 'un 'e used to get Miss Pye, 'is governess, to read to 'im a fairy tyle about a little mermaid what fell in love with a prince on land. Bein' in love with 'im she wanted to be with 'im, natural like; but there she was in one element, as you might sye, and 'im in another."

"That'd be like me."

"Which is why I'm tellin' madam of the story. Well, off the little mermaid goes to the sea-witch to find out 'ow she could get rid of 'er fish's tyle and 'ave two feet for to walk about in the prince's palace. Well, the sea-witch she up and tells 'er what she'd 'ave to do. Only, says she, if you do that you'll 'ave to pye for it with every step you tykes; for every step you tykes'll be like walkin' on sharp blydes. Now, says she, to the little mermaid, do you think it'd be worth while?"

In Letty's eyes all the stars glittered with her eagerness for the dénouement. "And did she think it was worth while—the little mermaid?"

"She did; but I'll give madam the tyle to read for 'erself. It's in the syme little book what Miss Pye used to read out of—up in Mr. Rash's old nursery."

With the pride of a royal thing conscious of its royalty the car rolled to the door and stopped. It was the prince's car, while she, Letty, was a mermaid born in an element different from his, and encumbered with a fish's tail. She must have shown this in her face, for Steptoe said, with his fatherly smile:

"Madam may 'ave to walk on blydes—but it'll be in the Prince's palace."

It'll be in the Prince's palace! Letty repeated this to herself as she followed him out to the car. Holding the door open for her, Eugene, who had been told of her romance, touched his cap respectfully. When she had taken her seat he tucked the robe round her, respectfully again. Steptoe marked the social difference between them by sitting beside Eugene.

THE DUST FLOWER

Rolling down Fifth Avenue Letty was as much at a loss to account for herself as Elijah must have been in the chariot of fire. She didn't know where she was going. She was not even able to ask. The succession of wonders within twenty-four hours blocked the working of her faculties. She thought of the girls who sneered at her in the studios—she thought of Judson Flack—and of what they would say if they were to catch a glimpse of her.

She was not so unsophisticated as to be without some appreciation of the quarter of New York in which she found herself. She knew it was the "swell" quarter. She knew that the world's symbols of money and display were concentrated here, and that in some queer way she, poor waif, had been given a command of them. One day homeless, friendless, and penniless, and the next driving down Fifth Avenue in a limousine which might be called her own!

The motor was slowing down. It was drawing to the curb. They had reached the place to which Steptoe had directed Eugene. Letty didn't have to look at the name-plate to know she was where the great stars got their gowns, and that she was being invited into Margot's!

You know Margot's, of course. A great international house, Margot—the secret is an open one—is but the incognita of a business-like English countess who finds it financially profitable to sign articles on costume written by someone else, and be sponsor for the newest fashions which someone else designs. As a way of turning an impoverished historic title to account it is as good as any other.

THE DUST FLOWER

Without knowing who Margot was Letty knew what she was. She couldn't have frequented studios without hearing that much, and once or twice in her wanderings about the city she had paused to admire the door. It was all there was to admire, since Margot, to Letty's regret, didn't display confections behind plate-glass.

It was a Flemish château which had been a residence before business had traveled above Forty-second Street. A man in livery would have barred them from passing the wrought-iron grille had it not been for the car from which they had emerged. Only people worthy of being customers of the house could afford such cars, and he saw that Steptoe was a servant. What Letty was he couldn't see, for servants of great houses never looked so nondescript.

In the great hall a beautiful staircase swept to an upper floor, but apart from a Louis Seize mirror and console flanked by two Louis Seize chairs there was nothing and no one to be seen. Steptoe turned to the right into a vast saloon with a cinnamon-colored carpet and walls of cool French gray. A group of gilded chairs were the only furnishings, except for a gilded canapé between two French windows draped with cinnamon-colored hangings. A French fender with French andirons filled the fireplace, and on the white marble mantelpiece stood a *garniture de cheminée,* a clock and two vases, in biscuit de Sèvres.

At the end of the room opposite the windows a woman in black, with coiffure à la Marcel, sat at a white-enamelled desk working with a ledger. A second woman in black, also with coiffure à la Marcel, stood holding open the doors of a white-enamelled wardrobe, gazing at its multi-colored contents. Two other women in black, still with coiffure à la Marcel, were bending over a white-enamelled drawer in a series of white-enamelled drawers, discussing in low tones. There were no customers. For such a house the season had not yet begun. Though in this saloon voices were pitched as low as for conversation in a church, the sharp catgut calls of Frenchwomen—and of French dressmakers especially—came from a room beyond.

Overawed by this vastness, simplicity, and solemnity, Steptoe and Letty stood barely within the door, waiting till someone noticed them. No one did so till the woman holding open the wardrobe doors closed them and turned round. She did not come forward at once; she only stared at them. Still keeping her eye on the newcomers she called the attention of the ladies occupied with the drawer, who lifted themselves up. They too stared. The lady at the desk stared also.

It was the lady of the wardrobe who advanced at last, slowly, with dignity, her hands genteelly clasped in front of her. She seemed to be saying, "No, we don't want any," or, "I'm sorry we've nothing to give you," by her very walk. Letty, with her gift for dramatic interpretation, could see this, though Steptoe, familiar as he was with ladies whom he would have classed as " 'igher," was not daunted. He too went forward, meeting madam half way.

Of what was said between them Letty could hear nothing, but the expression on the lady's face was

THE DUST FLOWER

dissuasive. She was telling Steptoe that he had come to the wrong place, while Steptoe was saying no. From time to time the lady would send a glance toward Letty, not in disdain, but in perplexity. It was perplexity which reached its climax when Steptoe drew from an inside pocket an impressive roll of bills.

The lady looked at the bills, but she also looked at Letty. The honor of a house like Margot's is not merely in making money; it is in its clientèle. To have a poor little waif step in from the street. . . .

And yet it was because she was a poor little waif that she interested the ladies looking on. She was so striking an exception to their rule that her very coming in amazed them. One of the two who had remained near the open drawer came forward into conference with her colleague, adding her dissuasions to those which Steptoe had already refused to listen to.

"There are plenty of other places to which you could go," Letty heard this second lady say, "and probably do better."

Steptoe smiled, that old man's smile which was rarely ineffective. "Madam don't 'ave to tell me as there's plenty of other plyces to which I could go; but there's none where I could do as well."

"What makes you think so?"

"I'm butler to a 'igh gentleman what 'e used to entertyne quite a bit when 'is mother was alive. I've listened to lydies talkin' at tyble. No one can't tell me. I *know*."

Both madams smiled. Each shot another glance at Letty. It was plain that they were curious as to her identity. One of them made a venture.

"And is this your—your daughter?"

Steptoe explained, not without dignity, that the young lady was not his daughter, but that she had come into quite a good bit of money, and had done it sudden like. She needed a 'igh, grand outfit, though for the present she would be content with three or four of the dresses most commonly worn by a lydy of stytion. He preferred to nyme no nymes, but he was sure that even Margot would not regret her confidence—and he had the cash, as they saw, in his pocket.

Of this the result was an exchange between the madams of comprehending looks, while, in French, one said to the other that it might be well to consult Madame Simone.

Madame Simone, who bustled in from the back room, was not in black, but in frowzy gray; her coiffure was not à la Marcel, but as Letty described it, "all anyway." A short, stout, practical Frenchwoman, she had progressed beyond the need to consider looks, and no longer considered them. The two shapely subordinates with whom Steptoe had been negotiating followed her at a distance like attendants.

She disposed of the whole matter quickly, addressing the attendants rather than the postulants for Margot's favor.

"Mademoiselle she want an outfit—good!—bon! We don't know her, but what difference does that make to me?—qu'est ce que c'est que cela me fait? Money is money, isn't it?—de l'argent c'est de l'argent, n'est-ce pas?—at this time of year especially—à cette saison de l'année surtout."

THE DUST FLOWER

To Steptoe and Letty she said: "'Ave the goodness to sit yourselves 'ere. Me, I will show you what we 'ave. A street costume first for mademoiselle. If mademoiselle will allow me to look at her—Ah, oui! Ze taille—what you call in Eenglish the figure—is excellent. Très chic. With ze proper closes mademoiselle would have style—de l'élégance naturelle—that sees itself—cela se voit—oui—oui ——"

Meditating to herself she studied Letty, indifferent apparently to the actual costume and atrocious hat, like a seeress not viewing what is at her feet but events of far away.

With a sudden start she sprang to her convictions. "I 'ave it. J'y suis." A shrill piercing cry like that of a wounded cockatoo went down the long room. "Alphonsine! Alphon*sine!*"

Someone appeared at the door of the communicating rooms. Madame Simone gave her orders in a few sharp staccato French sentences. After that Letty and Steptoe found themselves sitting on two of the gilded chairs, unexpectedly alone. The other ladies had returned to their tasks. Madame Simone had gone back to the place whence they had summoned her. Nothing had happened. It seemed to be all over. They waited.

"Ain't she goin' to show us nothin'?" Letty whispered anxiously. "They always do."

Steptoe was puzzled but recommended patience. He couldn't think that Madame could have begun so kindly, only to go off and leave them in the lurch. It was not what he had looked for, any more than she; but he had always found patient waiting advantageous.

THE DUST FLOWER

Perhaps ten minutes had gone by when a new figure wandered toward them. Strutted would perhaps be the better word, since she stepped like a person for whom stepping means a calculation. She was about Letty's height, and about Letty's figure. Moreover, she was pretty, with that haughtiness of mien which turns prettiness to beauty. What was most disconcerting was her coming straight toward Letty, and standing in front of her to stare.

Letty colored to the eyes—her deep, damask flush. The insult was worse than anything offered by Mrs. Courage; for Mrs. Courage after all was only a servant, and this a young lady of distinction. Letty had never seen anyone dressed with so much taste, not even the stars as they came on the studio lot in their everyday costumes. Indignant as she was she could appreciate this delicate seal-brown cloth, with its bits of gold braid, and darling glimpses of sage-green wherever the lining showed indiscreetly. The hat was a darling too, brown with a feather between brown and green, the one color or the other according as the wearer moved.

If it hadn't been for this cool insolence. . . . And then the young lady deliberately swung on her heel, which was high, to move some five or six yards away, where she stood with her back to them. It was a darling back—with just enough gold braid to relieve the simplicity, and the tiniest revelation of sage-green. Letty admired it the more poignantly for its cold contempt of herself.

Steptoe was not often put out of countenance, but it seemed to have happened now. "I *can't* think," he

THE DUST FLOWER

murmured, as one who contemplates the impossible, "that the French madam can 'ave been so civil to begin with, just to go and make a guy of us."

"If all her customers is like this ——" Letty began.

But the young lady of distinction turned again, stepping a few paces toward the back of the room, swinging on herself, stepping a few paces toward the front of the room, swinging on herself again, and all the while flinging at Letty glances which said: "If you want to see scorn, this is it."

Fascination kept Letty paralyzed. Steptoe grew uneasy.

"I wish the French madam'd come back agyne," he murmured, from half closed lips. "We 'aven't come 'ere to be myde a spectacle of—not for no one."

And just then the seal-brown figure strolled away, as serenely and impudently as she had come.

"Well, of all ——!"

Letty's exclamation was stifled by the fact that as the first young lady of distinction passed out a second crossed her coming in. They took no notice of each other, though the newcomer walked straight up to Letty, not to stare but to toss up her chin with a hint of laughter suppressed. Laughter, suppressed or unsuppressed, was her note. She was all fair-haired, blue-eyed vivacity. It was a relief to Letty that she didn't stare. She twitched, she twisted, she pirouetted, striking dull gleams from an embroidery studded with turquoise and jade—but she hadn't the hard unconscious arrogance of the other one.

All the same it pained Letty that great ladies should be so beautiful. Not that this one was beautiful of face—she wasn't—only piquant—but the general effect was beautiful. It showed what money and the dressmaker could do. If she, Letty could have had a dress and a hat like this!—a blue or a green, it was difficult to say which—with these strips of jade and turquoise on a ground of the purplish-greenish-blue she remembered as that of the monkshood in the old farm garden in Canada—and the darlingest hat, with one long feather beginning as green and graduating through every impossible shade of green and blue till it ended in a monkshood tip. . . .

No wonder the girl's blue eyes danced and quizzed and laughed. As a matter of fact, Letty commented, the eyes brought a little too much blue into the composition. It was her only criticism. As a whole it lacked contrast. If she herself had worn this costume —with her gold-stone eyes—and brown hair—and rich coloring, when she had any color—blue was always a favorite shade with her—when she could choose, which wasn't often—she remembered as a child on the farm how she used to plaster herself with the flowers of the blue succory—the dust-flower they called it down there because it seemed to thrive like the disinherited on the dust of the wayside—not but what the seal-brown was adorable. . . .

The spectacle grew dazzling, difficult for Steptoe to keep up with. He and Letty were plainly objects of interest to these grand folk, because there were now four or five of them. They advanced, receded, came up and studied them, wheeled away, smiled sometimes at each other with the high self-assurance of beauty and position, pranced, pawed, curveted, were noble or coquettish as the inner self impelled, but always the embodiment of overweening pride. Among the "real gentry," as he called them, there had unfailingly been for him and his colleagues a courtesy which might have been called only a distinction in equality, whereas these high-steppers. . . .

It was a relief to see the French madam bustling in again from the room at the back. Steptoe rose. He meant to express himself. Letty hoped he would. For people who brought money in their hands this treatment was too much. When Steptoe advanced to meet madam, she went with him. As her champion she must bear him out.

But madam forestalled them. "I 'ope that mademoiselle has seen something what she like. Me, I thought the brown costume—*cœur de le marguerite jaune* we call it ziz season ——"

Letty was quick. She had heard of mannequins, the living models, though so remotely as to give her no visualized impression. Suddenly knowing what they had been looking at she adapted herself before Steptoe could get his protest into words.

"I liked the seal-brown; but for me I thought the second one ——"

Madame Simone nodded, sagely. "Why shouldn't mademoiselle 'ave both?"

Chapter XI

WHILE this question was being put, and Steptoe was rising to what he saw as the real occasion, Rashleigh Allerton too was having a new experience. He couldn't understand it; he couldn't understand himself. Not that that was strange, since he had hardly ever understood himself at any time; but now he was, as he expressed it, "absolutely stumped."

He had put on the table the bottle on which the kilted Highlander was playing on the pipes; he had poured himself a glass. It was what he called a good stiff glass, meant, metaphorically, to kill or cure, and he hoped it would be to kill.

And that was all.

He had sat looking at it, or he had looked at it while walking about; but he had only looked at it. It was as far as he could go. Now that to go farther had become what he called a duty the perversity of his nerves was such that they refused. It was like him. He could always do the forbidden, the dare-devil, the crazily mad; but when it came to the reasonable and straightforward something in him balked. Here he was at what should have been the beginning of the end, and the demon which at another time would have driven him on was holding him back. Temptation had worked itself round the other way. It was temptation not to do, when saving grace lay in doing.

THE DUST FLOWER

An hour or more had gone by when Mr. Radbury knocked at the door, timidly.

"Come in, Radbury," Allerton cried, in a gayety he didn't feel. "Have a drink."

Mr. Radbury looked at the bottle and the glass. He looked at his young employer, who with his hands in his pockets, was again standing by the window. It was the first time in all the years of his service, first with the father and then with the son, that this invitation had been given him.

"Thanks, Mr. Rash," he said, with a thick, shaky utterance. "Liquor and I are strangers. I wish I could feel——"

But the old man's trembling anxiety forced on Allerton the fact that the foolish game was up. "All right, Radbury. Was only joking. No harm done. Had only taken the thing out to—to look at it."

Before sitting down to read and sign the letters he put both glass and bottle back into the keeping of Queen Caroline Murat, saying to himself as he did so: "I must find some other way."

He was thrown back thus on Barbara's suggestion of a few hours earlier. He must get rid of the girl! He had scarcely as yet considered this proposal, though not because he deemed it unworthy of himself. Nothing could be unworthy of himself. A man who was so little of a man as he was entitled to do anything, however base, and feel no shame. It was simply that his mind hadn't worked round to looking at the thing as feasible. And yet it was; plainly it was. The law allowed for it, if one only took advantage of the law's allowances. It would be beastly, of course; and more beastly for him than the average of men; but because it was beastly it were better done at once, before the girl got used to luxurious surroundings.

But even this resolution, speedy as it was, came a little late. By evening Letty was already growing used to luxurious surroundings, and finding herself at home in them.

First, there were no longer any women in the house, and with the three men—Steptoe's friends being already installed—she found herself safe from the prying and criticizing feminine.

Secondly, some of the new clothes had already come home, and she was now wearing the tea-gown she had long dreamt of but had never aspired to possess. It was of a blue so dark as to be almost black, with a flame colored bar across the breast, harmonizing with her hair and eyes. Of her eyes she wasn't thinking; but her hair. . . .

That, however, was another part of the day's fairy tale.

When the dresses had been bought and paid for madame presumed to Steptoe that mademoiselle was under some rich gentleman's protection. Taking words at their face value, as she, Letty, did herself, Steptoe admitted that she was. Madam made it plain that she understood this honor, which often came to girls of the humblest classes, and the need there could be for supplementing wardrobes suddenly. After that it was confidence for confidence. Madame had seen that in the matter of lingerie mademoiselle "left to desire," and though Margot made no specialty in this line, they happened to have on an upper floor a consignment just arrived from Paris, and if monsieur would allow mademoiselle to come up and inspect it.... Then it was Madame Simone's coiffeur. At least it was the coiffeur whom Madame Simone recommended, who came to the house, after Letty had donned a peignoir from the consignment just arrived from Paris.... And now, at half past nine in the evening, it was the memory of a day of mingled agony and enchantment.

Having looked her over as he summoned her to dinner, Steptoe had approved of her. He had approved of her with an inner emphasis stronger than he expressed. Letty didn't know how she knew this; but she knew. She knew that her transformation was a surprise to him. She knew that though he had hoped much from her she was giving him more than he had hoped. Nothing that he said told her this, but something in his manner—in his yearning as he passed her the various dishes and tactfully showed her how to help herself, in the tenderness with which he repeated correctly her little slips in words—something in this betrayed it.

She knew it, too, when after dinner he begged her not to escape to the little back room, but to take her place in the drawing-room.

"Madam'll find that it'll pass the time for 'er. Maybe too Mr. Rashleigh'll come in. 'E does sometimes—early like. I've known 'im to come 'ome by 'alf past nine, and if 'is ma wasn't sittin' in the drorin' room 'e'd be quite put out. Lydies mostly wytes till their 'usbands comes in; and in cyse madam'd feel

THE DUST FLOWER

lonely I'll leave the door open to the back part of the 'ouse, and she'll 'ear me talkin' to the boys."

The October evening being chilly he lit a fire. Drawing up in front of it a small armchair, suited for a lady's use, he placed behind it a table with an electric lamp. Letty smiled up at him. He had never seen her smile before, and now that he did he made to himself another comment of approval.

"You're awful good to me."

He reflected as to how he could bring home to her the grammatical mistake.

"Madam finds me *horfly* good, does she? P'rhaps that's because madam don't know that 'er comin' to this 'ouse gratifies a tyste o' mine for which I ain't never 'ad no gratificytion."

As he put a footstool to her feet he caught the question she so easily transmitted by her eyes.

"P'raps madam can hunderstand that after doin' things all my life for people as is used to 'em I've 'ad a kind o' cryvin' to do 'em for them as 'aven't 'ad nothink, and who could enjoy them more. I told madam yesterday I was somethink of a anarchist, and that's 'ow I am—wantin' to give the poor a wee little bit of what the rich 'as to throw awye."

Later he brought her an old red book, open at a page on which she read, *The Little Mermaid*.

Her heart leaped. It was from this volume that Miss Pye had read to the Prince when he was a child. She let her eyes run along the opening words.

"Far out in the sea the water is as blue as the petals of the cornflower, and clear as the purest glass."

She liked this sentence. It took her into a blue

THE DUST FLOWER

world. It was curious, she thought, how much meaning there was in colors. If you looked through red glass the world was angry; if through yellow, it was lit with an extraordinary sun; if through blue, you had the sensation of universal happiness. She supposed that that was why blue flowers always made you feel that there was a want in life which ought to be supplied—and wasn't.

She remembered a woman who had a farm near them in Canada, who grew only blue flowers in her garden. The neighbors said she was crazy; but she, Letty, had liked that garden better than all the gardens she knew. She would go there and talk to that woman, and listen to what she had to say of Nature's peculiar love of blue. The sea and sky were loveliest when they were blue, and so were the birds. There were blue stones, the woman said, precious stones, and other stones that were little more than rocks, which said something to the heart when pearls and diamonds spoke only to the eyes. In the fields, orchards, and gardens, white flowers, yellow flowers, red flowers were common; but blue flowers were rare and retiring, as if they guarded a secret which men should come and search out.

To this there was only one exception. Letty would notice as she trudged back to her father's farm that along the August roadsides there was a blue flower— of a blue you would never see anywhere else, not even in the sky—which grew in the dust, and lived on dust, and out of the dust drew elements of beauty such as roses and lilies couldn't boast of. "That means," the crazy woman said, "that there's nothing so dry, or

THE DUST FLOWER

parched, or sterile, that God can't take it and fashion from it the most priceless treasures of loveliness, if we only had the eyes to see them."

Letty never forgot this, and during all the intervening years the dust flower, with its heavenly color, had been the wild growing thing she loved best. It spoke to her. It not only responded to the ache she felt within herself, but gave a promise of assuagement. She had never expected the fulfilment of that promise, but was it possible that now it was going to be kept?

With her eyes on the fire she saw the color of the dust flower close to the flaming wood. It was the closest of all the colors, the one the burning heart kept nearest to itself. It seemed to be, as the crazy woman said, dear to Nature itself, its own beloved secret, the secret which, even when written in the dust of the wayside, or in the fire on the hearth, hardly anyone read or found out.

And as she was dreaming of this and of her Prince, Rashleigh was walking up the avenue, saying to himself that he must make an end of it. He was walking home because, having dined at the Club, he found himself too restless to stay there. Walking relieved his nerves, and enabled him to think. He must have the thing over and done with. She would go decently, of course, since, as he had promised her, she would have plenty of money to go with—plenty of money for the rest of her life—and that was the sole consideration. She would doubtless be as glad to escape as he to have her disappear. After that, so his lawyer had assured him in the afternoon, the legal steps would be relatively easy.

THE DUST FLOWER

Letting himself in with his latchkey he was surprised to see a light in the drawing-room. It had not been lighted up at night, as far as he could remember, since the days when his mother was accustomed to sit there. If he came home early he had always used the library, which was on the other side of the house and at the back.

He went into the front drawing-room, which was empty; but a fire burnt in the back one, and before it someone was seated. It was not the girl he had found in the park. It was a lady whom he didn't recognize, but clearly a lady. She was reading a book, and had evidently not heard his entrance or his step.

With the shadows of the front drawing-room behind him he stood between the portieres, and looked. He had looked for some seconds before the lady raised her eyes. She raised them with a start. Slowly there stole into her cheek the dark red of confusion. She dropped the book. She rose.

It wasn't till she rose that he knew her. It wasn't till he knew her that he was seized by an astonishment which almost made him laugh. It wasn't till he almost laughed that he went forward with the words, which insensibly bridged some of the gulf between them:

"Oh! So this is—*you!*"

Chapter XII

LETTY had not heard Allerton's entrance or approach because for the first time in her life she was lost in the magic of Hans Andersen.

"The sun had just gone down as the little mermaid lifted her head above the water. The clouds were brilliant in purple and gold, and through the pale, rose-tinged air the evening star shone clear and bright. The air was warm and mild; the sea at rest. A great ship with three masts lay close by, only one sail unfurled, for there was no breath of air, and the sailors sat aloft in the rigging or leaned lazily over the bulwarks. Music and singing filled the air, and as the sky darkened hundreds of Chinese lanterns were lighted. It seemed as if the flags of every nation were hung out. The little mermaid swam up to the cabin window, and every time she rose upon the waves she could see through the clear glass that the room was full of brilliantly dressed people. Handsomest of all was the young prince with the great dark eyes."

Allerton's eyes were dark, and though she did not consider him precisely young, the analogy between him and the hero of the tale was sufficient to take her eyes from the book and to set her to dreaming.

"He could not be more than sixteen years old, and this was his birthday. All this gaiety was in honor of him; the sailors danced upon the deck; and when the young prince came out a myriad of rockets flew

THE DUST FLOWER

high in the air, with a glitter like the brightest noontide, and the little mermaid was so frightened that she dived deep down under the water. She soon rose up again, however, and it seemed as if all the stars of heaven were falling round her in golden showers. Never had she seen such fireworks; great, glittering suns wheeled by her, fiery fishes darted through the blue air, and all was reflected back from the quiet sea. The ship was lighted up so that one could see the smallest rope. How handsome the young prince looked! He shook hands with everybody, and smiled, as the music rang out into the glorious night. It grew late, but the little mermaid could not turn her eyes away from the ship and the handsome prince."

Once more Letty's thought wandered from the page. She too would have watched her handsome prince, no matter what the temptation to look elsewhere.

"The colored lanterns were put out, no rocket rose in the air, no cannon boomed from the portholes; but deep below there was a surging and a murmuring. The mermaid sat still, cradled by the waves, so that she could look in at the cabin window. But now the ship began to make more way. One sail after another was unfurled; the waves rose higher; clouds gathered in the sky; and there was a distant flash of lightning. The storm came nearer. All the sails were taken in, and the ship rocked giddily, as she flew over the foaming billows; the waves rose mountain-high, as if they would swallow up the very masts, but the good ship dived like a swan into the deep black trough, and rose bravely to the foaming crest. The little mermaid thought it was a merry journey, but the sailors were of a different opinion. The ship strained and creaked; the timbers shivered as the thunder strokes of the waves fell fast; heavy seas swept the decks; the mainmast snapped like a reed; and the ship lurched heavily, while the water rushed into the hold. Then the young princess began to understand the danger, and she herself was often threatened by the falling masts, yards, and spars. One moment it was so dark that she could see nothing, but when the lightning flamed out the ship was as bright as day. She sought for the young prince, and saw him sinking down through the water as the ship parted. The sight pleased her, for she knew he must sink down to her home. But suddenly she remembered that men cannot live in the water, and that he would only reach her father's palace a lifeless corpse. No; he must not die! She swam to and fro among the drifting spars, forgetting that they might crush her with their weight; she dived and rose again, and reached the prince just when he felt that he could swim no longer in the stormy sea. His arms were beginning to fail him, his beautiful eyes were closed; in another moment he must have sunk, had not the little mermaid come to his aid. She kept his head above water, and let the waves carry them whither they would."

Letty didn't want Allerton's life to be in danger, but she would have loved saving it. She fell to pondering possible conditions in which she could perform this feat, while he ran no risk whatever.

"The next day the storm was over; not a spar of the ship was left in sight. The sun rose red and glowing upon the waves, and seemed to pour down

THE DUST FLOWER

new life upon the prince, though his eyes remained closed. The little mermaid kissed his fair white forehead and stroked back his wet hair. He was like the marble statue in her little garden, she thought. She kissed him again, and prayed that he might live."

Letty saw herself seated somewhere in a mead, Allerton lying unconscious with his head in her lap, though the circumstances that brought them so together remained vague.

"Suddenly the dry land came in sight before her, high blue mountains on whose peaks the snow lay white, as if a flock of swans had settled there. On the coast below were lovely green woods, and close on shore a building of some kind, the mermaid didn't know whether it was church or cloister. Citrons and orange trees grew in the garden, and before the porch were stately palm trees. The sea ran in here and formed a quiet bay, unruffled, but very deep. The little mermaid swam with the prince to the white sandy shore, laid him on the warm sand, taking care that his head was left where the sun shone warmest. Bells began to chime and ring through all parts of the building, and several young girls entered the garden. The little mermaid swam farther out, behind a tiny cliff that rose above the waves. She showered sea-foam on her hair that no one might see its golden glory, and then waited patiently to see if anyone would come to the aid of the young prince."

To Letty that was the heart-breaking part of the story, the leaving the beloved one to others. It was what she and the little mermaid had in common, unless she too could get rid of her fish's tail at the cost of

THE DUST FLOWER

walking on blades. But for the little mermaid there the necessity was, as she, Letty read on.

"Before long a young girl came by; she gave a start of terror and ran back to call for assistance. Several people came to her aid, and after a while the little mermaid saw the prince recover his consciousness, and smile upon the group around him. But he had no smile for her; he did not even know that she had saved him. Her heart sank, and when she had seen him carried into the large building, she dived sorrowfully down to her father's palace."

Lifting her eyes to meditate on this situation Letty saw Allerton standing between the portières. Her dream of being little mermaid to his prince went out like a pricked bubble. Though he neither smiled nor sneered she knew he was amused at her, with a bitterness in his amusement. In an instant she saw her transformation as it must appear to him. She had spent his money recklessly, and made herself look ridiculous. All the many kinds of shame she had ever known focused on her now, making her a glowing brand of humiliations. She stood helpless. Hans Andersen dropped to the floor with a soft thud. Nevertheless, it was she who spoke first.

"I suppose you—you think it funny to see me rigged up like this?"

He took time to pick up the book she had dropped and hand it back to her. "Won't you sit down again?"

While she seated herself and he followed her example she continued to stammer on. "I—I thought I ought to—to look proper for the house as long as I was in it."

THE DUST FLOWER

Her phrasing gave him an opening. "You're quite right. I should like you to get whatever would help you in—in your profession before you—before you leave us."

Quick to seize the implications here she took them with the submission of those whose lots have always depended on other people's wills.

"I'll go whenever you want me to."

Relieved as he was by this willingness he was anxious not to seem brutal. "I'd—I'd rather you consulted your own wishes about that."

She put on a show of nonchalance. "Oh, I don't care. It'll be just—just as you say *when*."

He would have liked to say when at that instant, but a pretense at courtesy had to be maintained. "There's no hurry—for a day or two."

"You said a week or two yesterday."

"Oh, did I? Well, then, we'll say a week or two now."

"Oh, not for me," she hastened to assure him. "I'd just as soon go to-night."

"Have you hated it as much as that?"

"I've hated some of it."

"Ah, well! You needn't be bothered with it long."

Her candor was of the kind which asks questions frankly. "Haven't you got any more use for me?"

"I'm afraid—" it was not easy to put it into the right words—"I'm afraid I was mistaken yesterday. I put you in—in a false position with no necessity for doing so."

It took her a few seconds to get the force of this. "Do you mean that you didn't need me to be—to be a shame and a disgrace to you *at all?*"

"Did I put it in that way?"

"Well, didn't you?"

The fact that she was now dressed as she was made it more embarrassing to him to be crude than it had been when addressing the homeless and shabby little "drab."

"I don't know what I said then. I was—I was upset."

"And you're upset very easy, ain't you?" She corrected herself quickly: "aren't you?"

"I suppose that's true. What of it?"

"Oh, nothing. I—I just happen to know a way you can get over that—if you want to."

He smiled. "I'm afraid my nervousness is too deeply seated—I may as well admit that I'm nervous—you saw it for yourself ——"

"Oh, I saw you was—you were—sick up here—" she touched her forehead—"as soon as you begun to talk to me."

Grateful for this comprehension he tried to use it to his advantage. "So that you understand how I could go off the hooks ——"

"Sure! My mother'd go off 'em the least little thing, till—till she done—till she did—the way I told her."

"Then some of these days I may ask you to—but just now perhaps we'd better talk about ——"

"When I'm to get out."

Her bluntness of expression hurt him. "That's not the way I should have put it ——"

"But it's the way you'd 'a' meant, isn't it?"

He was the more disconcerted because she said this

gently, with the same longing in her face and eyes as in that of the little mermaid bending over the unconscious prince.

The unconscious prince of the moment merely said: "You mustn't think me more brutal than I am ——"

"Oh, I don't think you're brutal. You're just a little dippy, ain't—aren't—you? But that's because you let yourself go. If when you feel it comin' on you'd just—but perhaps you'd rather *be* dippy. Would you?"

If he could have called these wide goldstone eyes with their tiny flames maternal it is the word he would have chosen. In spite of the difficulty of the minute he was conscious of a flicker of amusement.

"I don't know that I would, but ——"

"After I'm gone shall we—shall we *stay* married?"

This being the real question he was glad she faced it with the directness which gave her a kind of charm. He admitted that. She had the charm of everything which is genuine of its kind. She made no pretense. Her expression, her voice, her lack of sophistication, all had the limpidity of water. He felt himself thanking God for it. "He alone knows what kind of hands I might have fallen into yesterday, crazy fool that I am." Of this child, crude as she was, he could make his own disposition.

So in answer to her question he told her he had seen his lawyer in the afternoon—he was a lawyer himself but he didn't practice—and the great man had explained to him that of all the processes known to American jurisprudence the retracing of such steps as they had taken on the previous day was one of the simplest. What the law had joined the law could put asunder, and was well disposed toward doing so. There being several courses which they could adopt, he put them before her one by one. She listened with the sort of attention which shows the mind of the listener to be fixed on the speaker, rather than on anything he says. Not being obliged to ask questions or to make answers she could again see him as the handsome, dark-eyed prince whom she would have loved to save from drowning or any other fate.

Of all he said she could attach a meaning to but one word: "desertion." Even in the technical marital sense she knew vaguely its significance. She thought of it with a tightening about the heart. Any desertion of him of which she would be capable would be like that of the little mermaid when she dived sorrowfully down to her father's palace, leaving him with those to whom he belonged. It was this thought which prompted a question flung in among his observations, though the link in the train of thought was barely traceable:

"Is she takin' you back—the girl you told me about yesterday?"

He looked puzzled. "Did I tell you about a girl yesterday?"

"Why, sure! You said she kicked you out ——"

"Well, she hadn't. I—I didn't know I'd gone so far as to say ——"

"Oh, you went a lot farther than that. You said you were goin' to the devil. Ain't you? I mean, aren't you?"

"I—I don't seem able to."

THE DUST FLOWER

"You're the first fellow I've ever heard say that."

"I'm the first fellow I've ever heard say it myself. But I tried to-day—and I couldn't."

"What did you do?"

"I tried to get drunk."

She half rose, shrinking away from him. "Not—not *you!*"

"Yes. Why not? I've been drunk before—not often, but ——"

"Don't tell me," she cried, hastily. "I don't want to know. It's too ——"

"But I thought it was just the sort of thing you'd be ——"

"I'd be used to. So it is. But that's the reason. You're—you're different. I can't bear to think of it—not with you."

"But I'm just like any other man."

"Oh, no, you're not."

He looked at her curiously. "How am I—how am I—different?"

"Oh, other men are just men, and you're a—a kind of prince."

"You wouldn't think so if you were to know me better."

"But I'm not goin' to know you better, and I'd rather think of you as I see you are." She dropped this theme to say: "So the other girl ——"

"She didn't mean it at all."

"She'd be crazy if she did. But what made her let you think so?"

"She's—she's simply that sort; goes off the hooks too."

"Oh! So there'll be a pair of you."

"I'm afraid so."

"That'll be bloody murder, won't it? Momma was that way with Judson Flack. Hammer and tongs—the both of them—till I took her in hand, and ——"

"And what happened then?"

"She calmed down and—and died."

"So that it didn't do her much good, did it?"

"It did her that much good that she died. Death was better than the way she was livin' with Judson Flack—and it wasn't always his fault. I do' wanta defend him, but momma got so that if he did have a quiet spell she'd go and stir him up. There's not much hope for two married people that lives like that, do you think?"

"But you say your mother, under your instruction, got over it."

"Yes, but it was too late. The more she got over it the more he'd lambaste her, and when her money was all gone ——"

"But do you think all—all hot-tempered couples have to go it in that way?"

She made a little hunching movement of the shoulders. "It's mostly cat and dog anyhow. You and her—the other girl—won't be much worse than others."

"But you think we'll be worse, to some extent at least."

She ignored this to say, wistfully: "I suppose you're awful fond of her."

"I think I can say as much as that."

"And is she fond of you?"

THE DUST FLOWER

"She says so."

"If she is I don't see how she could——" Her voice trailed away. Her eyes forsook his face to roam the shadows of the room. She added to herself rather than to him: "I couldn't ha' done it if it was me."

"Oh, if you were in love ——"

The eyes wandered back from the shadows to rest on him again. They were sorrowful eyes, and unabashed. A child's would have had this unreproachful ache in them, or a dog's. Though he didn't know what it meant it disturbed him into leaving his sentence there.

It occurred to him then that they were forgetting the subject in hand. He had not expected to be able to converse with her, yet something like conversation had been taking place. It had come to him, too, that she had a mind, and now that he really looked at her he saw that the face was intelligent. Yesterday that face had been no more to him than a smudge, without character, and almost featureless, while to-day. . . .

The train of his thought being twofold he could think along one line, and speak along another. "So if you go to see my lawyer he'll suggest different things that you could do ——"

"I'd rather do whatever 'ud make it easiest for you."

"You're very kind, but I think I'd better not suggest. I'll leave that to him and you. He knows already that he's to supply you with whatever money you need for the present; and after everything is settled I'll see that you have ——"

THE DUST FLOWER

The damask flush which Steptoe had admired stole over a face flooded with alarm. She spoke as she rose, drawing a little back from him. "I do' want any money."

He looked up at her in protestation. "Oh, but you must take it."

She was still drawing back, as if he was threatening her with something that would hurt. "I do' want to."

"But it was part of our bargain. You don't understand that I couldn't ——"

"I didn't make no such—" She checked herself. Her mother had rebuked her for this form of speech a thousand times. She said the sentence over as she felt he would have said it, as the people would have said it among whom she had lived as a child. The cadence of his speech, the half forgotten cadences of theirs, helped her ear and her intuitions. "I didn't make any such bargain," she managed to bring out, at last. "You said you'd give me money; but I never said I'd take it."

He too rose. He began to feel troubled. Perhaps she wouldn't be at his disposition after all. "But— but I couldn't stand it if you didn't let me ——"

"And I couldn't stand it if I did."

"But that's not reasonable. It's part of the whole thing that I should look out for your future after what ——"

"I know what you mean," she declared, tremblingly. "You think that because I'm—I'm beneath you that I ain't got—that I haven't got—no sense of what a girl should do and what she shouldn't do. But you're

THE DUST FLOWER

wrong. Do you suppose I didn't know all about how crazy it was when I went with you yesterday? Of course I did. I was as much to blame as you."

"Oh, no, you weren't. Apart from your being what you call beneath me—and I don't admit that you are—I'm a great deal older than you———"

"You're only older in years. In livin' I'm twice your age. Besides I'm all right here—" she touched her forehead again—"and I could see first thing that you was a fellow that needed to be took—to be taken—care of."

"Oh, you did!"

She strengthened her statement with an affirmative nod. "Yes, I did."

"Well, then, I've always paid the people who've taken care of me ———"

"Oh, but you didn't ask me to take care of you, and I didn't take no care. You wanted me to be a disgrace to you, and I thought so little of myself that I said I'd go and be it. Now I've got to pay for that, not be paid for it."

Her head was up with what Steptoe considered to be mettle. Though the picture she presented was stamped on his mind as resembling the proud mien of the girl in Whistler's Yellow Buskin, he didn't think of that till later.

"There's one thing I must ask you to remember," he said, in a tone he tried to make firm, "that I couldn't possibly accept from you anything in the way of sacrifice."

Her eyes were wide and earnest. "But I never thought of *makin'* anything in the way of sacrifice."

THE DUST FLOWER

"It would be sacrifice for you to help me get out of this scrape, and have nothing at all to the good."

"But I'd have lots to the good." She reflected. "I'd have rememberin'."

"What have you got to remember?"

With her child's lack of self-consciousness she looked him straight in the eyes. "You—for one thing."

"Me!" He had hardly the words for his amazement. "For heaven's sake, what can you have to remember about me that—that could give you any pleasure?"

"Oh, I didn't say it would give me any pleasure. I said I'd *have* it. It'd be mine—something no one couldn't take away from me."

"But if it doesn't do you any good ——"

"It does me good if it makes me richer, don't it?"

"Richer to—to remember *me?*"

She nodded, with a little twisted smile, beginning to move toward the door. Over her shoulder she said: "And it isn't only you. There's—there's Steptoe."

Chapter XIII

MAKING her nod suffice for a good-night, Letty, with the red volume of Hans Andersen under her arm, passed out into the hall. It was not easy to carry herself with the necessary nonchalance, but she got strength by saying inwardly: "Here's where I begin to walk on blades." The knowledge that she was doing it, and that she was doing it toward an end, gave her a dignity of carriage which Allerton watched with sharpened observation.

Reaching the little back spare room she found the door open, and Steptoe sweeping up the hearth before a newly lighted fire. Beppo, whose basket had been established here, jumped from his shelter to paw up at her caressingly. With the hearth-brush in his hand Steptoe raised himself to say:

"Madam'll excuse me, but I thought as the evenin' was chilly ——"

"He doesn't want me to stay."

She brought out the fact abruptly, lifelessly, because she couldn't keep it back. The calm she had been able to maintain downstairs was breaking up, with a quivering of the lip and two rolling tears.

Slowly and absently Steptoe dusted his left hand with the hearth-brush held in his right. "If madam's goin' to decide 'er life by what another person wants she ain't never goin' to get nowhere."

THE DUST FLOWER

There were tears now in the voice. "Yes, but when it's—*him*."

" 'Im or anybody else, we all 'ave to fight for what we means to myke of our own life. It's a poor gyme in which I don't plye my 'and for all I think it'll win."

"Do you mean that I should—act independent?"

" 'Aven't madam an independent life?"

"Havin' an independent life don't make it easier to stay where you're not wanted."

"Oh, if madam's lookin' first for what's easy ——"

"I'm not. I'm lookin' first for what he'll *like*."

Hanging the hearth-brush in its place he took the tongs to adjust a smoking log. "I've been lookin' for what 'e'd like ever since 'e was born; and now I see that gettin' so much of what 'e liked 'asn't been good for 'im. If madam'd strike out on 'er own line, whether 'e liked it or not, and keep at it till 'e 'ad to like it ——"

"Oh, but when it's—" she sought for the right word—"when it's so humiliatin' ——"

"Humiliatin' things is not so 'ard to bear, once you've myde up your mind as they're to be borne." He put up the tongs, to busy himself with the poker. "Madam'll find that humiliation is a good deal like that there quinine; bitter to the tyste, but strengthenin'. I've swallered lots of it; and look at me to-dye."

"I know as well as he does that it's all been a crazy mistake ——"

"I was readin' the other day—I'm fond of a good book, I am—occupies the mind like—but I was readin' about a circus man in South Africa, what 'e myde a mistyke and took the wrong tryle—and just when 'e was a-givin' 'imself up for lost among the tigers and

THE DUST FLOWER

the colored savages 'e found 'e'd tumbled on a mine of diamonds. Big 'ouse in Park Lyne in London now, and 'is daughter married to a Lord."

"Oh, I've tumbled into the mine of diamonds all right. The question is ———"

"If madam really tumbled, or was led by the 'and of Providence."

She laughed, ruefully. "If that was it the hand of Providence 'd have to have some pretty funny ways."

"I've often 'eard as the wyes of Providence was strynge; but I ain't so often 'eard as Providence 'ad got to myke 'em strynge to keep pyce with the wyes of men. Now if the 'and of Providence 'ad picked out madam for Mr. Rash, it'd 'ave to do somethink out of the common, as you might sye, to bring together them as man had put so far apart." He looked round the room with the eye of a head-waiter inspecting a table in a restaurant. "Madam 'as everythink? Well, if there's anythink else she's only got to ring."

Bowing himself out he went down the stairs to attend to those duties of the evening which followed the return of the master of the house. In the library and dining room he saw to the window fastenings, and put out the one light left burning in each room. In the hall he locked the door with the complicated locks which had helped to guarantee the late Mrs. Allerton against burglars. There was not only a bolt, a chain, and an ordinary lock, but there was an ingenious double lock which turned the wrong way when you thought you were turning it the right, and could otherwise baffle the unskilful. Occupied with this task he could peep over his shoulder, through the unlighted front drawing-room, and see his adored one standing on the hearthrug, his hands clasped behind him, and his head bent, in an attitude of meditation.

Steptoe, having much to say to him, felt the nervousness of a prime minister going into the presence of a sovereign who might or might not approve his acts. It was at once the weakness and the strength of his position that his rule was based on an unwritten constitution. Being unwritten it allowed of a borderland where powers were undefined. Powers being undefined his scope was the more easily enlarged, though now and then he found that the sovereign rebelled against the mayor of the palace and had to be allowed his way.

But the sovereign was nursing no seeds of the kind of discontent which Steptoe was afraid of. As a matter of fact he was thinking of the way in which Letty had left the room. The perspective, the teagown, the effectively dressed hair, enabled him to perceive the combination of results which Madame Simone had called *de l'élégance naturelle*. She had that; he could see it as he hadn't seen it hitherto. It must have given what value there was to her poor little rôles in motion pictures. Now that his eye had caught it, it surprised, and to some degree disturbed, him. It was more than the show-girl's inane prettiness, or the comely wax-work face of the girl on the cover of a magazine. With due allowance for her Anglo-Saxonism and honesty, she was the type of woman to whom "things happen." Things would happen to her, Allerton surmised, beyond anything she could experience in his cumbrous and antiquated house.

THE DUST FLOWER

This queer episode would drop behind her as an episode and no more, and in the multitude of future incidents she would almost forget that she had known him. He hoped to God that it would be so, and yet. . . .

He was noting too that she hadn't taxed him, in the way of calling on his small supply of nervous energy. Rather she had spared it, and he felt himself rested. After a talk with Barbara he was always spent. Her emotional furies demanded so much of him that they used him up. This girl, on the contrary, was soothing. He didn't know how she was soothing; but she was. He couldn't remember when he had talked to a woman with so little thought of what he was to say and how he was to say it, and heaven only knew that the things to be said between them were nerve-racking enough. But they had come out of their own accord, those nerve-racking things, probably, he reasoned, because she was a girl of inferior class with whom he didn't have to be particular.

She was quick, too, to catch the difference between his speech and her own. She was quick—and pathetic. Her self-correction amused him, with a strain of pity in his amusement. If a girl like that had only had a chance. . . . And just then Steptoe broke in on his musing by entering the room.

The first subject to be aired was that of the changes in the household staff, and Steptoe raised it diplomatically. Mrs. Courage and Jane had taken offense at the young lydy's presence, and packed themselves off in dishonorable haste. Had it not been that two men friends of his own were ready to come at an hour's notice the house would have been servantless

THE DUST FLOWER

till he had procured strangers. No condemnation could be too severe for Mrs. Courage and Jane, for not content with leaving the house in dudgeon they had insulted the young lydy before they went.

"Sooner or lyter they would 'a' went any'ow. For this long time back they've been too big for their boots, as you might sye. If Mr. Rash 'ad married the other young lydy she wouldn't 'a' stood 'em a week. It don't do to keep servants too long, not when they've got no more than a menial mind, which Jynie and Mrs. Courage 'aven't. The minute they 'eard that this young lydy was in the 'ouse. . . . And beautiful the wye she took it, Mr. Rash. I never see nothink finer on the styge nor in the movin' pictures. Like a young queen she was, a-tellin' 'em that she 'adn't come to this 'ouse to turn out of it them as 'ad 'ad it as their 'ome, like, and that she'd put it up to them. If they went she'd stye; but if they styed she'd go ——"

"She's going anyhow."

Steptoe moved away to feel the fastenings of the back windows. "That'll be a relief to us, sir, won't it?" he said, without turning his head.

"It'll make things easier—certainly."

"I was just 'opin' that it mightn't be—well, not too soon."

"What do you mean by too soon?"

"Well, sir, I've been thinkin' it over through the dye, just as you told me to do this mornin,' and I figger out—" on a table near him he began to arrange the disordered books and magazines—"I figger out that if she was to go it'd better be in a wye agreeable

152

THE DUST FLOWER

to all concerned. It wouldn't do, I syes to myself, for Mr. Rash to bring a young woman into this 'ouse and 'ave 'er go awye feelin' anythink but glad she'd come."

"That'll be some job."

"It'll be some job, sir; but it'll be worth it. It ain't only on the young lydy's account; it'll be on Mr. Rash's."

"On Mr. Rash's—how?"

The magazines lapping over each other in two long lines, he straightened them with little pats. "What I suppose you mean to do, sir, is to get out o' this matrimony and enter into the other as you thought as you wasn't goin' to enter into."

"Well?"

"And when you'd entered into the other you wouldn't want it on your mind—on your conscience, as you might sye—that there was a young lydy in the world as you'd done a kind o' wrong to."

Allerton took three strides across the corner of the room, and three strides back to the fireplace again. "How am I going to escape that? She says she won't let me give her any money."

"Oh, money!" Steptoe brushed money aside as if it had no value. "She wouldn't of course. Not 'er sort."

"But what *is* 'er sort. She seemed one thing yesterday, and to-day she's another."

"That's somethink like what I mean. That young lydy 'as growed more in twenty-four hours than lots'd grow in twenty-four years." He considered how best to express himself further. "Did Mr. Rash ever

THE DUST FLOWER

notice that it isn't bein' born of a certain kind o' family as'll myke a man a gentleman? Of course 'e did. But did 'e ever notice that a man'll often *not* be born of a certain kind o' family, and yet be a gentleman all the syme?"

"I know what you're driving at; but it depends on what you mean by a gentleman."

"And I couldn't 'ardly sye—not no more than I could tell you what the smell of a flower was, not even while you was a-smellin' of it. You know a gentleman's a gentleman, and you may think it's this or that what mykes 'im so, but there ain't no wye to put it into words. Now you, Mr. Rash, anybody'd know you was a gentleman what merely looked at you through a telescope; but you couldn't explyne it, not if you was took all to pieces like the works of a clock. It ain't nothink you do and nothink you sye, because if we was to go by that——"

"Good Lord, stop! We're not talking about me."

"No, Mr. Rash. We're talkin' about the queer thing it is what mykes a gentleman, and I sye that I can't sye. But I *know*. Now, tyke Eugene. 'E's just a chauffeur. But no one couldn't be ten minutes with Eugene and not know 'e's a gentleman through and through. Obligin'—good-mannered—modest—polite to the very cat 'e is—and always with that nice smile—wouldn't *you* sye as Eugene was a gentleman, if anybody was to arsk you, Mr. Rash?"

"If they asked me from that point of view—yes—probably. But what has that to do with it?"

"It 'as this to do with it that when you arsk me what sort that young lydy is I 'ave to reply as she's not the sort to accept money from strynge gentlemen, because it ain't what she's after."

"Then what on earth *is* she after? Whatever it is she can have it, if I can only find out what it is."

Steptoe answered this in his own way. "It's very 'ard for the poor to see so much that's good and beautiful in the world, and know that they can't 'ave none of it. I felt that myself before I worked up to where I am now. 'Ere in New York a poor boy or a poor girl can't go out into the street without seein' the things they're cryvin' for in their insides flaunted at 'em like—shook in their fyces—while the law and the police and the church and everythink what mykes our life says to 'em, 'There's none o' this for you.'"

"Well, money would buy it, wouldn't it?"

"Money'd buy it if money knew what to buy. But it don't. Mr. Rash must 'ave noticed that there's nothink 'elplesser than the people with money what don't know 'ow to spend it. I used to be that wye myself when I'd 'ave a little cash. I wouldn't know what to blow myself to what wouldn't be like them vulgar new-rich. But the new-rich is vulgar only because our life 'as put the 'orse before the cart with 'em, as you might sye, in givin' them the money before showin' 'em what to do with it."

Having straightened the lines of magazines to the last fraction of an inch he found a further excuse for lingering by moving back into their accustomed places the chairs which had been disarranged.

"You 'ave to get the syme kind of 'ang of things as you and me've got, Mr. Rash, to know what it is you want, and 'ow to spend your money wise like. Pleasure isn't just in 'avin' things; it's in knowin' what's good to 'ave and what ain't. Now this young lydy'd be like a child with a dime sent into a ten-cent store to buy whatever 'e'd like. There's so many things, and all the syme price, that 'e's kind of confused like. First 'e thinks it'll be one thing, and then 'e thinks it'll be another, and 'e ends by tykin' the wrong thing, because 'e didn't 'ave nothink to tell 'im 'ow to choose. Mr. Rash wouldn't want a young lydy to whom 'e's indebted, as you might sye, to be like that, now would 'e?"

"It doesn't seem to me that I've got anything to do with it. If I offer her the money, and can get her to take it ——"

"That's where she strikes me as wiser than Mr. Rash, for all she don't know but so little. That much she knows by hinstinck."

"Then what am I going to do?"

"That'd be for Mr. Rash to sye. If it was me——"

The necessity for getting an armchair exactly beneath a portrait seemed to cut this sentence short.

"Well, if it was you—what then?"

"Before I'd give 'er money I'd teach 'er the 'ang of our kind o' life, like. That's what she's aichin' and cryvin' for. A born lydy she is, and 'ankerin' after a lydy's wyes, and with no one to learn 'em to 'er ——"

"But, good heavens, I can't do that."

"No, Mr. Rash, but I could, if you was to leave 'er 'ere for a bit. I could learn 'er to be a lydy in the course of a few weeks, and 'er so quick to pick up.

Then if you was to settle a little hincome on 'er she wouldn't——"

Allerton took the bull by the horns. "She wouldn't be so likely to go to the bad. That's what you mean, isn't it?"

Moving behind Allerton, who continued to stand on the hearthrug, Steptoe began poking the embers, making them safe for the night.

"Did Mr. Rash ever notice that goin' to the bad, as 'e calls it, ain't the syme for them as 'ave nothink as it looks to them as 'ave everythink? When you're 'ungry for food you heats the first thing you can lie your 'ands on; and when you're 'ungry for life you do the first thing as'll promise you the good you're lookin' for. What people like you and me is hapt to call goin' to the bad ain't mostly no more than a 'ankerin' for good which nothink don't seem to feed."

Allerton smiled. "That sounds to me as if it might be dangerous doctrine."

"What excuses the poor'll often seem dyngerous doctrine to the rich, Mr. Rash. Our kind is awful afryde of their kind gettin' a little bit of what they're longin' for, and especially 'ere in America. When we've took from them most of the means of 'aving a little pleasure lawful, we call it dyngerous if they tyke it unlawful like, and we go to work and pass laws agynst them. Protectin' them agynst theirselves we sye it is, and we go at it with a gun."

"But we're talking of——"

"Of the young lydy, sir. Quite so. It's on 'er account as I'm syin' what I'm syin'. You arsk me if

THE DUST FLOWER

I think she'll go to the bad in cyse we turn 'er out, and I sye that ———"

Allerton started. "There's no question of our turning her out. She's sick of it."

"Then that'd be my point, wouldn't it, sir? If she goes because she's sick of it, why, then, natural like, she'll look somewhere else for what—for what she didn't find with us. You may call it goin' to the bad, but it'll be no more than tryin' to find in a wrong wye what life 'as denied 'er in a right one."

Allerton, who had never in his life been asked to bear moral responsibility, was uneasy at this philosophy, changing the subject abruptly.

"Where did she get the clothes?"

"Me and 'er, Mr. Rash, went to Margot's this mornin' and bought a bunch of 'em."

"The deuce you did! And you used my name?"

"No, sir," Steptoe returned, with dignity, "I used mine. I didn't give no 'andle to gossip. I pyde for the things out o' some money I 'ad in 'and—my own money, Mr. Rash—and 'ad 'em all sent to me. I thought as we was mykin' a mistyke the young lydy'd better look proper while we was mykin' it; and I knew Mr. Rash'd feel the syme."

The situation was that in which the *fainéant* king accepts the act of the mayor of the palace because it is Hobson's choice. Moreover, he was willing that she should have the clothes. If she wouldn't take money she would at least apparently take them, which, in a measure, would amount to the same thing. He was dwelling on this bit of satisfaction when Steptoe continued.

THE DUST FLOWER

"And as long as the young lydy remynes with us, Mr. Rash, I thought it'd be discreeter like not to 'ave no more women pokin' about, and tryin' to find out what 'ad better not be known. It mykes it simpler as she 'erself arsks to be called Miss Gravely ——"

"Oh, she does?"

"Yes, sir; and that's what I've told William and Golightly, the waiter and the chef, is 'er nyme. It mykes it all plyne to 'em ——"

"Plain? Why, they'll think ——"

"No, sir. They won't think. When it comes to what's no one's business but your own women thinks; men just haccepts. They tykes things for granted, and don't feel it none of their affair. Mr. Rash'll 'ave noticed that there's a different kind of honor among women from what there is among men. I don't sye but what the women's is all right, only the men's is easier to get on with."

There being no response to these observations Steptoe made ready to withdraw. "And shall you stye 'ome for breakfast, sir?"

"I'll see in the morning."

"Very good, sir. I've locked up the 'ouse and seen to everythink, if you'll switch off the lights as you come up. Good-night, Mr. Rash."

"Good-night."

Chapter XIV

WHILE this conversation was taking place Letty, in the back spare room, was conducting a ceremonial too poignant for tears. There were tears in her heart, but her eyes only smarted.

Taking off the blue-black tea-gown, she clasped it in her arms and kissed it. Then, on one of the padded silk hangers, she hung it far in the depths of the closet, where it wouldn't scorch her sight in the morning.

Next she arrayed herself in a filmy breakfast thing, white with a copper-colored sash matching some of the tones in her hair and eyes, and simple with an angelic simplicity. Standing before the long mirror she surveyed herself mournfully. But this robe too she took off, kissed, and laid away.

Lastly she put on the blue-green costume, with the turquoise and jade embroidery. She put on also the hat with the feather which shaded itself from green into monkshood blue. She put on a veil, and a pair of white gloves. For once she would look as well as she was capable of looking, though no one should see her but herself.

Viewing her reflection she grew frightened. It was the first time she had ever seen her personal potentialities. She had long known that with "half a chance" she could emerge from the cocoon stage of the old gray rag and be at least the equal of the average; but

THE DUST FLOWER

she hadn't expected so radical a change. She was not the same Letty Gravely. She didn't know what she was, since she was neither a "star" nor a "lady," the two degrees of elevation of which she had had experience. All she could feel was that with the advantages here presented she had the capacity to be either. Since, apparently, the becoming a lady was now excluded from her choice of careers, "stardom" would still have been within her reach, only that she was not to get the necessary "half a chance." That was the bitter truth of it. That was to be the result of her walking on blades. All the same, as walking on blades would help her prince she was resolved to walk on them. For her mother's sake, even for Judson Flack's, she had done things nearly as hard, when she had not had this incentive.

The incentive nerved her to take off the blue-green costume, kissing it a last farewell, and laying it to rest, as a mother a dead baby in its coffin. Into the closet went the bits of lingerie from the consignment just arrived from Paris, and the other spoils of the day. When everything was buried she shut the door upon it, as in her heart she was shutting the door on her poor little fledgling hopes. Nothing remained to torment her vision, or distract her from what she had to do. The old gray rag and the battered black hat were all she had now to deal with.

She slept little that night, since she was watching not for daylight but for that first stirring in the streets which tells that daylight is approaching. Having neither watch nor clock the stirring was all she had to go by. When it began to rumble and creak and throb faintly in and above the town she got up and dressed.

So far had she travelled in less than forty-eight hours that the old gray rag, and not the blue-green costume, was now the disguise. In other words, once having tasted the prosperous she had found it the natural. To go back to poverty was not merely hard; it was contrary to all spontaneous dictates. Dimly she had supposed that in reverting to the harness she had worn she would find herself again; but she only discovered that she was more than ever lost.

Very softly she unlocked her door to peep out at the landing. The house was ghostly and still, but it was another sign of her development that she was no longer afraid of it. Space too had become natural, while dignity of setting had seemed to belong to her ever since she was born. Turning her back on these conditions was far more like turning her back on home than it had been when she walked away from Judson Flack's.

She crept out. It was so dark that she was obliged to wait till objects defined themselves black against black before she could see the stairs. She listened too. There were sounds, but only such sounds as all houses make when everyone is sleeping. She guessed, it was pure guessing, that it must be about five o'clock.

She stole down the stairs. The necessity for keeping her mind on moving noiselessly deadened her thought to anything else. She neither looked back to what she was leaving behind, nor forward to what she was going to. Once she had reached the street it would be time enough to think of both. She had the

THE DUST FLOWER

fact in the back of her consciousness, but she kept it there. Out in the street she would feel grief for the prince and his palace, and terror at the void before her; but she couldn't feel them yet. Her one impulse was to escape.

At the great street door she could see nothing; but she could feel. She found the key and turned it easily. As the door did not then yield to the knob she fumbled till she touched the chain. Slipping that out of its socket she tried the door again, but it still refused to open. There must be something else! Rich houses were naturally fortresses! She discovered the bolt and pulled it back.

Still the door was fixed like a rock. She couldn't make it out. A lock, a chain, a bolt! Surely that must be everything! Perhaps she had turned the key the wrong way. She turned it again, but only with the same result. She found she could turn the key either way, and still leave the door immovable.

Perhaps she didn't pull it hard enough. Doors sometimes stuck. She pulled harder; she pulled with her whole might and main. She could shake the door; she could make it rattle. The hanging chain dangled against the woodwork with a terrifying clank. If anyone was lying awake she would sound like a burglar—and yet she must get out.

Now that she was balked, to get out became an obsession. It became more of an obsession the more she was balked. It made her first impatient, and then frantic. She turned the key this way and that way. She pulled and tugged. The perspiration came out on her forehead. She panted for breath; she almost sobbed. She knew there was a "trick" to it. She knew it was a simple trick because she had seen Steptoe perform it on the previous day; but she couldn't find out what it was. The effort made her only the more desperate.

She was not crying; she was only gasping—in raucous, exhausted, nervous sobs. They came shorter and harder as she pitted her impotence against this unyielding passivity. She knew it was impotence, and yet she couldn't desist; and she couldn't desist because she grew more and more frenzied. It was the kind of frenzy in which she would have dashed herself wildly, vainly against the force that blocked her with its pitiless resistance, only that the whole hall was suddenly flooded with a blaze of light.

It was light that came so unexpectedly that her efforts were cut short. Even her hard gasps were silenced, not in relief but in amazement. She remained so motionless that she could practically see herself, thrown against this brutal door, her arms spread out on it imploringly.

Seconds that seemed like minutes went by before she found strength to detach herself and turn.

Amazement became terror. On the halfway landing of the stairs stood a figure robed in scarlet from head to foot, with flying indigo lapels. He was girt with an indigo girdle, while the mass of his hair stood up as in tongues of forked black flame. The countenance was terrible, in mingled perplexity and wrath.

She saw it was the prince, but a prince transformed by condemnation.

"What on earth does this mean?"

THE DUST FLOWER

He came down the rest of the stairs till he stood on the lowest step. She advanced toward him pleadingly.

"I was—I was trying to get out."

"What for?"

"I—I—I must get away."

"Well, even so; is this the way to do it? I thought someone was tearing the house down. It woke me up."

"I was goin' this way because—because I didn't want you to know what'd become of me."

"Yes, and have you on my mind."

"I hoped I'd be takin' myself off your mind."

"If you want to take yourself off my mind there's a perfectly simple means of doing it."

"I'll do anything—but take money."

"And taking money is the only thing I ask of you."

"I can't. It'd—it'd—shame me."

"Shame you? What nonsense!"

She reflected fast. "There's two ways a woman can take money from a man. The man may love her and marry her; or perhaps he don't marry her, but loves her just the same. Then she can take it; but when——"

"When she only renders him a—a great service——"

"Ah, but that's just what I didn't do. You said you wanted me to send you to the devil—and now you ain't a-goin' to go."

He grew excited. "But, good Lord, girl, you don't expect me to go to the devil just to keep my word to you."

"I don't want you to do anything just to keep your word to me," she returned, fiercely. "I only want you to let me get away."

THE DUST FLOWER

He came down the remaining step, beginning to pace back and forth as he always did when approaching the condition he called "going off the hooks." Letty found him a marvelous figure in his scarlet robe, and with his mass of diabolic black hair.

"Yes, and if I let you get away, where would you get away *to?*"

"Oh, I'll find a place."

"A place in jail as a vagrant, as I said the other day."

"I'd rather be in jail," she flung back at him, "than stay where I'm not wanted."

"That's not the question."

"It's the biggest question of all for me. It'd be the biggest for you too if you were in my place." She stretched out her hands to him. "Oh, please show me how to work the door, and let me go."

He flared as he was in the habit of flaring whenever he was opposed. "You can go when we've settled the question of what you'll have to live on."

"I'll have myself to live on—just as I had before I met you in the Park."

"Nothing is the same for you or for me as before I met you in the Park."

"No, but we want to make it the same, don't we? You can't—can't marry the other girl till it is."

"I can't marry the other girl till I know you're taken care of."

"Money wouldn't take care of me. That's where you're makin' your mistake. You rich people think that money will do anything. So it will for you; but it don't mean so awful much to me." Her eyes, her

THE DUST FLOWER

lips, her hands besought him together. "Think now! What would I do with money if I had it? It ain't as if I was a lady. A lady has ways of doin' nothin' and livin' all the same; but a girl like me don't know anything about them. I'd go crazy if I didn't work— or I'd die—or I'd do somethin' worse."

It was because his nerves were on edge that he cried out: "I don't care a button what you do. I'm thinking of myself."

She betrayed the sharpness of the wound only by a deepening of the damask flush. "I'm thinkin' of you, too. Wouldn't you rather have everything come right again—so that you could marry the other girl—and know that I'd done it for you *free*—and not that you'd just bought me off?"

"You mean, wouldn't I rather that all the generosity should be on your side ——"

"I don't care anything about generosity. I wouldn't be doin' it for that. It'd be because ——"

He flung out his arms. "Well—why?"

"Because I'd like to do something *for* you ——"

"Do something for me by making me a cad." He was beside himself. "That's what it would come to. That's what you're playing for. I should be a cad. You dress yourself up again in this ridiculous rig ——"

"It's not a ridic'lous rig. It's my own clothes ——"

"Your own clothes *now* are—are what I saw you in when I came home last evening. You can't go back to that thing. We can't go back in any way." He seemed to make a discovery. "It's no use trying to be what we were in the Park, because we can't be.

THE DUST FLOWER

Whatever we do must be in the way of—of going on to something else."

"Well, that'd be something else, if you'd just let me go, and do the desertion stunt you talked to me about ———"

"I'll not let you do it unless I pay you for it."

"But it'd be payin' me for it if—if you'd just let me do it. Don't you see I *want* to?"

"I can see that you want to keep me in your debt. I can see that I'd never have another easy moment in my life. Whatever I did, and whoever I married, I should have to owe it to *you*."

"Well, couldn't you—when I owe so much to you?"

"There you go! What do you owe to me? Nothing but getting you into an infernal scrape ———"

"Oh, no! It's not been that at all. You'd have to be me to understand what it *has* been. It'll be something to think of all the rest of my life—whatever I do."

"Yes, and I know how you'll think of it."

"Oh, no, you don't. You couldn't. It's nothin' to you to come into this beautiful house and see its lovely kind of life; but for me ———"

"Oh, don't throw that sort of thing at me," he flamed out, striding up and down. "Steptoe's been putting that into your head. He's strong on the sentimental stuff. You and he are in a conspiracy against me. That's what it is. It's a conspiracy. He's got something up his sleeve—I don't know what—and he's using you as his tool. But you don't come it over me. I'm wise, I am. I'm a fool too. I know it well enough. But I'm not such a fool as to ———"

THE DUST FLOWER

She was frightened. He was going "off the hooks." She knew the signs of it. This rapid speech, one word leading to another, had always been her mother's first sign of super-excitement, until it ended in a scream. If he were to scream she would be more terrified than she had ever been in her life. She had never heard a man scream; but then she had never seen a man grow hysterical.

His utterance was the more clear-cut and distinct the faster it became.

"I know what it is. Steptoe thinks I'm going insane, and he's made you think so too. That's why you want to get away. You're afraid of me. Well, I don't wonder at it; but you're not going. See? You're not going. You'll go when I send you; but you'll not go before. See? I've married you, haven't I? When all is said and done you're my wife. My wife!" He laughed, between gritted teeth. "My wife! That's my wife!" He pointed at her. "Rashleigh Allerton who thought so much of himself has married *that*—and she's trying to do the generous by him ——"

Going up to him timidly, she laid her hand on his arm. "Say, mister, would you mind countin' ten?"

The appeal took him so much by surprise that, both in his speech and in his walk, he stopped abruptly. She began to count, slowly, and marking time with her forefinger. "One—two—three—four—five—six—seven—eight—nine—ten."

He stared at her as if it was she who had gone "off the hooks." "What do you mean by that?"

"Oh, nothin'. Now you can begin again."

"Begin what?"

"What you was—what you were sayin'."

"What I was saying?" He rubbed his hand across his forehead, which was wet with cold perspiration. "Well, what was I saying?"

He was not only dazed, but a pallor stole over his skin, the more ghastly in contrast with his black hair and his scarlet dressing-gown.

"Isn't there no place you can lay down? I always laid momma down after a spell of this kind. It did her good to sleep and she always slept."

He said, absently: "There's a couch in the library. I can't go back to bed."

"No, you don't want to go back to bed," she agreed, as if she was humoring a child. "You wouldn't sleep there ———"

"I haven't slept for two nights," he pleaded, in excuse for himself, "not since ———"

Taking him by the arm she led him into the library, which was in an ell behind the back drawing-room. It was a big, book-lined room with worn, shiny, leather-covered furnishings. On the shiny, leather-covered couch was a cushion which she shook up and smoothed out. Over its foot lay an afghan the work of the late Mrs. Allerton.

"Now, lay down."

He stretched himself out obediently, after which she covered him with the afghan. When he had closed his eyes she passed her hand across his forehead, on which the perspiration was still thick and cold. She remembered that a bottle of Florida water and a paper fan were among the luxuries of the back spare room.

THE DUST FLOWER

"Don't you stir," she warned him. "I'm goin' to get you something."

Absorbed in her tasks as nurse she forgot to make the sentimental reflections in which she would otherwise have indulged. Back to the room from which she had fled she hurried with no thought that she was doing so. From the grave of hope she disinterred a half dozen of the spider-web handkerchiefs to which a few hours previously she had bid a touching adieu. With handkerchiefs, fan, and Florida water, she flew back to her patient, who opened his eyes as she approached.

"I don't want to be fussed over ——" he was beginning, fretfully.

"Lie still," she commanded. "I know what to do. I'm used to people who are sick—up here."

"Up here" was plainly the forehead which she mopped softly with a specimen from Margot's Parisian consignment. He closed his eyes. His features relaxed to an expression of relief. Relief gave place to repose when he felt her hand with the cool scented essence on his brow. It passed and passed again, lightly, soothingly, consolingly. Drowsily he thought that it was Barbara's hand, but a Barbara somehow transformed, and grown tenderer.

He was asleep. She sat fanning him till a feeble daylight through an uncurtained window warned her to switch off the electricity. Coming back to her place, she continued to fan him, quietly and deftly, with no more than a motion of the wrist. She had the nurse's wrist, slender, flexible; the nurse's hand, strong, shapely, with practical spatulated finger-tips. After all, he was in some degree the drowning unconscious prince, and she the little mermaid.

"He'll be ashamed when he wakes up. He'll not like to find me sittin' here."

It was broad daylight now. He was as sound asleep as a child. Since she couldn't disturb him by rising she rose. Since she couldn't disturb him even by kissing him she kissed him. But she wouldn't kiss his lips, nor so much as his cheek or his brow. Very humbly she knelt and kissed his feet, outlined beneath the afghan. Then she stole away.

Chapter XV

THE interlacing of destinies is such that you will not be surprised to learn that the further careers of Letty Gravely, of Barbara Walbrook, of Rashleigh Allerton now turned on Mademoiselle Odette Coucoul, whose name not one of the three was ever destined to hear.

On his couch in the library Allerton slept till after nine, waking in a confusion which did not preclude a sense of refreshment. At the same minute Madame Simone was finishing her explanations to Mademoiselle Coucoul as to what was to be done to the sealbrown costume, which Steptoe had added to Letty's wardrobe, in order to conceal the fact that it was a model of a season old, and not the new creation its purchasers supposed. Taking in her instructions with Gallic precision mademoiselle was already at work when Miss Tina Vanzetti paused at her door. The door was that of a small French-paneled room, once the boudoir of the owner of the Flemish chateau, but set apart now by Madame Simone for jobs requiring deftness.

Miss Vanzetti, whose Neapolitan grandfather had begun his American career as a boot-black in Brooklyn, was of the Americanized type of her race. She could not, of course, eliminate her Latinity of eye and tress nor her wild luxuriance of bust, but English was her mother-tongue, and the chewing of gum

THE DUST FLOWER

her national pastime. She chewed it now, slowly, thoughtfully, as she stood looking in on Mademoiselle Odette, who was turning the skirt this way and that, searching out the almost invisible traces of use which were to be removed.

"So she's give you that to do, has she? Some stunt, I'll say. Gee, she's got her gall with her, old Simone, puttin' that off on the public as something new. If I had a dollar for every time Mamie Gunn has walked in and out to show it to customers I'd buy a set of silver fox."

Mademoiselle's smile was radiant, not because she had radiance to shed, but because her lips and teeth framed themselves that way. She too was of her race, alert, vivacious, and as neat as a trivet, as became a former midinette of the rue de la Paix and a daughter of Batignolles.

"Madame she t'ink it all in de beezeness," she contented herself with saying.

With her left hand Miss Vanzetti put soft touches to the big black coils of her back hair. "See that kid that all these things is goin' to? Gee, but she's beginnin' to step out. I know her. Spotted her the minute she come in to try on. Me and she went to the same school. Lived in the same street. Name of Letty Gravely."

Seeing that she was expected to make a response mademoiselle could think of nothing better than to repeat in her pretty staccato English: "Name of Let-ty Grav-el-ly."

"Stepfather's name was Judson Flack. Company-promoter he called himself. Mother croaked three or

THE DUST FLOWER

four years ago, just before we moved to Harlem. Never saw no more of her till she walked in here with the old white slaver what's payin' for the outfit. Gee, you needn't tell me! S'pose she'll hit the pace till some fella chucks her. Gee, I'm sorry. Awful slim chance a girl'll get when some guy with a wad blows along and wants her." The theme exhausted Miss Vanzetti asked suddenly: "Why don't you never come to the Lantern?"

In her broken English mademoiselle explained that she didn't know the American dances, but that a fella had promised to teach her the steps. She had met him at the house of a cousin who was married to a waiter chez Bouquin. Ver' beautiful fella, he was, and had invited her to a chop suey dinner that evening, with the dance at the Lantern to wind up with. Most ver' beautiful fella, single, and a detective.

"Good for you," Miss Vanzetti commanded. "If you don't dance you might as well be dead, I'll say. Keeps you thin, too; and the music at the Lantern is swell."

The incident is so slight that to get its significance you must link it up with the sound of the telephone which, as a simultaneous happening, was waking Judson Flack from his first real sleep after an uncomfortable night. Nothing but the fear lest by ignoring the call the great North Dakota Oil Company whose shares would soon be on the market, would be definitely launched without his assistance dragged him from his bed.

"Hello?"

A woman's voice inquired: "Is this Hudson 283-J?"

"You bet."

"Is Miss Gravely in?"

"Just gone out. Only round the corner. Back in a few minutes. Say, sister, I'm her stepfather, and 'll take the message."

"Tell her to come right over to the Excelsior Studio. Castin' director's got a part for her. Real part. Small but a stunner. Outcast girl. I s'pose she's got some old duds to dress it in?"

"Sure thing!"

"Well, tell her to bring 'em along. And say, listen! I don't mind passing you the tip that the castin' director has his eye on that girl for doin' the pathetic stunt; so see she ain't late."

"Y'betcha."

That an ambitious man, growing anxious about his future, was thus placed in a trying situation will be seen at once. The chance of a lifetime was there and he was unable to seize it. Everyone knew that by these small condensations of nebular promise stars were eventually evolved, and to have at his disposal the earnings of a star. . . .

It seemed providential then that on dropping into the basement eating place at which he had begun to take his breakfasts he should fall in with Gorry Larrabin. They were not friends, or rather they were better than friends; they were enemies who found each other useful. Mutually antipathetic, they quarrelled, but could not afford to quarrel long. A few days or a few weeks having gone by, they met with a nod, as if no hot words had been passed.

It was such an occasion now. Ten days earlier

THE DUST FLOWER

Judson had called Gorry to his teeth "no detective, but a hired sneak." Gorry had retorted that, hired sneak as he was, he would have Judson Flack "in the jug" as a promoter of faked companies before the year was out. One word had led to another, and only the intervention of friends to both parties had kept the high-spirited fellows from exchanging blows. But the moment had come round again when each had an axe to grind, so that as Judson hung up his hat near the table at which Gorry, having finished his breakfast, was smoking and picking his teeth, the nod of reconciliation was given and returned.

"Say, why don't you sit down here?"

Politely Gorry indicated the unoccupied side of his own table. It was a small table covered with a white oil-cloth, and tolerably clean.

"Don't mind if I do," was the other's return of courtesy, friendly relations being thus re-established.

Having given his order to a stunted Hebrew maid of Polish culture, Judson Flack launched at once into the subject of Letty. He did this for a two-fold reason. First, his grievance made the expression of itself imperative, and next, Gorry being a hanger-on of that profession which lives by knowing what other people don't might be in a position to throw light on Letty's disappearance. If he was he gave no sign of it. As a matter of fact he was not, but he meant to be. He remembered the girl; had admired her; had pointed out to several of his friends that she had only to doll herself up in order to knock spots out of a lot of good lookers of recognized supremacy.

Odette Coucoul's description of him as "most ver'

beautiful fella" was not without some justification. Regular, clean-cut features, long and thin, were the complement of a slight well-knit figure, of which the only criticism one could make was that it looked slippery. Slipperiness was perhaps his ruling characteristic, a softness of movement suggesting a cat, and a habit of putting out and drawing back a long, supple, snake-like hand which made you think of a pickpocket. Eyes that looked at you steadily enough impressed you as untrustworthy chiefly because of a dropping of the pupil of the left, through muscular inability.

"Awful sorry, Judson," was his summing up of sympathy with his companion's narrative. "Any dope I get I'll pass along to you."

Between gentlemen, however, there are understandings which need not be put into words, the principle of nothing for nothing being one of them. The conversation had not progressed much further before Gorry felt at liberty to say:

"Now, about this North Dakota Oil, Judson. I'd like awful well to get in on the ground floor of that. I've got a little something to blow in; and there's a lot of suckers ready to snap up that stock before you print the certificates."

Diplomacy being necessary here Judson practiced it. Gorry might indeed be seeking a way of turning an honest penny; but then again he might mean to sell out the whole show. On the one hand you couldn't trust him, and on the other it wouldn't do to offend him so long as there was a chance of his getting news of the girl. Judson could only temporize, pleading his lack of influence with the bunch who were getting up the company. At the same time he would do his utmost to work Gorry in, on the tacit understanding that nothing would be done for nothing.

Allerton too had breakfasted late, at the New Netherlands Club, and was now with Miss Barbara Walbrook, who received him in the same room, and wearing the same hydrangea-colored robe, as on the previous morning. He had called her up from the Club, asking to be allowed to come once more at this unconventional hour in order to communicate good news.

"She's willing to do anything," he stated at once, making the announcement with the glee of evident relief. "In fact, it was by pure main force that I kept her from running away from the house this morning."

He was dashed that she did not take these tidings with his own buoyancy. "What made you stop her?" she asked, in some wonder. "Sit down, Rash. Tell me the whole thing."

Though she took a chair he was unable to do so. His excitement now was over the ease with which the difficulty was going to be met. He could only talk about it in a standing position, leaning on the mantelpiece, or stroking the head of the Manship terra cotta child, while she gazed up at him, nervously beating her left palm with the black and gold fringe of her girdle.

"I stopped her because—well, because it wouldn't have done."

"Why wouldn't it have done? I should think that it's just what would have done."

"Let her slip away penniless, and—and without friends?"

"She'd be no more penniless and without friends than she was when—when you—" she sought for the right word—"when you picked her up."

"No, of course not; only now the—the situation is different."

"I don't see that it is—much. Besides, if you were to let her run away first, so that you get—whatever the law wants you to get, you could see that she wasn't penniless and without friends afterwards. Most likely that's what she was expecting."

His countenance fell. "I—I don't think so."

"Oh, you wouldn't think so as long as she could bamboozle you. I was simply thinking of your getting what she probably wants to give you—for a price."

"I don't think you do her justice, Barbe. If you'd seen her ———"

"Very well; I shall see her. But seeing her won't make any difference in my opinion."

"She'll not strike you as anything wonderful of course; but I know she's as straight as they make 'em. And so long as she is ———"

"Well, what then?"

"Why, then, it seems to me, we must be straight on our side."

"We'll be straight enough if we pay her her price."

"There's more to it than that."

"Oh, there is? Then how much more?"

"I don't know that I can explain it." He lifted one of the Stiegel candlesticks and put it back in its place. "I simply feel that we can't—that we can't let all the

THE DUST FLOWER

magnanimity be on her side. If she plays high, we've got to play higher."

"I see. So she's got you there, has she?"

"I wish you wouldn't be disagreeable about it, Barbe."

"My dear Rash," she expostulated, "it isn't being disagreeable to have common sense. It's all the more necessary for me not to abnegate that, for the simple reason that you do."

He hurled himself to the other end of the mantelpiece, picking up the second candlestick and putting it down with force. "It's surely not abnegating common sense just to—to recognize honesty."

"Please don't fiddle with those candlesticks. They're the rarest American workmanship, and if you were to break one of them Aunt Marion would kill me. I'll feel safer about you if you sit down."

"All right. I'll sit down." He drew to him a small frail chair, sitting astride on it. "Only please don't fidget me."

"Would you mind taking *that* chair?" She pointed to something solid and masculine by Phyffe. "That little thing is one of Aunt Marion's pet pieces of old Dutch colonial. If anything were to happen to it—But you were talking about recognizing honesty," she continued, as he moved obediently. "That's exactly what I should like you to do, Rash, dear—with your eyes open. If I'm not looking anyone can pull the wool over them, whether it's this girl or someone else."

"In other words I'm a fool, as you were good enough to say——"

"Oh, do forget that. I couldn't help saying it, as I think you ought to admit; but don't keep bringing it up every time I do my best to meet you pleasantly. I'm not going to quarrel with you any more, Rash. I've made a vow to that effect and I'm going to keep it. But if I'm to keep it on my side you mustn't badger me on yours. It doesn't do me any good, and it does yourself a lot of harm." Having delivered this homily she took a tone of brisk cheerfulness. "Now, you said over the phone that you were coming to tell me good news."

"Well, that was it."

"What was it?"

"That she was ready to do anything—even to disappear."

"And you wouldn't let her."

"That I couldn't let her—with nothing to show for it."

"But she will have something to show for it—in the end. She knows that as well as I do. Do you suppose for a minute that she doesn't understand the kind of man she's dealing with?"

"You mean that ——?"

"Rash, dear, no girl who knows as much as this girl knows could help seeing at a glance that she's got a pigeon to pluck, as the French say, and of course she means to pluck it. You can't blame her for that, being what she is; but for heaven's sake let her pluck it in her own way. Don't be a simpleton. Angels shouldn't rush in where fools would fear to tread—and you *are* an angel, Rash, though I suppose I'm the only one in the world who sees it."

"Thank you, Barbe. I know you feel kindly toward me, and that, as you say, you're the only one in the world who does. That's all right, I acknowledge it, and I'm grateful. What I don't like is to see you taking it for granted that this girl is merely playing a game——"

"Rash, do you remember those two winters I worked in the Bleary Street Settlement? and do you remember that the third winter I said that I'd rather enlist in the Navy that go back to it again? You all thought that I was cynical and hard-hearted, but I'll tell you now what the trouble was. I went down there thinking I could teach those girls—that I could do them good—and raise them up—and have them call me blessed—and all that. Well, there wasn't one of them who hadn't forgotten more than I ever knew—who wasn't working me when I supposed she was hanging on my wisdom—who wasn't laughing at me behind my back when I was under the delusion that she was following my good example. And if you've got one of them on your hands she'll fool the eyes out of your head."

"You think so," he said, drily. "Then I don't."

"In that case there's no use discussing it any further."

"There may be after you've seen her."

"How can I see her?"

"You can go to the house."

"And tell her I know everything?"

"If you like. You could say I told you in confidence—that you're an old friend of mine."

"And nothing else?"

"Since you only want to size her up I should think that would be enough."

She nodded, slowly. "Yes, I think you're right. Better not give anything away we can keep to ourselves. Now tell me what happened this morning. You haven't done it yet."

He told her everything—how he had been waked by hearing someone fumbling with the lock of the door, whether inside or outside the house he couldn't tell—how he had gone to the head of the stairs and switched on the lower hall light—how she had flung herself against the door as a little gray bird might dash itself against its cage in its passion to escape.

"She staged it well, didn't she? She must have brains."

"She has brains all right, but I don't think ——"

"She knew of course that if she made enough noise someone would come, and she'd get the credit for good intentions."

"I really don't think, Barbe. . . . Now let me tell you. You'll *see* what she's like. I felt very much as you do. I was right on the jump. Got all worked up. Would have gone clean off the hooks if ——"

There followed the narrative of his loss of temper, of his wild talk, of her clever strategy in counting ten—"just like a cold douche it was"—and the faint turn he so often had after spells of emotion. To convince Miss Walbrook of the queer little thing's ingenuousness he told how she had made him lie down on the library couch, covered him up, rubbed his brow with Florida water, and induced the best sleep he had had in months.

THE DUST FLOWER

She surprised him by springing to her feet, her arms outspread. "You great big idiot! Really there's no other name for you!"

He gazed up at her in amazement. "What's the matter now?"

Flinging her hands about she made inarticulate sounds of exasperation beyond words.

"There, there; that'll do," she threw off, when he jumped to her side, to calm her by taking her in his arms. "*I'm* not off the hooks. *I* don't want anyone to rub Florida water on my brow—and hold my hand —and cradle me to sleep ———"

"She didn't," he exclaimed, with indignation. "She never touched my hand. She just ———"

"Oh, I know what she did—and of course I'm grateful. I'm delighted that she was there to do it— *delighted*. I quite see now why you couldn't let her go, when you knew your fit was coming on. I've seen you pretty bad, but I've never seen you as bad as that; and I must say I never should have thought of counting ten as a cure for it."

"Well, *she* did."

"Quite so! And if I were you I'd never go anywhere without her. I'd keep her on hand in case I took a turn ———"

He was looking more and more reproachful. "I must say, Barbe, I don't think you're very reasonable."

She pushed him from her with both hands against his shoulders. "Go away, for heaven's sake! You'll drive me crazy. I'm *not* going to lose my temper with you. I'll never do it again. I've got you to bear with, and I'm going to bear with you. But go! No, go now! Don't stop to make explanations. You can do that later. I'll lay in a supply of Florida water and an afghan. . . ."

He went with that look on his face which a well meaning dog will wear when his good intentions are being misinterpreted. On his way to the office he kept saying to himself: "Well *I* don't know what to do. Whatever I say she takes me up the wrong way. All I wanted was for her to understand that the little thing is a *good* little thing. . . ."

Chapter XVI

WHILE Allerton was making these reflections Steptoe was summoned to the telephone.

"Is this you, Steptoe? I'm Miss Barbara Walbrook."

Steptoe braced himself. In conversing with Miss Barbara Walbrook he always felt the need of inner strengthening. "Yes, Miss Walbrook?"

"Mr. Allerton tells me you've a young woman at the house."

"We 'ave a young lydy. Certainly, miss."

"And Mr. Allerton has asked me to call on her."

Steptoe's training as a servant permitted him no lapses of surprise. "Quite so, miss. And when was it you'd be likely to call?"

"This afternoon about four-thirty. Perhaps you could arrange to have me see her alone."

"Oh, there ain't likely to be no one 'ere, miss."

"And another thing, Steptoe. Mr. Allerton has asked me just to call as an old friend of his. So you'll please not say to her that—well, anything about me. I'm sure you understand."

Steptoe replied that he did understand, and having put up the receiver he pondered.

What could it mean? What could be back of it? How would this unsophisticated girl meet so skilful an antagonist. That Miss Walbrook was coming as an antagonist he had no doubt. In his own occasional meetings with her she had always been a superior, a commander, to whom even he, 'Enery Steptoe, had been a servitor requiring no further consideration. With so gentle an opponent as madam she would order and be obeyed.

At the same time he could not alarm madam, or allow her to shirk the encounter. She had that in her, he was sure, which couldn't but win out, however much she might be at a disadvantage. His part would be to reduce her disadvantages to a minimum, allowing her strong points to tell. Her strong points, he reckoned, were innocence, an absence of self-consciousness, and, to the worldly-wise, a disconcerting candor. Steptoe analyzed in the spirit and not verbally; but he analyzed.

For Letty the morning had been feverish, chiefly because of her uncertainty. Was it the wish of the prince that she should go, or was it not? If it was his wish, why had he not let her? If, on the other hand, he desired her to stay, what did he mean to do with her? He had passed her on the way out to breakfast at the Club—she had been standing in the hall— and he had smiled.

What was the significance of that smile? She sat down in the library to think. She sat down in the chair she had occupied while he lay on the couch, and reconstructed that scene which now, for all her life, would thrill her with emotional memories. There he had lain, his head on the very indentation which the cushion still bore, his feet here, where she had pressed her lips to them. She had actually had her hand on his brow, she had smoothed back his hair, and had hardly noted at the time that such was her extraordinary privilege.

She came back to the fact that he had smiled at her. It would have been an enchanting smile from anyone, but coming from a prince it had all the romantic effulgence with which princes' smiles are infused. How much of that romantic effulgence came automatically from the prince because he was a prince, and how much of it was inspired by herself? Was any of it inspired by herself? When all was said and done this last was the great question.

It brought her where so many things brought her, to the dream of love at first sight. Could it have happened to him as it had happened to herself? It was so much in her mental order of things that she was far from considering it impossible. Improbable, yes; she would admit as much as that; but impossible, no! To be sure she had been in the old gray rag; but Steptoe had informed her that there were kings who went about falling in love with beggar-maids. She would have loved being one of those beggar-maids; and after all, was she not?

True, there was the other girl; but Letty found it hard to see her as a reality. Besides, she had, in appearance at least, treated him badly. Might it not easily have come about that she, Letty, had caught his heart in the rebound? She quite understood that if the prince *had* fallen in love with her at first sight, there might be convulsion in his inner self without, as yet, a comprehension on his part of the nature of his passion.

She had reached this point when Steptoe entered the

library on one of his endless tasks of re-arranging that which seemed to be in sufficiently good order. Putting the big desk to rights he said over his shoulder:

"Perhaps I'd better tell madam as she's to 'ave a caller this afternoon."

Letty sprang up in alarm. "A—*what?*"

"A lydy what'll myke a call. Oh, madam don't need to be afryde. She's an old friend o' Mr. Rash's, and'll want, no doubt, to be a friend o' madam too."

"But what does she know about me?"

"Mr. Rash must 'a told 'er. She spoke to me just now on the telephone, and seemed to know everything. She said she'd be 'ere this afternoon about four-thirty, if madam'd be so good as to give 'er a cup o' tea."

"Me?"

Having invented the cup of tea for his own purpose Steptoe went on to explain further. "It's what the 'igh lydies mostly gives each other about 'alf past four or five o'clock, and madam couldn't homit it without seemin' as if she didn't know what's what. It'll be very important for madam to tyke 'er position from the start. If the lydy is comin' friendly like she'd be 'urt if madam wasn't friendly too."

Letty had seen the giving and taking of tea in more than one scene in the movies, and had also, from a discreet corner, witnessed the enacting of it right in the "set" on the studio lot. She remembered one time in particular when Luciline Lynch, the star in *Our Crimson Sins,* had driven Frank Redgar, the director, almost out of his senses by her inability to get the right turn of the wrist. Letty, too, had been almost

THE DUST FLOWER

out of her senses with the longing to be in Luciline Lynch's place, to do the thing in what was obviously the way. But now that she was confronted with the opportunity in real life she saw the situation otherwise.

"And I won't be able to talk right," was the difficulty she raised next.

"That'll be a chance for madam to listen and ketch on. She's horfly quick, madam is, and by listenin' to Miss Walbrook, that's the lydy's nyme, and listenin' to 'erself—" He broke off to emphasize this line of suggestion—"it's listenin' to 'erself that'll 'elp madam most. It's a thing as 'ardly no one does. If they did they'd be 'orrified at their squawky voices and bad pernounciation. If I didn't listen to myself, why, I'd talk as bad as anyone, but—Well, as I sye, this'll give madam a chance. All the time what Miss Walbrook is speakin' madam can be listenin' to 'er and listenin' to 'erself too, and if she mykes mistykes this time she'll myke fewer the next."

Letty was pondering these hints as he continued.

"Now if madam wouldn't think me steppin' out of my plyce I'd suggest that me and 'er 'as a little tea of our own like—right now—in the drorin' room—and I'll be Miss Walbrook—and William'll be William—and madam'll be madam—and we'll get it letter-perfect before 'and, just as with Mary Ann Courage and Jyne."

No sooner said than done. Letty was already wearing the white filmy thing with the copper-sash, buried with solemn rites on the previous night, but disinterred that morning, which did very well as a tea-gown. Steptoe placed her in the corner of the sofa which the lyte Mrs. Allerton had generally occupied when "receivin' company", and William brought in the tea-equipage on a gorgeous silver tray.

Before he did this it had been necessary to school William to his part, which, to do him justice, he carried out with becoming gravity. Any reserves he might have felt were expressed to Golightly by a wink behind Steptoe's back before he left the kitchen. The wink was the more expressive owing to the fact that Golightly and William had already summed up the old fellow as "balmy on the bean," while their part was to humor him. Plain as a bursting shell seemed to William Miss Gravely's position in the household, and Steptoe's chivalry toward her an eccentricity which a sense of humor could enjoy. Otherwise they justified his reading of the fundamental non-morality of men, in bringing no condemnation to bear on anyone concerned. Being themselves two almost incapacitated heroes, with jobs likely to prove "soft," it was wise, they felt, to enter into Steptoe's comedy. At half past ten in the morning, therefore, Golightly prepared tea and buttered toast, while William arranged the tea-tray with those over-magnificent appointments which had been "the lyte Mrs. Allerton's tyste."

From her corner of the sofa Letty heard the butler announce, in a voice stately but not stentorian: "Miss Barbara Walbrook."

He was so near the door that to step out and step in again was the work of a second. In stepping in again he trod daintily, wriggling the back part of his person, better to simulate the feminine. In order that Letty should nowhere be caught unaware he put out his hand languidly, back upward, as princesses do when they expect it to be kissed.

"So delighted to find you at 'ome, Mrs. Allerton. It's such a very fine dye I was sure as you'd be out."

Rising from her corner Letty shook the relaxed hand as she might have shaken a dog's tail. "Very pleased to meet you."

From the histrionic Steptoe lapsed at once into the critical. "I think if madam was to sye, 'So glad to be *at* 'ome, Miss Walbrook; do let me ring for tea,' it'd be more like the lyte Mrs. Allerton."

Obediently Letty repeated this formula, had the bell pointed out to her, and rang. The ladies having seated themselves, Miss Walbrook continued to improvise on the subject of the weather.

"Some o' these October dyes'll be just like summer time! and then agyne there'll be a nip in the wind as'll fairly freeze you. A good time o' year to get out your furs, and I'm sure I 'ope as 'ow the moths 'aven't gone and got at 'em. Horfly nasty things them moths. They sye as everything in the world 'as a use; but I'm sure I don't see what use there is for moths, eatin' 'oles in the seats of gentlemen's trousers, no matter what you do to keep the coat-closet aired—and everything like that. What do you sye, Mrs. Allerton?"

Letty was relieved of the necessity of answering by the entrance of William with the tray, after which her task became easier. Used to making "a good cup of tea" in an ordinary way, the doing it with this formal ceremoniousness was only a matter of revision. As if it was yesterday she recalled the instructions given to Luciline Lynch, "Lemon?—cream?—one lump?—two lumps?" so that Miss Walbrook was startled by her readiness. She, Miss Walbrook, was betrayed, in fact, into some confusion of personality, stating that she would have cream and no sugar, and that furthermore Englishmen like herself 'ardly ever took lemon in their tea, and in her opinion no one ever did to whom the tea-drinking 'abit was 'abitual.

"It's a question of tyste," Miss Walbrook continued, sipping with a soft siffling noise in the way he considered to be ladylike. "Them that 'as drunk tea with their mother's milk, as you might sye, 'll tyke cream and sugar, one or both; but them that 'as picked up the 'abit in lyter life 'll often condescend to lemon."

What the rehearsal did for Letty was to make the mechanical task familiar, while she concentrated her attention on Miss Walbrook.

It has to be admitted that to Barbara Walbrook Letty was a shock. Having worked for two years in the Bleary Street Settlement she had her preconceived ideas of what she was to find, and she found something so different that her first consciousness was that of being "sold."

Steptoe had received her at the door, and having ushered her into the drawing-room announced, "Miss Barbara Walbrook," as if she had been calling on a duchess. From the semi-obscurity of the back drawing-room a small lithe figure came forward a step or two. The small lithe figure was wearing a tea-gown of which so practiced an eye as Miss Walbrook's could not but estimate the provenance and value, while a sweet voice said:

THE DUST FLOWER

"I'm so glad to be at home, Miss Walbrook. Do let me ring for tea."

Before a protest could be voiced the bell had been rung, so that Miss Walbrook found herself sitting in the chair Steptoe had used in the morning, and listening to her hostess as you listen to people in a dream.

"Beautiful weather for October, isn't it? Some of these October days'll be just like summer time. And then again there'll be a nip in the wind that'll fairly freeze you. A good time of year to get out your furs, isn't it? and I'm sure I hope the moths ain't—haven't —got at them. Awfully nasty things moths ——"

Letty's further efforts were interrupted by William bearing the tray as he had borne it in the morning, and in the minutes of silence while he placed it Miss Walbrook could go through the mental process known as pulling oneself together.

But she couldn't pull herself together without a sense of outrage. She had expected to feel shame, vicariously for Rash; she had not expected to be asked to take part in a horrible bit of play-acting. This dressing-up; this mock hospitality; this desecration of the things which "dear Mrs. Allerton" had used; this mingling of ignorance and pretentiousness, inspired a rage prompting her to fling the back of her hand at the ridiculous creature's face. She couldn't do that, of course. She couldn't even express herself as she felt. She had come on a mission, and she must carry out that mission; and to carry out the mission she must be as suave as her indignation would allow of. *She* was morally the mistress of this house. Rash and all

195

Rash owned belonged to *her*. To see this strumpet sitting in her place. . . .

It did nothing to calm her that while she was pressing Rash's ring into her flesh, beneath her glove, this vile thing was wearing a plain gold band, just as if she was married. She could understand that if they had absurdly walked through an absurd ceremony the absurd minister who performed it might have insisted on this absurd symbol; but it should have been snatched from the creature's hand the minute the business was ended. They owed that to *her*. *Hers* was the only claim Rash had to consider, and to allow this farce to be enacted beneath his roof. . . .

But she remembered that Letty didn't know who she was, or why she had come, or the degree to which she, Barbara Walbrook, saw through this foolery.

Letty repeated her little formula: "Lemon?—cream?—one lump?—two lumps?" though before she reached the end of it her voice began to fail. Catching the hostility in the other woman's bearing, she felt it the more acutely because in style, dress, and carriage this was the model she would have chosen for herself.

Miss Walbrook waved hospitality aside. "Thank you, no; nothing in the way of tea." She nodded over her shoulder towards William's retreating form. "Who's that man?"

Her tone was that of a person with the right to inquire. Letty didn't question that right, knowing the extent to which she herself was an usurper. "His name is William."

"How did he come here?"

"I—I don't know."

"Where are Nettie and Jane?"

"They've—they've left."

"Left? Why?"

"I—I don't know."

"And has Mrs. Courage left too?"

Letty nodded, the damask flush flooding her cheeks darkly.

"When? Since—since you came?"

Letty nodded again. She knew now that this was the bar of social judgment of which she had been afraid.

The social judge continued. "That must be very hard on Mr. Allerton."

Letty bowed her head. "I suppose it is."

"He's not used to new people about him, and it's not good for him. I don't know whether you've seen enough of him to know that he's something of an invalid."

"I know—" she touched her forehead—"that he's sick up here."

"Oh, do you? Then I shouldn't have thought that you'd have—" but she dropped this line to take up another. "Yes, he's always been so. When he was a boy they were afraid he might be epileptic; and though he never was as bad as that he's always needed to be taken care of. He can do very wild and foolish things as—as you've discovered for yourself."

Letty felt herself now a little shameful lump of misery. This woman was so experienced, so right. She spoke with a decision and an authority which made love at first sight a fancy to blush at. Letty could say nothing because there was nothing to say, and meanwhile the determined voice went on.

"It's terrible for a man like him to make such a mistake, because being what he is he can't grapple with it as a stronger or a coarser man would do."

But here Letty saw something that might be faintly pleaded in her own defence. "He says he wouldn't ha' made the mistake if that—that other girl hadn't been crazy."

Barbara drew herself up. "Did he—did he say that?"

"He said something like it. He said she went off the hooks, just like he did himself." She raised her eyes. "Do you know her, Miss Walbrook?"

"Yes, I know her."

"She must be an awful fool."

Barbara prayed for patience. "What—what makes you say so?"

"Oh, just what *he's* said."

"And what has he said? Has he talked about her to *you?*"

"He hasn't talked about her. He's just—just let things out."

"What sort of things?"

"Only that sort." She added, as if to herself: "I don't believe he thinks much of her."

Barbara's self-control was miraculous. "I've understood that he was very much in love with her."

"Well, perhaps he is." Letty's little movement of the shoulders hinted that an expert wouldn't be of this opinion. "He may think he is, anyhow."

"But if he thinks he is ——"

THE DUST FLOWER

Letty's eyes rested on her visitor with their compelling candor. "I don't believe men know much about love, do you, Miss Walbrook?"

"It depends. All men haven't had as much experience of it as I suppose you've had——"

"Oh, I haven't had any." The candor of the eyes was now in the whole of the truthful face. "Nobody was ever in love with me—never. I never had a fella—nor nothing."

In spite of herself Barbara believed this. She couldn't help herself. She could hear Rash saying that whatever else was wrong in the ridiculous business the girl herself was straight. All the same the discussion was beneath her. It was beneath her to listen to opinions of herself coming from such a source. If Rash didn't "think much of her" there was something to "have out" with him, not with this little street-waif dressed up with this ludicrous mummery. The sooner she ended the business on which she had come the sooner she would get a legitimate outlet for the passion of jealousy and rage consuming her.

"But we're wandering away from my errand. I won't pretend that I've come of my own accord. I'm a very old friend of Mr. Allerton's, and he's asked me—or practically asked me—to come and find out——"

For what she was to come and find out she lacked for a minute the right word, and so held up the sentence.

"What I'd take to let him off?"

The form of expression was so crude that once more Barbara was startled. "Well, that's what it would come to."

THE DUST FLOWER

"But I've told him already that—that I want to let him off anyhow."

"Yes? And on what terms?"

"I don't want any terms."

"Oh, but there must be *terms*. He couldn't let you do it ——"

"He could let me do it for *him,* couldn't he? I'd go through fire, if it'd make him a bit more comfortable than he is."

Barbara could not believe her ears. "Do you want me to understand that ——?"

"That I'll do whatever will make him happy just to *make* him happy? Yes. That's it. He didn't need to send no one—to send anyone—to ask me, because I've told him so already. He wants me to get out. Well, I'm ready to get out. He wants me to go to the bad. Well, I'm ready ——"

"Yes; he understands all that. But, don't you see? a man in his position couldn't take such a sacrifice from a girl in yours ——"

"Unless he pays me for it in cash."

"That's putting it in a nutshell. If you owned a house, for instance, and I wanted it, I'd buy it from you and pay you for it; but I couldn't take it as a gift, no matter how liberal you were nor how much I needed it."

"I can see that about a house; but your own self is different. I could sell a house when I couldn't sell—myself."

"Oh, but would you call that selling yourself?"

"It'd be selling myself—the way I look at it. When I'm so ready to do what he wants I can't see why he

THE DUST FLOWER

don't let me." She added, tearfully: "Did he tell you about this morning?"

She nodded. "Yes, he told me about that."

"Well, I would have gone then if—if I'd known how to work the door."

"Oh, that's easy enough."

"Do you know?"

"Why, yes."

"Will you show me?"

Miss Walbrook rose. "It's so simple." She continued, as they went toward the door: "You see, Mr. Allerton's mother always kept a lot of valuable jewelry in the house, and she was afraid of burglars. She had the most wonderful pearls. I suppose Mr. Allerton has them still, locked away in some bank. Burglars would never come in by the front door, my aunt used to tell her, but—" They reached the door itself. "Now, you see, there's a common lock, a bolt, and a chain ——"

Letty explained that she had discovered them already.

"But, you see these two little brass knobs over here? That's the trick. You push this one this way, and that one that way, and the door is locked with an extra double lock, which hardly anyone would suspect. See?"

She shook the door which resisted as it had resisted Letty in the morning.

"Now! You push that one this way, and this one that way—and there you are!"

She opened the door to show how easily the thing could be done; and the door being open she passed out.

THE DUST FLOWER

She had not intended to go in this way; but, after all, was not her mission accomplished? It was nothing to her whether this girl accepted money, or whether she did not. The one thing essential was that she should take herself away; and if she was sincere in what she said she had now the means of doing it. Without troubling herself to take her leave Miss Walbrook went down the steps.

Before turning toward Fifth Avenue she glanced back. Letty was standing in the open doorway, her flaming eyes wide, her expression puzzled and wounded. "It's nothing to me," Barbara repeated to herself firmly; but because she was a lady, as she understood the word lady, almost before she was a woman, she smiled faintly, with a distant, and yet not discourteous, inclination of the head.

Chapter XVII

IT was because she was a lady, as she understood the word lady, that by the time she had walked the few steps into Fifth Avenue Miss Walbrook already felt the inner reproach of having done something mean. To do anything mean was so strange to her that she didn't at first recognize the sensation. She only found herself repeating two words, and repeating them uneasily: *"Noblesse oblige!"*

Nevertheless, on the principle that all's fair in love and war, she fought this off. "Either she must go or I must." That she herself should go was not to be considered; therefore the other must go, and by the shortest way. The shortest way was the way she had shown her, and which the girl herself was desirous to take. There was no more than that to the situation.

There was no more than that to the situation unless it was that the strong was taking a poor advantage of the weak. But then, why shouldn't the strong take any advantage it possessed? What otherwise was the use of being strong? The strong prevailed, and the weak went under. That was the law of life. To suppose that the weak must prevail because it was weak was sheer sentimentality. All the same, those two inconvenient words kept dinning in her ears: *"Noblesse oblige!"*

She began to question the honesty which in Letty's presence had convinced her. It was probably not honesty at all. She had known girls in the Bleary Street Settlement who could persuade her that black was white, but who had proved on further knowledge to be lying all round the compass. When it wasn't lying it was bluff. It was possible that Letty was only bluffing, that in her pretense at magnanimity she was simply scheming for a bigger price. In that case she, Barbara, had called the bluff very skilfully. She had put her in a position in which she could be taken at her word. Since she was ready to go, she could go. Since she was ready to go to the bad. . . .

Miss Walbrook was not prim. She knew too much of the world to be easily shocked, in the old conventional sense. Besides, her Bleary Street work had brought her into contact with girls who had gone to the bad, and she had not found them different from other girls. If she hadn't known. . . .

She could contemplate without horror, therefore, Letty's taking desperate steps—if indeed she hadn't taken them long ago—and yet she herself didn't want to be involved in the proceeding. It was one thing to view an unfortunate situation from which you stood detached, and another to be in a certain sense the cause of it. She would not really be the cause of it, whatever the girl did, since she, the girl, was a free agent, and of an age to know her own mind. Moreover, the secret of the door was one which she couldn't help finding out in any case. She, Miss Walbrook, could dismiss these scruples; and yet there was that uncomfortable sing-song humming through her brain: *"Noblesse oblige! Noblesse oblige!"*

"I must get rid of it," she said to herself, as Wild-

THE DUST FLOWER

goose admitted her. "I've got to be on the safe side. I can't have it on my mind."

Going to the telephone before she had so much as taken off her gloves she was answered by Steptoe. "This is Miss Walbrook again, Steptoe. I should like to speak to—to the young woman."

Steptoe who had found Letty crying after Miss Walbrook's departure answered with resentful politeness. "I'll speak to Mrs. Allerton, miss. She *may* be aible to come to the telephone."

"Ye-es?" came later, in a feeble, teary voice.

"This is Miss Walbrook again. I'm sorry to trouble you the second time."

"Oh, that doesn't matter."

"I merely wanted to say, what perhaps I should have said before I left, that I hope you won't—won't *use* the information I gave you as I was leaving—at any rate not at once."

"Do you mean the door?"

"Exactly. I was afraid after I came away that you might do something in a hurry——"

"It'll have to be in a hurry if I do it at all."

"Oh, I don't see that. In any case, I'd—I'd think it over. Perhaps we could have another talk about it, and then——"

Something was said which sounded like a faint, "Very well," so that Barbara put up the receiver.

Her conscience relieved she could open the dams keeping back the fiercer tides of her anger. Rash had talked about her to this girl! He had given her to understand that she was a fool! He had allowed it to appear that "he didn't think much of her!" No matter what he had said, the girl had been able to make these inferences. What was more, these inferences might be true. Perhaps he *didn't* think much of her! Perhaps he only *thought* he was in love with her! The idea was so terrible that it stilled her, as approaching seismic storm will still the elements. She moved about the drawing-room, taking off her gloves, her veil, her hat, and laying them together on a table, as if she was afraid to make a sound. She was standing beside that table, not knowing what to do next, or where to go, when Wildgoose came to the door to announce, "Mr. Allerton."

"I've seen her." Without other form of greeting, or moving from beside the table, she picked up her gloves, threw them down again, picked them up again, threw them down again, with the nervous action of the hands which betrayed suppressed excitement. "I didn't believe her—quite."

"But you didn't disbelieve her—wholly?"

"It's a difficult case."

"I've got you into an awful scrape, Barbe."

She threw down the gloves with special vigor. "Oh, don't begin on that. The scrape's there. What we have to find is the way out."

"Well, do you see it any more clearly?"

"Do you?"

He came near to her. "I see this—that I can't let her throw herself away for me. I've been thinking it over, and I want to ask your opinion of this plan. Let's sit down."

She thought his plan the maddest that was ever proposed, and yet she accepted it. She accepted it because she was suspicious, jealous, and unhappy. "It'll give me the chance to watch—and *see*," she said to herself, as he talked.

In his opinion Letty couldn't take their point of view because she was so inexperienced. It seemed to her a simple thing to go away, leaving them with the responsibilities of her future on their consciences; and it would not seem other than a simple thing till she saw life more as they did. To bring her to this degree of culture they must be subtle with her, and patient. They musn't rush things. They mustn't let her rush them. To end the situation in such a way as to make for happiness they must end it at a point where all would be best for all concerned. For Barbara and himself nothing would be best which was not also best for the girl. What would be best for the girl would be some degree of education, of knowledge of the world, so that she might go back to the life whence they had plucked her less likely to be a prey to the vicious. In that case, if they supplied her with a little income she would know what to do with it, and would perhaps marry some man in her own class able to take care of her.

Barbara's impulse was to cry out: "That's the most preposterous suggestion I ever heard of in my life!" But she controlled this quite reasonable prompting because another voice said to her: "This will give you the opportunity to keep an eye on them. If he's not true in his love for you—if there *is* an infatuation on his part for this common and vulgar creature—you'll be able to detect it." Jealousy loving to suffer she was willing to inflict torture on herself for the sake of catching him in disloyalty.

THE DUST FLOWER

Expecting a storm, and bringing out what he considered his wise proposals with great embarrassment, Allerton was surprised and pleased at the sympathetic calm in which she received them.

"So that you'd suggest ——?"

"Our keeping her on a while longer, and making friends with her. I'd like it tremendously if you'd be a friend to her, because you could do more for her than anyone."

"More than you?"

"Oh, I'd do my bit too," he assured her, innocently. "I could put her up to a lot of things, seeing her every day as I should. But you're the one I should really count on."

Because the words hurt her more than any she could utter, she said, quietly: "I suppose you remember sometimes that after all she's your wife."

He sprang to his feet. Knowing that he did at times remember it he tried to deny it. "No, I don't. She's not. I don't admit it. I don't acknowledge it. If you care anything about me, Barbe, you'll never say that again."

He came and knelt beside her, taking her hands and kissing them. Laying his head in her lap, he begged to be caressed, as if he had been a dog.

Nevertheless by half past nine that evening he was at home, sitting by the fireside with Letty, and beginning his special part in the great experiment.

"She's not my wife," he kept repeating to himself poignantly, as he walked up the Avenue from the Club; "she's not—she's *not*. But she *is* a poor child toward whom I've undertaken grave responsibilities."

THE DUST FLOWER

Because the responsibilities were grave, and she was a poor child, his attitude toward her began to be paternal. It was the more freely paternal because Barbe approved of what he was undertaking. Had she disapproved he might have undertaken it all the same, but he couldn't have done it with this whole-heartedness. He would have been haunted by the fear of her displeasure; whereas now he could let himself go.

"We don't want to keep you a prisoner, or detain you against your will," he said, with regard to the incident of the morning, "but if you'll stay with us a little longer, I think we can convince you of our good intentions."

"Who's—we?"

She shot the question at him, as she lay back in her chair, the red book in her lap. He smiled inwardly at the ready pertinence with which she went to a point he didn't care to discuss.

"Well, then, suppose I said—I? That'll do, won't it?"

She shot another question, her flaming eyes half veiled. "How long would you want me to stay?"

"Suppose we didn't fix a time? Suppose we just left it—like that?"

The question rose to her lips: "But in the end I'm to go?" only, on second thoughts she repressed it. She preferred that the situation should be left "like that," since it meant that she was not at once to be separated from the prince. The fact that she was legally the prince's wife had as little reality to her as to him. Could she have had what she yearned for law or no law would have been the same to her. But since she couldn't have that, it was much that he should come like this and sit with her by the fire in the evening.

He leaned forward and took the book from her lap. "What are you reading? Oh, this! I haven't looked at it for years." He glanced at the title. *"The Little Mermaid!* That used to be my favorite. It still is. When I was in Copenhagen I went to see the little bronze mermaid sitting on a rock on the shore. It's a memorial to Hans Andersen. She's quite startling for a minute—till you know what it is. Where are you at?"

Pointing out the line at which she had stopped her hand touched his, but all the consciousness of the accident was on her side. He seemed to notice nothing, beginning to read aloud to her, with no suspicion that sentiment existed.

"Many an evening and morning she rose to the place where she had left the prince. She watched the fruits in the garden ripen and fall; she saw the snow melt from the high mountains; but the prince she never saw, and she came home sadder than ever. Her one consolation was to sit in her little garden, with her arms clasped round the marble statue which was like the prince ———"

"That'd be me," Letty whispered to herself; "my arms clasped round a marble statue—like my prince—but only a marble statue."

"Her flowers were neglected," Allerton read on, "and grew wild in a luxuriant tangle of stem and blossom, reaching the branches of the willow-tree, and making the whole place dark and dim. At last she could bear it no longer and she told one of her sisters——"

"I wouldn't tell my sister, if I had one," Letty assured herself. "I'd never tell no one. It's more like my own secret when I keep it to myself. Nobody'll ever know—not even him."

"The other sisters learned the story then, but they told it to no one but a few other mermaids, who told it to their intimate friends. One of these friends knew who the prince was, and told the princess where he came from and where his kingdom lay. Now she knew where he lived; and many a night she spent there, floating on the water. She ventured nearer to the land than any of her sisters had done. She swam up the narrow lagoon, under the carved marble balcony; and there she sat and watched the prince when he thought himself alone in the moonlight. She remembered how his head had rested on her breast, and how she had kissed his brow; but he would never know, and could not even dream of her."

Letty had not kissed her prince's brow, but she had kissed his feet; but he would never know that, and would dream of her no more than this other prince of the little thing who loved him.

Allerton continued to read on, partly because the old tale came back to him with its enchanting loveliness, partly because reading aloud would be a feature of his educational scheme, and partly because it soothed him to be doing it. He could never read to Barbara. Once, when he tried it, the sound of his voice and the monotony of his cadences, so got on her nerves that she stopped him in the middle of a word. But this girl with her uncritical mind, and her gratitude for small bits of kindliness, gave him confidence in himself by her rapt way of listening.

She did listen raptly, since a prince's reading must always be more arresting than that of ordinary mortals, and also because, both consciously and subconsciously, she was taking his pronunciation as a standard.

And just at this minute her name was under discussion in a brilliant gathering at The Hindoo Lantern, in another quarter of New York.

If you know The Hindoo Lantern you know how much it depends on atmosphere. Once a disused warehouse in a section of the city which commerce had forsaken, the enthusiasm for the dance which arose about 1910, has made it a temple. It gains, too, by being a temple of the esoteric. The Hindoo Lantern is not everybody's lantern, and does not swing in the open vulgar street. You might live in New York a hundred years and unless you were one of the initiated and privileged, you might never know of its existence.

You could not so much as approach it were it not first explained to you what you ought to do. You must pass through a tobacconist's, which from the street looks like any other tobacconist's, after which you traverse a yard, which looks like any other yard, except that it is bounded by a wall in which there is a small and unobtrusive door. Beside the small and unobtrusive door there hangs a bell-rope, of the ancient

THE DUST FLOWER

kind suggesting the convent or the Orient. The bellrope pulls a bell; the bell clangs overhead; the door is opened cautiously by a Hindoo lad, or, as some say, a mulatto boy dressed as a Hindoo. If you are with a friend of the institution you will be admitted without more inspection; but should you be a stranger there will be a scrutiny of your passports. Assuming, however, that you go in, you will find a small courtyard, in which at last The Hindoo Lantern hangs mystic, suggestive, in oriental iron-work, and panels of colored glass.

Having passed beneath this symbol you will enter an antechamber rich in the magic of the East. In a reverent obscurity you will find Buddha on the right, Vishnu on the left, with flowers set before the one, while incense burns before the other. Somewhere in the darkness an Oriental woman will be seated on the ground, twanging on a sarabar, and now and then crooning a chant of invitation to come and share in darksome rites. You will thus be "worked up" to a sense of the mysterious before you pass the third gate of privilege into the shrine itself.

Here you will discover the large empty oval of floor, surrounded by little tables for segregation and refreshment, with which the past ten years have made us familiar. The place will be buzzing with the hum of voices, merry with duologues of laughter, and steaming with tobacco smoke. A jazz-band will strike up, coughing out the nauseated, retching intervals so stimulating to our feet, and two by two, in driblets, streamlets, and lastly in a volume, the guests will take the floor.

THE DUST FLOWER

In the way of "steps" all the latest will be on exhibition. You will see the cow-trot, the rabbit-jump, the broom-stick, the washerwoman's dip. Everyone who is anyone will be here, if not on one night then on another, in a jovial fraternity steeped in the spirit of democracy. Revelry will be sustained on lemonade and a resinous astringent known locally as beer, while a sense of doing the forbidden will be in the air. For commercial reasons it will be needful to keep it in the air, since in the proceedings themselves there will be nothing more occult, or more inciting to iniquity, than a kindergarten game.

Hither Mr. Gorry Larrabin had brought Mademoiselle Odette Coucoul, to teach her the new dances. As a matter of fact, he had just led her back to their little table, inconspicuously placed in the front row, after putting her through the paces of the camel-step. Mademoiselle had found it entrancing, so much more novel in the motion than the antiquated valses she had danced in France. Mr. Larrabin had retreated like a camel walking backwards, while she had advanced like a camel going forwards. The art was in lifting the foot quite high, throwing it slightly backwards, and setting it down with a delicate deliberation, while you craned the neck before you with a shake of the Adam's apple. To incite you to produce this effect the jazz-band urged you onward with a sob, a gulp, a moan, an effect of strangulation, till finally it tore up the seat of your being as if you had been suddenly struck sea-sick.

"Mon Dieu, but it is lofely," mademoiselle gurgled, laughing in her breathlessness. "It is terr-i-bul to call no one a camel—*un chameau*—in France; but here am I a—*chameau!*"

Gorry took this with puzzled amusement. "What's the matter with calling anyone a camel? I don't see any harm in that."

Mademoiselle hid her face in confusion. "Oh, but it is terr-i-bul, terr-i-bul! It is almost so worse as to call no one a—how you say zat word in Eenglish? —a cow, n'est ce pas?—*une vache*—and zat is the most bad name what you can call no one."

Looking across the room Gorry was struck with an idea. "Well, there's a—what d'ye call it—*a vashe*— over there. See that guy with the girl with the cream-colored hair—fella with a big black mustache, like a brigand in a play? There's a *vashe* all-righty; and yet I've got to keep in with him."

As he explained his reasons for keeping in with the "vashe" in question mademoiselle contented herself with shedding radiance and paying no attention. Neither did she pay attention when he went on to tell of the girl who had disappeared, and of her stepfather's reasons for finding her. She woke to cognizance of the subject only when Gorry repeated the exact words of Miss Tina Vanzetti that morning: "Name of Letty Gravely."

It was mademoiselle's turn for repetition. "But me, I know dat name. I 'ear it not so long ago. Name of Let-ty Grav-el-ly! I sure 'ear zat name all recently." She reflected, tapping her forehead with vivacity. "Mais quand? Mais oui? C'était—Ah!" The exclamation was the sharp cry of discovery. "Tina Vanzetti—my frien'! She tell me zis morning. Zat girl—Let-ty Grav-el-ly—she come chez Margot with ole man—what he keep ze white slave—and he command her grand beautiful trousseau—Tina Vanzetti she will give me ze address—and I will tell you—and you will tell him—and he will put you on to *riche affairs* ——"

"It'll be dollars and cents in the box office for me," Gorry interpreted, forcibly, while the band belched forth a chord like the groan of a dying monster, calling them again to their feet.

" 'Remember,' said the witch," Allerton continued to read, " 'when you have once assumed a human form you can never again be a mermaid—never return to your home or to your sisters more. Should you fail to win the prince's love, so that he leaves father and mother for your sake, and lays his hand in yours before the priest, an immortal soul will never be granted you. On the same day that he marries another your heart will break, and you will drift as seafoam on the water.' 'So let it be,' said the little mermaid, turning pale as death.' "

Allerton lifted his eyes from the book. "Does it bore you?"

There was no mistaking her sincerity. "*No! I love* it."

"Then perhaps we'll read a lot of things. After this we'll find a good novel, and then possibly somebody's life. You'd like that, wouldn't you?"

Her joy was such that he could hardly hear the "Yes," for which he was listening. He listened because he was so accustomed to boring people that to know he was not boring them was a consolation.

THE DUST FLOWER

"Is there anybody's life—his biography—that you'd be specially interested in?"

She answered timidly and yet daringly. "Could we—could we read the life of the late Queen Victoria —when she was a girl?"

"Oh, easily! I'll hunt round for one to-day. Now let me tell you about Hans Andersen. He was born in Denmark, so that he was a Dane. You know where Denmark is on the map, don't you?"

"I think I do. It's there by Germany isn't it?"

"Quite right. But let me get the atlas, and we'll look it up."

He was on his feet when she summoned her forces for a question. "Do you read like this to—to the girl you're engaged to?"

"No," he said, reddening. "She—she doesn't like it. She won't let me. But wait a minute. I'll go and get the atlas."

" 'On the same day that he marries another,' Letty repeated to herself, as she sat alone, 'your heart will break, and you will drift as sea-foam on the water.' 'So let it be,' said the little mermaid."

Chapter XVIII

ON the next afternoon Allerton reported to Miss Walbrook the success of his first educational evening.

"She's very intelligent, very. You'd really be pleased with her, Barbe. Her mind is so starved that it absorbs everything you say to her, as a dry soil will drink up rain."

Regarding him with the mysterious Egyptian expression which had at times suggested the reincarnation of some ancient spirit Barbara maintained the stillness which had come upon her on the previous day. "That must be very satisfactory to you, Rash."

He agreed the more enthusiastically because of believing her at one with him in this endeavor. "You bet! The whole thing is going to work out. She'll pick up our point of view as if she was born to it."

"And you're not afraid of her picking up anything else?"

"Anything else of what kind?"

"She might fall in love with you, mightn't she?"

"With me? Nonsense! No one would fall in love with me who ——"

Her mysterious Egyptian smile came and went. "You can stop there, Rash. It's no use being more uncomplimentary than you need to be. And then, too, you might fall in love with her."

"Barbe!" He cried out, as if wounded. "You're

THE DUST FLOWER

really too absurd. She's a good little thing, and she's had the devil's own luck ——"

"They always do have. That was one thing I learnt in Bleary Street. It was never a girl's own fault. It was always the devil's own luck."

"Well, isn't it, now, when you come to think of it? You can't take everything away from people, and expect them to have the same standards as you and me. Think of the mess that people of our sort make of things, even with every advantage."

"We've our own temptations, of course."

"And they've got theirs—without our pull in the way of carrying them off. You should hear Steptoe ——"

"I don't want to hear Steptoe. I've heard him too much already."

"What do you mean by that?"

"What can I mean by it but just what I say? I should think you'd get rid of him."

Having first looked puzzled, with a suggestion of pain, he ended with a laugh. "You might as well expect me to get rid of an old grandfather. Steptoe wouldn't let me, if I wanted to."

"He doesn't like me."

"Oh, that's just your imagination, Barbe. I'll answer for him when it comes to ——"

"You needn't take the trouble to do that, because I don't like him."

"Oh, but you will when you come to understand him."

"Possibly; but I don't mean to come to understand him. Old servants can be an awful nuisance, Rash ——"

THE DUST FLOWER

"But Steptoe isn't exactly an old servant. He's more like——"

"Oh, I know what he's like. He's a habit; and habits are always dangerous, even when they're good. But we're not going to quarrel about Steptoe yet. I just thought I'd put you on your guard——"

"Against him?"

"He's a horrid old schemer, if that's what you want me to say; but then it may be what you like."

"Well, I do," he laughed, "when it comes to him. He's been a horrid old schemer as long as I remember him, but always for my good."

"For your good as he sees it."

"For my good as a kind old nurse might see it. He's limited, of course; but then kind old nurses generally are."

To be true to her vow of keeping the peace she forced back her irritations, and smiled. "You're an awful goose, Rash; but then you're a lovable goose, aren't you?" She beckoned, imperiously. "Come here."

When he was on his knees beside her chair she pressed back his face framed by her two hands. "Now tell me. Which do you love most—Steptoe or me?"

He cast about him for two of her special preferences. "And you tell me; which do you love most, a saddle-horse or an opera?"

"If I told you, which should I be?—the opera or the saddle-horse?"

"If I told you, which would you give up?"

So they talked foolishly, as lovers do in the chaffing stage, she trying to charm him into promising to get

THE DUST FLOWER

rid of Steptoe, he charmed by her willingness to charm him. Neither remembered that technically he was a married man; but then neither had ever taken his marriage to Letty as a serious breach in their relations.

While he was thus on his knees the kindly old nurse was giving to Letty a kindly old nurse's advice.

"If madam 'ud go out and tyke a walk I think it'd do madam good."

To madam the suggestion had elements of mingled terror and attraction. "But, Steptoe, I couldn't go out and take a walk unless I dressed up in the new outdoor suit."

"And what did madam buy it for?—with the 'at and the vyle, and everythink, just like the lyte Mrs. Allerton."

It was the argument she was hoping for. In the first place she was used to the freedom of the streets; and in the second the outdoor suit was calling her. Letty's love of dress was more than a love of appearing at her best, though that love was part of it; it was a love of the clothes themselves, of fabrics, colors, and fashions. When her dreams were not of wandering knights who loved her at a glance—bankers, millionaires, casting directors in motion-picture studios, or, in high flights of imagination, incognito English lords—they dealt in costumes of magic tissue, of hues suited to her hair and eyes, in which the world saw and greeted her, not as the poor little waif whom Judson Flack had put out of doors, but the true Letty Gravely of romance. The Letty Gravely of romance was the real Letty Gravely, a being set free from the cruel, the ugly, the carking, the sordid, to flourish in a sunlight she knew to be shining somewhere.

Oddly enough her vision had come partly true; and yet so out of focus that she couldn't see its truth. It was like the sunlight which she knew to be shining somewhere, with a wrong refraction in its rays. The world into which she had been carried was like that in a cubist picture which someone had shown her at the studio. It bore a relation to the world she knew, but a relation in which whatever she had supposed to be perpendicular was oblique, and whatever she had supposed to be oblique was horizontal, and nothing as she had been accustomed to find it. It made her head swim. It was literally true that she was afraid to move lest she should make a misstep through an error in her sense of planes.

But clothes she understood. In the swirling of her universe they formed a rock to which her intelligence could cling. They kept her sane. In a sense they kept her happy. When all outside was confusion and topsy-turvyness she could retire among Margot's cartons, and find herself on solid ground. I should be sorry to record the hours she spent before the long mirror in the little back spare room. Here her imagination could give itself free range. She was Luciline Lynch, and Mercola Merch, and Lisabel Anstey, and any other star of whom she admired the attainments; she could play a whole series of parts from which her lack of a wardrobe had hitherto excluded her. From time to time she ventured, like Steptoe, to be Barbara

THE DUST FLOWER

Walbrook herself, though assuming the role with less intrepidity than he.

It was easier, she found, to be any of the stars than Barbara Walbrook, for the reason that the latter was "the real thing." She was living her part, not playing it. She was "letter perfect," in Steptoe's sense, not because a director moved her person this way, or turned her head that way, but because life had so infused her that she did what was right unconsciously. Letty, by pretending to enter at the door and come forward to the mirror as to a living presence, studied what was right by imitation. Miss Walbrook walked with a swift, easy gait which suggested the precision of certain strong birds when swooping on their prey. Between the door and the mirror Letty aimed at the same effect till she made a discovery.

"I can't do it her way; I can only do it my way."

The ways were different; yet each could be effective. That too was a discovery. Nature had no rule to which every individual was obliged to conform. The individual was, in a measure, his own rule, and got his attractiveness from being so. The minute you abandoned your own gifts to cultivate those with which Nature had blessed someone else you lost not only your identity but your charm.

Letty worked this out as something like a principle. However many the hints she took it would be folly to try to be anything but herself. After all, it was what gave her value to a star, her personality. If Luciline Lynch whom Nature had endowed with the grand manner had tried to be Mercola Merch who was all vivacious wickedness—well, anyone could see! So, if Barbara Walbrook suggested an eagle on the wing and she, Letty Gravely, was only a sparrow in the street, the sparrow would be more successful as a sparrow than in trying to emulate the eagle.

And yet there was a value to good models which at first she found difficult to reconcile with this truth of personal independence. This too she thought out. "It's like a way to do your hair," was her method of expressing it. "You do what's in fashion, but you twist it so that it suits your own style. It isn't the fashion that makes you look right; it's in being true to what suits you."

There was, however, in Barbara Walbrook a something deeper than this which at first eluded her. It was in Rashleigh Allerton too. It was in Lisabel Anstey, and in a few other stars, but not in Mercola Merch, nor in Luciline Lynch. "It's the whole business," Letty summed up to herself, "and yet I don't know what it is. Unless I can put my finger on it . . ."

She was just at this point when Steptoe addressed her on the subject of going out. That she do so was part of his programme. Madam would not be madam till she felt herself free to come and go; and till madam was madam Mr. Rash would not understand who it was they had in the 'ouse. That he didn't understand it yet was partly due to madam 'erself who didn't understand it on 'er side. To cultivate this understanding in madam was Steptoe's immediate aim, in which Beppo, the little cocker spaniel, unexpectedly came to his assistance.

As the two stood conversing at the foot of the stairs Beppo lilted down, with that air of having no

THE DUST FLOWER

one to love which he had worn during all the eighteen months since his mistress had died. The cocker spaniel's heart, as everyone knows, is imbued with the principle of one life, one love. It has no room for two loves; it has still less room for that general amiability to which most dogs are born. Among the human race it singles out one; and to that one it is faithful. In separation it seeks no substitute; in bereavement it rarely forms a second tie. To everyone but Beppo the removal of Mrs. Allerton had made the world brighter. He alone had mourned that presence with a grief which sought neither comfort nor mitigation. He had followed his routine; he had eaten and slept; he had gone out when he was taken out and come in when he was brought in; but he had lived shut up within himself, aloof in his sorrow. For the first time in all those eighteen months he had come out of this proud gloom when Rashleigh's key had turned in the door that night, and Letty had entered the house.

The secret call which Beppo had heard can never be understood by men till men have developed more of their latent faculties. As he lay in his basket something reached him which he recognized as a summons to a new phase of usefulness. Out of the lethargy of mourning he had jumped with an obedient leap that took him through the obscurity of the house to where a frightened girl had need of a little dog's sympathy. Of that sympathy he had been lavish; and now that there was new discussion in the air he came with his contribution.

In words Steptoe had to be his interpreter. "That

THE DUST FLOWER

poor little dog as 'as growed so fond of madam don't get 'alf the exercise he ought to be give. If madam was to tyke 'im out like for a little stroll up the Havenue. . . ."

Thus it happened that in less than half an hour Letty found herself out in the October sunlight, dressed in her blue-green costume, with all the details to "correspond," and leading Beppo on the leash. To lead Beppo on the leash, as Steptoe had perceived, gave a reason for an excursion which would otherwise have seemed motiveless. But she was out. She was out in conditions in which even Judson Flack, had he met her, could hardly have detected her. Gorgeously arrayed as she seemed to herself she was dressed with the simplicity which stamps the French taste. There was nothing to make her remarked, especially in a double procession of women so many of whom were remarkable. Had you looked at her twice you would have noted that while skill counted for much in her gentle, well-bred appearance, a subtle, unobtrusive, native distinction counted for most; but you would have been obliged to look at her twice before noting anything about her. She was a neatly dressed girl, with an air; but on that bright afternoon in Fifth Avenue neatly dressed girls with an air were as buttercups in June.

Seizing this fact Letty felt more at her ease. No one was thinking her conspicuous. She was passing in the crowd. She was not being "spotted" as the girl who a short time before had had nothing but the old gray rag to appear in. She could enjoy the walk—and forget herself.

THE DUST FLOWER

Then it came to her suddenly that this was the secret of which she was in search, the power to forget herself. She must learn to do things so easily that she would have no self-consciousness in doing them. In big things Barbara Walbrook might think of herself; but in all little things, in the way she spoke and walked and bore herself toward others, she acted as she breathed. It seemed wonderful to Letty, this assurance that you were right in all the fundamentals. It was precisely in the fundamentals that she was so likely to be wrong. It was where girls of her sort suffered most; in the lack of the elementary. One could bluff the advanced, or make a shot at it; but the elementary couldn't be bluffed, and no shot at it would tell. It betrayed you at once. You must *have* it. You must have it as you had the circulation of your blood, as something so basic that you didn't need to consider it. That was her next discovery, as with Beppo tugging at the end of his tether she walked onward.

She was used to walking; she walked strongly, and with a trudging sturdiness, not without its grace. She came to the part of Fifth Avenue where the great houses begin to thin out, and vacant lots, as if ashamed of their vacancy, shrink behind boardings vivid with the news of picture-plays. It was the year when they were advertising the screen-masterpiece, *Passion Aflame;* and here was depicted Luciline Lynch, a torch in her hand, her hair in maenadic dishevelment, leading on a mob to set fire to a town. Letty herself having been in that mob paused in search of her face among the horde of the great star's followers. It was a blob of scarlet and green from which she dropped her eyes, only to have them encounter a friend of long standing.

At the foot of the boarding, and all in a row, was a straggling band of dust-flowers. It was late in the season, yet not too late for their bit of blue heaven to press in among the ways of men. She was not surprised to find them there. Ever since the crazy woman had pointed out the mission of this humble little helper of the human race she had noted its persistency in haunting the spots which beauty had deserted. You found it in the fields, it was true; but you found it rarely, sparsely, raggedly, blooming, you might say, with but little heart for its bloom. Where other flowers had been frightened away; where the poor crowded; where factories flared; where junk-heaps rusted; where backyards baked; where smoke defiled; where wretchedness stalked; where crime brooded; where the land was unkempt; where the human spirit was sodden—there the celestial thing multiplied its celestial growths, blessing the eyes and making the heart leap. It mattered little that so few gave it a thought or regarded it as other than a weed; there were always those few, who knew that it spelled beauty, who knew that it spelled something more.

Letty was of those few. She was of those few for old sake's sake, but also for the sake of a new yearning. Slipping off a glove she picked a few of the dusty stalks, even though she knew that once taken from their task of glorifying the dishonored the blue stars would shut almost instantly. "They'll wither in a few days now," she said, in self-excuse; "and any-

THE DUST FLOWER

how I'll leave most of them." Having shaken off the dust she fastened them in her corsage, blue against her blue-green.

They were her symbol for happiness springing up in the face of despair, and from a soil where you would expect it to be choked. She herself was happy to-day as she could not remember ever to have been happy in her life. For the first time she was passing among decent people decently; and then—it was the great hope beyond which she didn't look—the prince might read with her again that evening.

But as she turned from Fifth Avenue into East Sixty-seventh Street the prince was approaching his door from the other direction. Even she was aware that it was contrary to his habits to appear at home by five in the afternoon. She didn't know, of course, that Barbara had so stimulated his enthusiasm for the educational course that he had come on the chance of taking it up at the tea hour. He could not remember that Barbara had ever before been so sympathetic to one of his ideas. The fact encouraged his feeble belief in himself, and made him love her with richer tenderness.

In the gentle girl of quietly distinguished mien he saw nothing but a stranger till Beppo strained at his leash and barked. Even then it took him half a minute to get his powers of recognition into play. He stopped at the foot of his steps, watching her approach.

By doing so he made the approach more difficult for her. The heart seemed to stop in her body. She could scarcely breathe. Each step was like walking on blades, yet like walking on blades with a kind of

THE DUST FLOWER

ecstasy. Luckily Beppo pranced and pulled in such a way that she was forced to give him some attention.

The prince's first words were also a distraction from terrors and enchantments which made her feel faint.

"Where did you get the poor man's coffee?"

The question by puzzling her gave her some relief. Pointing at the sprays in her corsage he went on:

"That's what the country people often call the chicory weed in France."

She was able to gasp feebly: "Oh, does it grow there?"

"I think it grows pretty nearly everywhere. It's one of the most classic wild flowers we know anything about. The ancient Egyptians dried its leaves to give flavor to their salad, and I remember being told at Luxor that the modern Copts and Arabs do the same. You see it's quite a friendly little beast to man."

It eased her other feelings to tell him about the crazy woman in Canada, and her reading of the dust-flower's significance.

"That's a good idea too," Allerton agreed, smiling down into her eyes. "There are people like that—little dust-flowers cheering up the wayside for the rest of us poor brutes."

She said, wistfully: "I suppose you've known a lot of them."

As he laughed his eyes rested on a man sauntering toward them from the direction of Fifth Avenue. "I've known about two—" his eyes came back to smile again down into hers—"or *one*." He started as a man starts who receives a new suggestion. "I say! Let's go in and look up chicory and succory in the encyclopedia. Then we'll know all about it. It seems to me, too," he went on, reminiscently, "that I read a little poem about this very blue flower—by Margaret Deland, I think it was—only a few weeks ago. I believe I could put my hand on it. Come along."

As he sprang up the steps the pearly gates were opening again before Letty when the man whom Allerton had seen sauntering toward them actually passed by. Passing he lifted his hat politely, smiled, and said, "Good afternoon, Miss Gravely," like any other gentleman. He was a good-looking slippery young man, with a cast in his left eye.

Because she was a woman before she was a lady, as she understood the word lady, Letty responded with, "Good afternoon," and a little inclination of the head. He was several doors off before she bethought herself sufficiently to take alarm.

"Who's that?" Allerton demanded, looking down from the third or fourth step.

"I'm sure I haven't an idea. I think he must be some camera-man who's seen me when they've been shooting the pitch—" she made the correction almost in time—"who's seen me when they've been shooting the *pick-tures*. I can't think of anything else."

They watched the retreating form till, without a backward glance, it turned into Madison Avenue.

"Come along in," Allerton called then, in a tone intended to disperse misgiving, "and let's begin."

Ten minutes later he was reading in the library, from a big volume open on his knees, how for over a

THE DUST FLOWER

century the chicory root had been dried and ground in France, and used to strengthen the cheaper grades of coffee, when Letty broke in, as if she had not been following him:

"I don't think that fella could have been a camera-man after all. No camera-man would ha' noticed me in the great big bunch I was always in."

"Oh, well, he can't do you any harm anyhow," Allerton assured her. "I'll just finish this, and then I'll look for the poem by Mrs. Deland."

With her veil and gloves in her lap Letty sat thoughtful while he passed from shelf to shelf in search of the smaller volume. Of her real suspicion, that the man was a friend of Judson Flack's, she decided not to speak.

Seated once more in front of her, and bending slightly toward her, Allerton read:

> "Oh, not in ladies' gardens,
>   My peasant posy!
>   Smile thy dear blue eyes,
>   Nor only—nearer to the skies—
>   In upland pastures, dim and sweet—
>   But by the dusty road
>   Where tired feet
>   Toil to and fro;
>   Where flaunting Sin
>   May see thy heavenly hue,
>   Or weary Sorrow look from thee
>   Toward a more tender blue."

Allerton glanced up from the book. "Pretty, isn't it?"

She admitted that it was, and then added: "And yet there was the times when the castin' director put me right in the front, to register what the crowd behind me was thinkin' about. He might ha' noticed me then."

"Yes, of course; that must have been it. Now wouldn't you like me to read that again? You must always read a poem a second or third time to really know what it's about."

Meanwhile a poem of another sort was being read to Miss Barbara Walbrook by her aunt, who had entered the drawing-room within five minutes after Allerton had left it. During those five minutes Barbara had remained seated, plunged into reverie. The problem with which she had to deal was the degree to which she was right or wrong in permitting Rashleigh to go on in his crazy course. That this outcast girl was twining herself round his heart was a fact growing too obtrusive to be ignored. Had Rashleigh been as other men decisive action would have been imperative. But he was not as other men, and there lay the possibilities she found difficult.

If the aunt couldn't help the niece to solve the difficult question she at least could compel her to take a stand.

As she entered the drawing-room she came from out of doors, a slender, unfleshly figure, all intellect and idea. Her vices being wholly of the spirit were not recognized as vices, so that she passed as the highest type of the good woman which the continent of America knows anything about. Being the highest type of the good woman she had, moreover, the privilege which American usage accords to all good women of being good aggressively. No other good woman in the world enjoys this right to the same degree, a fact to which we can point with pride. The good English woman, the good French woman, the good Italian woman, are obliged by the customs of their countries to direct their goodness into channels in which it is relatively curbed. The good American woman, on the other hand, is never so much at home as when she is on the warpath. Her goodness being the only standard of goodness which the country accepts she has the right to impose it by any means she can harness to her purposes. She is the inspiration of our churches, and the terror of our constituencies. She is behind state legislatures and federal congresses and presidential cabinets. They may elude her lofty purposes, falsify her trust, and for a time hoodwink her with male chicaneries; but they are always afraid of her, and in the end they do as she commands. Among the coarsely, stupidly, viciously masculine countries of the world the American Republic is the single and conspicuous matriarchate, ruled by its good women. Of these rulers Miss Marion Walbrook was as representative a type as could be found, high, pure, zealous, intolerant of men's weaknesses, and with only spiritual immoralities of her own.

Seated in one of her slender upright armchairs she had the impressiveness of goodness fully conscious of itself. A document she held in her hand gave her the judicial air of one entitled to pass sentence.

THE DUST FLOWER

"I'm sorry, Barbara; but I've some disagreeable news for you."

Barbara woke. "Indeed?"

"I've just come from Augusta Chancellor's. She talked about—that man."

"What did she say?"

"She said two or three things. One was that she'd met him one day in the Park when he decidedly wasn't himself."

"Oh, it's hard to say when he's himself and when he isn't. He's what the French would call *un original.*"

"Oh, I don't know about that. The originality of men is commonplace as it's most novel. This man is on a par with the rest, if you call it original for him to have a woman in the house."

Barbara feigned languidness. "Well, it is—the way he has her there."

"The way he has her there? What do you mean by that?"

"I mean what I say. There's no one else in the world who would take a girl under his roof in the way Rash has taken this girl."

"How, may I ask, did he take her?"

Having foreseen that one day she should be in this position Barbara had made up her mind as to how much she should say. "He found her."

"Oh, they all do that. They generally find them in the Park."

"Exactly; it's just what he did."

"I guessed—it was only guessing mind you—that he also tried to find Augusta Chancellor."

"Oh, possibly. He'd go as far as that, if he saw her doing anything he thought not respectable."

"Barbara, please! You're talking about a friend of mine, one of my colleagues. Let's return to—I hope you won't find the French phrase invidious—to our mutton."

"Oh, very well! Rash found the girl homeless—penniless—with no friends. Her stepfather had turned her out. Another man would have left her there, or turned her over to the police. Rash took her to his own house, and since then we've both been helping her to—to get on her feet."

"Helping her to get on her feet in a way that's driven from the house the good old women who've been there for nearly thirty years."

"Oh, you know that too, do you?"

"Why, certainly. Jane, that was the parlor maid, is very intimate with Augusta Chancellor's cook; and she says—Jane does—that he's actually married the creature."

Barbara shrugged her shoulders. "I can't help what the servants say, Aunt Marion. I'm trying to be a friend to the girl, and help her to pull herself together. Of course I recognize the fact that Rash has been foolish—quixotic—or whatever you like to call it; but he hasn't kept anything from me."

"And you're still engaged to him?"

"Of course I'm still engaged to him." She held out her left hand. "Look at his ring."

"Then why don't you get married?"

"Are you in such a hurry to get rid of me?"

The question being a pleasantry Miss Walbrook

took it with a gentle smile. When she resumed it was with a slight flourish of the document in her hand, and another turn to the conversation.

"I went to the bank this morning. I've brought home my will. I'm thinking of making some changes in it."

Barbara looked non-committal, as if the subject had nothing to do with herself.

"The question I have to decide," Miss Walbrook pursued, "is whether to leave everything to you, in the hope that you'll carry on my work——"

"I shouldn't know how."

"Or whether to establish a trust——"

"I should do that decidedly."

"And let it fall into the hands of a pack of men."

"It will fall into the hands of a pack of men, whatever you do with it."

"And yet if you had it in charge——"

"Some man would get hold of it, Aunt Marion."

"Which is what I'm debating. I'm not so very sure——"

"That I shall marry in the end?"

"Well, you're not married yet . . . and if you were to change your mind . . . the world has such a need of consecrated women with men so unscrupulous and irresponsible . . . we must break their power some day . . . and now that we've got the opportunity . . . all I want you to understand is that if you shouldn't marry there'd be a great career in store for you. . . ."

Chapter XIX

BY the end of twenty-four hours the possibility of this great career quickened Barbara's zeal for taking a hand in Letty's education. Not only did that impulse of furious jealousy, by which she meant at first to leave it wholly to Rash, begin to seem dangerous, but there was a world to consider and throw off the scent. Now that Augusta Chancellor knew that the girl was beneath Rash's roof all their acquaintances would sooner or later be in possession of the fact. It was Barbara's part, therefore, to play the game in such a way that a bit of quixotism would be the most foolish thing of which Rash would be suspected.

That she would be playing a game she knew in advance. She must hide her suspicions; she must control her sufferings. She must pretend to have confidence in Rash, when at heart she cried against him as an infant and a fool. Never was woman in such a ridiculous situation as that into which she had been thrust; never was heart so wild to ease itself by invective and denunciation; and never was the padlock fixed so firmly on the lips. Hour by hour the man she loved was being weaned and won away from her; and she must stand by with grimacing smiles, instead of throwing up her arms in dramatic gestures and calling on her gods to smite and smash and annihilate.

Since, however, she had a game to play, a game she would play, though she did it quivering with protest and repulsion.

THE PRINCE'S FIRST WORDS WERE ALSO A DISTRACTION FROM TERRORS AND ENCHANTMENTS WHICH MADE HER FEEL FAINT

"Do you mind if I take the car this afternoon, Aunt Marion, since you're not going to use it."

"Take it of course; but where are you going?"

"I thought I would ask that protégée of Rash Allerton's, of whom we were speaking yesterday, to come for a drive with me. But if you'd rather I didn't ——"

"I've nothing to do with it. It's entirely for you to say. The car is yours, of course."

The invitation being transmitted by telephone Steptoe urged Letty to accept it. "It'll be all in the wye of madam's gettin' used to things—a bit at a time like."

"But I don't think she likes me."

"If madam won't stop to think whether people likes 'er or not I think madam 'd get for'arder. Besides madam'll pretty generally always find as love-call wykes love-echo, as the syin' goes."

Which, as a matter of fact, was what Letty did find. She found it from the minute of entering the car and taking her seat, when Miss Walbrook exclaimed heartily: "What a lovely dress! And the hat's too sweet! Suits you exactly, doesn't it? My dear, I've the greatest bother ever to find a hat that doesn't make me look like a scarecrow."

From the naturalness of the tone there was no suspecting the cost of these words to the speaker, and the subject was one in which Letty was at home. In turn she could compliment Miss Walbrook's appearance, duly admiring the toque of prune-colored velvet, with a little bunch of roses artfully disposed, and the coat of prune-colored Harris tweed. In further discussing the length of the new skirts and the chances of the tight corset coming back they found topics of common interest. The fact that they were the topics which came readiest to the lips of both made it possible to maintain the conversation at its normal give-and-take, while each could pursue the line of her own summing up of the other.

To Letty Miss Walbrook seemed friendlier than she had expected, only spasmodically so. Her kindly moods came in spurts of which the inspiration soon gave out. "I think she's sad," was Letty's comment to herself. Sadness, in Letty's use of words, covered all the emotions not distinctly cheerful or hilarious.

She knew nothing about Miss Walbrook, except that it appeared from this conversation that she lived with an aunt, whose car they were using. That she was a friend of the prince's had been several times repeated, but all information ended there. To Letty she seemed old—between thirty and forty. Had she known her actual age she would still have seemed old from her knowledge of the world and general sophistication. Letty's own lack of sophistication kept her a child when she was nearly twenty-three. That Miss Walbrook was the girl to whom the prince was engaged had not yet crossed her thought.

At the same time, since she knew that girl she brought her to the forefront of Letty's consciousness. She was never far from the forefront of her consciousness, and of late speculation concerning her had become more active. If she approached the subject with the prince he reddened and grew ill at ease. The present seemed, therefore, an opportunity to be utilized.

THE DUST FLOWER

They were deep in the northerly avenues of the Park, when apropos of the dress topic, Letty said, suddenly: "I suppose she's awfully stylish—the girl he's engaged to."

The response was laconic: "She's said to be."

"Is she pretty?"

"I don't think you could say that."

"Then what does he see in her?"

"Whatever people do see in those they're in love with. I'm afraid I'm not able to define it."

Dropping back into her corner Letty sighed. She knew this mystery existed, the mystery of falling in love for reasons no one was able to explain. It was the ground on which she hoped that at first sight someone would fall in love with her. If he didn't do it for reasons beyond explanation he would, of course, not do it at all.

It was some minutes before another question trembled to her lips. "Does she—does she know about me?"

"Oh, naturally."

"And did she—did she feel very bad?"

Barbara's long eyes slid round in Letty's direction, though the head was not turned. "How should you feel yourself, if it had happened to you?"

"It'd kill me."

"Well, then?" She let Letty draw her own conclusions before adding: "It's nearly killed her."

Letty cowered. She had never thought of this. That she herself suffered she knew; that the prince suffered she also knew; but that this unknown girl, whatever her folly, lay smitten to the heart brought a new complication into her ideas. "Even if he ever did come to—" she held up her unspoken sentence there—"I'd ha' stolen him from her."

There was little more conversation after that. Each had her motives for reflections and silences. They were nearing the end of the drive when Letty said again:

"What would you do if you was—if you were—me?"

"I'd do whatever I felt to be highest."

To Letty this was a beautiful reply, and proof of a beautiful nature. Moreover, it was indirectly a compliment to herself, in that she could be credited with doing what she felt to be highest as well as anyone else. In her life hitherto she had been figuratively kicked and beaten into doing what she couldn't resist. Now she was considered capable of acting worthily of her own accord. It inspired a new sentiment toward Miss Walbrook.

She thought, too, that Miss Walbrook liked her a little better. Perhaps it was the fulfillment of Steptoe's adage, love-call wakes love-echo. She was sure that somehow this call had gone out from her to Miss Walbrook, and that it hadn't gone out in vain.

It hadn't gone out in vain, in that Miss Walbrook was able to say to herself, with some conviction, "That's the way it will have to be done." It was a way of which her experiences in Bleary Street had made her skeptical. Among those whom she called the lower orders innocence, ingenuousness, and integrity were qualities for which she had ceased to look. She didn't look for them anywhere with much confidence; but she had long ago come to the conclusion that the poor were schemers, and were obliged to be schemers because they were poor. Something in Letty impressed her otherwise. "That's the way," she continued to nod to herself. "It's no use trusting to Rash. I'll get her; and she'll get him; and so we shall work it."

Arrived in East Sixty-seventh Street she went in with Letty and had tea. But it was she who sat in dear Mrs. Allerton's corner of the sofa, and when William brought in the tray she said, "Put it here, William," as one who speaks with authority. Of this usurpation of the right to dispense hospitality Letty did not see the significance, being glad to have it taken off her hands.

Not so, however, with Steptoe who came in with a covered dish of muffins. Having placed it before Miss Walbrook he turned to Letty.

"Madam ain't feelin' well?"

Letty's tone expressed her surprise. "Why, yes."

"Madam'll excuse me. As madam ain't presidin' at 'er own tyble I was afryde ——"

It being unnecessary to say more he tiptoed out, leaving behind him a declaration of war, which Miss Walbrook, without saying anything in words, was not slow to pick up. "Insufferable," was her comment to herself. Of the hostile forces against her this, she knew, was the most powerful.

Neither did Rash perceive the significance of Barbara's place at the tea-table when he entered about five o'clock, though she was quick to perceive the significance of his arrival. It was not, however, a point to note outwardly, so that she lifted her hand above the tea-kettle, letting him bend over it, as she exclaimed:

"Welcome to our city! Do sit down and make yourself at home. Letty and I have been for a drive, and are all ready to enjoy a little male society."

The easy tone helped Allerton over his embarrassment, first in finding the two women face to face, then in coming so unexpectedly face to face with them, and lastly in being caught by Barbara coming home at this unexpected hour. Knowing what the situation must mean to her he admired her the more for her sangfroid and social flexibility.

She took all the difficulties on herself. "Letty and I have been making friends, and are going to know each other awfully well, aren't we?" A smile at Letty drew forth Letty's smile, to Rashleigh's satisfaction, and somewhat to his bewilderment. But Barbara, handing him a cup of tea, addressed him directly. "Who do you think is engaged? Guess."

He guessed, and guessed wrong. He guessed a second time, and guessed wrong. There followed a conversation about people they knew, with regard to which Letty was altogether an outsider. Now and then she recognized great names which she had read in the papers, tossed back and forth without prefixes of Mr. or Miss, and often with pet diminutives. The whole represented a closed corporation of intimacies into which she could no more force her way than a worm into a billiard ball. Rash who was at first beguiled by the interchange of personalities began to experience a sense of discomfort that Letty should

THE DUST FLOWER

be so discourteously left out; but Barbara knew that it was best for both to force the lesson home. Rash must be given to understand how lost he would be with any outsider as his companion; and Letty must be made to realize how hopelessly an outsider she would always be.

But no lesson should be urged to the quick at a single sitting, so that Barbara broke off suddenly to ask why he had come home. In the same way as she had given the order to William she spoke with the authority of one at liberty to ask the question. Not to give the real reason he said that it was to write a letter and change his clothes.

"And you're going back to the Club?"

He replied that he was going to dine with a bachelor friend at his apartment.

"Then I'll wait and drop you at the Club. You can go on from there afterwards. I've got the time."

This too was said with an authority against which he felt himself unable to appeal.

Having written a note and changed to his dinner jacket he rejoined them in the drawing-room. Barbara held out her hand to Letty, with a briskness indicating relief.

"So glad we had our drive. I shall come soon again. I wish it could be to-morrow, but my aunt will be using the car."

"There's my car," Allerton suggested.

"Oh, so there is." Barbara took this proposal as a matter of course. "Then we'll say to-morrow. I'll call up Eugene and tell him when to come for me."

With Allerton beside her, and driving down Fifth

THE DUST FLOWER

Avenue, she said: "I see how to do it, Rash. You must leave it to me."

He replied in the tone of a child threatened with the loss of his rôle in a game. "I can't leave it to you altogether."

"Then leave it to me as much as you can. I see what to do and you don't. Furthermore, I know just how to do it."

"You're wonderful, Barbe," he said, humbly.

"I'm wonderful so long as you don't interfere with me."

"Oh, well, I shan't do that."

She turned to him sharply. "Is that a promise?"

"Why do you want a promise?" he asked, in some wonder.

"Because I do."

"That is, you can't trust me."

"My dear Rash, who *could* trust you after what ———?"

"Oh, well, then, I promise."

"Then that's understood. And if anything happens, you won't go hedging and saying you didn't mean it in that way?"

"It seems to me you're very suspicious."

"One's obliged to foresee everything with you, Rash. It isn't as if one was dealing with an ordinary man."

"You mean that I'm to give you carte blanche, and have no will of my own at all."

"I mean that when I'm so reasonable, you must try to be reasonable on your side."

"Well, I will."

THE DUST FLOWER

As they drew up in front of the New Netherlands Club, he escaped without committing himself further.

If he dined with a bachelor friend that night he must have cut the evening short, for at half past nine he re-entered the back drawing-room where Letty was sitting before the fire, her red book in her lap. She sat as a lover stands at a tryst as to which there is no positive engagement. To fortify herself against disappointment she had been trying to persuade herself that he wouldn't come, and that she didn't expect him.

He came, but he came as a man who has something on his mind. Almost without greeting he sat down, took the book from her lap and proceeded to look up the place at which he had left off.

"Miss Walbrook's lovely, isn't she?" she said, before he had found the page.

"She's a very fine woman," he assented. "Do you remember where we stopped?"

"It was at, 'So let it be, said the little mermaid, turning pale as death.' You know her very well, don't you?"

"Oh, very well indeed. I think we begin here: 'But you will have to pay me also ——' "

"Have you known her very long?"

"All my life, more or less."

"She says she knows the girl you're engaged to."

"Yes, of course. We all know each other in our little set. Now, if you're ready, I'll begin to read."

" 'But you will have to pay me also,' said the witch; 'and it is not a little that I ask. Yours is the loveliest voice in the world, and you trust to that, I dare say, to charm your love. But you must give it to me. For my costly drink I claim the best thing you possess. I shall give you my own blood, so that my draught may be as sharp as a two-edged sword.' 'But if you take my voice from me, what have I left?' asked the little mermaid, piteously. 'Your loveliness, your graceful movements, your speaking eyes. Those are enough to win a man's heart. Well, is your courage gone? Stretch out your little tongue, that I may cut it off, and you shall have my magic potion.' 'I consent,' said the little mermaid."

Letty cried out: "So that when she'd be with him she'd understand everything, and not be able to tell him anything."

"I'm afraid," he smiled, "that that's what's ahead of her, poor thing."

"Oh, but that—" she could hardly utter her distress—"Oh, but that's worse than anything in the world."

He looked up at her curiously. "Would you rather I didn't go on?"

"No, no; please. I—I want to hear it all."

At The Hindoo Lantern Mr. Gorry Larrabin and Mr. Judson Flack found themselves elbow to elbow outside the rooms where their respective ladies were putting the final touches to their hats and hair before entering the grand circle. It was an opportunity especially on Gorry's part, to seal the peace which had been signed so recently.

"Hello, Judson. What's the prospects in oil?"

Judson's tone was pessimistic. "Not a thing doin',

THE DUST FLOWER

Gorry. Awful slow bunch, that lump of nuts I'm in with on this. Mentioned your name to one or two of 'em; but no enterprise. Boneheads that wouldn't know a white man from a crane." That he understood what Gorry understood became clear as he continued: "Friend o' mine at the Excelsior passes me the tip that they've held up that play they were goin' to put my girl into. Can't get anyone else that would swing the part. Waitin' for her to turn up again. I suppose you haven't heard anything, Gorry?"

Gorry looked him in the eyes as straight as was possible for a man with a cast in the left one. "Not a thing, Judson; not a thing."

The accent was so truthful that Judson gave his friend a long comprehending look. He was sure that Gorry would never speak with such sincerity if he was sincere.

"Well, I'm on the job, Gorry," he assured him, "and one of these days you'll hear from me."

"I'm on the job too, Judson; and one of these days ——"

But as Mademoiselle Coucoul emerged from the dressing-room and shed radiance, Gorry was obliged to go forward.

Chapter XX

IT was May.

In spite of her conviction that she knew what to do and how it to do it, Barbara perceived that at the end of seven months they were much where they had been in the previous October. If there was a change it was that all three, Rashleigh, Letty, and herself, had grown strained and intense.

Outwardly they strove to maintain a semblance of friendship. For that Barbara had worked hard, and in a measure had succeeded. She had held Rash; she had won Letty.

She had more than won Letty; she had trained her. All that in seven months a woman of the world could do for an unformed and ignorant child she had done. Her experience at Bleary Street had helped her in this; and Letty had been quick. She had seized not only those small points of speech and action foundational to rising in the world, but the point of view of those who had risen. She knew how, Barbara was sure, that there were certain things impossible to people such as those among whom she had been thrown.

Since it was May it was the end of a season, and the minute Barbara had long ago chosen for a masterstroke. Each of the others felt the crisis as near as she did herself.

"It's got to end," Letty confessed to her, as amid

THE DUST FLOWER

the soft loveliness of springtime, they were again driving in the Park.

Barbara chose her words. "I suppose he feels that too."

"Then why don't he let me end it?"

"I fancy that that's a difficult position for a man. If you ask his permission beforehand he feels obliged to say ——"

"And perhaps," Letty suggested, "he's too tender-hearted."

"That's part of it. He *is* tender-hearted. Besides that, his position is grotesque—a man with whom two women are in love. To one of them he's been nominally married, while to the other he's bound by every tie of honor. No wonder he doesn't see his way. If he moves toward the one he hurts the other—a man to whom it's agony to hurt a fly."

"Does the other girl still feel the way she did?"

"She's killing herself. She's breaking her heart. Nobody knows it but him and her—and even he doesn't take it in. But she is."

"I suppose she thinks I'm something awful."

"Does it matter to you what she thinks?"

"I don't want her to hate me."

"Oh, I shouldn't say she did that. She feels that, considering everything, you might have acted with more decision."

"But he won't let me."

"And he never will, if you wait for that."

"Then what do you think I ought to do?"

"That's where I find you weak, Letty, since you ask me the question. No one can tell you what to do—and he least of all. It's a situation in which one of you must withdraw—either you or the other girl. But, don't you see? he can't say so to either."

"And if one of us must withdraw you think it should be me."

"I have to leave that to you. You're the one who butted in. I know it wasn't your fault—that the fault was his entirely; but we recognize the fact that he's—how shall I put it?—not quite responsible. We women have to take the burden of the thing on ourselves, if it's ever to be put right."

In her corner of the car Letty thought this over. The impression on her mind was the deeper since, for several months past, she had watched the prince growing more and more unhappy. He was less nervous than he used to be, less excitable; and for that he had told her the credit was due to herself. "You soothe me," he had once said to her, in words she would always treasure; and yet as his irritability decreased his unhappiness seemed to grow. She could only infer that he was mourning over the girl to whom he was engaged, and on whom he had inflicted a great wrong. For the last few weeks Letty's mind had occupied itself with her almost more than with the prince himself.

"Do you think I shall ever see her?" she asked, suddenly now.

Barbara reflected. "I think you could if you wanted to."

"Should you arrange it?"

"I could."

"You're sure she'd be willing to see me?"

THE DUST FLOWER

"Yes; I know she would."

"When could you do it?"

"Whenever you like."

"Soon?"

"Yes; sooner perhaps than—" Barbara spoke absently, as if a new idea was taking possession of her mind—"sooner perhaps than you think."

"And you say she's breaking her heart?"

"A little more, and it will be broken."

By the time Letty had been set down at the door in East Sixty-seventh Street the afternoon had grown chilly. In the back drawing-room Steptoe was on his knees lighting the fire. Letty came and stood behind him. Without preliminary of any kind she said, quietly:

"Steptoe, it's got to end."

Expecting a protest she was surprised that he should merely blow on the shivering flame, saying, in the interval between two long breaths: "I agrees with madam."

"And it's me that must end it."

He blew gently again. "I guess that'd be so too."

She thought of the little mermaid leaping into the sea, and trembling away into foam. "If he wants to marry the girl he's in love with he'll never do it the way we're living now."

He rose from his knees, dusting one hand against the other. "Madam's quite right. 'E won't—not never."

She threw out her arms, and moaned. "And, O Steptoe! I'm so tired of it."

"Madam's tired of ——?"

THE DUST FLOWER

"Of living here, and doing nothing, and just watching and waiting, and nothing never happening——"

"Does madam remember that, the dye when she first come I said there was two reasons why I wanted to myke 'er into a lydy?"

Letty nodded.

"The one I told 'er was that I wanted to 'elp someone who was like what I used to be myself."

"I remember."

"And the other, what I didn't tell madam, I'll tell 'er now. It was—it was I was 'opin' that a woman'd come into my poor boy's life as'd comfort 'im like——"

"And she didn't come."

"'E ain't seen that she's come. I said it'd be a tough job to bring 'im to fallin' in love with 'er like; but it's been tougher than what I thought it'd be."

"So that I must—must do something."

"Looks as if madam'd 'ave to."

"I suppose you know that there's an easy way for me to do it?"

"Nothink ain't so very easy; but if madam 'as a big enough reason——"

She felt the necessity of being plain. "I suppose that if he hadn't picked me up in the Park that day I'd have gone to the bad anyhow."

"If madam's thinkin' about goin' to the bad——"

She threw up her head defiantly. "Well, I am. What of it?"

"I was just thinkin' as I might 'elp 'er a bit about that."

She was puzzled. "I don't think you know what I said. I said I was——"

THE DUST FLOWER

"Goin' to the bad, madam. That's what I understood. But madam won't find it so easy, not 'avin 'ad no experience like, as you might sye."

"I didn't know you needed experience—for that."

"All good people thinks that wye, madam; but when you tackle it deliberate like, there's quite a trick to it."

"And do you know the trick?" was all she could think of saying.

"I may not know the very hidentical trick madam'd be in want of—'er bein' a lydy, as you might sye—but I could put 'er in the wye of findin' out."

"You don't think I could find out for myself?"

"You see, it's like this. I used to know a young man what everythink went ag'in' 'im. And one dye 'e started out for to be a forgerer like—so as 'e'd be put in jyle—and be took care of—board and lodgin' free—and all that. Well, out 'e starts, and not knowin' the little ins and outs, as you might sye, everythink went agin 'im, just as it done before. And, would madam believe it? that young man 'e hended by studying for the ministry. Madam wouldn't want to myke a mistyke like that, now would she?"

Letty turned this over in her mind. A career parallel to that of this young man would effect none of the results she was aiming at.

"Then what would you suggest?" she asked, at last.

"I could give madam the address of a lydy—an awful wicked lydy, she is—what'd put madam up to all the ropes. If madam was to go out into the cold world, like, this lydy'd give 'er a home. Besides the address I'd give madam a sign like—so as the lydy'd know it was somethink special."

"A sign? I don't know what you mean."

"It'd be this, madam." He drew from his pocket a small silver thimble. "This'd be a password to the lydy. The minute she'd see it she'd know that the time 'ad come."

"What time?"

"That's somethink madam'd find out. I couldn't explyne it before'and."

"It sounds very queer."

"It'd *be* very queer. Goin' to the bad is always queer. Madam wouldn't look for it to be like 'avin' a gentleman lead 'er in to dinner."

"What's she like—the lady?"

"That's somethink madam'd 'ave to wyte and see. She wouldn't *seem* so wicked, not at first sight, as you might sye. But time'd tell. If madam'd be pytient—well, I wouldn't like to sye." He eyed the fire. "I think that fire'll burn now, madam; and if it don't, madam'll only 'ave to ring."

He was at the door when Letty, feeling the end of all things to be at hand, ran after him, laying her fingers on his sleeve.

"Oh, Steptoe; you've been so good to me!"

He relaxed from his dignity sufficiently to let his hand rest on hers, which he patted gently. "I've been madam's servant—and my boy's."

"I shall never think of you as a servant—never."

The frosty color rose into his cheeks. "Then madam'll do me a great wrong."

"To me you're so much higher than a servant———"

THE DUST FLOWER

"Madam'll find that there ain't nothink 'igher than a servant. There's a lot about service in the pypers nowadyes, crackin' it up, like; but nobody don't seem to remember that servants knows more about that than what other people do, and servants don't remember it theirselves. So long as I can serve madam, just as I've served my boy ——"

"Oh, but, Steptoe, I shall have gone to the bad."

"That'd be all the syme to me, madam. At my time o' life I don't see no difference between them as 'as gone to the bad and them as 'as gone to the good, as you might sye. I only sees—people."

Left alone Letty went back to the fire, and stood gazing down at it, her foot on the fender. So it was the end. Even Steptoe said so. In a sense she was relieved.

She was relieved at the prospect of being freed from her daily torture. The little mermaid walking on blades in the palace of the prince, and forever dumb, had known bliss, but bliss so akin to anguish that her heart was consumed by it. The very fact that the prince himself suffered from the indefinable misery which her presence seemed to bring made escape the more enticing.

She was so buried in this reflection as to have heard no sound in the house, when Steptoe announced in his stately voice: "Miss Barbara Walbrook." Having parted from this lady half an hour earlier Letty turned in some surprise.

"I've come back again," was the explanation, sent down the long room. "Don't let William bring in tea," the imperious voice commanded Steptoe. "We wish to be alone." There was the same abruptness as

THE DUST FLOWER

she halted within two or three feet of where Letty stood, supporting herself with a hand on the edge of the mantelpiece. "I've come back to tell you something. I made up my mind to it all at once—after I left you a few minutes ago. Now that I've done it I feel easier."

Letty didn't know which was uppermost in her mind, curiosity or fear. "What—what is it?" she asked, trembling.

"I've given up the fight. I'm out of it."

Letty crept forward. "You've—you've done *what?*"

"I told you in the Park that one or the other of us would have to withdraw ——"

"One or the other of—of *us?*"

"Exactly and I've done it."

With horror in her face and eyes Letty crept nearer still. "But—but I don't understand."

"Oh, yes, you do. How can you help understanding. You must have seen all along that ——"

"Not that—that you were—the other girl. Oh, not that!"

"Yes, that; of course; why not?"

"Because—because I—I couldn't bear it."

"You can bear it if I can, can't you—if I've had to bear it all these weeks and months."

"Yes, but that's—" she covered her face with her hands—"that's what makes it so terrible."

"Of course it makes it terrible; but it isn't as terrible now as it was—to you anyhow."

"But why do you withdraw when—when you love him—and he loves you ——?"

THE DUST FLOWER

"I do it because I want to throw all the cards on the table. It's what my common sense has been telling me to do all along, only I've never worked round to it till we had our talk this afternoon. Now I see——"

"What do you see, Miss Walbrook?"

"I see that we've got to give him a clean sheet, or he'll never know where he is. He can't decide between us because he's in an impossible position. We'll have to set him absolutely free, so that he may begin again. I'll do it on my side. You can do—what you like."

She went as abruptly as she came, leaving Letty clearer than ever as to her new course.

By midnight she was ready. In the back spare room she waited only to be sure that all in the house were asleep.

She had heard Allerton come in about half past nine, and the whispering of voices told that Steptoe was making his explanations, that she was out of sorts, had dined in her room, and begged not to be disturbed. At about half past ten she heard the prince go upstairs to his own room, though she fancied that outside her door he had paused for a second to listen. That was the culminating minute of her self-repression. Once it was over, and he had gone on his way, she knew the rest would be easier.

By midnight she had only to wait quietly. In the old gray rag and the battered black hat she surveyed herself without emotion. Since making her last attempt to escape her relation to all these things had changed. They had become less significant, less im-

THE DUST FLOWER

portant. The emblems of the higher life which in the previous autumn she had buried with ritual and regret she now packed away in the closet, with hardly a second thought. The old gray rag which had then seemed the livery of a degraded life was now no more than the resumption of her reality.

"I'll go as I came," she had been saying to herself, all the evening. "I know he'd like me to take the things he's given me; but I'd rather be just what I was."

If there was any ritual in what she had done since Miss Walbrook had left her it was in the putting away of small things by which she didn't want to be haunted.

"I couldn't do it with this on," she said of the plain gold band on her finger, to which, as a symbol of marriage, she had never attached significance in any case.

She took it off, therefore, and laid it on the dressing table.

"I couldn't do it with this in my pocket," she said of the purse containing a few dollars, with which Steptoe had kept her supplied.

This too she laid on the dressing table, becoming as penniless as when Judson Flack had put her out of doors. Somehow, to be penniless seemed to her an element in her new task, and an excuse for it.

Since Allerton had never made her a present there was nothing of this kind to discard. It had been part of his non-committal, impersonal attitude toward her that he had never given her a concrete sign that she meant anything to him whatever. He had thanked her on occasions for the comforting quality he found in her presence. He had, in so many words, recognized the fact that when he got into a tantrum of nerves she could bring him out of it as no one else had ever done. He had also imparted to her the discovery that in reading to her, and trying to show her the point of view of a life superior to her own, he had for the first time in his life done something for someone else; but he had never gone beyond all this or allowed her to think that his heart was not given to "the girl he was engaged to." In that at least he had been loyal to the mysterious princess, as the little mermaid could not but see.

She was not consciously denuded, as she would have felt herself six months earlier. As to that she was not thinking anything at all. Her motive, in setting free the prince from the "drag" on him which she now recognized herself to be, filled all her mental horizons. So dominated was she by this overwhelming impulse as to have no thought even for self-pity.

When a clock somewhere struck one she took it as the summons. From the dressing-table she picked up the scrawl in Steptoe's hand, giving the name of Miss Henrietta Towell, at an address at Red Point, L. I. She knew Red Point, on the tip of Long Island, as a distant, partially developed suburb of Brooklyn. In the previous year she had gone with a half dozen other girl "supes" from the Excelsior Studio to "blow in" a quarter looking at the ocean steamers passing in and out. She had no intention of intruding on Miss Towell, but she couldn't hurt Steptoe's feelings by leaving the address behind her.

For the same reason she took the silver thimble which stood on the scrap of paper. On its rim she read the inscription, "H.T. from H.S." but she made no attempt to unravel the romance behind it. She merely slipped the scrawl and the thimble into the pocket of her jacket, and stood up.

She took no farewells. To do so would have unnerved her. On the landing outside her door she listened for a possible sound of the prince's breathing, but the house was still. In the lower hall she resisted the impulse to slip into the library and kiss the place where she had kissed his feet on the memorable morning when her hand had been on his brow. "That won't help me any," were the prosaic words with which she put the suggestion away from her. If the little mermaid was to leap over the ship's side and dissolve into foam the best thing she could do was to leap.

The door no longer held secrets. She had locked it and unlocked it a thousand times. Feeling for the chain in the darkness she slipped it out of its socket; she drew back the bolt; she turned the key. Her fingers found the two little brass knobs, pressing this one that way, and that one this way. The door rolled softly as she turned the handle.

Over the threshold she passed into a world of silence, darkness, electricity, and stars. She closed the door noiselessly. She went down the steps,

Chapter XXI

HAVING the choice between going southward either by Fifth Avenue or by Madison Avenue, Letty took the former for the reason that there were no electric cars crashing through it, so that she would be less observed. It seemed to her important to get as far from East Sixty-seventh Street as possible before letting a human glance take note of her personality, even as a drifting silhouette.

In this she was fortunate. For the hour between one and two in the early morning this part of Fifth Avenue was unusually empty. There was not a pedestrian, and only a rare motor car. When one of the latter flashed by she shrank into the shadow of a great house, lest some eye of miraculous discernment should light on her. It seemed to her that all New York must be ready to read her secret, and be on the watch to turn her back.

She didn't know why she was going southward rather than northward, except that southward lay the Brooklyn Bridge, and beyond the Brooklyn Bridge lay Beehive Valley, and within Beehive Valley the Excelsior Studio, and in the Excelsior Studio the faint possibility of a job. She was already thinking in the terms that went with the old gray rag and the battered hat, and had come back to them as to her mother-tongue. In forsaking paradise for the limbo of outcast souls she was at least supported by the fact that in the limbo of outcast souls she was at home.

She was not frightened. Now that she was out of the prince's palace she had suddenly become sensationless. She was like a soul which having reached the other side of death is conscious only of release from pain. She was no longer walking on blades; she was no longer attempting the impossible. Between her and the life which Barbara Walbrook understood the few steps she had taken had already marked the gulf. The gulf had always been there, yawning, unbridgable, only that she, Letty Gravely, had tried to shut her eyes to it. She had tried to shut her eyes to it in the hope that the man she loved might come to do the same. She knew now how utterly foolish any such hope had been.

She would have perceived this earlier had he not from time to time revived the hope when it was about to flicker out. More than once he had confessed to depending on her sympathy. More than once he had told her that she drew out something he had hardly dared think he possessed, but which made him more of a man. Once he harked back to the dust flower, saying that as its humble and heavenly bloom brightened the spots bereft of beauty so she cheered the lonely and comfortless places in his heart. He had said these things not as one who is in love, but as one who is grateful, only that between gratitude and love she had purposely kept from drawing the distinction.

She did not reproach him. On the contrary, she blessed him even for being grateful. That meed he gave her at least, and that he should give her anything at all was happiness. Leaving his palace she did so with nothing but grateful thoughts on her own side. He had smiled on her always; he had been considerate, kindly, and very nearly tender. For what he called the wrong he had done her, which she held to be no wrong at all, he would have made amends so magnificent that the mere acceptance would have overwhelmed her. Since he couldn't give her the one thing she craved her best course was like the little mermaid to tremble into foam, and become a spirit of the wind.

It was what she was doing. She was going without leaving a trace. A girl more important than she couldn't have done it so easily. A Barbara Walbrook had she attempted a freak so mad, would be discovered within twenty-four hours. It was one of the advantages of extreme obscurity that you came and went without notice. No matter how conspicuously a Letty Gravely passed it would not be remembered that she had gone by.

With regard to this, however, she made one reserve. She couldn't disappear forever, not any more than Judith of Bethulia when she went to the tent of Holofernes. The history of Judith was not in Letty's mind, because she had never heard of it; there was only the impulse to the same sort of sacrifice. Since Israel could be delivered only in one way, that way Judith had been ready to take. To Letty her prince was her Israel. One day she would have to inform him that the Holofernes of his captivity was slain—that at last he was free.

There were lines along which Letty was not imaginative, and one of those lines ran parallel to Judith's experience. When it came to love at first sight, she could invent as many situations as there were millionaires in the subway. In interpreting a part she had views of her own beyond any held by Luciline Lynch. As to matters of dress her fancy was boundless.

Her limitations were in the practical. Among practical things "going to the bad" was now her chief preoccupation. She had always understood that when you made up your mind to do it you had only to present yourself. The way was broad; the gate wide open. There were wicked people on every side eager to pull you through. You had only to go out into the street, after dark especially—and there you were!

Having walked some three or four blocks she made out the figure of a man coming up the hill toward her. Her heart stopped beating; her knees quaked. This was doom. She would meet it, of course, since her doom would be the prince's salvation; but she couldn't help trembling as she watched it coming on.

By the light of an arc-lamp she saw that he was in evening dress. The wicked millionaires who, in motion-pictures, were the peril of young girls, were always so attired. Iphigenia could not have trodden to the altar with a more consuming mental anguish than Letty as she dragged herself toward this approaching fate; but she did so drag herself without mercy. For a minute as he drew near she was on the point of begging him to spare her; but she saved herself in time from this frustration of her task.

The man, a young stock-broker in a bad financial plight, scarcely noticed that a female figure was passing him. Had the morrow's market been less a matter of life and death to him he might have thrown her a

THE DUST FLOWER

glance; but as it was she did not come within the range of his consciousness. To her amazement, and even to her consternation, Letty saw him go onward up the hill, his eyes straight before him, and his profile sharply cut in the electric light.

She explained the situation by the fact that he hadn't seen her at all. That a man could actually *see* a girl, in such unusual conditions, and still go by inoffensively, was as contrary to all she had heard of life as it would have been to the principles of a Turkish woman to suppose that one of this sex could behold her face and not fall fiercely in love with her. As, however, two men were now coming up the hill together Letty was obliged to re-organize her forces to meet the new advance.

She couldn't reason this time that they hadn't seen her, because their heads turned in her direction, and the intonation of the words she couldn't articulately hear was that of faint surprise. Further than that there was no incident. They were young men too, also in evening dress, and of the very type of which all her warnings had bidden her beware. The immunity from insult was almost a matter for chagrin.

As she approached Fifty-ninth Street encounters were nearly as numerous as they would have been in daylight; but Letty went on her way as if, instead of the old gray rag, she wore the magic cloak of invisibility. So it was during the whole of the long half mile between Fifty-ninth Street and Forty-second Street. In spite of the fact that she was the only unescorted woman she saw, no invitation "to go to the bad" was proffered her. "There's quite a trick to it,"

Steptoe had said, in the afternoon; and she began to think that there was.

At Forty-second Street, for no reason that she could explain, she turned into the lower and quieter spur of Madison Avenue, climbing and descending Murray Hill. Here she was almost alone. Motor-car traffic had practically ceased; foot-passengers there were none; on each side of the street the houses were somber and somnolent. The electric lamps flared as elsewhere, but with little to light up.

Her sense of being lost became awesome. It began to urge itself in on her that she was going nowhere, and had nowhere to go. She was back in the days when she had walked away from Judson Flack's, without the same heart in the adventure. She recalled now that on that day she had felt young, daring, equal to anything that fate might send; now she felt curiously old and experienced. All her illusions had been dished up to her at once and been blown away as by a hurricane. The little mermaid who had loved the prince and failed to win his love in return could have nothing more to look forward to.

She was drifting, drifting, when suddenly from the shadow of a flight of broad steps a man stalked out and confronted her. He confronted her with such evident intention that she stopped. Not till she stopped could she see that he was a policeman in his summer uniform.

"Where you goin', sister?"

"I ain't goin' nowheres."

She fell back on the old form of speech as on another tongue.

THE DUST FLOWER

"Where you come from then?"

Feeling now that she had gone to the bad, or was at the beginning of that process, she made a reply that would seem probable. "I come from a fella I've been—I've been livin' with."

"Gee!" The tone was of deepest pity. "Darned sorry to hear you're in that box, a nice girl like you."

"I ain't such a nice girl as you might think."

"Gee! Anyone can see you're a nice girl, just from the way you walk."

Letty was astounded. Was the way you walked part of Steptoe's "trick to it?" In the hope of getting information she said, still in the secondary tongue: "What's the matter with the way I walk?"

"There's nothin' the matter with it. That's the trouble. Anyone can see that you're not a girl that's used to bein' on the street at this hour of the night. Ain't you goin' *anywheres?*"

Fear of the police-station suddenly made her faint. If she wasn't going *anywheres* he might arrest her. She bethought her of Steptoe's scrawled address. "Yes, I'm goin' there."

As he stepped under the arc-light to read it she saw that he was a fatherly man, on the distant outskirts of youth, who might well have a family of growing boys and girls.

"That's a long ways from here," he said, handing the scrap of paper back to her. "Why don't you take the subway? At this time of night there's a train every quarter of an hour."

"I ain't got no bones. I'm footin' it."

"Footin' it all the way to Red Point? You? Gee!"

THE DUST FLOWER

Once more Letty felt that about her there was something which put her out of the key of her adventure.

"Well, what's there against *me* footin' it?"

"There's nothin' against you footin' it—on'y you don't seem that sort. Haven't you got as much as two bits? It wouldn't come to that if you took the subway over here at ——"

"Well, I haven't got two bits; nor one bit; nor nothin' at all; so I guess I'll be lightin' out."

She had nodded and passed, when a stride of his long legs brought him up to her again. "Well, see here, sister! If you haven't got two bits, take this. I can't have you trampin' all the way over to Red Point—not *you!*"

Before knowing what had happened Letty found her hand closing over a silver half-dollar, while her benefactor, as if ashamed of his act, was off again on his beat. She ran after him. Her excitement was such that she forgot the secondary language.

"Oh, I couldn't accept this from you. Please! Don't make me take it. I'm—" She felt it the moment for making the confession, and possibly getting hints—"I'm—I'm goin' to the bad, anyhow."

"Oh, so that's the talk! I thought you said you'd gone to the bad already. Oh, no, sister; you don't put that over on me, not a nice looker like you!"

She was almost sobbing. "Well, I'm going—if—if I can find the way. I wish you'd tell me if there's a trick to it."

"There's one trick I'll tell you, and that's the way to Red Point."

"I know that already."

THE DUST FLOWER

"Then, if you know that already, you've got my four bits, which is more than enough to take you there decent." He lifted his hand, with a warning forefinger. "Remember now, little sister, as long as you spend that half dollar it'll bind you to keep good."

He tramped off into the darkness, leaving Letty perplexed at the ways of wickedness, as she began once more to drift southward.

But she drifted southward with a new sense of misgiving. Danger was mysteriously coy, and she didn't know how to court it. True, there was still time enough, but the début was not encouraging. When she had gone forth from Judson Flack's she had felt sure that adventure lay in wait for her, and Rashleigh Allerton had responded almost instantaneously. Now she had no such confidence. On the contrary; all her premonitions worked the other way. Perhaps it was the old gray rag. Perhaps it was her lack of feminine appeal. Men had never flocked about her as they flocked about some girls, like bees about flowers. If she was a flower, she was a dust flower, a humble thing, at home in the humblest places, and never regarded as other than a weed.

She wandered into Fourth Avenue, reaching Astor Place. From Astor Place she descended the city by the long artery of Lafayette Street, in which teams rumbled heavily, and all-night workers shouted raucously to each other in foreign lauguages. One of a band of Italians digging in the roadway, with colored lanterns about them, called out something at her, the nature of which she could only infer from the laughter of his compatriots. Here too she began to notice other women like herself, shabby, furtive, unescorted, with terrible eyes, aimlessly drifting from nowhere to nowhere. There were not many of them; only one at long intervals; but they frightened her more than the men.

They frightened her because she saw what she must look like herself, a thing too degraded for any man to want. She was not that yet, perhaps; but it was what she might become. They were not wholly new to her, these women; and they all had begun at some such point as that from which she was starting out. Very well! She was ready to go this road, if only by this road her prince could be freed from her. Since she couldn't give up everything for him in one way, she would do it in another. The way itself was more or less a matter of indifference—not entirely, perhaps, but more or less. If she could set him free in any way she would be content.

The rumble and stir of Lafayette Street alarmed her because it was so foreign. The upper part of the town had been empty and eerie. This quarter was eerie, alien, and occupied. It was difficult for her to tell what so many people were doing abroad because their aims seemed different from those of daylight. What she couldn't understand struck her as nefarious; and what struck her as nefarious filled her with the kind of terror that comes in dreams.

By these Italians, Slavs, and Semites she was more closely scrutinized than she had been elsewhere. She was scrutinized, too, with a hint of hostility in the scrutiny. In their jabber of tongues they said things about her as she passed. Wild-eyed women, working by the flare of torches with their men, resented her presence in the street. They insulted her in terms she couldn't understand, while the men laughed in frightful, significant jocosity. The unescorted women alone looked at her with a hint of friendliness. One of them, painted, haggard, desperate, awful, stopped as if to speak to her; but Letty sped away like a snow-bird from a shrike.

At a corner where the cross-street was empty she turned out of this haunted highway, presently finding herself lost in a congeries of old-time streets of which she had never heard. Her only knowledge of New York was of streets crossing each other at right angles, numbered, prosaic, leaving no more play to the fancy than a sum in arithmetic. Here the ways were narrow, the buildings tall, the night effects fantastic. In the lamp light she could read signs bearing names as unpronounceable as the gibbering monkey-speech in Lafayette Street. Warehouses, offices, big wholesale premises, lairs of highly specialized businesses which only the few knew anything about, offered no place for human beings to sleep, and little invitation to the prowler. Now and then a marauding cat darted from shadow to shadow, but otherwise she was as nearly alone as she could imagine herself being in the heart of a great city.

Still she went on and on. In the effort to escape this overpowering solitude she turned one corner and then another, now coming out beneath the elevated trains, now on the outskirts of docks where she was afraid of sailors. She was afraid of being alone, and afraid of the thoroughfares where there were people.

THE DUST FLOWER

On the whole she was more afraid of the thoroughfares where there were people, though her fear soon entered the unreasoning phase, in which it is fear and nothing else. Still headed vaguely southward she zigzagged from street to street, helpless, terrified, longing for day.

She was in a narrow street of which the high weird gables on either side recalled her impressions on opening a copy of *Faust,* illustrated by Gustave Doré, which she found on the library table in East Sixty-seventh Street. On her right the elevated and the docks were not far away, on the left she could catch, through an occasional side street the distant gleam of Broadway. Being afraid of both she kept to the deep canyon of unreality and solitude, though she was afraid of that. At least she was alone; and yet to be alone chilled her marrow and curdled her blood.

Suddenly she heard the clank of footsteps. She stopped to listen, making them out as being on the other side of the street, and advancing. Before she had dared to move on again a man emerged from the half light and came abreast of her. As he stopped to look across at her, Letty hurried on.

The man also went on, but on glancing over her shoulder to make sure that she was safe she saw him pause, cross to her side of the street, and begin to follow her. That he followed her was plain from his whole plan of action. The ring of his footsteps told her that he was walking faster than she, though in no precise hurry to overtake her. Rather, he seemed to be keeping her in sight, and watching for some opportunity.

THE DUST FLOWER

It was exactly what men did when they robbed and murdered unprotected women. She had read of scores of such cases, and had often imagined herself as being stalked by this kind of ghoul. Now the thing which she had greatly feared having come upon her she was nearly hysterical. If she ran he would run after her. If she only walked on he would overtake her. Before she could reach the docks on one side or Broadway on the other, where she might find possible defenders, he could easily have strangled her and rifled her fifty cents.

It was still unreasoning fear, but fear in which there was another kind of prompting, which made her wheel suddenly and walk back towards him. She noticed that as she did so, he stopped, wavered, but came on again.

Before the obscurity allowed of her seeing what type of man he was she cried out, with a half sob:

"Oh, mister, I'm so afraid! I wish you'd help me."

"Sure!" The tone had the cheery fraternal ring of commonplace sincerity. "That's what I turned round for. I says, that girl's lost, I says. There's places down here that's dangerous, and she don't know where she is."

Hysterical fear became hysterical relief. "And you're not going to murder me?"

"Gee! Me? What'd I murder you for? I'm a plumber."

His tone making it seem impossible for a plumber to murder anyone she panted now from a sense of reassurance and security. She could see too that he was a decent looking young fellow in overalls, off on an early job.

"Where you goin' anyhow?" he asked, in kindly interest. "The minute I see you on the other side of the street, I says Gosh, I says! That girl's got to be watched, I says. She don't know that these streets down by the docks is dangerous."

She explained that she was on her way to Red Point, Long Island, and that having only fifty cents she was sparing of her money.

"Gee! I wouldn't be so economical if it was me. That ain't the only fifty cents in the world. Look-a-here! I've got a dollar. You must take that ——"

"Oh, I couldn't."

"Shucks! What's a dollar? You can pay me back some time. I'll give you my address. It's all right. I'm married. Three kids. And say, if you send me back the dollar, which you needn't do, you know—but if you *must*—sign a man's name to the letter, because my wife—well, she's all right, but if ——"

Letty escaped the necessity of accepting the dollar by assuring him that if he would tell her the way to the nearest subway station she would use a portion of her fifty cents.

"I'll go with you," he declared, with breezy fraternity. "No distance. They're expecting me on a job up there in Waddle Street, but they'll wait. Pipe burst—floodin' a loft where they've stored a lot of jute—but why worry?"

As they threaded the broken series of streets toward the subway he aired the matrimonial question.

"Some think as two can live on the same wages as

THE DUST FLOWER

one. All bunk, I'll say. My wife used to be in the hair line. Some little earner too. Had an electric machine that'd make hair grow like hay on a marsh. Two dollars a visit she got. When we was married she had nine hunderd saved. I had over five hunderd myself. We took a weddin' tour; Atlantic City. Gettin' married's a cinch; but *stayin'* married—she's all right, my wife is, only she's kind o' nervous like if I look sideways at any other woman—which I hardly ever do intentional—only my wife's got it into her head that. . . ."

At the entrance to the subway Letty shook hands with him and thanked him.

"Say," he responded, "I wish I could do something more for you; but I got to hike it back to Waddle Street. Look-a-here! You stick to the subway and the stations, and don't you be in a hurry to get to your address in Red Point till after daylight. They can't be killin' nobody over there, that you'd need to be in such a rush, and in the stations you'd be safe."

To a degree that was disconcerting Letty found this so. Having descended the stairs, purchased a ticket, and cast it into the receptacle appointed for that purpose, she saw herself examined by the colored man guarding the entry to the platform. He sat with his chair tilted back, his feet resting on the chain which protected part of the entrance, picking a set of brilliant teeth. Letty, trembling, nervous, and only partly comforted by the cavalier who was now on his way to Waddle Street, shrank from the colored man's gaze and was going down the platform where she could be away from it. Her progress was arrested by the sight

THE DUST FLOWER

of two men, also waiting for the train, who on perceiving her started in her direction.

The colored man lifted his feet lazily from the chain, brought his chair down to four legs, put his toothpick in his waistcoat pocket, and dragged himself up.

"Say, lady," he drawled, on approaching her, "I think them two fellas is tough. You stay here by me. I'll not let no one get fresh with you."

Languidly he went back to his former position and occupation, but when after long waiting, the train drew in he unhooked his feet again from the chain, rose lazily, and accompanied Letty across the otherwise empty platform.

"Say, brother," he said to the conductor, "don't let any fresh guy get busy with this lady. She's alone, and timid like."

"Sure thing," the conductor replied, closing the doors as Letty stepped within. "Sit in this corner, lady, next to me. The first mutt that wags his jaw at you'll get it on the bean."

Letty dropped as she was bidden into the corner, dazed by the brilliant lighting, and the greasy unoccupied seats. She was alone in the car, and the kindly conductor having closed his door she felt a certain sense of privacy. The train clattered off into the darkness.

Where was she going? Why was she there? How was she ever to accomplish the purpose with which two hours earlier she had stolen away from East Sixty-seventh Street? Was it only two hours earlier? It seemed like two years. It seemed like a space of time not to be reckoned. . . .

THE DUST FLOWER

She was tired as she had never been tired in her life. Her head sank back into the support made by the corner.

"There's quite a trick to it," she found herself repeating, though in what connection she scarcely knew. "An awful wicked lydy, she is, what'd put madam up to all the ropes." These words too drifted through her mind, foolishly, drowsily, without obvious connection. She began to wish that she was home again in the little back spare room—or anywhere—so long as she could lie down—and shut her eyes—and go to sleep. . . .

Chapter XXII

IT was Steptoe who discovered that the little back spare room was empty, though William had informed him that he thought it strange that madam didn't appear for breakfast. Steptoe knew then that what he had expected had come to pass, and if earlier than he had looked for it, perhaps it was just as well. Having tapped at madam's door and received no answer he ventured within. Everything there confirming his belief, he went to inform Mr. Rash.

As Mr. Rash was shaving in the bathroom Steptoe plodded round the bedroom, picking up scattered articles of clothing, putting outside the door the shoes which had been taken off on the previous night, digging another pair of shoes from the shoe-cupboard, and otherwise busying himself as usual. Even when Mr. Rash had re-entered the bedroom the valet made no immediate reference to what had happened in the house. He approached the subject indirectly by saying, as he laid out an old velvet house-jacket on the bed:

"I suppose if Mr. Rash ain't goin' out for 'is breakfast 'e'll put this on for 'ome."

Mr. Rash, who was buttoning his collar before the mirror said over his shoulder: "But I am going out for my breakfast. Why shouldn't I? I always do."

Steptoe carried the house-jacket back to the closet.

THE DUST FLOWER

"I thought as Mr. Rash only did that so as madam could 'ave the dinin' room to 'erself, private like."

As a way of expressing the fact that Allerton had never eaten a meal with Letty the choice of words was neat.

"Well? What then?"

"Oh, nothink, sir. I was only thinkin' that, as madam was no longer 'ere ——"

Allerton wheeled round, his fingers clawing at the collar-stud, his face growing bloodless. "No longer here? What the deuce do you mean?"

"Oh, didn't Mr. Rash know? Madam seems to 'ave left us. I supposed that after I'd gone upstairs last night Mr. Rash and 'er must 'ave 'ad some sort of hunderstandin'—and she went."

"Went?" Allerton's tone was almost a scream. Leaping on the old man he took him by the shoulders, shaking him. "Damn you! Get it out! What are you trying to tell me?"

Steptoe quaked and cowered. "Why, nothink, sir. Only when William said as madam didn't come down to 'er breakfast I went to 'er door and tapped—and there wasn't no one in the room. Mr. Rash 'ad better go and see for 'imself."

The young man not only released the older one, but pushed him aside with a force which sent him staggering backwards. Over the stairs he scrambled, he plunged. Though he had never entered the back spare room since allotting it to Letty as her own he threw the door open now as if the place was on fire.

But by the time Steptoe had followed and reached the threshold Allerton had calmed suddenly. He stood in front of the open closet vaguely examining its contents. He picked up the little gold band, chucked it a few inches into the air, caught it, and put it down. He looked into the little leather purse, poured out its notes and pennies into his hand, replaced them, and put that also down again. He opened the old red volume lying on the table by the bed, finding *The Little Mermaid* marked by two stiff dried sprays of dust flower, which more than ever merited its name. When he turned round to where Steptoe, white and scared by this time, was standing in the open doorway, his, Allerton's, face was drawn, in mingled convulsion and bewilderment. With two strides he was across the room.

"Tell me what you know about this, you confounded old schemer, before I kick you out."

Shivering and shaking, Steptoe nevertheless held himself with dignity. "I'll tell you what I know, Mr. Rash, though it ain't very much. I know that madam 'as 'ad it in 'er mind for some time past that unless she took steps Mr. Rash'd never be free to marry the young lydy what 'e was in love with."

"What did she mean by taking steps?"

"I don't know exactly, but I think it was the kind o' steps as'd give Mr. Rash 'is release quicker nor any other."

Allerton's arm was raised as if to strike a blow. "And you let her?"

The old face was set steadily. "I didn't do nothin' but what Mr. Rash 'imself told me to do."

"Told you to do?"

"Yes, Mr. Rash; six months ago; the mornin' after

THE DUST FLOWER

you'd brought madam into the 'ouse. I was to get you out of the marriage, you said; but I think madam 'as done it all of 'er own haccord."

"But why? Why should she?"

Steptoe smiled, dimly. "Oh, don't Mr. Rash see? Madam 'ad give 'erself to 'im 'eart and spirit and soul. If she couldn't go to the good for 'im, she'd go to the bad. So long as she served 'im, it didn't matter to madam what she done. And if I was Mr. Rash ———"

Allerton's spring was like that of a tiger. Before Steptoe felt that he had been seized he was on his back on the floor, with Allerton kneeling on his chest.

"You old reptile! I'm going to kill you."

"You may kill me, Mr. Rash, but it won't make no difference to madam 'avin' loved you ———"

Two strong hands at his throat choked back more words, till the sound of his strangling startled Allerton into a measure of self-control. He scrambled to his feet again.

"Get up."

Steptoe dragged himself up, and after dusting himself with his fingers stood once more passive and respectful, as if nothing violent had occurred.

"If I was Mr. Rash," he went on, imperturbably, "I'd let well enough alone."

It was Allerton who was breathless. "Wha—what do you mean by well enough alone?"

"Well the wye I see it, it's this wye. Mr. Rash is married to one young lydy and wants to marry another." He broke off to ask, significantly: "I suppose that'd be so, Mr. Rash?"

"Well, what then?"

THE DUST FLOWER

"Why, then, 'e can't marry the other young lydy till the young lydy what 'e's married to sets 'im free. Now that young lydy what 'e's married to 'as started out to set 'im free, and if I was Mr. Rash I'd let 'er."

"You'd let her throw herself away for me?"

"I'd let 'er do anythink what'd show I knowed my own mind, Mr. Rash. If it wouldn't be steppin' out of my place to sye so, I wish Mr. Rash could tell which of these two young lydies 'e wanted, and which 'e'd be willin' for to ——"

"How can I tell that when—when both have a claim on me?"

"Yes, but only one 'as a clyme on Mr. Rash now. Madam 'as given up 'er clyme, so as to myke things easier for *'im*. There's only one clyme now for Mr. Rash to think about, and that mykes everythink simple."

An embarrassed cough drew Steptoe's attention to the fact that someone was standing in the hall outside. It was William with a note on a silver tray. Beside the note stood a small square package, tied with a white ribbon, which looked as if it contained a piece of wedding cake. His whisper of explanation was the word, "Wildgoose," but a cocking of his eye gave Steptoe to understand that William was quite aware of wading in the current of his employer's love affairs. Moreover, the fact that Steptoe and his master should be making so free with the little back spare room was in William's judgment evidence of drama.

"What's this?"

Glancing at the hand-writing on the envelope, and taking in the fact that a small square package, looking like a bit of wedding cake stood beside it, Allerton jumped back. Steptoe might have been presenting him with a snake.

"I don't know, Mr. Rash. William 'as just brought it up. Someone seems to 'ave left it at the door."

As Steptoe continued to stand with his offering held out Allerton had no choice but to take up the letter and break the seal. He read it with little grunts intended to signify ironic laughter, but which betrayed no more than bitterness of soul.

"Dear Rash:

I have come to see that we shall never get out of the impasse in which we seem to have been caught unless someone takes a stand. I have therefore decided to take one. Of the three of us it is apparently easiest for me, so that I am definitely breaking our engagement and sending you back your ring. Any claim I may have had on you I give up of my own accord, so that as far as I am concerned you are free. This will simplify your situation, and enable you to act according to the dictates of your heart. Believe me, dear Rash, affectionately yours

Barbara Walbrook."

Though it was not his practice to take his valet into the secret of his correspondence the circumstances were exceptional. Allerton handed the letter to Steptoe without a word. As the old man was feeling for his glasses and adjusting them to his nose Mr. Rash turned absently away, picking up the volume of Hans

Andersen, from which the sprays of dust flower tumbled out. On putting them back his eyes fell upon the words, which someone had marked with a pencil:

"Day by day she grew dearer to the prince; but he loved her as one loves a child. The thought of making her his queen never crossed his mind."

A spasm passed over his face. He turned the page impatiently. Here he caught the words which had been underlined:

"I am with him every day. I will watch over him —love him—and sacrifice my life for him."

Shutting the book with a bang, and throwing it on the table, he wheeled round to where Steptoe, having folded the letter, was taking off his spectacles.

"Well, what do you say to that?"

"What I'd sye to that, Mr. Rash, is that it's as good as a legal document. If any young lydy what wrote that letter was to bring a haction for breach, this 'ere pyper'd nyle 'er."

"So where am I now?"

"Free as a lark, Mr. Rash. One young lydy 'as turned you down, and the other 'as gone to the bad for you; so if you was to begin agyne with a third you'd 'ave a clean sheet."

He groaned aloud. "Ah, go to ——"

But without stating the place to which Steptoe was to go he marched out of the room, and back to his dressing upstairs.

More dispassionate was the early morning scene in the little basement eating house in which the stunted Hebrew maid of Polish culture was serving breakfast to two gentlemen who had plainly met by appointment. Beside the one was an oblong packet, of which some of the contents, half displayed, had the opulent engraved decorations of stock certificates.

The other gentleman, resembling an operatic brigand a little the worse for wear, was saying with conviction: "Oil! Don't talk to me! No, sir! There's enough oil in Milligan Center alone to run every car in Europe and America at this present time; while if you include North Milligan, where it's beginnin' to shoot like the Old Faithful geyser ———"

"Awful obliged to you, Judson," the other took up, humbly. "I thought that bunch o' nuts 'd never ———"

"So did I, Gorry. I've sweated blood over this job all winter. Queer the way men are made. Now you'd hardly believe the work I've had to show that lot of boneheads that because a guy's a detective in one line, he ain't a detective in every line. Homicide, I said, was Gorry Larrabin's specialty, and where there's no homicide he's no more a detective than a busted rubber tire."

"You've said it," Gorry corroborated, earnestly. "One of the cussed things about detectin' is that fellas gets afraid of you. Think because you're keepin' up your end you must be down on every little thing, and that you ain't a sport."

"Must be hard," Judson said, sympathetically.

"I'll tell you it's hard. Lots of fun I'd like to be let in on—but you're kept outside."

The drawbacks of the detective profession not being what Judson chiefly had on his mind he allowed the subject to drop. An interval of silence for the con-

THE DUST FLOWER

sumption of a plateful of golden toasties permitted Gorry to begin again reminiscently.

"By the way, Judson, do you remember that about six months ago you was chewin' over that girl of yours, and what had become of her?"

To himself Judson said: "That's the talk; now we're comin' to business." Aloud he made it: "Why, yes. Seems to me I do. She's been gone so long I'd almost forgot her."

"Well, what d'ye know? Last night—lemme see, was it last night?—no, night before last—I kind o' got wind of her."

"Heaven's sake!"

"Guy I know was comin' through East Sixty-seventh Street, and there was my lady, dressed to beat the band, leadin' one of them little toy dogs, and talkin' to a swell toff that lives in one of them houses. Got the number here in my pocket-book."

While he was searching his pocket-book Judson asked, breathlessly: "Couldn't be no mistake?"

"It's nix on mistakes. That guy don't make 'em. Surest thing on the force. He said, 'Good afternoon, Miss Gravely'; and she said, 'Good afternoon' back to him—just like that. The guy walked on and turned a corner; but when he peeped back, there was the couple goin' into the house just like husband and wife. What d'ye know?"

"What do I know? I know I'll spill his claret for him before the week is out."

"Ah, here it is! Knew I had that address on me somewheres." He handed the scrap of paper across the table. "That's his name and number. Seems to

THE DUST FLOWER

me you may have a good thing there, Judson, if you know how to work it."

In another early morning scene the ermine was cleaning her nest; and you know how fastidious she is supposed to be as to personal spotlessness. The ermine in question did not belie her reputation, as you would have seen by a glance at the three or four rooms which made up what she called her "flat."

Nothing was ever whiter than the wood-work of the "flat" and its furnishings. Nothing was ever whiter than the little lady's dress. The hair was white, and even the complexion, the one like silver, the other like the camelia. Having breakfasted from white dishes placed on a white napkin, she was busy with a carpet-sweeper sweeping up possible crumbs. In an interval of the carpet-sweeper's buzz she heard the telephone.

"Hello!" The male voice was commanding.

"Yes?" The response was sweetly precise.

"Is this Red Point 3284-W?"

"It is."

"Can I speak to Miss Henrietta Towell?"

"This is Miss Henrietta Towell."

"This is the Brooklyn Bridge Emergency Hospital. Do you know a girl named Letitia Rashleigh?"

There was a second's hesitation. "I was once a lady's maid to a lady whose maiden name was Rashleigh. I think there may be a connection somewhere."

"She was found unconscious on a car in the subway last night and brought in here."

"And has she mentioned me?"

THE DUST FLOWER

"She hasn't mentioned anyone since she came to; but we find your address on a paper in her pocket."

"That seems singular, but I expect there's a purpose behind it. Is that everything she had?"

"No; she had forty-five cents and a thimble."

"A thimble! Just an ordinary thimble."

"Yes, an ordinary thimble, except that it has initials on the edge. 'H.T. from H.S.' Does that mean anything to you?"

"Yes; that means something to me. May I ask how to reach the hospital?"

This being explained Miss Towell promised to appear without delay, begging that in the meantime everything be done for Miss Rashleigh's comfort.

She was not perturbed. She was not surprised. She did not wonder who Letitia Rashleigh could be, or why her address should be found in the girl's pocket. She was as quiet and serene as if such incidents belonged to every day's work.

Dressed for the street she was all in black. A mantua covered with bugles and braid dropped from her shoulders, while a bonnet which rose to a pointed arch above her brow, and allowed the silver knob of her hair to escape behind, gave her a late nineteenth century dignity. Before leaving the house she took two volumes from her shelves—read first in one, then in the other—sat pensive for a while, with head bent and eyes shaded—after which she replaced her books, turned the key in her door, and set forth for Brooklyn Bridge.

Chapter XXIII

"WHY you should hold me responsible," Barbara was saying, "I can't begin to imagine. Surely I've done everything I could to simplify matters, to straighten them out, and to give you a chance to rectify your folly. I've effaced myself; I've broken my heart; I've promised Aunt Marion to go in for a job for which I'm not fitted and don't care a rap; and yet you come here, accusing me ——"

"But, Barbe, I'm *not* accusing you! If I'm accusing anyone it's myself. Only I can't speak without your taking me up ——"

"There you go! Oh, Rash, dear, if you'd only been able to control yourself nothing of this would have happened—not from the first."

She was pacing up and down the little reception room, and rubbing her hands together, while the twisting of the fish-tail of her hydrangea-colored robe, like an eel in agony, emphasized her agitation. Rashleigh was seated, his elbows on his knees, his head bowed between his hands, of which the fingers clutched and tore at the masses of his hair. Only when he spoke did he lift his woe-begone black eyes.

"Well, I didn't control myself," he admitted, impatiently; "that's settled. Why go back to it? The question is ——"

"Yes; why go back to it? That's you all over, Rash. You can do what no one else in his senses would ever think of doing; and when you've upset the whole apple cart it must never be referred to again. I'm to accept, and keep silence. Well, I've *kept* silence. I've gone all winter like a muzzled dog. I've wheedled that girl, and kow-towed to her, and made her think I was fond of her—which I am in a way—you may not believe it, but I am—and what's the result? She gets sick of the whole business; runs away; and you come here and throw the whole blame on me."

He tried to speak with special calmness. "Barbe, listen to me. What I said was this ——"

She came to a full stop in front of him, her arms outspread. "Oh, Rash, dear, I know perfectly well what you said. You don't have to go all over it again. I'm not deaf. If you would only not be so excitable ——"

He jumped to his feet. "I'm excitable, I know, Barbe. I confess it. Everybody knows it. What I'm trying to tell you is that I'm not excited *now*."

She laughed, a little mocking laugh, and started once more to pace up and down. "Oh, very well! You're not excited now. Then that's understood. You never are excited. You're as calm as a mountain." She paused again, though at a distance. "*Now?* What is it you're going to do? That's what you've come to ask me, isn't it? Are you going to run after her? Are you going to let her go? Are you going to divorce her, if she gives you the opportunity? If you divorce her are you going to ——?"

"But, Barbe, I can't decide all these questions now. What I want to do is to *find* her."

THE DUST FLOWER

"Well, I haven't got her here? Why don't you go after her? Why don't you apply to the police? Why don't you ——?"

"Yes, but that's just what I want to discuss with you. I don't *like* applying to the police. If I do it'll get into the papers, and the whole thing become so odious and vulgar ——"

"And it's such an exquisite idyll now!"

He threw back his head. *"She's* an exquisite idyll—in her way."

"There! That's what I wanted to hear you say! I've thought you were in love with her ——"

He remembered the penciled lines in Hans Andersen. "If I have been, it's as you may be in love with an innocent little child ——"

She laughed again, wildly, almost hysterically. "Oh, Rash, don't try to get that sort of thing off on me. I know how men love innocent little children. You can see the way they do it any night you choose to hang round the stage-door of a theatre where the exquisite idylls are playing in musical comedy."

"Don't Barbe! Not when you're talking about her! I know she's an ignorant little thing; but to me she's like a wild-flower ——"

"Wild-flowers can be cultivated, Rash."

"Yes, but the wild-flower she's most like is the one you see in the late summer all along the dusty highways ——"

She put up both palms in a gesture of protestation. "Oh, Rash, please don't be poetical. It gets on my nerves. I can't stand it. I like you in every mood but your sentimental one." She came to a halt beside the mantelpiece, on which she rested an elbow, turning to look at him. "Now tell me, Rash! Suppose I wasn't in the world at all. Or suppose you'd never heard of me. And suppose you found yourself married to this girl, just as you are—nominally—legally—but not really. Would you—would you make it—really?"

They exchanged a long silent look. His eyes had not left hers when he said: "I—I might."

"Good! Now suppose she wasn't in the world at all, or that you'd never heard of her. And suppose that you and I were—were on just the same terms that we are to-day. Would you—would you want to marry me? Answer me truly."

"Why, yes; of course."

"Now suppose that she and I were standing together, and you were led in to choose between us. And suppose you were absolutely free and untrammelled in your choice, with no question as to her feelings or mine to trouble you. Which would you take? Answer me just as truly and sincerely as you can."

He took time to think, wheeling away from her, and walking up and down the little room with his hands behind his back. It occurred to neither that Barbara having broken the "engagement," and returned the ring, the choice before him was purely hypothetical. Their relations were no more affected by the note she had written him that morning than by the ceremony through which he and Letty had walked in the previous year.

To Barbara the suspense was almost unbearable. In a minute or two, and with a word or two, she would know how life for the future was to be cast. She would have before her the possibility of some day becoming a happy wife—or a great career like her aunt's.

Pausing in his walk he confronted her just as he stood, his hands still clasped behind his back. Her own attitude, with elbow resting on the mantelpiece, was that of a woman equal to anything.

He spoke slowly. "Just as truly and sincerely as I can answer you—I don't know."

She stirred slightly, but otherwise gave no sign of her impatience. "And is there anything that would help you to find out?"

He shook his head. "Nothing that I can think of, unless——"

"Yes? Unless—what?"

"Unless it's something that would unlock what's locked in my subconsciousness."

"And what would that be?"

"I haven't the faintest idea."

She moved from the mantelpiece with a gesture of despair. "Rash, you're absolutely and hopelessly impossible."

"I know that," he admitted, humbly.

With both fists clenched she stood in front of him. "I could kill you."

He hung his head. "Not half so easily as I could kill myself."

Letty's judgment on Miss Henrietta Towell was different from yours and mine. She found her just what she had expected to see from the warnings long ago issued by Mrs. Judson Flack in putting her

THE DUST FLOWER

daughter on her guard. In going about the city she, Letty, was always to be suspicious of elderly ladies, respectably dressed, enticingly mannered, and with what seemed like maternal intentions. The more any one of these traits was developed, the more suspicious Letty was to be. With these instructions carefully at heart she would have been suspicious of Henrietta Towell in any case; but with Steptoe's description to fall back upon she couldn't but feel sure.

By the time Miss Towell had arrived at the hospital Letitia Rashleigh had sufficiently recovered to be dressed and seated in the armchair placed beside the bed in the small white ward. On one low bedpost the jacket had been hung, and on the other the battered black hat.

"There's nothing the matter with her," the nurse explained to Miss Towell, before entering the ward. "She had fainted in the subway, but I think it was only from fatigue, and perhaps from lack of food. She's quite well nourished, only she didn't seem to have eaten any supper, and was evidently tired from a long and frightening walk. She gives us no explanation of herself, and is disinclined to talk, and if it hadn't been that she had your address in her pocket ——"

"I think I know how she got that. From her name I judge that she's a relative of the family in which I used to be employed; but as they were all very wealthy people ——"

"Even very wealthy people often have poor relations."

"Yes, of course; but I was with this family for so many years that if there'd been any such connection

THE DUST FLOWER

I think I must have heard of it. However, it makes no difference to me, and I shall be glad to be of use to her, especially as she has in her possession an article—a thimble it is—which once belonged to me."

At the bedside the nurse made the introduction. "This is the lady whose address you had in your pocket. She very kindly said she'd come and see what she could do for you."

Having placed a chair for Miss Towell the nurse withdrew to attend to other patients in the ward, of whom there were three or four.

Letty regarded the newcomer with eyes that seemed lustreless in spite of their tiny gold flames. Having a shrewd idea of what she would mean to her visitor she felt it unnecessary to express gratitude. In a certain sense she hated her at sight. She hated her bugles and braid and the shape of her bonnet, as the criminal about to be put to death might hate the executioner's mask and gaberdine. The more Miss Towell was sweet-spoken and respectable, the more Letty shrank from these tokens of hypocrisy in one who was wicked to the core. "She wouldn't seem so wicked, not at first," Steptoe had predicted, "but time'd tell." Well, Letty didn't need time to tell, since she could see for herself already. She could see from the first words addressed to her.

"You needn't tell me anything about yourself, dear, that you don't want me to know. If you're without a place to go to, I shall be glad if you'll come home with me."

It was the invitation Letty had expected, and to which she meant to respond. Knowing, however, what was behind it she replied more ungraciously than she would otherwise have done. "Oh, I don't mind talking about myself. I'm a picture-actress, only I've been out of a job. I haven't worked for over six months. I've been—I've been visiting."

Miss Towell lowered her eyes, and spoke with modesty. "I suppose you were visiting people who knew —who knew the person who—who gave you my address and the thimble?"

This question being more direct than she cared for Letty was careful to answer no more than, "Yes."

Miss Towell continued to sit with eyes downcast, and as if musing. Two or three minutes went by before she said, softly: "How is he?"

Letty replied that he was very well, and in the same place where he had been so long. Another interval of musing was followed by the simple statement: "We differed about religion."

This remark had no modifying effect on Letty's estimate of Miss Towell's character, since religion was little more to her than a word. Neither was she interested in dead romance between Steptoe and Miss Towell, all romance being summed up in her prince. That flame burned with a pure and single purpose to wed him to the princess with whom he was in love, while the little mermaid became first foam, and then a spirit of the air. It took little from the poetry of this dissolution that it could be achieved only by trundling over Brooklyn Bridge, and through a nexus of dreary streets. In Letty's outlook on her mission the end glorified the means, however shady or degraded.

It was precisely this spirit—mistaken, if you choose

THE DUST FLOWER

to call it so—which animated Judith of Bethulia, Monna Vanna, and Boule de Suif. Letty didn't class herself with these heroines; she only felt as they did, that there was something to be done. On that something a man's happiness depended; on it another woman's happiness depended too; on it her own happiness depended, since if it wasn't done she would feel herself a clog to be cursed. To be cursed by the prince would mean anguish far more terrible than any punishment society could mete out to her.

"If you feel equal to it we might go now, dear," Miss Towell suggested, on waking from her dreams of what might have been. "I wish I could take you in a taxi; but I daresay you won't mind the tram."

Letty rose briskly. "No, I shan't mind it at all." She looked Miss Towell significantly in the eyes, hoping that her words would carry all the meaning she was putting into them. "I shan't mind—anything you want me to do, no matter what."

Miss Towell smiled, sweetly. "Thank you, dear. That'll be very nice. I shan't ask you to do much, because it's your problem, you know, and you must work it out. I'll stand by; but standing by is about all we can do for each other, when problems have to be faced. Don't you think it is?"

As this language meant nothing to Letty, she thanked the nurse, smiled at the other patients, and, trudging at Miss Towell's side with her quaintly sturdy grace, went forth to her great sacrifice.

Allerton had drawn from his conversation with Barbara this one practical suggestion. As he had months before consulted his lawyer, Mr. Nailes, as to ways of losing Letty after she had been found, he might consult him as to ways of finding her now that she had been lost. Mr. Nailes would not go to the police. He would apply to some discreet house of detectives who would do the work discreetly.

"Then, I presume, you've changed your mind about this marriage," was Mr. Nailes' not unnatural inference, "and mean to go on with it."

"N-not exactly." Allerton was still unable to define his intentions. "I only don't want her to disappear—like this."

Mr. Nailes pondered. He was a tall, raw-boned man, of raw-boned countenance, to whom the law represented no system of divine justice, but a means by which Eugene Nailes could make money, as his father had made it before him. Having inherited his father's practice he had inherited Rashleigh Allerton, the two fathers having had a long-standing business connection. Mr. Nailes had no high opinion of Rashleigh Allerton—in which he was not peculiar—but a client with so much money was entitled to his way. At the same time he couldn't have been human without urging a point of common sense.

"If you *don't* want to—to continue your—your relation with this—this lady, doesn't it strike you that now might be a happy opportunity——?"

Allerton did what he did rarely; he struck the table with his fist. "I want to find her."

The words were spoken with so much force that to Mr. Nailes they were conclusive. It was far from his intention to compel anyone to common sense, and least of all a man whose folly might bring increased fees to the firm of Nailes, Nailes, and Nailes.

It was agreed that steps should be taken at once, and that Mr. Nailes would report in the evening. Gravely was the name Allerton was sure she would use, and the only one that needed to be mentioned. It needed only to be mentioned too that Mr. Nailes was acting for a client who preferred to remain anonymous.

It was further agreed that Mr. Nailes should report at Allerton's office at ten that evening, in person if there was anything to discuss, by telephone if there was nothing. This was convenient for Mr. Nailes, who lived in the neighborhood of Washington Square, while it protected Rash from household curiosity. At ten that night he was, therefore, in the unusual position of pacing the rooms he had hardly ever seen except by daylight.

Not Letty's disappearance was uppermost in his mind, for the moment, but his own inhibitions.

"My God, what's the matter with me?" he was muttering to himself. "Am I going insane? Have I been insane all along? Why *can't* I say which of these two women I want, when I can have either?"

He placed over against each other the special set of spells which each threw upon his heart.

Barbara was of his own world; she knew the people he knew; she had the same interests, and the same way of showing them. Moreover, she had in a measure grown into his life. Their friendship was not only intimate it was one of long standing. Though she worried, hectored, and exasperated him, she had fits of generous repentance, in which she mothered him adorably. This double-harness of comradeship had worked for so many years that he couldn't imagine wearing it with another.

And yet Letty pulled so piteously at his heart that he fairly melted in tenderness toward her. Everything he knew as appeal was summed up in her soft voice, her gentle manner, her humility, her unquestioning faith in himself. No one had ever had faith in him before. To Barbe he was a booby when he was not a baby. To Letty he was a hero, strong, wise, commanding. It wasn't merely his vanity that she touched; it was his manliness. Barbe suppressed his manliness, because she herself was so imperious. Letty depended on it, and therefore drew it out. Because she believed him a man, he could be a man; whereas with Barbe, as with everyone else, he was a creature to be liked, humored, laughed at, and good-naturedly despised. He was sick of being liked, humored, and laughed at; he rebelled with every atom in him that was masculine at being good-naturedly despised. To find anyone who thought him big and vigorous was to his starved spirit, as the psalmist says, sweeter also than honey and the honeycomb. In having her weakness to hold up he could for the first time in his life feel himself of use.

If there was no Barbe in the world he could have taken Letty as the mate his soul was longing for. Yet how could he deal such a blow at Barbe's loyalty? She had protected him during all his life, from boyhood upwards. Between him and derision she had stood like a young lioness. How could he deny her now?

THE DUST FLOWER

—no matter what frail, gentle hands were clinging around his heart?

"How can I? How can I? How can I?"

He was torturing himself with this question when the telephone rang, and he knew that Letty had not been found.

"No; nothing," were the words of Mr. Nailes. "No one of the name has been reported at any of the hospitals, or police stations, or any other public institution. They've applied at all the motion-picture studios round New York; but still with no result. This, of course, is only the preliminary search, as much as they've been able to accomplish in one afternoon and evening. You mustn't be disappointed. To-morrow is likely to be more successful."

Rash was, therefore, thrown back on another phase of his situation. Letty was lost. She was not only lost, but she had run away from him. She had not only run away from him, but she had done it so that he might be rid of her. She had not only done it so that he might be rid of her, but. . . .

His spirit balked. His imagination could work no further. Horror staggered him. A mother who knows that her child is in the hands of kidnappers who will have no mercy might feel something like the despair and helplessness which sent him chafing and champing up and down the suite of rooms, cursing himself uselessly.

Suddenly he paused. He was in front of the cabinet which had come via Bordentown from Queen Caroline Murat. Behind its closed door there was still the bottle on the label of which a kilted Highlander was dancing. He must have a refuge from his thoughts, or else he would go mad. He was already as near madness as a man could come and still be reckoned sane.

He opened the door of the cabinet. The bottle and the glass stood exactly where he had placed them on that morning when he had tried to begin going to the devil, and had failed. Now there was no longer that same mysterious restraint. He was not thinking of the devil; he was thinking only of himself. He must still the working of his mind. Anything would do that would drug his faculties, and so. . . .

It was after midnight when he dragged himself out of a stupor which had not been sleep. Being stupor, however, it was that much to the good. He had stopped thinking. He couldn't think. His head didn't ache; it was merely sore. He might have been dashing it against the wall, as figuratively he had done. His body was sore too—stiff from long sitting in the same posture, and bruised as if from beating. All that was nothing, however, since misery only stunned him. To be stunned was what he had been working for.

Out in the air the wind of the May night was comforting. It soothed his nerves without waking the dormant brain. Instead of looking for a taxi he began walking up the Avenue. Walking too was a relief. It allowed him to remain as stupefied as at first, and yet stirred the circulation in his limbs. He meant to walk till he grew tired, after which he would jump on an electric bus.

But he did not grow tired. He passed the great

milestones, Fourteenth Street, Twenty-third Street, Forty-second Street, Fifty-ninth Street, and not till crossing the last did he begin to feel fagged. He was then so near home that the impulse of doggedness kept him on foot. He was a strong walker, and physically in good condition, without being wholly robust. Had it not been for the kilted Highlander he would hardly have felt fatigue; but as it was, the corner of East Sixty-seventh Street found him as spent as he cared to be.

Advancing toward his door he saw a man coming in the other direction. There was nothing in that, and he would scarcely have noticed him, only for the fact that at this hour of the night pedestrians in the quarter were rare. In addition to that the man, having reached the foot of Allerton's own steps, stood there waiting, as if with intention.

Through the obscurity Rash could see only that the man was well built, flashily dressed, and that he wore a sweeping mustache. In his manner of standing and waiting there was something significant and menacing. Arrived at the foot of the steps Allerton could do no less than pause to ask if the stranger was looking for anyone.

"Is your name Allerton?"

"Yes; it is."

"Then I want my girl."

It was some seconds before Rash could get his dulled mind into play. Moreover, the encounter was of a kind which made him feel sick and disgusted.

"Whom do you mean?" he managed to ask, at last.

"You know very well who I mean. I mean Letty Gravely. I'm her father; and by God, if you don't give her up—with big damages——"

"I can't give her up, because she's not here."

"Not here? She was damn well here the day before yesterday."

"Yes; she was here the day before yesterday; but she disappeared last night."

"Ah, cut that kind o' talk. I'm wise, I am. You can't put that bunk over on me. She's in there, and I'm goin' to get her."

"I wish she was in there; but she's not."

"How do I know she's not?"

"I'm afraid you'll have to take my word for it."

"Like hell I'll take your word for it. I'm goin' to see for myself."

"I don't see how you're going to do that."

"I'm goin' in with you."

"That wouldn't do you any good. Besides, I can't let you."

The man became more bullying. "See here, son. This game is my game. Did j'ever see a thing like this?"

Watching the movement of his hand Rash saw the handle of a revolver displayed in a side pocket.

"Yes, I've seen a thing like that; but even if it was loaded—which I don't believe it is—you've too much sense to use it. You might shoot me, of course; but you wouldn't find the girl in the house, because she isn't there."

"Well, I'm goin' to see. You march. Up you go, and open that door, and I'll follow you."

THE DUST FLOWER

"Oh, no, you won't." Allerton looked round for the policeman who occasionally passed that way; but though a lighted car crashed down Madison Avenue there was no one in sight. He might have called in the hope of waking the men upstairs, but that seemed cowardly. Though in a physical encounter with a ruffian like this he could hardly help getting the worst of it—especially in his state of half intoxication—it was the encounter itself that he loathed, even more than the defeat. "Oh, no, you won't," he repeated, taking one step upward, and turning to defend his premises. "I don't mean that you shall come into this house, or ever see the girl again, if I can prevent it."

"Oh, you don't, don't you?"

"No, I don't."

"Then take that."

The words were so quickly spoken, and the blow in his face so unexpected, that Rash staggered backwards. Being on a step he had little or no footing, and having been drinking his balance was the more quickly lost.

"And that!"

A second blow in the face sent him down like a stone, without a struggle or a cry.

He fell limply on his back, his feet slipping to the sidewalk, his body sagging on the steps like a bit of string, accidentally dropped there. The hat, which fell off, remained on the step beside the head it had been covering.

The man leaped backward, as if surprised at his own deed. He looked this way and that, to see if he had been observed. A lighted car crashed up Madison Avenue, but otherwise the street remained empty. Creeping nearer the steps he bent over his victim, whose left hand lay helpless and outstretched. Timidly, gingerly, he put his fingers to the pulse, starting back from it with a shock. He spoke but two words, but he spoke them half aloud.

"Dead! God!"

Then he walked swiftly away into Madison Avenue, where he soon found a car going southward.

Chapter XXIV

BARBARA was late for breakfast. Miss Walbrook, the aunt, was scanning the morning paper, her refined, austere Americanism being as noticeable in the dining-room as elsewhere in the house. Everything was slender and strong; everything was American, unless it was the Persian rug. On the paneled walls there were but three portraits, a Boston ancestress, in lace cap and satins, painted by Copley; a Philadelphia ancestor in the Continental uniform, painted by Gilbert Stuart; and her New York grandmother, painted by Thomas Sully, looking over her shoulder with the wild backward glance that artist gives to the girl Victoria in the Metropolitan Museum. In a flat cabinet along a wall was the largest collection of old American glass to be found in the country.

Barbara rushed in, with apologies for being late. "I didn't sleep a wink. It doesn't seem to me as if I should ever sleep again. Where's my cup?"

"Wildgoose will bring it. As the coffee had grown cold he took that and the cup to keep warm. What's the matter?"

Wildgoose stepped in with the missing essentials. A full-fed, round-faced, rubicund man of fifty-odd he looked a perennial twenty-five. Barbara began to minister to herself.

"Oh, everything's the matter. I told you yesterday that that girl had run away. Well, I begin to wish she'd run back again."

THE DUST FLOWER

Miss Walbrook, the elder, had this in common with Miss Henrietta Towell, that she believed it best for everyone to work out his own salvation. Barbara had her personal life to live, and while her aunt would help her to live it, she wouldn't guide her choice. She continued, therefore, to scan the paper till her niece should say something more.

She said it, not because she wanted to give information, but because she was temperamentally outspoken. "I begin to wish there were no men in the world. If women are men in a higher stage of development, why didn't men die out, so that we could be rid of them? Isn't that what we generally get from the survival of the fittest?"

Miss Walbrook's thin, clear smile suggested the edge of a keenly tempered blade. "I've never said that women were men in a higher stage of development. I've said that in their parallel states of development women had advanced a stage beyond men. You may say of every generation born that women begin where men leave off. I suppose that that's what's meant by the myth of Eve springing from Adam's side. It was to be noticed even then, in the prehistoric, in the age that formed the great legends. Adam was asleep, when Eve as a vital force leaped away from him. If it wasn't for Eve's vitality the human race would still be in the Stone Age."

Barbara harked back to what for her was the practical. "Some of us are in the Stone Age as it is. I'm sure Rash Allerton is as nearly an elemental as one can be, and still belong to clubs and drive in motorcars."

THE DUST FLOWER

Miss Walbrook risked her principles of non-interference so far as to say: "It's part of our feminine lack of development that we're always inclined to look back on the elemental with pity, and even with regret. The woman was never born who didn't have in her something of Lot's wife."

"Thank you, Aunt Marion. In a way that lets me out. If I'm no weaker than the rest of my sex ———"

"Than many of the rest of your sex."

"Very well, then; than many of the rest of my sex; if I'm no weaker than that I don't have to lose my self-respect."

"You don't have to lose your self-respect; you only risk—your reason."

Barbara stared at her. "That's the very thing I'm afraid of. I'd give anything for peace of mind. How did you know?"

"Oh, it doesn't call for much astuteness. I don't suppose there's a married woman in the world in full command of her wits. You've noticed how foolish most of them are. That's why. It isn't that they were born foolish. They've simply been addled by enforced adaptation to mates of lower intelligence. Oh, I'm not scolding. I'm merely stating a natural, observed, psychological fact. The woman who marries says good-bye to the orderly working of her faculties. For that she may get compensations, with which I don't intend to find fault. But compensations or no, to a clear-thinking woman like ———"

"Like yourself, Aunt Marion."

"Very well; like myself, if you will; but to a clear-

THE DUST FLOWER

thinking woman it's as obvious as daylight that her married sisters are partially demented. They may not know it; the partially demented never do. And it's no good telling them, because they don't believe you. I'm only saying it to you to warn you in advance. If you part with your reason, it's something to know that you do it of your own free will."

Once more Barbara confined herself to the case in hand. "Still, I don't believe every man is as trying as Rash Allerton."

"Not in his particular way, perhaps. But if it's not in one way then it's in another."

"Even he wouldn't be so bad if he could control himself. At the minute when he's tearing down the house he wants you to tell him that he's calm."

"If he didn't want you to tell him that it would be something equally preposterous. There's little to choose between men."

Barbara grew thoughtful. "Still, if people didn't marry the human race would die out."

"And would there be any harm in that? It's not a danger, of course; but if it was, would anyone in his senses want to stop it? Looking round on the human race to-day one can hardly help saying that the sooner it dies out the better. Since we can't kill it off, it's well to remember ——"

"To remember what, Aunt Marion?"

Miss Walbrook reflected as to how to express herself cautiously. "To remember that—in marrying—and having children—children who will have to face the highly probable miseries of the next generation —Well, I'm glad there'll be no one to reproach me

THE DUST FLOWER

with his being in the world, either as his mother or his ancestress."

"They say Rash's father and mother didn't want *him* in the world, and I sometimes wish they'd had their way. If he wasn't here—or if he was dead—I believe I could be happier. I shouldn't be forever worrying about him. I shouldn't have him on my mind. I often wonder if it's—if it's love I feel for him—or only an agonizing sense of responsibility."

The door being open Walter Wildgoose waddled to the threshold, where he stood with his right hand clasped in his left. "Mr. Steptoe at Mr. Allerton's to speak to Miss Barbara on the telyphone, please."

Barbara gasped. "Oh, Lord! I wonder what it is now!"

Left to herself Miss Walbrook resumed her scanning of the paper, but she resumed it with the faintest quiver of a smile on her thin, cleanly-cut lips. It was the kind of smile which indicates patient hope, or the anticipation of something satisfactory.

"Oh!"

The exclamation was so loud as to be heard all the way from the telephone, which was in another part of the house. Miss Walbrook let the paper fall, sat bolt upright, and listened.

"Oh! Oh!"

It was like a second, and repeated, explosion. Miss Walbrook rose to her feet; the paper rustled to the floor.

"Oh! Oh!"

The sound was that which human beings make when the thing told them is more than they can bear.

Barbara cried out as if someone was beating her with clubs, and she was coming to her knees.

She was not coming to her knees. When her aunt reached her she was still standing by the little table in the hall which held the telephone, on which she had hung up the receiver. She supported herself with one hand on the table, as a woman does when all she can do is not to fall senseless.

"It's—it's Rash," she panted, as she saw her aunt appear. "Somebody has—has killed him."

Miss Walbrook stood with hands clasped, like one transfixed. "He's dead?—after all?"

Barbara nodded, tearlessly. She could stammer out the words, but no more. "Yes—all but!"

In the flat at Red Point there was another and dissimilar breakfast scene. For the first time in her life Letty was having coffee and toast in bed. The window was open, and between the muslin curtains, which puffed in the soft May wind, she could see the ocean with steamers and ships on it.

The room was tiny, but it was spotless. Everything was white, except where here and there it was tied up with a baby-blue ribbon. Anything that could be tied with a baby-blue ribbon was so tied.

Letty thought she had never seen anything so dainty, though her experienced eye could detect the fact that nothing had really cost money. As an opening to the career on which she had embarked the setting was unexpected, while the method of her treatment was bewildering. In the black recesses of her heart Miss Henrietta Towell might be hiding all

THE DUST FLOWER

those feline machinations which Mrs. Judson Flack had led Letty to believe a part of the great world's stock-in-trade; but it couldn't be denied that she hid them well. Letty didn't know what to make of it. "There's quite a trick to it," Steptoe had warned her; but the explanation seemed inadequate to the phenomena.

Sipping her coffee and crunching her toast she was driven to ponder on the ways of wickedness. She had expected them to be more obvious. All her information was to the effect that an unprotected girl in a world of males was a lamb among lions, a victim with no way of escape. That she was a lamb among lions, and a victim with no way of escape, she was still prepared to believe; only the preliminaries puzzled her. Instead of being crude, direct, indelicate, they were subtle and misleading. After twenty-four hours in Miss Towell's spare room there was still no hint of anything but coddling.

"You see, my dear," Miss Towell had said, "if I don't nurse you back to real 'ealth, him that gave you the thimble might be displeased with me."

It was not often that Miss Towell dropped an *h* or added one; but in moments of emotion early habit was too strong for her.

Coming into the room now, on some ermine's errand of neatness, she threw a glance at Letty, and said: "You don't *look* like a Rashleigh, do you, dear? But then you never can tell anything about families from looks, can you?"

It was her nearest approach as yet to the personal, and Letty considered as to how she was to meet it. "I'm not a Rashleigh—not really—only by—by marriage. Rashleigh isn't my real name. It's—it's the name I'm going by in pictures."

"Oh!"

Miss Towell's exclamation was the subdued one of acquiescence. She knew that ladies in pictures often preferred names other than their own, and if Letty was not a Rashleigh it "explained things." That is, it explained how anyone called Rashleigh could be wandering about in this friendless way, though it made 'Enery Steptoe's intervention the more mysterious. It was conceivable that he might act on behalf of a genuine Rashleigh, however out at elbow; but that he should take such pains for a spurious one, and go to the length of sending the sacred silver thimble as a pledge, rendered the situation puzzling.

Schooled by her religious precepts to taking her duties as those of a minute at a time Miss Towell made no effort to force the girl's confidence, and especially since Letty, like most young people in trouble, was on her guard against giving it. So long as she preferred to be shut up within herself, shut up within herself she should remain. Miss Towell felt that, for the moment at least, her own responsibility was limited to making the child feel that someone cared for her.

At the same time she couldn't have been a lonely woman with a love-story behind her without the impulse to dwell a little longingly on the one romantic incident in her experience. Though it had never come to anything, the fact that it had once opened its shy little flower made a sweet bright place to which her thoughts could retire.

The references came spasmodically and without context, as the little white lady busied herself in waiting on Letty or in the care of her room.

"I haven't seen him since a short time after the mistress went away."

Letty felt herself coloring. Though not prudish there were words she couldn't get used to. Besides which she had never thought that Steptoe. . . . But Miss Towell pursued her memories.

"It always worried him that I should hold views different from his but I couldn't submit to dictation, now, could I, dear?"

Once more Letty felt herself awkwardly placed. The only interpretation she could put on Miss Towell's words referring to moral reformation on her hostess's part she said, as non-committally as might be: "He's a good deal of a stickler."

"He's been so long in a high position that he becomes—well, I won't be 'arsh—but he becomes a little harbitrary. That's where it was. He was a little harbitrary. With a mistress who allowed him a great deal of his own way—well, you can hardly blame him, can you, dear?"

Letty forced herself to accept the linguistic standard of the world. "I suppose if she hadn't allowed him a great deal of his own way he'd have looked somewhere else."

"That he could easily have done. He had temptations enough—a man like him. Why, dear, there was a lady in Park Avenue did everything she could that wasn't positively dishonorable to win him away——"

"He must have been younger and better looking than he is now," Letty hazarded, bluntly.

"Oh, it wasn't a question of looks. Of course if she'd considered that, why, any foolish young fellow—but she knew what she would have got."

Not being at her ease in this kind of conversation, and finding the effort to see Steptoe as Lothario difficult, Letty became blunt again. "He must have had an awful crush on the first one."

"It wasn't her exactly; it was the boy."

"Oh, there was a boy?"

"Why of course, dear! Didn't you know that?"

"Whose boy was it?"

"Why, the mistress's boy; but I don't think *he*——" Letty understood the pronoun as applying to Steptoe—"I don't think *he* ever realized that he wasn't his very own." Straightening the white cover on the chest of drawers Miss Towell shook her head. "It was a sad case."

"What made it sad?"

"A lovely boy he was. Had a kind word for everyone, even for the cat. But somehow his father and mother—well, they were people of the world, and they hadn't wanted a child, and when he came—and he so delicate always—I could have cried over him."

Letty's heart began to swell; her lip trembled. "I know someone like that myself."

"Do you, dear? Then I'm sure you understand."

Partly because the minute was emotional, and partly from a sense that she needed to explain herself, Letty murmured, more or less indistinctly: "It's on his account that I'm here."

Failing to see the force of this Miss Towell was content to say: "I'm glad you were led to me, dear.

"BUT BY AND BY I CREEPS OUT AND DOWN THE STEPS, AND THERE 'E WAS, ALL 'UDDLED EVERY WYE."

THE DUST FLOWER

There's always a power to shepherd us along, if we'll only let ourselves be guided."

To Letty the moment had arrived when plainness of speech was imperative. Leaning across the tray, which still stood on her lap, she gazed up at her hostess with eager, misty eyes. "*He* said you'd teach me all the ropes."

Miss Towell paused beside the bed, to look inquiringly at the tense little face. "The ropes of what, dear?"

"Of what—" it was hard to express—"of what you—you used to be yourself. You don't seem like it now," she added, desperately, "but you were, weren't you?"

"Oh, that!" The surprise was in the discovery that an American girl of Letty's age could entertain so sensible a purpose. "Why, of course, dear! I'll tell you all I know, and welcome."

"There's quite a trick to it, isn't there?"

"Well, it's more than a trick. There are two or three things which you simply *have* to be."

"Oh, I know that. That's what frightens me."

"You needn't be afraid, once you've made up your mind to it." She leaned above the bed to relieve Letty of the tray. "For instance—you don't mind my asking questions do you?"

"Oh, no! You can ask me anything."

"Then the first thing is this: "Are you pretty good as a needle-woman?"

Letty was astounded. "Why—why you don't have to *sew*, do you?"

"Certainly, dear. That's one of the most important

things you'd be called on to do. You'd never get anywhere if you weren't quick with your needle and thread. And then there'd be hair-dressing. You have to know something about that. I don't say that you must be a professional; but for the simpler occasions—after that there's packing. That's something we often overlook, and where French girls have us at a disadvantage. They pack so beautifully."

Letty was entirely at sea. "Pack what?"

"Pack trunks, dear."

"What for?"

"For travel; for moving from town to country; or from country to town; or making visits; you see you're always on the go. Oh, it's more than a trick; it's quite an art; only—" She smiled at Letty as she stood holding the tray, before carrying it out—"only, I shouldn't have supposed you'd be thinking of that when you act in moving pictures."

"I—I thought I might do both."

"Now, I should say that that's one thing you couldn't do, dear. If you took up this at all you'd find it so absorbing——"

"And you're very unhappy too, aren't you? I've always heard you were."

"Well, that would depend a good deal on yourself. There's nothing in the thing itself to make you unhappy; but sometimes there are other women——"

Letty's eyes were flaming. "They say they're awful."

"Oh, not always. It's a good deal as you carry yourself. I made it a point to keep my position and respect the position of others. It wasn't always easy,

THE DUST FLOWER

especially with Mary Ann Courage and Janie Cakebread; but——"

Letty's head fell back on the pillow. Her eyes closed. A merry-go-round was spinning in her head. Where was she? How had she come there? What was she there *for?* Where was the wickedness she had been told to look for everywhere? Having gone in search of it, and expected to find it lying in wait from the first minute of passing the protecting door, she had been shuffled along from one to another, with exasperating kindness, only to be brought face to face with Jane Cakebread and Mary Ann Courage at the end.

Miss Towell having borne away the tray, Letty struggled out of bed, and put on the woollen dressing gown thrown over a chair by the bedside. This was no place for her. Beehive Valley was not far off, and her forty-five cents would more than suffice to take her there. She would see the casting director. She would get a job. With food to eat and a place to sleep as a starting point she would find her own way to wickedness, releasing the prince in spite of all the mishaps which kept her as she was.

But she trembled so that having wrapped the dressing gown about her she was obliged to sit down again. She would have to be crafty. She must get this woman to help her with her dressing, without suspecting what she meant to do. How could she manage that? She must try to think.

She was trying to think when she heard the ring of the telephone. It suggested an idea. Some time— not this time, of course—when the telephone rang and

THE DUST FLOWER

the woman was answering it, she, Letty, would be able to slip away. The important thing was to do her hair and get her clothes on.

"Yes? . . . Yes?" There was a little catch to the breath, a smothered laugh, a smothered sigh. "Oh, so this is you! . . . Yes, I got it. . . Seeing it again gave me quite a turn. . . . I never expected that you'd keep it all this time, but. . . . Yes, she's here. . . . No; she didn't come exactly of her own accord, but I—I found her. . . . I could tell you about it easier if you were—it's so hard on the telephone when there's so much to say—but perhaps you don't care to. . . . Yes, she's quite well—only a little tired—been worked up somehow—but a day or so in bed. . . . Oh, very sensible . . . and she wants me to teach her how to be a lady's maid. . . ."

So that was it! Steptoe had been treacherous. Letty would never believe in anyone again. She could make these reflections hurriedly because the voice at the telephone was silent.

"Oh!"

It was the same exclamation as that of Barbara Walbrook, but in another tone—a tone of distress, sharp, sympathetic. Pulling the dressing gown about her, frightened, tense, Letty knew that something had gone wrong.

"Oh! Oh! . . . last night, did you say? . . . early this morning. . . ."

Letty crept to where her hostess was seated at the telephone. "What is it?"

But Miss Towell either didn't hear the question or was too absorbed to answer it. "Oh, 'Enery, *try* to remember that God is his life—that there can be no death to be afraid of when——"

Letty snatched the receiver from the other woman's hands, and fell on her knees beside the little table. "Oh, what is it? What is it? It's me; Letty! Something's happened. I've got to know."

Amazed and awed by the force of this intrusion Miss Towell stood up, and moved a little back.

Over the wire Steptoe's voice sounded to Letty like the ghost of his voice, broken, dead.

"I think if I was madam I'd come back."

"But what's happened? Tell me that first."

"It's Mr. Rash."

"Yes, I know it's Mr. Rash. But what is it? Tell me quickly, for God's sake."

"'E's been 'it."

Her utterance was as nearly as possible a cry. "But he hasn't been *killed?*"

"Madam'd find 'im alive—if she 'urried."

When Letty rose from her knees she was strong. She was calm, too, and competent. She further surprised Miss Towell by the way in which she took command.

"I must hurry. They want me at once. Would you mind helping me to dress?"

Chapter XXV

"THE queer thing about it, miss," Steptoe was saying to Barbara, "is that I didn't 'ear no noise. My winder is just above the front door, two floors up, and it was open. I always likes an open winder, especially when the weather begins to get warm—makes it 'ealthier like, and so——"

"Yes, but tell me just how he is."

"That's what I'm comin' to, miss. The minute I see what an awful styte we was in, I says, Miss Walbrook, she'll 'ave to know, I says; and so I called up. Well, as I was a-tellin you, miss, I couldn't sleep all night, 'ardly not any, thinkin of all what 'ad 'appened in the 'ouse, in the course of a few months, as you might sye—and madam run awye—and Mr. Rash 'e not 'ome—and it one o'clock and lyter. Not but what 'e's often lyter than that, only last night I 'ad that kind of a feelin' which you'll get when you know things is not right, and you don't 'ardly know 'ow you know it."

"Yes, Steptoe," she interposed, eagerly; "but is he conscious now? That's what I want to hear about."

Steptoe's expression of grief lay in working up to a dramatic climax dramatically. He didn't understand the hurried leaps and bounds by which you took the tragic on the skip, as if it were not portentous. In his response to Miss Walbrook there was a hint of irritation, and perhaps of rebuke.

THE DUST FLOWER

"I couldn't sye what 'e is now, miss, as the doctor and the nurse is with 'im, and won't let nobody in till they decides whether 'e's to live or die." Rocking himself back and forth in his chair he moaned in stricken anticipation. "If 'e goes, I shan't be long after 'im. I may linger a bit, but the good Lord won't move me on too soon."

Barbara curbed her impatience to reach the end, going back to the beginning. "Well, then, was it you who found 'im?"

"It was this wye, miss. Knowin' 'e wasn't in the 'ouse, I kep' goin' to my winder and listenin'—and then goin' back to bed agyne—I couldn't tell you 'ow many times; and then, if you'd believe it I must 'ave fell asleep. No; I can't believe as I was asleep. I just seemed to come to, like, and as I laid there wonderin' what time it was, seems to me as if I 'eard a kind of a snore, like, not in the 'ouse, but comin' up from the street."

"What time was that?"

"That'd be about 'alf past one. Well, up I gets and creeps to the winder, and sure enough the snore come right up from the steps. Seems to me, too, I could see somethink layin' there, all up and down the steps, just as if it 'ad been dropped by haccident like. My blood freezes. I slips into my thick dressin' gown—no, it was my thin dressin' gown—I always keeps two—one for winter and one for summer—and this spring bein' so early like——"

"But in the end you got down stairs."

"If I didn't, miss, 'ow could I 'a' found 'im? I ain't one to be afryde of dynger, not even 'ere in New

THE DUST FLOWER

York, where you can be robbed and murdered without 'ardly knowin' it—and the police that slow about follerin' up a clue——"

"And what happened when you'd opened the front door?"

"I didn't open it at once, miss. I put my hear to the crack and listened. And there it was, a long kind of snore, like—only it wasn't just what you'd call a snore. It was more like this." He drew a deep, rasping, stertorous breath. "Awful, it was, miss, just like somebody in liquor. 'It's liquor,' I says, and not wantin' to be mixed up in no low company I wasn't for openin' the door at all——"

"But you did?"

"Not till I'd gone 'alf wye upstairs and down agyne. I'm like that. I often thinks I'll not do a thing, and then I'll sye to myself, 'Now, perhaps I'd better, and so it was that time. 'E's out, I says, and who knows but what 'e's fell in a fynt like?' So back I goes, and I peeps out a little bit—just my nose out, as you might sye, not knowin' but what if there was low company——"

"When did you find out who it was?"

"I knowed the 'at, like. It was that 'at what 'e bought afore 'e bought the last one. No; I don't know but what 'e's bought two since 'e bought that one—a soft felt, and a cowboy what he never wore but once or twice because it wasn't becomin'. You'll 'ave noticed, miss, that 'e 'ad one o' them fyces what don't look well in nothink rakish—a real gentleman's fyce 'e 'ad—and them cowboy 'ats——"

"Well, when you saw that hat, what did you do?"

"For quite a spell I didn't do nothink. I was all blood-curdled, as you might sye. But by and by I creeps out, and down the steps, and there 'e was, all 'uddled every wye ——"

His lip trembled. In trying to go on he produced only a few incoherent sounds. Reaching for his handkerchief, he blew his nose, before being able to say more.

"Well, the first thing I says to myself, miss, was, Is 'e dead? It was a terrible thing to sye of one that's everythink in the world to me; but seein' 'im there, all crumpled up, with one leg one wye, and the other leg another wye, and a harm throwed out 'elpless like—well, what was I to think? miss—and 'im not aible to sye a word, and me shykin' like a leaf, and out of doors in my thin dressin' gown—if I'd 'ad on my thick one I wouldn't 'a' felt so kind of shymeful like——"

"You might have known he wasn't dead when you heard him breathing."

"I didn't think o' that. I thought as 'e was. And when I see 'is poor harm stretched out so wild like I creeps nearer and nearer, and me 'ardly aible to move —I felt so bad—and I puts my finger on 'is pulse. Might as well 'ave put it on that there fender. Then I looks at 'is fyce and I see blood on 'is lip and 'is cheek. "Somethink's struck 'im, I says; and then I just loses consciousness, and puts back my 'ead, as you'll see a dog do when 'e 'owls, and I yells, Police!"

"Oh, you did that, did you?"

"I'm ashymed to sye it, miss, but I did; and who should come runnin' along but the policeman what in the night goes up and down our beat. By that time

I'd got my 'and on 'is 'eart, and the policeman 'e calls out from a distance, 'Hi, there! What you doin' to that man?' Thought I was murderin' 'im, you see. I says, 'My boy, 'e is, and I'm tryin' to syve 'is life.' Well, the policeman 'e sees I'm in my dressin' gown, and don't look as if I'd do 'im any 'arm, so 'e kind o' picks up 'is courage, and blows 'is whistle, and another policeman 'e runs up from the wye of the Havenue. Then when there's two of 'em they ain't afryde no more, so that the first one 'e comes up to me quite bold like, and arsks me who's killed, and what's killed 'im, and I tells 'im 'ow I was layin' awyke, with the winder open, and Mr. Rash bein' out I couldn't sleep like ——"

"How long did they let him lie there?"

"Oh, not long. First they was for callin' a hambulance; but when I tells 'em that 'e's my boy, and lives in my 'ouse, they brings 'im in and we lays 'im on the sofa in the libery, and I rings up Dr. Lancing, and ——"

But something in Barbara snapped. She could stand no more. Not to cry out or break down she sprang to her feet. "That'll do, Steptoe. I know now all I need to know. Thank you for telling me. I shall stay here till the doctor or the nurse comes down. If I want you again I'll ring."

Lashing up and down the drawing-room, wringing her hands and moaning inwardly, Barbara reflected on the speed with which Nemesis had overtaken her. "If he wasn't here—or if he was dead," she had said, "I believe I could be happier." As long as she lived she would hear the curious intonation in Aunt

THE DUST FLOWER

Marion's voice: "He's dead?—after all?" It was in that *after all* that she read the unspeakable accusation of herself.

Waiting for the doctor was not long. On hearing his step on the stair Barbara went out to meet him. "How is he?" she asked, without wasting time over self-introductions.

"It's a little difficult to say as yet. The case is serious. Just how serious we can't tell to-day—perhaps not to-morrow. I find no trace of fracture of the cranium, or of laceration of the brain; but it's too soon to be sure. Dr. Brace and Dr. Wisdom, who've both been here, are inclined to think that it may be no more than a simple concussion. We must wait and see."

Relieved to this extent Barbara went on to explain herself. "I'm Miss Walbrook. I was engaged to Mr. Allerton till—till quite recently. We're still great friends—the greatest friends. He had no near relations—only cousins—and I doubt if any of them are in New York as late in the season as this—and even if they are he hardly knows them——"

The doctor, a cheery, robust man in the late thirties, in his own line one of the ablest specialists in New York, had a foible for social position and his success in it. Even now, with such grave news to communicate, he couldn't divest himself of his dinner-party manner or his smile.

"I've had the pleasure of meeting Miss Walbrook, at the Essingtons' dinner—the big one for Isabel—and afterwards at the dance."

"Oh, of course," Barbara corroborated, though with no recollection of the encounter. "I knew it was somewhere, but I couldn't quite recall—So I felt, when the butler called me up, that I should be here——"

"Quite so! quite so! You'll find Miss Gallifer, who's with him now, a most competent nurse, and I shall bring a good night nurse before evening." The professional side of the situation disposed of, he touched tactfully on the romantic. "It will be a great thing for me to know that in a masculine household like this a woman with knowledge and authority is running in and out. The more you can be here, Miss Walbrook, the more responsibility you'll take off my hands."

"May I be in his room—and help the nurse—or do anything like that?"

"Quite so! quite so! I'm sure Miss Gallifer, who can't be there every minute of the time, you understand, will be glad to feel that there's someone she can trust——"

"And he couldn't know I was there?"

"Not unless he returned unexpectedly to consciousness, which is possible, you understand——"

Her distress was so great that she hazarded a question on which she would not otherwise have ventured. "Doctor, you're a physician. I can speak to you as I shouldn't speak to everyone. Suppose he did return unexpectedly to consciousness, and found me there in the room, do you think he'd be—annoyed?"

It was the sort of situation he liked, a part in the intimate affairs of people of the first quality. "As to his being annoyed I can't say. It might be the very opposite. What I know is this, that in the coming

THE DUST FLOWER

back of the mind to its regular functions inhibitions are often suspended ——"

"And you mean by that ——?"

"That the first few minutes in which the mind revives are likely to be minutes of genuine reality. I don't say that the mind could keep it up. Very few of us can be our genuine selves for more than flashes at a time; but a returning consciousness doesn't put on its inhibitions till ——"

"So that what you see in those few minutes you can take as the truth."

"I should say so. I'm not in a position to affirm it; but the probabilities point that way."

"And if there had been, let us say, a lesser affection, something of recent origin, and lower in every way ——"

"I think that until it forged its influence again—if it ever did—you'd see it forgotten or disowned."

She tried to be even more explicit. "He's perfectly free, in every way. I broke off my engagement just to make him free. The—the other woman, she, too, has—has left him ——"

"So that," he summed up, "if in those first instants of returning to the world you could read his choice you'd be relieved of doubts for the future."

Having made one or two small professional recommendations he was about to go when Barbara's mind worked to another point. "You know, he's been very excitable."

"So I've understood. I go a good deal to the Chancellors'. You know them, of course. I've heard about him there."

THE DUST FLOWER

"Well, then, if he got better, is there anything we could do about that?"

"In a general way, yes. If you're gentle with him——"

"Oh, I am."

"And if you try to smooth him down when you see him beginning to be ruffled——"

"That's just what I do, only it seems to excite him the more."

"Then, in that case, I should say, break the conversation off. Go away from him. Let him alone. Let him work out of it. Begin again later."

"Ye-es, only——" she was wistful, unconvinced—"only later it's so likely to be the same thing over again."

He dodged the further issue by running up to explain to the nurse Miss Walbrook's position in the house, and as helper in case of necessity. By the time he had come down again Barbara's anguish was visible. "Oh, doctor, you think he *will* get better, don't you?"

He was at the front door. "I hope he will. Quite—quite possibly he will. His pulse isn't very strong as yet, but—Well, Dr. Brace and Dr. Wisdom are coming for another consultation this afternoon; only his condition, you understand, is—well, serious."

Barbara divined the malice beneath Steptoe's indications, as he conducted her upstairs. "That was the lyte Mrs. Allerton's room; that's the front spare room; and that's our present madam's room—when she's 'ere—heach with its barth. I'm sure if Miss Walbrook was inclined to use the front spare room I'd be entirely

THE DUST FLOWER

welcome, and 'ave put in clean towels, and everythink, a-purpose."

When Rash's door was pointed out to her she tapped. Miss Gallifer opened it, receiving her colleague with a great big hearty smile. Great, big, and hearty were the traits by which Miss Gallifer was known among the doctors. Healthy, skilful, jolly, and offhand, she carried the issues of life and death, in which she was at home, with a lightness which made her easy to work with. Some nurses would have resented the intrusion of an outsider—professionally speaking—like Miss Walbrook; but to Miss Gallifer it was the more the merrier, even in the sickroom. The very fact of coming to close quarters with the type she knew as a "society girl" added spice to the association.

For the first few seconds Barbara found her breeziness a shock. She had expected something subdued, hushed, funereal. Miss Gallifer hardly lowered her voice, which was naturally loud, or quieted her manner, which, when off duty, could be boisterous. It was not boisterous now, of course; only quick, free, spontaneous. Then Barbara saw the reason.

There was no need to lower the voice or quiet the manner or soften the swish of rustling to and fro, in presence of that still white form composed in the very attitude of death. If Barbara hadn't known he was alive she wouldn't have supposed it. She had seen dead men before—her father, two brothers, other relatives. They looked like this; this looked like them. She said *this* to herself, and not *he,* because it seemed the word.

But by the time she had moved forward and was standing by the bed Miss Gallifer's businesslike tone became a comfort. You couldn't take such a tone if you thought there was danger; and in spite of the hemming and hawing of the doctors Miss Gallifer didn't think there was.

"Oh, I've seen lots of such cases, and *I* say it's a simple concussion. Old Wisdom, he doesn't know anything. I wouldn't consult him about an accident to a cat. Laceration of the brain is always his first diagnosis; and if the patient didn't have it he'd get it to him before he'd admit that he was wrong."

Barbara put the question in which all her other questions were enfolded. "Then you think he'll get better?"

"I shouldn't be surprised."

"Would you be surprised—the other way?"

"I think I should—on the whole. Pulse is poor. That's the worst sign." She picked up the hand lying outside the coverlet and put her finger-tips to the wrist, doing it with the easy nonchalant carelessness with which she might have seized an inanimate object, yet knowing exactly what she was about. "H'm! Fifty-six! That's pretty low. If we could get it above sixty—but still!" Dropping the hand with the same indifference, yet continuing to know what she was about, Miss Gallifer tossed aside the index of the pulse as wholly non-convincing. "I've known cases where the pulse would go down till there was almost no pulse at all, and *yet* it would come up again."

"So that you feel ——?"

"Oh, he'll do. I shouldn't worry—yet. If he

wasn't going to pull through there would be something——"

"Something to tell you?"

"Well, yes—if you put it that way. I most always know with a patient. It isn't anything in his condition. It's more like a hunch. There's often the difference between a doctor and a nurse. The doctor goes by what he sees, the nurse by what she feels. Nine times out of ten the doctor'll see wrong and the nurse'll feel right—and there you are! You can't go by doctors. A lot of guess-work gumps, I often think; and yet the laity need them for comfort."

Making the most of all this Barbara asked, timidly: "Is there anything I could do?"

"Well, no! There isn't much that anyone can do. You've just got to wait. If you're going to stay——"

"I should like to."

Then you can be somewhere else in the house so that I could call you—or you could sit right here—whichever you preferred."

"I'd rather sit right here, if I shouldn't be in the way."

"Oh, when you're in the way I'll tell you."

On this understanding Barbara sat down, in a small low armchair not far from the foot of the bed. Miss Gallifer also sat down, nearer to the window, taking up a book which, as Barbara could see from the "jacket" on the cover, bore the title, *The Secret of Violet Pryde*. It was clear that there was nothing to be done, since Miss Gallifer could so easily lose herself in her novel.

Not till her jumble of impressions began to arrange

themselves did Barbara realize that she was in Rash's room, surrounded by the objects most intimate to his person. Here the poor boy slept and dressed, and lived the portion of his life which no one else could share with him. In a sense they were rifling his privacy, the secrecy with which every human being has in some measure to surround himself. She recalled a day in her childhood, after her parents and both her brothers had died, when their house with its contents was put up for sale. She remembered the horror with which she had seen strangers walking about in the rooms sanctified by loved presences, and endeared to her holiest memories. Something of that she felt now, as Miss Gallifer threw aside her book, sprang lightly to her feet, hurried into Rash's bathroom, and came out with a towel slightly damped, which she passed over the patient's brow. She was so horribly at ease! It was as if Rash no longer had a personality whose rights one must respect.

But he might get better! Miss Gallifer believed that he would! Barbara clung to that as an anchor in this tempest of emotions. If he got better he would open his eyes. If he opened his eyes it would be, for a little while at least, with his inhibitions suspended. If his inhibitions were suspended the thing he most wanted would be in his first glance; and if his first glance fell on her. . . .

Chapter XXVI

WAITING was becoming dreamlike. She didn't find it tedious, or over-fraught with suspense. On the contrary, it was soothing. It was a little trance-like, too, almost as if she had been enwrapped in Rash's stillness.

It was so strange to see him still. It was so strange to be still herself. Of her own being, as of his, she had hardly any concept apart from the high winds of excitement. Calm like this was new to her, and because new it was appeasing, wonderful. It was not unlike content, only the content which comes in sleep, to be broken up by waking. Somewhere in her nature she liked seeing him as he was, helpless, inert, with no power of enraging her by being restive to her will. It was, in its way, a repetition of what she had said that morning: "If he wasn't here—or if he was dead!" Longing for peace, her stormy soul seemed to know by instinct the price she would have to pay for it. For peace to be possible Rash must pass out of her life, and the thought of Rash passing out of her life was agony.

While Miss Gallifer was downstairs at lunch Barbara had the sweet, unusual sense of having him all to herself. She had never so had him in their hours together because the violence of their clashes had prevented communion. Seated in this silence, in this quietude, she felt him hers. There was no one to dispute her claim, no one whose claim she had in any way to recognize as superior. Letty's claim she had never recognized at all. It was accidental, spurious. Letty herself didn't put it forth—and even she was gone. If Rash were to open his eyes he would see no one but herself.

She was sorry when Miss Gallifer came back, though there was no help for that; but Miss Gallifer was obtrusive only when she chatted or moved about. For much of the time she pursued the secret of Violet Pryde with such assiduity that the room became quiescent, and communion with Rash could be re-established.

The awesome silence was disturbed only by the turning of Miss Gallifer's pages. It might have been three o'clock. Once more Barbara was lost in the unaccustomed hush, her eyes fixed on the white face on the pillow, in almost hypnotic restfulness. The pushing open of the door behind was so soft that she didn't notice. Miss Gallifer turned another page.

It was the sense that someone was in the room which made Barbara glance over her shoulder and Miss Gallifer look up. A little gray figure in a battered black hat stood just within the door. She stood just within the door, but with no consciousness of anything or anyone in the room. She saw only the upturned face and its deathlike fixity.

With slow, spellbound movement she began to come forward. Barbara, who had never seen the Letty who used to be, knew her now only by a terrified intuition. Miss Gallifer was entirely at a loss, and somewhat indignant. The little gray vagrant was

THE DUST FLOWER

not of the type she had been used to treating with respect.

"What are you doing here?" she asked quickly, as soon as speech came to her.

Letty didn't look at her, or remove her eyes from the face on the pillow. A woman in a trance could not have spoken with greater detachment or self-control. "I came—to see."

"Well, now that you've seen, won't you please go away, before I call the police?"

Of this Letty took no notice, going straight to the bedside, while Miss Gallifer moved toward Barbara, who stood as she had risen from her chair.

"Do you know who she is?" Miss Gallifer asked, with curiosity greater than her indignation.

Barbara nodded. "Yes, I know who she is. I thought she'd—disappeared."

"Oh, they never disappear for long—not that kind. What had I better do? Is she anything—to *him?*"

Barbara was saved the necessity of answering because Letty, who was on the other side of the bed, bent over and kissed the feet, as she had kissed them once before.

"Is she dotty?" Miss Gallifer whispered. "Ought I to take her by the shoulders and put her out the door? I could, you know—a scrap of a thing like that."

Barbara whispered back. "I can't tell you who she is, but—but I wouldn't interfere with her."

"Oh, the doctor'll do that. *He'll* not——"

But Letty raised herself, addressing the nurse. "Is he—dead?"

THE DUST FLOWER

Miss Gallifer's tone was the curt one we use to inferiors. "No, he's not dead."

"Is he going to die?"

"Not this time, I think."

Letty looked round her. "Well, I'll just sit over here." She went to a chair at the back of the room, in a corner on a line with the door. "I won't give any trouble. The minute he begins to—to live I'll go."

It was Barbara who arranged the matter peaceably, mollifying Miss Gallifer. Without explaining who Letty was she insisted on her right to remain. If Miss Gallifer was mystified, it was no more than Miss Towell was, or anyone else who touched the situation at a tangent. To that Barbara was indifferent, while Letty didn't think of it.

In rallying her forces Barbara's first recollection had been, "I must be a sport." With theoretical sporting instincts she knew herself the kind of sport who doesn't always run true to form. Hating meanness she could lapse into the mean, and toward Letty herself had so lapsed. That accident she must guard against. The issues were so big that whatever happened, she couldn't afford to reproach herself. Self-reproach would not only magnify defeat but poison success, since, if she availed herself of her advantages, no success would ever prove worth while.

For her own sake rather than for Letty's she made use of the hour while the doctors were again in consultation to explain the possibilities. She would have the whole thing clearly understood. Whether or not Letty did understand it she wasn't quite sure, since she seemed cut off from thought-communication. She listened, nodded, was docile to instructions, but made no response.

To be as lucid as possible Barbara put it in this way: "Since you've left him, and I've broken my engagement he'll be absolutely free to choose; and yet, you must remember, we may—we may both lose him."

That both should lose him seemed indeed the more probable after the consultation. All the doctors looked grave, even Dr. Lancing. His dinner-party manner had forsaken him as he talked to Barbara, his emphasis being thrown on the word "prepared." It was still one of those cases in which you couldn't tell, though so far the symptoms were not encouraging. He felt himself bound in honor to say as much as that, hoping, however, for the best.

Closing the front door on him Barbara felt herself shaken by a frightful possibility. If he never regained consciousness that would "settle it." The suspense would be over. Her fate would be determined. She would no longer have to wonder and doubt, to strive or to cry. No longer would she run the risk of seeing another woman get him. She would find that which her tempestuous nature craved before everything—rest, peace, release from the impulse to battle and dominate. Not by words, not so much as by thought, but only in wild emotion she knew that, as far as she was concerned, it might be better for him to die. If he lived, and chose herself, the storm would only begin again. If he lived and chose the other. . . .

But as to that she could see no reasonable prospect. She had only to look at Letty, shrinking in her corner of the bedroom, to judge any such mischance impossible. She was so humble; so negligible; so much a bit of flotsam of the streets. She had an appeal of her own, of course; but an appeal so lowly as to be obscured by the wayside dust which covered it. What was the flower to which Rash had now and then compared her? Wasn't that what he called it—the dust flower?—that ragged blue thing of byways and backyards, which you couldn't touch without washing your hands afterwards. No, no! Not even the legal tie which nominally bound them could hold in the face of this inequality. It would be too grotesque.

The hours passed. The night nurse was now installed, and was reading *Keith Macdermot's Destiny*. She was one of those tall, slender women whom you see to be all bone. As businesslike as Miss Gallifer, and quite as detached, Miss Moines was brisk and systematic. It being her habit to subdue a household to herself before she entered on her duties her eyes regarded Miss Walbrook and Letty with the startled glance of a horse's.

For before going Miss Gallifer had given her a hint. "You'll have to do a lot of side-stepping here. This is the famous House of Mystery. You'll find two nuts upstairs—that's what I'd call them if they were men—but they're women—girls, sort of—and you've just got to leave them alone. One's a high-stepper—regular society—was engaged to the patient and now acts as if she'd married him; and the other—well, perhaps you can make her out; I can't. Seems a little off. May be the poor castaway, once loved, and now broken-hearted but faithful, you read about in books. Anyhow, there they are, and you'd best let them be.

It won't be for more than—well, I give him twenty-four hours at the most. I begin to think that for once old Wisdom is right. Good-looker too, poor fellow, and can't be more than thirty-five. I wonder what could have happened? I suppose they'll go into that at the inquest."

But Miss Moines was too systematic to have companions in the room without marshaling them to some form of duty. They needed to eat; they needed to sleep. Now and then someone had to go out on the landing and comfort or reassure Steptoe, who sat on the attic stairs like a grief-stricken dog.

Letty was the first to consent to go and lie down. She did so about nine o'clock, extracting a promise that whatever happened she would be called at twelve. If there was any change in the meantime—but that, Miss Moines assured her, was understood in all such ride-and-tie arrangements. At twelve Letty was to return and Barbara lie down till three, with the same proviso in case of the unexpected. But, so to put it, the unexpected seemed improbable, in view of that rigid form, and the white, upturned face.

"And yet," Miss Moines confided to Barbara, "I don't think he's as far gone as they think. Miss Gallifer only changed her mind when they talked her round. A doctor just sees the patient in glimpses, whereas a nurse lives with him, and knows what he can stand."

About eleven Miss Moines closed *Keith Macdermot's Destiny,* and took the pulse. She nodded as she did so, with a slight exclamation of triumph. "Ah, ha! Fifty-eight! That's the first good sign. It may not mean anything, but———"

THE DUST FLOWER

Barbara was too exhausted to feel more than a gleam of comfort. The lassitude being emotional rather than physical Miss Moines detected it easily enough, and sent her to rest before the hour agreed upon. She went the more willingly, since the pulse had risen and hope could begin once more.

On the stairs Steptoe raised his bowed head, with a dazed stare. Seeing Miss Walbrook he stumbled to his feet.

" 'Ow is 'e now, miss?"

She told him the good news.

"Ah, thank God! Perhaps after all 'E'll spare 'im."

Steptoe informed Letty, who right on the stroke of midnight returned to her post. "Pulse gone up two of them degrees, madam. 'E's goin' to pull through!"

To Letty this was a signal. On going to rest in the little back spare room she had thrown off her street things, worn during all the hours of watching, and put on the dressing gown she had left there a few nights earlier. She was still wearing it, but at Steptoe's news she went back again. On passing him the second time she was clad in the old gray rag and the battered hat in which it would be easier to escape. Steptoe said nothing; but he nodded to himself comprehendingly.

A clock struck two. Miss Moines was hungry. Expecting to be hungry she had had a small tray, with what she called a "lunch," placed for her in the dining-room. Had there been immediate danger she would not have left her post; but with Letty there she saw no harm in taking ten or fifteen minutes to conserve her strength.

THE DUST FLOWER

For the first time in all those hours Letty was alone with him. Not expecting to be so left she was at first frightened, then audacious. Except for the one time when she had approached the bedside and kissed his feet she had remained in her corner, watching with the silent, motionless intentness of a little animal. Her eyes hardly ever left the white face; but at this distance even the white face was dim.

Now she was possessed by a great daring. She would steal to the bedside again. Again she would see the beloved features clearly. Again she would have the amazing bliss of kissing the coverlet that covered the dear feet. When Miss Moines returned she would be back again in her corner, as if she had never left it. If the pulse rose higher, if there was further hope, if he seemed to be reviving, she could slip away in the confusion of their joy.

She rose and listened. The house was as still as it had been at other times when she had listened in the night. She glided to the bed.

He lay as if he had been carved in stone, propped up with pillows to make breathing easier, his arms outside the coverlet. He was a little as he had been on the morning when she had passed her hand across his brow. As then, too, his hair rose in tongues of diabolic flame.

She was near him. She was bending over him. She was bending not above his feet, but above his head. She knew how mad she was, but she couldn't help herself. Stooping—stooping—closer—closer—her lips touched the forked black mane of his hair.

She leaped back. She leaped not only because of

her own boldness, but because he seemed to stir. It was as if this kiss, so light, so imperceptible, had sent a galvanic throbbing through his frame. She herself felt it, as now and then in winter she had felt an electric spark.

Her sin had found her out. She was terrified. He lay just as he had lain before—only not quite—not quite! His arms were not just as they had been; the coverlet was slightly, ever so slightly, disturbed. The nurse would see it and know that. . . .

There was a stirring of a hand. It was so little of a stirring that she thought her eyes must have deceived her when it stirred again—a restless toss, like a muscular contraction in sleep. She was not alarmed now, only excited, and wondering what she ought to do. She ought to run to the head of the stairs and call Miss Moines, only that she couldn't bring herself to leave him.

Then, as she stood in her attitude of doubt, the eyes opened and looked at her. They looked at her straight, and yet glassily. They looked at her with no gladness in the look, almost with no recognition. If anything there was a kind of sickness there, as if the finding her by his bedside was a disappointment.

"I know what it is," she said to herself. "He wants —*her*."

But the eyes closed again. The face was as white, the profile as rigid, as ever.

She sped to Barbara, who was lying on a couch in the front spare room. "Come! He woke up! He wants you!"

Back in the bedroom she effaced herself. They

THE DUST FLOWER

were all there now—Barbara, Steptoe, and Miss Moines.

"It's what he would do," Miss Moines corroborated, "if he was coming back."

Letty had told part of what she had seen, but only part of it. The rest was her secret. The little mermaid's kiss had left the prince as inanimate as before; hers had brought him back to life!

It was the moment to run away. Miss Moines had said that having once opened his eyes he would open them again. When he did he mustn't find her there. They were all so intent on watching that this was her opportunity.

They were all so intent—but Steptoe. She was buttoning her jacket when she saw his eyes steal round in her direction. A second later he had tiptoed back into the hall, and closed the door behind him.

It was vexing, but not fatal. He had probably gone for something. While he was getting it she would elude him. One thing was certain—she couldn't face the look of disappointment in those sick dark eyes again. She opened the door. She shut it noiselessly behind her. Steptoe wasn't there, and the way was free.

Barbara stood just where Letty had described herself as standing when the eyes had given her that glassy stare. To herself she seemed to stand there for ever, though the time could be counted in minutes. The pounding of her heart was like a pulsating of the house.

The eyes opened again. They opened, first wearily, and then with a fretful light which seemed to be searching for what they couldn't find.

THE DUST FLOWER

Barbara stood still.

There was another stirring of the hand, irritated, impatient. A little moan or groan was distinctly of complaint. The eyes having rolled hither and thither helplessly, the head turned slowly on the pillow so as to see the other side of the room.

"He's looking for something that he misses," Miss Moines explained, wonderingly. "What do you suppose it can be?"

"He wants—*her*."

Barbara found her at the street door, pleading with Steptoe, who actually held her by the arm. The loud whisper down the stairs was a cry as well as a command.

"Come!"

At the bedroom door they parted. With a light instinctive push Barbara forced Letty to go back to the spot on which she had stood earlier. She herself went to the other side of the bed, only to find that the head, in which the eyes were closed again, was now turned that way.

As if aware that some mysterious decision was approaching Miss Moines kept herself in the background. Steptoe had hardly advanced from the threshold. Neither of the women by the bedside seemed to breathe.

When the eyes opened for the third time the intelligence in them was keener. On Barbara they rested long, quietly, kindly, till memory came back.

With memory there was again that restless stirring, that complaining moan. Once more, slowly, distressfully, the head turned on the pillow.

THE DUST FLOWER

On Letty the long, quiet, kindly regard lay as it had lain on Barbara. They waited; but in the look there was no more than that.

From two hearts two silent prayers were going up.

"Oh, God, end it somehow—and let me have *peace!*"

"Oh, God, make him live again—and give them to each other!"

Then, when no one was expecting it, a faint smile quivered on the lips, as if the returning mind saw something long desired and comforting. Faintly, feebly, unsteadily, the hands were raised toward the dust flower. The lips moved, enough to form dumbly the one word, "Come!"

The invitation was beyond crediting. Letty trembled, and shrank back.

But from the support of the pillow the whole figure leaned forward. The hands were lifted higher, more firmly and more longingly. Strength came with the need for strength. A smile which was of life, not death, beamed on the features and brought color to the face which had all these hours seemed carved in stone.

"He'll do now," the nurse threw off, professionally. "He'll be up in a few days."

It was Barbara who gave the sign to both Steptoe and Miss Moines. By the imperiousness of her gesture and her uplifted head she swept them out before her. If she was leaving all behind her she was leaving it superbly; but she wasn't leaving all. Back of her tumultuous passions a spirit was crying to her spirit, "Now you'll get what you want far more than you want this—rest from vain desire."

THE DUST FLOWER

Letty approached the bedside slowly, as if drawn by an enchantment. To the outstretched hands she stretched out hers. The door was closed, and once more she was alone with him.

But neither saw that for the space of a few inches the closed door was opened again, and that an old profile peered within. Then, as slowly, slowly, slowly, Letty sank on her knees, bowing her head on the hands which drew her closer, and closer still, a pair of old lips smiled contentedly.

When the head drew back, the door was closed again.

THE END

Mrs. Frances Wilson